SPYDER WEB

SPYDER WEB

TOM GRACE

WARNER BOOKS

A Time Warner Company

Warner Books, Inc., 1271 Avenue of the Americas, New York, NY 10020

Visit our Web site at http://warnerbooks.com

 A Time Warner Company

Printed in the United States of America
First Printing: January 1999
10 9 8 7 6 5 4 3 2 1

Library of Congress Cataloging-in-Publication Data

Grace, Tom.
Spyder web / Tom Grace.
    p.   cm.
    ISBN 0-446-52407-7
    I. Title
[PS3557.R1177S68   1999]
813'.54—dc21   98-5226
                                    CIP

In loving memory of
Marcia Grace
April 9, 1938–April 1, 1988
My mother and my friend

ACKNOWLEDGMENTS

While I may be the architect of this story, I would be remiss if I failed to recognize the contributions of those who helped me along the way. I give my wholehearted thanks to:

Mel Parker and Larry Kirshbaum of Warner Books, who turned my avocation into my occupation.

Esther Margolis, a woman of charm, intelligence, and insight, who introduced me to New York and changed my world.

My wife, Kathy, and our children. Your incredible support throughout the creation of this book is what made it possible.

The Warner Books crew, whose efforts on every aspect of this project are immeasurable.

Marcie Klaus-Gates, a tough literary critic, an enthusiastic audience, and a good friend.

Dr. David H. Gorski, who helped immensely with all things medical.

Denise Landis, Dean Pode, and the staff of the UMMC Survival Flight Program. Keep 'em flying, guys.

The researchers of the University of Michigan's Ultrafast Optics Laboratory. The future of computer technology will be born in places like this.

My father, Tom Grace, and my uncle, Don Saunders, who share with me the love of a good adventure.

SPYDER WEB

Prologue

Hong Kong, PRC

"Thank you," Lin Mei said absently as the owner of the restaurant brought her tea and a bowl of noodles with fish.

She had arrived early at the tiny dockside restaurant, the anticipation of word from her brother in Beijing being almost more than she could contain. Since the handover last summer, each new day brought with it the reality of Hong Kong's transformation from British Crown Colony into a Red Chinese city. Despite Beijing's assurances that little would change, residents of capitalism's strongest beachhead on the Chinese mainland still carried a nagging sense of uncertainty about the future.

Like Hong Kong, Lin was as much a part of China as she was of the West, and the delicate balance between those conflicting forces was difficult for both. An attractive young woman in her mid-twenties, she had been fortunate to study in the United States and was soon to marry a young man from San Francisco. On a personal level, Lin Mei's future was full of promise.

She picked at her food, but the anxiety she felt made eating difficult. Instead, she resigned herself to quietly sipping tea while she waited for her brother's emissary.

She spoke with Zhenyi as often as she could, but getting a phone connection to Beijing was still no simple task. Most of her communication with him was through letters carried by private couriers across the slowly dissolving border.

Lin Zhenyi had surprised her when he joined the Party and took a position with the PRC government rather than going West, as she had. He believed that China could change but that the change would have to come from within the government.

Despite his Party membership, Zhenyi maintained discreet contact with democratic reformers. His belief that change was coming deepened with the expansion of China's economy and the return of Hong Kong and, soon, Macao. He felt that strong international ties would draw China out of her self-imposed isolation. When Lin Mei received his call three nights before, she sensed that her brother's optimism had been crushed.

"Mei, I can't talk now," Zhenyi had apologized at the end of that brief conversation, "but my next letter will explain everything. You can pick it up at the usual place on Tuesday, at eight o'clock. Read it carefully and you'll understand. I've also enclosed some important research for a friend of mine. He will make arrangements to meet with you. It is crucial that you give him what I found."

Tonight, she waited, just as he had asked.

Kang Fa circled the restaurant for twenty minutes, looking for watchers before entering. Hong Kong was still

Hong Kong, and he knew that there were many eyes in the city that still worked for foreign intelligence services. Through the window, he saw twelve cramped seats, half-filled with evening diners. Near the window sat Lin Mei.

She is beautiful, Kang thought as he approached, more so than any photograph could render.

Her long black hair was drawn back in a French braid that descended to the small of her back like a silken cord against the red satin of her dress. Life in Hong Kong had been very kind to this exquisite young woman.

As Kang entered the restaurant, he saw her look cautiously in his direction.

She's expecting me, he thought, and he smiled back to acknowledge her attention.

"Lin Mei?" he asked politely as he approached her table.

"Yes," she replied. The man was older than she, well over forty, with graying black hair and a kind face.

"My name is Kang Fa. I am an acquaintance of your brother. I apologize if I have kept you waiting."

Lin only nodded, almost afraid to speak. Kang sat in the lacquer chair beside hers and ordered tea from the owner of the tiny restaurant.

"Zhenyi asked me to bring you this letter. I know he wished that he could have delivered it himself."

Lin Mei accepted a sealed envelope that bore the characters of her name; the handwriting was Zhenyi's. She opened it and began to read, devouring each of her brother's quickly drawn characters. He spoke of his disillusion with China, of his lost hope for the future. As she read, she realized that the rambling letter was her brother's final confession; he wrote as a man facing certain death. She began to weep as the depth of her brother's despair unfolded before her. Zhenyi ended the letter by imploring her to deliver the attached pages to a friend, who, he said, would know what to do with them.

She turned to the next page of the letter. It was a grainy photocopy of an official document that authorized the relocation of the listed individuals into Mainland China for an undetermined period of time. All those named were members of Hong Kong's most prominent Chinese families. The pages were excerpts from Beijing's ten-year plan for the pacification of Hong Kong.

China is going to take hostages to keep Hong Kong in line, Lin Mei realized. The Communists are no different from the warlord emperors who held key families at court to prevent rebellion.

She placed the letter and the list in her purse while struggling to maintain her composure. "Thank you for delivering this letter."

Kang saw that she was visibly shaken by what she'd read. "You must share an uncommonly strong bond with Zhenyi. He has expressed his deepest fears to you, and his news is quite disturbing."

She looked at Kang's bowed head and sensed that he, too, was concerned for her brother. "Do you know him well?"

"I've only known Lin for a short time, but it has been long enough to know that he cares a great deal for you."

"Mr. Kang, I really don't feel much like eating right now, and I have another appointment not far from here. If you have the time, I'd like you to walk with me there. I haven't seen Zhenyi in months, and I want to hear more about him from a friend."

"I would be honored."

Kang accompanied her on a meandering walk through the narrow streets of Hong Kong. They talked about Lin

Zhenyi, and she was grateful for his presence; Kang was a sympathetic audience. The list had given her a glimpse of something terrible, and she felt as if she held the lives of those people in her hands. Lin hoped that the man she was to meet would know what to do with the list.

An hour slipped by quickly, and Lin ended their walk at the dock where she was to wait. Vessels of all kinds were tied up along the pier, aging junks, fishing boats, and small barges. As evening slipped into darkness, odd circles and squares of light from the boats illuminated the dock in an irregular rhythm of light and shadow.

Lin turned to Kang as they approached the site of her expected rendezvous. "I would like to thank you for the kindness you have shown me tonight."

"The pleasure was all mine. Your brother was a decent man."

Lin nodded and prepared to part company, when a sudden icy fear swept over her. She looked carefully at Kang. He smiled back pleasantly, but his eyes spoke of something deeper and darker beyond the innocent facade. He read her fear and his smile widened.

"Why do you say my brother *was* a decent man? What has happened to him?"

"Your brother was arrested for espionage."

Lin swallowed back her fears. "Is he dead?"

"Yes," Kang replied.

She looked into his eyes and saw the truth, and beyond the truth, she saw something else; Kang Fa seemed to be taking pleasure in her anguish, as only a truly evil person could.

A single tear fell from her eye as she stood there, paralyzed with fear of this man. Kang gently brushed her cheek with his hand to collect the droplet, his touch nearly causing her to faint.

"A tear for the fallen, how poetic. Zhenyi shed many tears before he died, especially when I told him that I would be visiting you."

The certainty with which he confirmed her brother's death caused Lin's worst fears to explode in her mind. She was in the presence of a sadistic monster.

"I broke your brother's pitiful group of subversives. I infiltrated it with my own agents and destroyed each cell of resistance. With your brother's help, I intercepted the courier who was to meet you tonight. Everyone involved has been captured or killed, and you, my beautiful flower, are all that remains of Lin Zhenyi's ring of spies."

This man is a killer! her mind screamed out. *Run!*

Lin bolted to one side, trying to escape, but Kang just laughed and grabbed her as she tried to pass, locking his left arm tightly around her torso. His forearm clamped over her breasts, holding her back firmly against his chest. Her warmth aroused him as she trembled in his crushing embrace.

"You are a very beautiful woman, more beautiful than your brother described. When I told him that I would visit you, he pleaded with me not to harm you. He said that you were not involved in his crimes." Kang pulled at her dress and ran his hand slowly, intimately across her thigh. "This was the image that I placed in your brother's mind, the single thought that forced him to tell me *everything*."

"You bastard!" She choked, sobbing.

Kang's free hand moved away from beneath her dress, and with it went the fear of a brutal rape. He'd brought her on a journey from trust to fear, enjoying each subtle turn and its effect upon her, but time grew short and Lin's contact would soon arrive. His grip tightened and her sobbing abruptly halted with the violent snap of her neck.

Neville Axton walked confidently down the darkened pier. Every place in this city held its own special dangers for the inattentive, and a man had to know how to carry himself if he expected to walk about unaccosted. His thirty years as an agent in Her Majesty's Secret Service, most of which had been spent in Hong Kong, allowed him to project an outward demeanor that, while not overtly hostile, left the impression that he was not someone to be trifled with.

He had been worried about tonight's exchange from the moment he learned that Lin Mei would be involved. Axton had warned his Chinese agent about the dangers of using his sister as a mule, but Zhenyi's situation had become desperate and there was simply no alternative.

He strolled along the pier, ignoring the private lives going on inside the floating homes to either side of him. Near the end of the long dock, he saw the silhouette of a woman in the reflected lights of Hong Kong. The woman made no move, no glance toward him as he approached.

At ten feet, he knew that it was Lin Mei seated on the crates near the end of the jetty. Axton sensed something amiss and approached cautiously.

Crouching down in front of her, he stared into the quiet of her eyes. In place of the animation that usually shone out of someone her age, there was emptiness. Her lips were slightly parted, as if to speak, but no words or warning came.

In Lin Mei's hands, Axton found Zhenyi's letter held out like an offering. The list was gone. Axton placed his

8 TOM GRACE

hand upon her shoulder. His gentle touch caused her to topple forward, crumpling in his arms like a rag doll.

"Lin Mei," Axton vowed, his mind filling with rage and sorrow, "I swear to you that I will find your murderer."

Langley, Virginia

Jackson Barnett wiped the offending smudge from the right lens of his wire-framed bifocals and, satisfied that his vision would be hampered by nothing more than his aging eyes, perched them back on his face. His face was long and thin, favoring his mother's side of the family, and framed with a full head of neatly trimmed silver hair. Barnett possessed the look and demeanor of a lifelong scholar: physically unimposing yet possessing the confidence of a well-trained mind.

Barnett read the intelligence report a second time to clarify his grasp of the details. The report identified the means used to divert the shipment of an American-made supercomputer to a North Korean military testing facility. The machine's sale was restricted to only the closest allies of the United States, and its theft was considered a serious breech of national security. Unfortunately, this was just one of the many problems facing the Director of Central Intelligence this afternoon, problems well beyond those he had faced as a prosecutor in South Carolina a quarter of a century ago.

As Barnett studied the mechanics of the computer theft, his speaker phone buzzed.

"Yes, Sally?" he answered.

"Phillip Moy is here to see you."

Barnett glanced at his wristwatch and quickly noticed two things. First, the hours between 1:00 and

4:30 P.M. had passed very quickly today, and, second, Phillip Moy was as punctual as ever. "Show him right in."

Sally Kirsch escorted an Asian man of average height and build into Barnett's office. The man wore the corporate uniform of highly paid executives around the world—a well-tailored conservative gray suit with a starched white shirt, a floral-print silk tie, and a pair of black Italian loafers whose sheen cast no doubt about the suppleness of the leather. Phillip Moy's face was nearly round and had, as its most dominating feature, a pair of dark brown eyes that burned with a fiery intelligence.

Moy was the founder and CEO of the computer corporation that bore his name. He looked remarkably sharp and unperturbed following a day of briefings and testimony on Capitol Hill. Today's session had, no doubt, added a few more gray hairs to his otherwise blue-black mane.

Kirsch placed several pink message slips on Barnett's desk and collected a small stack of classified files from his out-basket for a return trip to the file room.

Barnett rose to greet his guest. Both men, who had started from humble beginnings, were in their early fifties and nearing the pinnacle of their careers.

"Can I get you a drink, Phillip?" Barnett asked as he poured himself a scotch and soda.

"Sure, just splash a little scotch over some ice. Keep the water."

Barnett brought the drinks over and sat in a brown leather chair opposite Moy. He sipped on his drink, then loosened his tie, signaling an end to any formality for this meeting. "How are things going with the Gatekeeper Project?"

"We're still on schedule, so far. Our initial tests show the device is capable of monitoring all the signal traffic moving over a major computer network without degrading that network's performance. The defensive aspects of the Gatekeeper appear to be equally impressive."

"I'm glad to hear that. Lord knows that we need to get those units in place ASAP. Just last week, some kid broke through an Internet server into one of the Pentagon's low-level computers." Barnett took a hard swallow of scotch and smacked his lips, sighing.

"She spoofed the router, a real nice hack. It was dumb luck she got caught." Moy noticed Barnett's eyebrow arch slightly. "Professional admiration, Jackson—the young lady has talent."

"Maybe you should hire her."

"She'd fit right in. Some of my best and brightest programmers have a similar wild, inventive streak. I just give them a constructive way to express their creativity. It's a good thing she wasn't working for someone else, like Ames."

Barnett nodded in agreement, recalling as if it were yesterday the arrest of the CIA counterintelligence officer on charges of spying for the Soviets. By exploiting the weak internal security on Langley's computer network, Ames used his office PC to steal dozens of files classified beyond his clearance. It was in the aftermath of the Aldrich Ames affair that Moy's security projects with the government began.

"We've come a long way since the early nineties, but the memory of Ames won't soon be forgotten."

"I understand and share your concerns, Jackson. The Gatekeepers will provide our government's computers with the security they need."

Moy was a firm believer in the Gatekeeper vision, a strategy for protecting the government's vast computer networks by providing those machines with the tools necessary to thwart a computer-based attack and pursue the attacker. The Gatekeeper vision was born from a fortunate accident in the Moy Electronics research labs. Almost a year earlier, a group of engineers working on a method to increase the flow of information inside a new type of parallel-processing computer hit an impasse. Unlike traditional computer designs, which relied upon a single chip to perform each instruction one after another, the new design linked hundreds of individual chips together like the oarsmen of a Roman galley. Each chip in the new design would tackle just a piece of a larger problem, allowing the team of small processors to outperform the massive single processor of a supercomputer.

The problem the engineers encountered was a simple matter of communication. The faster they tried to run the team of parallel processors, the more tangled the flow of information among individual chips became. They were ready to start over, when the project leader of the parallel-processing team had a discussion about their problems with the young woman who led Moy Electronics' most esoteric group of researchers—the neural and cognitive sciences team.

Over a two-hour lunch, the two project leaders brainstormed an idea that later evolved into the Gatekeeper, an artificially intelligent device capable of learning and adapting itself to its host computer's environment.

It was a giant step in programming, giving the Gatekeeper the ability to determine from where a user was calling and if the user was legitimate. In its current form, the device could discover a hacker trying to break into its host computer and trace the connection back to its source. Like taking a picture of a burglar in your house, Moy's Gatekeeper could follow the electronic trail to the hacker's computer and even strip evidence from the intruder's machine. The hacker wouldn't know he had been traced until the police showed up at the front door.

"Phillip, I've been thinking about something since you first explained these neural-network systems to me. Given that a Gatekeeper is capable of learning everything about the computer environment that it's attached to—and I believe you said that includes every machine that it comes into contact with—can it be taught to look for *other things* while it's out there?"

Moy arched an eyebrow at his friend as he thought about the question. "You want to turn my Gatekeeper into a hacker?"

Barnett nodded and took another sip of his drink as Moy settled back a little farther into the soft leather chair to consider the idea. He didn't disturb his colleague, knowing that Moy's outward calm belied the furious pace of thought within. True geniuses, he mused, seemed to possess a remarkable ability to block out distractions and focus their minds completely. While different thoughts floated in and out of his consciousness, Barnett knew that Moy's mind was racing through the possibilities posed by his question. After a few quiet moments, Moy looked up from his swirling glass with a mischievous smile.

Barnett broke the silence. "Judging from that look on your face, I assume you've found an answer. Can you program your Gatekeeper to break into another computer?"

"Of course, the tools are already there." To Moy, the technical issues seemed trivial. "The Gatekeeper is driven to learn about its computer environment in order to protect that environment. This includes the host computer and every system within its network. Each time another computer comes into contact with the Gatekeeper, it becomes a learned part of the Gatekeeper's experience. This mutant Gatekeeper would share a similar thirst to learn, but the intentions behind its actions would be markedly different."

"Give me an example, Phillip."

"Okay," Moy replied, relishing his role as computer villain. "Say I wanted to break into the network here at Langley. Your high-security computers aren't on the Net, so I can't hack my way in. And breaking into this building is obviously a little more difficult than getting into the English Department at Podunk State University."

"Obviously," Barnett agreed, playing along.

"If I wanted to get into your information, and I had one of these devices, I would find out where the CIA buys their personal computers and laptops. Then I would get a job at that company, say testing the computers before they get delivered. As soon as an order for the CIA came through, I'd plant my device in one of your computers and ship it. With any luck, that computer would be connected to the information that I'm interested in. The odds are also very high that the CIA's well-protected intranet has at least one dedicated phone line to the outside world. My device would find that line and stealthily contact me for further instructions."

Barnett was intrigued by the hacker-Gatekeeper scenario Moy proposed. "Could such a device be easily detected?"

Moy shook his head. "I envision this device as something very similar physically to our Gatekeeper, just one of a hundred anonymous black chips on a circuit board. Operationally, it would be completely invisible, and it would have total control over its host. In all likelihood, no one would ever know the device was there. Even if its

activities could be detected, they would be dismissed as the work of a person. After all, who in their right mind would suspect a computer of espionage?"

Barnett sipped his drink, then smiled. "I think you've reached the conclusion that I was hoping for. Recent international events are forcing the White House to reevaluate our diplomatic and trade relations with several countries, including Iraq, Iran, North Korea, and the People's Republic of China."

"The Red Chinese will rot in hell before I sell them any of my computers, regardless of what the White House thinks of them."

Barnett showed no surprise at Moy's reaction. The defection of Moy's father, a Chinese Oppenheimer, had resulted in the imprisonment of several relatives. Little word ever came out of China about the people they left behind.

"I would never ask you to deal with the PRC. I know your family history well enough not to make such a request." With that assurance made, Barnett returned to his original point. "What I wanted you to consider is what might happen if a computer equipped with one of these devices was to *disappear* in shipment and find itself someplace that we don't officially want it. Further suppose that once our electronic spy had learned its way around this hostile nation's computer network, it found a way to call home."

"Interesting." Moy's eyes narrowed as he studied the DCI's face. "Is China to be a target for this type of operation?"

Barnett just shrugged his shoulders. "This is purely speculation on my part, nothing more than an exercise in wishful thinking. I will admit that our current shortage of intelligence assets in the PRC, coupled with their desire for high-end computers, make them an ideal target."

Moy took the hint. "The modifications you propose would require significant funding and man-hours—at least a year of software development and testing. I expect that you'll want the accounting for this little venture kept separate from the Gatekeeper Project."

"That's correct. We'll assign some of our technical people to work with yours on developing the . . ." Barnett paused as he found himself at a momentary loss for words. "What shall we call this new device?"

"I'm not sure. What's the word you used to describe someone like Aldrich Ames, a hidden spy working for your enemies?"

"Ames was a mole. Like its namesake, intelligence moles burrow deep and are difficult to root out."

"Mole," Moy mused. "I'm sure my marketing people could dream up something from that, but it just doesn't sound right. It's too cute. The device we're talking about is coldly logical, calculating and precise. It's a finely tuned machine."

"Sounds like one of your sports cars."

"Exactly." A glint then appeared in Moy's eyes, a flash of inspiration that could only have been more obvious had a cartoonist drawn a lightbulb over his head. He flipped to a blank page on his legal pad and sketched something very quickly. "I recently acquired an old Porsche, one identical to the car that James Dean drove into oblivion. This particular model had a very unique name. If the goal of this project is to create an electronic spy, one that operates exclusively in a World Wide Web of networked computers, then the resulting device would be a . . ."

Moy paused dramatically as he handed the legal pad

to Barnett. Barnett saw on it a menacing arachnid leering at him, and one word in large block letters.

"*Spyder*," Barnett said, finishing the sentence. He thought about the name for a minute as Moy sat back, pleased with his quick wit. "I give up, Phillip; Spyder it is. I'll get everything arranged on this end to get you started. I'll fund the project through my discretionary budget. That should keep it hidden long enough for us to complete development."

Chapter 1

Ann Arbor, Michigan
November 17

The masonry walls of the Canham Natatorium reverberated with the rhythmic sound of swimmers pounding the shimmering surface of the fifty-meter pool into a froth. All the lanes were occupied by members of the defending Big Ten Champion Michigan women's swim team. At the far end of the pool, Kelsey Newton carefully studied the strokes of the young women who swam the eight-hundred-meter freestyle relay.

The sophomore who normally swam the third leg of the four-part event was lagging slightly behind the others, hampered no doubt by a badly bruised thigh that she had injured while traying. Traying was the collegiate version of sledding, in which trays borrowed from dormitory cafeterias were used instead of toboggans. The injured swimmer had lost control of her tray and tumbled harshly near the bottom of the hill. Kelsey barely suppressed a smile as she thought about her own pathetic attempts to steer those unwieldy slabs of fiberglass down the bumpy hills of the Nichols Arboretum.

These morning workouts were for conditioning and building endurance; the girls essentially swam on autopilot. Kelsey made a few notes on her clipboard and returned to the poolside office. She remembered these early-morning sessions from her four years as an undergraduate at Michigan and from the thousands of miles she had swum before and since. A wall in the basement of her parents' home bore the trophies, medals, and ribbons from her days as a competitive swimmer. As a senior, she had been the captain of this team and had led it to a Big Ten Championship and earned for herself the title of all-American.

All the years of swimming had molded Kelsey Newton, sculpting every muscle of her five-nine body into curvaceous perfection. Her shoulders were broad, which only served to accentuate the curves of her chest, waist, and hips. A waterfall of straight blond hair, which she normally wore in a French braid, fell just below the level of her shoulder blades, and her eyes glittered with a shade of blue that she described scientifically as "lapis lazuli."

The door of the men's locker room opened and out came a man dressed in a dark gray swimsuit. A pair of swim goggles dangled loosely around his neck and a towel was draped like a rope across his shoulders. He looked over the cavernous space, as if it was the first time he'd been here, and then began walking toward the office where Kelsey Newton sat.

Like Newton, the man's physique was the product of years spent in the water. His fair, freckled skin was tightly stretched over a lean base of chiseled muscles that were well defined, but not to the point of a bodybuilder's exaggeration. There was a harshness to his form that suggested that the waters he was drawn from were far more turbulent than those of a fifty-meter pool. The scars that marked various points of impact on his body clearly indicated that this man was a product of the forge of violence.

He was six feet tall and his clean-shaven face was accented by a thick crop of flaming red hair that he wore short. The final evidence of his Irish heritage were the green eyes that sparkled with recognition when he reached the office.

"Morning, Kelsey," he said, leaning against the door frame.

"I see you found the place. How are you feeling, Nolan?"

"A little rough around the edges, but not too bad. How about you?"

"I'm fine, thanks to your grandmother. After the first toast, she and I switched from whiskey to ginger ale. There is no way I can keep up with a bunch of Irish mourners."

" 'Tis true, lass, and there are quite a few casualties at the Kilkenny home this morning." Nolan then glanced down, suddenly struck by the real truth in his reply. "I still can't believe my mother is gone. Every time I turn a corner, or walk into a room in that house, I expect to see her. It's so strange not to find her there."

"I know, Nolan," Kelsey said as she clasped his hand. "I know."

Kelsey had spent most of the previous day with Nolan and his family, grieving with them and paying her last respects to Nolan's mother, Meghan Kilkenny, who was laid to rest. Kelsey's parents had been close friends with Nolan's since college, and the bond between the families was, in many ways, stronger than blood. Kelsey and Nolan had been close friends during childhood. Both were highly intelligent and, to the chagrin of their mothers, equally uninterested in romantic social encounters throughout their adolescence. Together, they went to proms and other gatherings that seemed to require a couple, but theirs was a friendship more of the mind than the heart, and both seemed reluctant to risk what they had for the elusive promise of the unknown.

Since graduating from high school, both had taken different paths. Kelsey had attended the University of Michigan, where she swam and majored in what she called "John Galt studies," physics and philosophy. Her keen mind and aggressive determination had brought her to the point where, at the age of thirty, she had earned a Ph.D., a position as associate professor of physics at the university, and a sizable grant for her research into the young field of optical electronics. Her position as assistant coach of the women's swim team, which brought her to the pool in the wee hours of the morning, was something she did out of her love for the sport.

Nolan had stripped his life to the bare essentials and left the comfortable upper-middle-class world of his parents to enter the United States Naval Academy at Annapolis. His success as a swimmer paralleled Kelsey's, and a wall in his old bedroom was similarly adorned with the symbols of his athletic accomplishments. Nolan's brilliance in the field of computer science had led the navy to defer his enlistment for two years while he pursued a graduate degree at the Massachusetts Institute of Technology. After that, Nolan's life took what many considered to be an unexpected turn—the quiet scholar-athlete joined the navy's elite Special Warfare Command and became a SEAL. Assignment to the SEAL teams was considered the most demanding mental and physical challenge the navy offered—it was precisely the kind of challenge that Nolan Kilkenny found irresistible.

From Kelsey's point of view, Nolan's assignment caused him to go from distant to secretive, but their friendship endured and their short, infrequent reunions were something they both enjoyed.

"Are you ready to swim some laps?" Kelsey asked.

"I can wait until practice is done."

"It's not a problem, I can clear a lane for you."

Kelsey walked over to the pool's edge and waited in front of the far lane. As the first swimmer from the relay team approached, she blew the whistle that dangled from a yellow cord around her neck.

Startled, the girl's head popped out of the water. "What's up, coach?"

"You guys are done for the day. Hit the showers." One by one, the swimmers stopped at the end of the pool.

"Lisa," Kelsey called out as the bruised swimmer emerged from the water, "have the trainer take a look at your leg. Maybe he can loosen it up a little."

"Sure, Kelsey," the swimmer replied as she gingerly climbed the ladder. "Is this your new boyfriend?"

"No," Kelsey replied, in a tone that said the matter was none of the girl's business. The girl joined her teammates and a few giggles were heard as they entered the locker room.

"What happened to your last boyfriend—what's his name?"

"Scott," Kelsey answered. "Scott and I broke up over a month ago."

"I thought you said he had real potential, that he might even be the one."

"There were glimmers of hope there. In the end,

though, he was intimidated by me. For some reason, he felt that my accomplishments made him less of a man."

"Doesn't sound like much of a man to start with."

"How about you? Any luck?"

"Nope, my social life is just as barren as always. I've dated a lot of women, but there was no depth to them. I guess I'm looking for someone who is more than the sum of her fashion accessories."

"Well, quit moping and hit the water. I'll join you in a few minutes."

Nolan tossed his towel against the wall, where the floor was dry, adjusted his goggles, loosened up his arms, and dove in. The water was brisk, deliberately cool to keep the swimmers moving. His heart rate quickened as he pulled himself through the water, accelerating to match his muscles' increased demand for oxygen.

He swam four miles every day, an effort more a mental exercise than a physical one. Then again, so much of Kilkenny's life over the past six years had been that way. As a Navy SEAL, his life was designed to be *that way*.

This was Kilkenny's eighth day home, his eighth day as a civilian. "Technically a civilian," his captain had cautioned. Kilkenny had returned to Ann Arbor on a compassionate leave to help care for his ailing mother. "Technically a civilian" meant that he could still be called back to duty should a crisis arise. Thankfully, the world looked calm on this November day in Ann Arbor.

He counted off the distance in his mind, tuning out the world beyond. The rhythm of his stroke and the surging of the water around his body had an almost hypnotic effect, allowing him to enter a calm, meditative state. Kilkenny found that he did his best thinking while swimming long distances, and today he had a lot on his mind.

Death had always been an abstraction for him—

something he had understood intellectually but not emotionally. Prior to his mother's death from cancer, he'd never lost anyone so close as to feel the hurt of death, to understand its meaning. Until he became a SEAL, he'd never known how it felt to be the cause of death.

Kilkenny's entire tour of duty with the navy had been spent training and working with the SEALs. In their company, he had mastered the skills necessary to achieve military objectives, skills that would keep himself and his squad alive behind enemy lines, skills that included killing.

The medals and ribbons on Kilkenny's dress uniform bespoke his leadership on missions recorded only in the classified files of the Pentagon, but they also served as reminders of those he had killed. Each of those deaths was a necessity required by either the mission's objectives or the safety of his squad. Killing was a part of his job, but he took no pleasure from it. He had never boasted of his kills, never bragged about how many of the enemy he'd "taken out" on a mission, but he also felt no emotion, no connection to those who died.

In reaching out to take his mother, death had taken on a new meaning for Nolan Kilkenny, one that numbed his heart with cruel grief and denied his mind a sensible reason. And for the first time in his life, death was personal. Kilkenny wanted to strike out against his mother's killer, but the disease was as efficient and unemotional about death as he had been. In another part of his mind, Kilkenny now questioned whether or not he could again take another life.

Nearing the end of the pool, he reached out for the side and prepared to flip-turn into another lap. Instead of touching the smooth tile wall, his hand grazed a warm, firm leg. Startled, he abruptly stopped and lifted his goggled face out of the water. On the pool's edge sat Kelsey Newton, smiling back at him.

"I've been trying to get your attention for the last two laps. If this didn't work, I was going to jump in after you. You've got a phone call," she said, her voice both sympathetic and concerned. "It's Captain Dawson."

Kilkenny nodded and stripped off his goggles as Newton pulled her supple legs from the water and walked back to the pool office.

He pulled himself from the cool water and quickly ran a towel over his dripping body before entering the office and picking up the phone. "Kilkenny here, sir."

"Nolan, I know you're on leave, but a situation has developed that requires our immediate attention. Tickets have already been cut and are waiting for you at the airport."

Part of his mind cursed at the thought of being pulled back, but he knew Dawson wouldn't have called unless he'd had to. *I hope it's a quick one,* Nolan thought as he copied down the flight information, knowing he couldn't refuse the summons. *Next month, I'm a full-time civilian.*

"I'm under way, sir."

Chapter 2

Little Creek Naval Amphibious Base, Virginia

Kilkenny followed the yeoman into Capt. Jack Dawson's office. Kilkenny stood two inches taller than his commanding officer, but the difference in their physiques exaggerated the distance. Dawson's sturdy, well-muscled ebony frame and severely cropped hair often caused complete strangers to mistake him for one of the Washington Redskins. In contrast, Kilkenny's taut, lean carriage and freckled Irish skin reminded people of nothing more than a marathon runner in need of a strong sunblock.

An unexpected wave of nostalgia swept over Dawson as Kilkenny reported for duty. They'd first met six years earlier, when Ens. Nolan Kilkenny reported to Coronado for BUD/S, Basic Underwater Demolition/ SEALs training. Dawson had taken one look at this wiry red-haired college kid and saw nothing more than a future Pentagon technoweenie who'd wash out before Hell Week. Dawson had been wrong.

"Take a seat, Lieutenant," Dawson ordered as he returned Kilkenny's salute. "Nolan, do you remember why you became a SEAL?"

Kilkenny knew this wasn't small talk, and he wondered about the motivation behind Dawson's question. "Yes, sir, it was the challenge. I knew that command of the SEAL squad would test my limits, both physically and mentally."

"And do you remember who encouraged you to undertake this challenge?"

"Yes, sir. Rear Adm. Roger Hopwood."

Like Kilkenny, Rear Admiral Hopwood was a graduate of the U.S. Naval Academy. Hopwood had also swum for the Midshipmen, and Kilkenny's performance with the team during his senior year caught the admiral's attention. The admiral was also a decorated SEAL, and he now served as NavSpecWarGruCom, commander of the navy's Special Warfare Group.

Upon learning that Kilkenny was both an accomplished scuba diver and a black belt in the Isshinryu style of karate, Hopwood took the future ensign under his wing and encouraged him to join the SEALs. It was Hopwood who also made sure that Dawson, who then oversaw SEAL training in Coronado, received a carefully edited file regarding Kilkenny's background. It wasn't until Kilkenny flattened the hand-to-hand combat instructor that Dawson became suspicious. Roger Hopwood loved surprises, and the quiet Ensign Kilkenny was a *ringer*. Kilkenny not only survived SEAL training, but excelled and eventually became one of Dawson's most valued squad leaders.

"That's right, Admiral Hopwood is one of your sea daddies. Now here's the situation."

"Situation" was Dawson's polite way of saying that

the Pentagon had an ugly job that needed to be done quickly and quietly.

"How well do you remember Haiti?"

"Well enough to get around if I had to, sir, but why Haiti now? I thought things were pretty quiet down there."

"Take a look at this tape and I think you'll understand."

Dawson punched the play button on the VCR and the image of a Haitian fishing village filled the screen. Center frame was the recognizable face of Jean Arno, the junior Republican congressman from Florida. Arno was smiling and talking in fluent Haitian French, which was no surprise, since the lawmaker was the youngest son of Haitian immigrants.

Accompanying the congressman were his aides, relief workers, and a few military officers. An officer near the rear of the group caught Kilkenny's attention; it was Admiral Hopwood. The whole scene looked like a well-choreographed photo opportunity designed to show the viewing audience at home how well American aid was working in Haiti. A loud popping sound from the jungle preceded a dizzying spin by the camera before it struck the ground. Though now skewed at a bizarre upward angle, the camera kept rolling, recording the screams of people and rapid blasts of approaching gunfire. Legs rushed past the lens, captured in their panicked flight. Then a group of men in black emerged from the jungle, spraying bullets wildly into the crowd as they entered the camera's view. Soon, the only sounds to be heard were those of gunfire and the cries of the dying.

One of the figures in black stood alone in the center of the village, dispassionately watching the carnage unfold. What struck Kilkenny most about the man was his eyes; they displayed nothing save a ruthless efficiency.

Are those my eyes in battle? Kilkenny wondered.

Three minutes into the massacre, several of the black-garbed men dragged Arno and the surviving Americans before their leader. This man looked over the prisoners, stopping at the congressman, whom he viewed with disgust.

"Fool!" he spat in Arno's face. "Will you *never* learn that your kind are not welcome in Haiti!"

Arno and the others remained silent, denying the man any satisfaction he might find in their pleas for mercy. The leader studied his prisoners carefully as he finished a cigarette, weighing their fate in his mind. A flick of his fingers sent the smoldering butt arcing to the ground. He stared down for a moment, then pulled the machete from his belt and swung furiously into Arno's neck. The others joined their leader, quickly hacking the Americans to death in an orgy of blood and violence.

Once the Americans were dead, the leader raised his bloodstained machete and ordered his men back into the jungle. The raiding party left with their plunder and several female captives. Soon, the only sound that remained was the buzzing of flies under the hot Caribbean sun.

Kilkenny swallowed back the bile in his throat as Dawson stopped the tape.

"What you just saw happened yesterday. The central figure in this massacre is Etienne Masson, the leader of a tribe, for lack of a better word, that controls a large piece of rain forest surrounding Jacmel. He was a twenty-year veteran of the Haitian military and even attended the Green Beret program at Bragg before going native."

"So he's not one of those cardboard generals we usually find in Third World hellholes."

"Just the opposite. Masson doesn't seem to be after anything. While our troops were there, he laid low. He doesn't care who is ruling Port-au-Prince as long as they stay out of his way. His cabal doesn't even have a name, but the people living in their shadow call them la Mort Noir, the Black Death. What you just saw was the first bit of carelessness on Masson's part."

"The camera," Kilkenny answered, the gruesome images still playing in his mind.

"Right. His men took out the cameraman first, but nobody bothered to get the tape. This is the first time that anyone outside of Haiti has seen Masson in nine years. The Haitians have tried to deal quietly with him on their own, without much luck. After yesterday, the Haitian government not only approves of the United States taking action; they expect it. We've got carte blanche, as long as we're quiet about it. Everyone over there is scared shitless of this guy."

"Understandably so; it looks like he actually enjoys killing people."

Dawson sensed something beneath the surface of Kilkenny's comment. He knew that Nolan was taking his mother's death hard. He'd experienced similar feelings of self-doubt following his own parents' deaths several years ago.

"Masson does enjoy killing, and he's good at it, but he's not like you and me. We're trained to kill, but we do it only when we have to. Masson is something else altogether." Dawson slid a folder bearing the CIA logo across his desk to Kilkenny. "Here's the intelligence briefing on Masson. What's known of his activities reads like a voodoo version of *Apocalypse Now,* with Masson playing the role of Colonel Kurtz."

Kilkenny began thumbing through the intelligence report. "Fine, what's the op?"

Dawson slipped a thick binder of materials across the desk to Kilkenny, then leaned back in his chair. "Quiet in, quiet out. You and your squad will launch in minisubs, SDVs, from the *Columbia,* six miles off Haiti's southern coast. You'll land on a remote beach and go hunting in-country. Your orders are to seek out and destroy the enemy."

Kilkenny looked over the preliminary mission time line. "A three-week op in December is cutting it a little close, sir. My tour is up at the end of next month."

"I'm well aware of your status, Lieutenant, and I know that you're ready to get on with your life. I want you to know that I wouldn't have called you back without a damn good reason."

"I know," Kilkenny replied, staring at the picture of a pair of young SEALs in Vietnam that Dawson proudly displayed on his wall. "Adm. Roger Hopwood."

Dawson looked over at the picture. "Jolly Roger and I go way back; we toured Nam together. I owe that man my life. He's the reason JSOC chose us to carry out this mission. This is *war,* Nolan, and we need some meat-eaters on this op."

Dawson stood up and Kilkenny snapped to attention. "Lieutenant Kilkenny, you are to assemble your squad and brief them on this assignment. Go over the plan and be ready to brief me on your deployment preparations at eighteen hundred hours. Whatever you need, you'll get. This one's for Hopwood."

"Aye, aye, sir."

Chapter 3

New York
November 25

Alex Roe slipped out of bed and into the oversized Georgia Bulldog sweatshirt that she'd left on the floor the night before. The shirt draped from her softly curved shoulders to a point on her thigh that was an inch below immodest. She pushed the sleeves up past her elbows, ran her fingers through her disheveled shoulder-length brunette hair, and set about finding something to eat. Roe firmly believed that her daily regimen of diet and exercise had kept her lithe body free of the fatty deposits that accumulate on so many people over the age of forty.

Inside the master bathroom, Randall Johnson was in the midst of his morning ablutions. She marveled at the beauty of the renovated turn-of-the-century factory that now housed Johnson's multilevel condominium. Many of the building's original architectural features remained exposed, lending an historic flavor to the contemporary elements of modern living.

The sun, barely over the horizon, poured light through the tall arched windows of the condo's great room. Long shadows cast by the morning light exaggerated the depth of the brickwork's relief; the terra-cotta details formed a study in contrast.

In the kitchen, she ground some fresh gourmet beans and started the coffeemaker. The morning was cold, but pleasant for November in New York, and, after digging out from an early snow, the city was preparing for tomorrow's Thanksgiving parade. Roe took an apple from the refrigerator, sat down at the sunlit kitchen table, and spread out the morning paper.

Twenty minutes later, she finished her morning reverie, poured another cup of coffee, and walked into the den, where her laptop computer sat waiting for her. With the machine switched on and herself recharged, she set about the task of completing her article by deadline.

Her story on Pangen Research was nearly complete, requiring only a few finishing touches. She was engrossed in a fine point of grammar when Randall Johnson entered quietly behind her, wearing only a robe cinched about his waist. He peered over her shoulder and read some of the text.

"You better not misquote me, Alex. I want to come across as an intelligent and decisive financial officer who just happens to be a great guy."

"Hmm, a CFO who is intelligent and decisive, yet still a great guy. Aren't those conflicting traits for someone in your position? I'm not sure the readers of *Net-Worth* magazine would believe that."

"From what you've told me, neither would your editors."

"That, my dear Randy," Roe replied while nuzzling his freshly shaven neck, "goes without saying. Editors, by their very nature, are a cynical lot, prone to doubt any journalist's objectivity."

"I would doubt your objectivity, too, if I knew you'd spent the night with a key player in your story."

Roe pulled away from Johnson's neck, feigning betrayed surprise. "*Et tu*, Randy? Though the occasional editor may criticize minor points of my work, none have ever questioned the quality of my research or the depth of my interviews."

Roe stood and pressed her hand into the matted hairs on his chest, pushed him back into a leather wing-back chair, and straddled his lap. Johnson was six inches taller than she, but the position of their bodies allowed her to gaze down at his salt-and-pepper hair. His body had softened slightly over the past twenty years, but neither of them were college students, and both found that the matured version of their old flame was still quite attractive.

Cradling him against her breasts, she began to kiss his forehead, slowly working her way down to his mouth. Johnson's arms caressed her back beneath the sweatshirt, gently massaging the muscles along her spine. Her mouth pressed deeply into his; their tongues engaged with a feverish intensity. Gradually, the kisses softened and the embrace grew gentle and close.

"I don't have a problem with the *depth* of your interviews, either." He pulled back enough so they were eye-to-eye. "Now remember, Pangen Research is the hottest biotech company you have ever seen and their CFO is both brilliant and a great guy."

"Yes, sir," she answered dutifully. "You know, this insecurity over my article is really unbecoming. I don't recall you ever being this nervous back in college."

Johnson slumped back in the chair. "Back in college, I didn't have twenty-five million dollars of venture capital and an IPO riding on some term paper. It's not your article that's got me on edge; it's everything with this little company. My little company."

Johnson stared through the window without really looking at anything. His mind instead focused on the events that had led to his present role as the financial shepherd of a hot young biotech research company.

"When those scientists came to me with a proposal to bring gene-therapy technologies out of the lab and into medical practice, I believed in them. They had these Nobel Prize–caliber ideas and no clue how to get a company going. I did a little investigation on their work and found what may be the next high-growth industry. It was like discovering Apple back when it was in the garage. I worked damn hard to design a workable business plan, and my board bought into it. In less than two years, I've built a company that's ready to go public, a company that owns a patented stable of purebred retroviruses that could start the biggest medical revolution since antibiotics."

"You have a serious case of mother-hen syndrome. Pangen is a textbook example of venture capitalism at its best. You've got a group of idealistic research scientists with a vision and no money, matched with a savvy young financier who makes the dream come true against incredible odds. When you're finished launching this company into the golden land of NASDAQ, we're writing a book about your adventures."

"Maybe," he replied coyly, "but only if I grant you

the rights to the story. I, of course, will retain the movie rights. I wonder whom we can get to play me."

Roe gave him a reassuring hug. In public, he was the Rock of Gibraltar—exuding confidence and focused leadership. Pangen Research owed its very existence to the forty-two-year-old man in her arms. He was preparing to let his fledgling company go out into the world on its own. Like any parent when a child finally leaves home, he felt the same pride in his work and the same worries about the future.

"Thanks, Alex, for everything. The past few weeks have been unbelievably tough for me. Your timing couldn't have been any better."

"Actually, it's an accident I came at all. I just happened to be available when *NetWorth* needed a piece on Pangen for a special issue. Freelancer's motto: Have Computer, Will Travel. Discovering a long-lost love was an unexpected bonus. I am glad that I found you again."

They held each other close in the morning light. "How did I ever let you get away?"

"As I recall, you felt it would be best if we started seeing other people."

"That, Little Miss Smart-Ass, was a rhetorical question. You don't answer those kinds of questions. You just nod your head politely." His expression softened as his thoughts retraced their shared history.

"I know, Randy. Harvard and UCLA were half a world apart then." Her mouth curled into a light smirk as she peered into his eyes. "You didn't have to take that scholarship."

"That's right," Johnson replied as he slipped her off his lap and leapt onto a long coffee table in front of the couch, balancing himself as if he were riding the California surf. "I could've tossed my Harvard MBA and gone surfin' with you. 'If everybody had an ocean, across the USA.'"

Roe laughed as Johnson butchered the Beach Boys classic and rode an imaginary curl of water across the den. Suddenly, she tackled him, and they both fell onto the couch.

"What the hell was that?" Johnson shouted as Roe smothered him with a pair of soft throw pillows.

"Wipeout." She laughed in her best Valley girl imitation. "If you're gonna surf, dude, you gotta, *like*, learn how to scope the waves and watch the curl or you'll end up fish food."

They held each other for several minutes, nibbling and kissing as the early-morning light streamed through the windows. Eventually, he gave her one last kiss and got up to ready himself for the day.

At the door, he turned and pointed toward her computer, whose colorful screen saver was randomly painting the active-matrix display. "Back to work, Hemingway. There's an editor just waiting for your wonderful story, and I'll be lucky to make the office by eight."

"Slave driver," Roe mumbled under her breath as she got up. "All right, I'll be good and finish my story, but I'd rather blow it off and have fun with you today. At least we have this weekend." Roe planted a quick kiss on his cheek and swatted his behind. "Now off to work with you. All those lawyers and stockbrokers are waiting to pour tons of new money into Pangen, and you don't want to disappoint them, do you?"

Johnson's quiet demeanor barely covered the enthusiasm he felt. "That *will* be exciting. Do you think you can make it? I'd love to have you there."

Alex tapped the keyboard, looked at the unfinished story, and shrugged her shoulders. "I don't think I'll be done with this in time, but I promise to watch your debut on CNN and write the appropriate closer for my piece. Editors just love it when my stories are timely."

Johnson departed by cab, leaving Roe to refine her prose. At the appointed hour, the CNN commentator switched to live coverage on the trading floor, where a member of the exchange's board formally welcomed Pangen Research to the roster of publicly traded companies.

In a brief announcement, Johnson confirmed rumors that the FDA had approved Pangen's latest generation of retroviruses for clinical trials in human-gene-therapy research. Pangen Research gained seven points in the first thirty minutes of trading.

Roe completed her article with a brief description of the company's frenzied debut on the New York Stock Exchange. She left a space for the final share price to be filled in later by the fact checkers. She then clicked on the appropriate icons to save the file and brought up the window for communications.

After a few keystrokes, she connected with the magazine's editorial computer and delivered her story. The combined effect of the stock's strong activity and the government's regulatory blessing gave her Pangen story an excellent shot at the cover. She imagined Johnson's surprise at receiving the "Biotech Special Issue" with his handsome face smiling back at him.

With her article completed, Roe set to work on her next task. She hadn't been completely truthful with Johnson about her reason for visiting Pangen, and this lack of honesty with an old friend bothered her. However, the piece for *NetWorth* provided an excellent cover for a more detailed search into Pangen's corporate secrets.

Using a SCSI cable, she wired her laptop directly to

Johnson's home computer and activated a linkup program. Immediately, her machine began to sift through the
data encoded on his hard drive, searching for the keys to
the Pangen mainframe. Twenty minutes later, she
cracked through the system security, posing as Pangen's
CFO.

The researchers at Pangen had provided her with as
much access as she desired, access that allowed her to develop an excellent understanding of their operational
strengths and weaknesses. After several months of working overtime, Pangen's computer group had taken a well-
deserved holiday to watch the day's excitement.

The stock offering also coincided with a major medical conference on human genetics in Washington, a
meeting that had drawn most of the company's research
staff away from their lab-office complex, leaving only a
skeleton crew behind to keep things running. Roe knew
that there would never be a better opportunity to steal
Pangen's secrets than today.

She located the scientific-research libraries and issued a backup command to the host computer. The dedicated data line from Johnson's home into Pangen's
computer network allowed Roe to take information as
fast as her computer could handle it.

In seconds, the magneto-optic disk drive attached to
her laptop began to spin, absorbing megabytes of information. In less than an hour, the sum of Pangen's intel-
lectual wealth lay on three blue-green disks.

Since Roe's connection to Pangen's computer flowed
over a dedicated data line, one that logged total time
usage rather than individual calls, there was no need for
her to access the phone company's billing computer to
erase any record of the call. The host computer, on the
other hand, did record the time she logged in and how

long she remained connected. That record held the only evidence that Pangen's computer system had been accessed.

Roe released two programs into Pangen's network. The first modified the network's system security, giving her access to the internal record-keeping files. After editing those files to remove all traces of her presence, she triggered the second. In less than a minute, the program logged Roe off the system, returned Pangen's network to its original configuration, and erased itself from memory.

Confident that she'd left no evidence of her intrusion, Roe disconnected the two machines and prepared to transfer the stolen information. Unlike the old days of le Carré–style espionage, there was no need for her to skulk around town in a trench coat to leave her stolen secrets in a hollowed-out tree trunk. No, in the modern world of espionage, a spy need only encrypt her data well and transmit it electronically.

Roe's transfer program incorporated a series of data-compression and encryption algorithms that left the stolen files looking more like random noise than any kind of coherent information. Once retrieved, an inverse series of the same algorithms returned the files to their original state. For images and digitized photographs, this process would cause a minor loss of clarity; for text and purely alphanumeric data, the retrieved files were identical to the originals.

Roe dialed into a local Internet server to keep Johnson's phone bill clear of a suspicious long-distance call. From there, she meandered through several other computer networks, carefully covering her electronic trail, before accessing a computer in the London office of business consultant Ian Parnell.

Once the data transfer was in process, Roe flipped on her cellular phone and dialed Parnell's office.

"Parnell Associates. How may I direct your call?" Parnell's assistant answered with cool British formality.

"Hi, Paulette. It's Alex. Is Ian in?"

"No. He's taking advantage of this lovely day on his boat. Hold on for a moment and I'll see if I can reach him."

Roe waited, listening to the antiseptic Muzak that filled the receiver beside her ear. Parnell certainly enjoyed his toys, the most prized of which was a deep metallic blue, offshore racing boat christened *Merlin*. She'd accompanied Parnell on several outings on the Thames and knew that he took his boat out on any fair day that London offered. Her brief visit to musical purgatory ended with Parnell's voice shouting over the roar of *Merlin's* engines.

"What's the good word, Alex?"

"The information is en route as we speak. It's everything your clients asked for."

"Absolutely smashing. I'll post your final payment by the end of business today." Parnell's voice returned to normal as the sound of the engines faded. "How's your schedule looking for the next couple of weeks?"

"Other than a long ski weekend in Vermont with an old friend, nothing special." A smiling picture of Johnson gazed back at her from the desktop.

"I've got another research project, one that I think you would be perfect for, if you're interested. It's worth fifty percent of a six-figure fee."

"You've got my attention, Ian."

"Good. An old client of mine, an electronics manufacturer in Hong Kong, has requested a little research into his main competitor's new product line. I'll E-mail you the background materials—usual encryption. Give me a call after you've had a chance to look them over, and we'll discuss specifics."

The file transfer ended and Roe logged off the various systems she had used to cover her tracks. It still amazed her how much easier, and safer, computers made espionage. Even though circumstances occasionally required that she physically break into the places that she was "researching," Roe found that she could complete most of her assignments by posing as a journalist or by using a computer and modem. The free flow of information in open, high-tech countries allowed them to outpace the more restrictive nations in nearly every measure of progress. This openness also made her job as an industrial spy much easier.

She felt a small twinge of guilt at the thought of stealing the information from her old flame's fledgling company, but she suppressed that reaction. She had harmed no one, and in a few years' time, most of Pangen's secrets would be well documented in scientific journals. Her consulting relationship with Ian Parnell simply allowed her to cash in on the impatience of Pangen's wealthiest rival.

Chapter 4

Roosevelt Roads Naval Station, Puerto Rico

The surf rolled in against the beach, four-foot waves cresting and crashing with a dull roar and the hiss of briny foam. The sky was partly overcast as the remnants of a late-season tropical storm drifted over the Caribbean island.

The long stretch of beach along Puerto Rico's eastern coastline was deserted, not because of the weather but because this area was off-limits. Traditional naval operations controlled a majority of the base real estate. The untamed jungle, just north of the docks and support facilities, was home to Navy Special Warfare Unit Three. It was here that Nolan Kilkenny's squad of SEALs had been sent to prepare for their mission.

It was late in the afternoon, with dusk only an hour away, when the first black shape emerged from the surf. A head peered out from beneath the waves, scanning the beach. As quickly as it appeared, it vanished. A moment later, seven black-suited figures emerged from the sea, riding an ebbing wave onto the sand. Black neoprene wet suits covered each of the men from head to toe, protecting them from the strength-sapping chill resulting from their long exposures to cool salt water. Their swim fins had been removed in the water and hooked to their dive belts in preparation for the transition from sea to land. All were armed and each focused his attention on a specific section of the beach. They thought and acted as one.

"Master Chief," Nolan Kilkenny called out, "did everybody make it home?"

"Hoo-yah, sir!" Master Chief Max Gates replied. "Just a walk in the park."

"Very well, then. This beach is secure and the exercise is over!" Kilkenny announced. "Stow your gear and clean your weapons."

Kilkenny slipped his mask down around his neck and stood to survey the beach. "Rodriguez."

"Yes, sir," replied a short fireplug of a man who had been born in a small town near the base.

"Nice job on point."

"No sweat, sir. I just followed the smell of my mama's cooking."

A pang of regret hit Kilkenny—that was a smell he would never follow home again.

Kilkenny's squad walked the short distance from the beach to the huts that served as their base of operation. Loose gear was removed first, dive belts, masks, and fins, and dunked in a large barrel of freshwater to rinse off the brine. Next off came the closed-circuit rebreathing units the SEALs used in place of the more common open-circuit scuba tanks. The rebreathing units, which recycled the diver's exhaled air for reuse, allowed the SEALs to approach a target from beneath the water without leaving a telltale stream of bubbles along the surface.

The men stripped their weapons down and carefully inspected and cleaned each component. This work was done quietly and with the utmost seriousness. Each member of the squad relied on the others, and none wanted a mission to fail or a buddy to be hurt because of something as preventable as a dirty weapon.

After reassembling and stowing his Heckler-Koch submachine gun and his 9-mm pistol, Kilkenny checked the in-basket in his hut. Inside, he found a manila envelope containing the latest satellite photos of the Haitian jungles. After a week of hard preparation, his team was beginning to gel. He had them eat, sleep, and breathe the mission twenty-four hours a day. Each piece of the equipment that they would use was becoming like a part of their bodies, each inch of Haitian rain forest as familiar as their own backyards.

This wasn't how Kilkenny had expected to spend his Thanksgiving, training in isolation with the six other men who made up his squad, but it was this kind of preparation that made the SEALs successful. Each mission was treated like a moon launch, with no detail so unimportant that it could be overlooked.

Gates approached and knocked on the door frame.

"Yo, Chief, come on in. I got the latest pictures."

Master Chief Max Gates entered the small hut and sat in the folding chair next to Kilkenny. Though junior in rank, Gates was Kilkenny's superior in age and combat experience. Like most SEALs, Gates was shorter than Kilkenny by half a head, but he made up for it with a barrel chest and a pair of forearms that would make Popeye proud. He was nearly bald, ruddy-faced, with a pair of dark brown eyes that peered out from beneath a pair of bushy brown eyebrows.

"The boys are looking good, Nolan." Twenty years in the navy hadn't softened Gates's Oklahoma drawl a bit. "They want this one."

"As they should," Kilkenny replied. "Hopwood was a SEAL legend, and the cocksucker who cut him down deserves to die."

"Actually, Nolan, they want this one for you."

"Why?"

"Because you've led these guys to hell and back and you never let them down. They just want you to go out the right way."

Before he could respond, a truck pulled up to their base. Kilkenny and Gates left the hut and walked over to the truck's tailgate.

"Listen up!" Kilkenny shouted. "D day is in ten days, which means ten more days of fun in the sun. Ten more glorious days of sweating, and marching and running SDV drills off the submarine. Ten more days"—Kilkenny paused, looking over his men—"starting tomorrow. Today, we quit early."

Cheers and excited profanities filled the air around him.

"I knew you'd like that. Since it's Thanksgiving, I cut a deal with the base commander to supplement our meager rations. Tonight, we dine on swordfish, steak, and beer."

Chapter 5

Chicago, Illinois
November 30

Alex Roe arrived for her interview with Phillip Moy at five minutes to ten. The silk suit she had chosen for this interview was stylish, sophisticated, and sexy. A few moments later, Moy's executive assistant ushered her into his office. Roe had interviewed the legendary computer genius five years ago, in a cramped, windowless office filled with used furniture. Today, his office was a little larger, the furniture was all new, and he finally had a window. Phillip Moy stood at his desk and waved to Roe as he finished a phone call.

"I apologize for the delay, Ms. Roe, but I had a minor problem to clear up. It's a pleasure to see you again." Moy's smile and handshake were genuine. "I greatly enjoyed the last article you wrote about my company."

"Please call me Alex, and the pleasure is all mine. For the record, we are starting the interview one minute early. I like what you've done with your new office. Quite an improvement over the old one."

"A few more creature comforts, but functional nonetheless. In the old building, there weren't enough spaces with windows, so I decided long ago that I wouldn't have windows until my staff did. I made good on that promise in this building."

As they took their seats, Moy's assistant entered and placed a silver tea service on the table and poured a cup for each before leaving. With the initial flattery over, the real interview began.

"I run my company by simple common sense," Moy announced proudly, setting the tone. "If you treat your people well, they will be loyal and work well for you. To illustrate that point, our employees control the largest block of shares in this company and, unlike the stock held by outside investors, these shares almost never trade. My people believe in their work and invest their own money into this company. It doesn't take a genius to understand that someone will work harder, and smarter, for something they care about."

"Well, that's what I'm here to look at," Roe explained. Moy's remarks were part of his corporate gospel and Roe's strategy was to make him feel that her article would be another public-relations coup. "At a time when other high-technology manufacturers' earnings are flat or even down, your company's soaring performance is nothing short of astonishing. Moy Electronics is one of only a few American firms that seems to have made the transition to true global competitiveness."

Moy smiled. Alex Roe had written a very positive piece about his company five years ago, one that, combined with their annual report, had caused Moy Electronics stock to rise several points. The publication of another glowing article about his company, followed by the announcement of the new product line, might work similar magic on Wall Street.

"Your praise is appreciated, but if you really want to find out about the reason for our success, you'll have to talk to the people who make it happen. I may carry the vision for where I think we should go, but it is all the other owners of this company who get us there." Moy picked up an itinerary from his desk and handed it to Roe. "You asked for permission to interview some of our employees. I have arranged for you to observe a few project teams in action during the next two weeks. My assistant will furnish you with the necessary information and security passes for your visit. In this way, I think you'll discover the real secret behind our success."

The interview continued for another thirty minutes, with Moy elaborating on world markets and events that defined the business climate in which the electronics giant competed. Roe thanked Moy for his time and collected the schedule and security materials from his assistant. The interview was a resounding success; Roe had achieved her primary goal of access to Moy's employees and most of the facility.

Roe spent the rest of the morning with the heads of the Personnel and Security departments, who ran her through a brief guest orientation. She signed the usual nondisclosure forms relating to proprietary materials she might come into contact with during her visit. Security finished processing her just before noon, allowing Roe to start her research in the employee cafeteria.

To her surprise, the food both looked and smelled fantastic, and, looking around the dining area, she noticed very few people brown-bagging their lunches. She selected a chef's salad and a cup of clam chowder and, at the register, discovered that the meal was heavily subsidized.

She found a seat near the window and began to browse through the new employee packet she'd been given. She knew Moy paid competitive wages, but she finally realized why their employee turnover was so low. Employees of Moy Electronics received fully paid health benefits, a retirement plan with generous employer contributions, favorable stock options, excellent vacation and medical time, an on-site fitness center, and an on-site child-care facility—all that *and* an inexpensive lunch. No wonder these people worked so hard to keep this place in business; working anywhere else might be considered a punishment.

When she was halfway through a folder on the current generation of Moy products, a small group of people approached her table.

"Mind if we join you?" an attractive, well-dressed woman with dark ebony skin asked politely. "It's too beautiful a day not to enjoy the view."

"Not at all, Miss Kearney," Roe replied, reading the woman's name off her picture ID. "I'm Alex Roe."

"Are you new?" Kearney inquired, glancing at Roe's orientation materials.

"No, I'm a freelance writer doing an article on the people who built Moy Electronics."

"Then you've come to the right place, but please call me Maria. I'm an industrial designer."

"She designs the pretty boxes that hide my beautiful chips," a heavyset blond-haired man commented as he cut into his burrito.

"That's Tim Otto," Kearney said, pointing at the man who'd just spoken, "a chip designer who simply hates to see his electronics covered up."

Otto nodded at Roe and continued eating his lunch.

"Next to him," Kearney continued, "is Josh Rad-wick, who also designs hardware, and Bill Iverson."

"Software god," Iverson added, offering his hand to Roe.

If there was a model of what corporate America looked like, the gangly Bill Iverson was the antithesis. Iverson's jeans were frayed and his athletic shoes were now stained a mottled shade of brown. He wore an un-buttoned red-checked flannel shirt over a black T-shirt promoting a heavy-metal band that had broken up over three years ago. Two days of stubble marred his otherwise smooth-featured face and a tangled eruption of frazzled brown hair crowned his head like a halo.

"Bill's a modest man who can program circles around most of the people here. The other two people on our team are coming." Kearney waited until a petite redhead and a tall man with a slight paunch and stringy blond hair arrived. "Natalie Geiss, Michael Cole, I'd like to in-troduce you to Alex Roe."

"Pleased to meet you, Alex," Geiss said with a smile. "Are you joining our project team?"

"Afraid not."

"Too bad, I could use another hand in working out the production sequence, but I'll get by."

"How about you, Michael?" Roe asked. "How do you fit into this merry bunch?"

Cole's sullen disposition was in contrast to the oth-ers. "Actually, I work for the government."

"Rumor has it that Michael's with the IRS," Iverson said with a laugh.

Cole glowered at Iverson as he bit into his club sand-wich. Less than a minute after he'd sat down, his pager went off.

"Damn, I hate these things," Cole said, and he

turned the alarm off and read the number. "Don't they know Chicago is an hour behind Washington? Well, I guess I'll see you all back in the lab."

Cole left with his tray, hoping to finish his lunch after he returned the call. The mood improved almost immediately after he left, though Roe found it hard to believe anyone could get this group down. It must be difficult for a wet-blanket bureaucrat like Cole to work with such enthusiastic people, she thought.

"So, you're working on some mysterious government project with Mr. Cole. Perhaps," Roe asked in a sinister mock-Russian accent, "you vould like to tell me your secrets, da?"

Everyone laughed as Roe arched an eyebrow and studied each of them suspiciously.

"Seriously," Maria said, "we shouldn't be talking about our project outside the lab. That's one offense this company does not forgive easily."

"I understand," Roe replied sympathetically. "If I went public with your secret projects, your competitors might catch up."

"Even if you did write about what we're doing, I doubt anyone could catch up with us," Iverson bragged, obviously proud of his work. "Only a handful of universities and specialty firms are even looking at neural-network processors."

"Bill"—Otto's voice was low and direct—"I think you're speaking out of class."

"It's okay," Geiss replied, coming to Iverson's defense. "He's just talking in generalities."

Roe dismissed their minor dispute over Iverson's off-hand remark, focusing instead on the revelation that they had made some kind of technological advance. "Since you've whetted my appetite, could you tell me *generally* what you're doing with neural-network systems? Most of the work I've seen is years away from any kind of marketable product. I assume, since you have industrial designers and product engineers on this team, that you are fairly close to something useful."

Everyone grew silent, unsure of what to say or not to say. Roe's speculation had struck too close to the mark about how far they'd come with their project.

The group's apparent leader, Maria Kearney, found her voice and spoke up. "Alex, you are correct on several points. Our project is based upon several major advances in neural-network computing that these three gentlemen made a year and a half ago."

Otto, Radwick, and Iverson beamed with pride at Kearney's praise.

"Now," Kearney continued, "without being rude, that is all that I am willing to say and more than I should."

Roe didn't press the issue any further. "I respect your candor, Maria, and don't worry about what you've said. I can't substantiate anything I've heard other than your names and job titles. For all I know, you may be pulling my leg and you're really working on a new mouse. Heck, Cole might just be a cranky government-standards hack here to verify that your new mouse is OSHA compliant."

"Cole's cranky all right, but don't be too hard on the guy. He recently went through a nasty divorce, and his ex-wife's lawyer wiped the floor with him." Iverson didn't particularly like Cole, but he did respect him. "On another note, you raised an interesting point. What would an OSHA-approved mouse look like?"

The remainder of the lunchtime conversation revolved around a series of napkin sketches that Kearney rapidly produced as the team designed their OSHA-compliant mouse. The humorous exercise taught Roe a lot about how Moy engineers used brainstorming as a creative tool. The final result was a hideous desk beast, covered with safety straps and carpal-tunnel guards, that bore little resemblance to the familiar computer device.

December 3

"Hello, Ian," Roe said over the phone. "Did you get a chance to review the materials I sent you?"

"Yes," Parnell replied, "I've got them right here in front of me, and now I understand your dilemma."

"I don't know if we're ever going to find someone with the kind of access we need who'll work with us."

"There wouldn't be another Randall Johnson on Moy's payroll, would there?"

"Ian, I don't have *that* many old boyfriends out there."

"Well, what do you suggest?"

"On the surface, I think Moy's senior-level employees are a dead end. They've got too much invested in stocks and the pension plan to risk working with us. I think Cole is our best bet."

"The government fellow?"

"Yes. He doesn't have the financial incentives to make him loyal to Moy, and I understand that he recently went through a rough divorce. He's precisely the kind of person we normally look for to help out with jobs like this. What do you think?"

Parnell sighed audibly over the phone. "I don't see that we have much choice. Check Cole out very thoroughly before you approach him. I'd hate to have this explode in our faces."

Chapter 6

Roe's investigation of Michael Cole began at his current address, an apartment in a deteriorating building on the fringe of D.C.'s drug-infested war zone.

Cole's divorce must have really pushed him into a hole, she thought.

The building manager glanced up briefly as Roe entered the lobby, then turned away, reminding herself that it was best not to notice unusual comings and goings in this neighborhood.

"It don't work," the woman's voice called out as Roe reached the elevator. "It's been broke for three days. You gotta take the stairs."

After climbing up to the third floor, Roe walked down the dimly lit hallway to apartment 315. After selecting the appropriate tool from a set of lock picks that she kept in her purse, Roe easily defeated the flimsy lock and entered Cole's apartment. The furnishings were sparse and inexpensive, all of the discount-store variety. The living room contained a battered leather recliner next to a reading lamp; a coffee table covered with a few paperback books and magazines; and a small color television propped up on a pair of plastic milk crates.

A thick layer of dust covered every horizontal surface in the apartment and an unusually repulsive odor filled the stale air. Roe found nothing in the kitchen that had been left out to decompose during Cole's absence. A quick search quickly identified the dried-out trap of the toilet bowl, which allowed rancid sewer gasses to vent through the fixture, as the source of the stench. Cole obviously hadn't been home in some time. Roe flushed the toilet to refill the trap and cracked a window in the bedroom to let in some fresh air. After a few minutes, the apartment seemed tolerable.

On the dresser, she noticed a low, flat bowl filled with change. Next to the bowl was a picture ID badge. Roe picked up the badge and studied it. The photo showed a man with a head of fine blond hair that was receding, thick, smooth cheeks, and just a hint of a double chin. "Cole, Michael H.," the badge read. Its color coding probably indicated areas to which Cole was permitted access. The job title read "Senior Systems Analyst." Roe let out a gasp when she tilted the badge to study the hologram in the corner.

"My God," she whispered to herself, recognizing the three-dimensional emblem in the hologram: the CIA logo.

She set the badge down and calmed herself. Cole is a programmer, she thought, not a spy or an analyst. With the right motivation, this can still work.

Focused back on her objective, Roe continued her search. In the smaller bedroom, she found Cole's home

office. A corner workstation with personal computer and
assorted electronic components occupied one end of the
room. Roe opened the closet doors and discovered a pair
of four-drawer gray metal file cabinets. Hanging beside
the file cabinets were a wet suit, an air tank, and a plunge
bag containing fins, a mask, and other scuba-diving para-
phernalia. Roe would have never guessed that Cole was a
sport diver, but, judging from the quality of the equipment, this was obviously one of his passions. She made a
mental note of the scuba gear and moved on to the file
cabinets.

The files were meticulously organized, making her
search fairly simple. The credit-card statements showed
him carrying a modest balance, but not wildly in debt.
His bank balances told another story. The bank accounts
he'd shared with his ex-wife had held respectable sums of
money until a year ago, when they had dropped to zero.
Their joint checking, certificates of deposit, IRAs—
every shared asset had suddenly evaporated. All the old
accounts had been closed, and the new ones bore only his
name, and very little money.

Cole had suddenly lost everything, which struck Roe
as odd. Both he and his ex-wife were working professionals; her deposits had been just as large as his. There were
no children, no risky investments, and, as near she could
figure, neither had joined a religious cult and given the
money away. D.C.'s divorce laws weren't that draconian
toward husbands, especially when the wife also has a solid
career. No, something else must have forced Cole to accept this outrageous settlement.

Roe skimmed further into the files and discovered
one with a handwritten label: *Divorce*. Among the papers, she found the suit for divorce and the settlement pa-

pers. She sat down at the desk and began to study the paper trail that marked the end of Cole's marriage.

The settlement confirmed what she'd begun to suspect; this divorce suit had never reached the courts. Cole and his wife had come to terms privately, leaving nothing for the court to do but grant the petition for divorce. She read through the terms, noting that Cole had initialed every item listed. He'd granted his ex-wife all but a few things that were of no interest to her.

In the final paragraph, Roe found what she was looking for. The settlement required that Barbara Cole remain silent about her reasons for the divorce; the official reason listed was "irreconcilable differences." The settlement also required that she deliver all materials, both originals and copies, of evidence related to Michael Cole's extramarital activities to her ex-husband.

He bought her off. She caught him with his hands in the cookie jar, and he bought her off. But why would Cole cave in over an affair, Roe thought, unless it was more than just an affair?

Michael Cole had a secret hidden somewhere in his divorce—something he wanted buried badly enough to pay for his wife's silence. As part of the settlement, a private investigator named Lou Gerty was to turn over all materials relating to the report he'd prepared for Cole's ex-wife. Barbara Cole had blackmailed her ex-husband, and whatever she had on him was precisely the kind of leverage Roe needed.

Chapter 7

Roe had returned to her hotel and changed into a smart, conservative blue business suit. She pulled her hair back and applied her makeup in an austere fashion. The effect she was looking for was cool, professional, and intimidating.

She had little trouble negotiating the major streets of the capital. She located Gerty's address at one of the recently restored office buildings along Pennsylvania Avenue. She parked her rental car in a nearby structure and walked up the street to the building.

"Excuse me," Roe said as she approached the portly security guard seated behind the reception desk, "where can I find the Gerty Agency?"

The guard smiled and pointed to a bank of elevators. "Lou Gerty's office is up on eight."

"Thank you."

*   *   *

The corridor was empty as Roe walked along the eighth floor toward Gerty's office. She found it tucked away near the end of the hallway. The matronly receptionist looked up from her computer as Roe entered.

"May I help you?" the woman asked politely.

"Yes. My name is Linda Ford and I'm with the FBI." Roe offered her credentials for the woman's inspection. The forged identity card was flawless and had been expensive, but worth the price. "I'm here to see Mr. Gerty."

"I'll see if he can be disturbed," the woman said with a hint of nervousness.

Lou Gerty ran a small one-man operation and appeared to make a decent living at his work. Several matted and framed photographs of D.C. monuments and historic sites graced the walls of the reception area. The lower-right-hand corner of each carried the signature *L. Gerty*; the man did more than take compromising pictures of adulterous spouses. If Gerty's eye for composition was as good with the dirty pictures as it was with these, he had a good shot at an NEA grant.

"Agent Ford," a baritone voice called out pleasantly, "I'm Lou Gerty. How can I help you?"

Gerty was middle-aged, somewhere around fifty. He was a few inches taller than Roe, but he carried almost twice her weight on a once-muscled body that had long ago declined. All that remained of his Afro was a fringe of gray that ran from ear to ear; the top of his head was bare and leathery.

"I need to discuss a case of yours in private."

"By all means. Please step into my office."

Gerty closed the door after she'd entered, then seated himself behind his desk.

"Which case are we talking about?"

"It's a divorce case from about a year ago. You were

hired by Barbara Cole to investigate her husband. In the course of your work, you uncovered something about Michael Cole that was so damaging that he gave his wife everything. I need to know what you discovered about Michael Cole."

"Frankly, Agent Ford, I'd like to help you, but I'm afraid I can't. My work for Mrs. Cole was a delicate family matter. The Coles have settled their differences and the issue is behind them both."

"Under normal circumstances, I'd be inclined to agree with you. Unfortunately, the situation I am dealing with is not in the realm of normal circumstances." Roe feigned a touch of irritation, then composed herself. "Are you aware of who employs Michael Cole?"

A sour look crossed Gerty's face, his lips pursing tightly beneath his mustache. "Yeah, I know who he works for. The CIA."

"That's where my concern lies, Mr. Gerty. I investigate cases of espionage committed within the United States."

"Is Cole spying for someone?"

"He's one of several suspects in an ongoing investigation."

"Damn, I hate traitors." Gerty's disgust was genuine. "I thought they cleaned the last of those rotten bastards out a couple years ago."

"Unfortunately, no, which brings us back to my request. I need to know what you know about Michael Cole."

Gerty considered her request carefully, and Roe could almost hear the debate raging in his head.

"I am sorry, Agent Ford, but I can't help you. The court ordered that everything I found out about Cole be turned over to him as part of the settlement."

"I appreciate your position, but let me try to explain mine to you." Roe took a slow deep breath and steeled herself. "I am investigating a matter of national security. You are in possession of information that I believe is vital to that investigation. If you do not provide this information to me, you will be guilty of obstruction of justice. In connection with an espionage investigation, such a charge would require jail time in a federal penitentiary. I will have your cooperation in this matter; it's your choice whether your cooperation is granted voluntarily or under the threat of legal action. With one phone call, I can have a search warrant delivered here in twenty minutes. So, are you sure that you turned over *everything* from your investigation?"

Gerty swallowed hard, his poker face cracking. "But what if Cole's not the one you're after? The things I found out about him weren't criminal, just something that neither of the Coles wants aired in public."

"I assure you that if Michael Cole is cleared as a suspect, whatever I learn about his private life will never see the light of day."

"This goes against what I feel to be right, but I don't see that I have much choice."

Gerty unlocked a high five-drawer file cabinet and pulled out a thick file.

"Mrs. Cole's attorney asked me to stash this away for her, as an insurance policy should her client ever need it."

Roe opened the file and skimmed over the investigation report. Gerty's prose was clear, precise, and unemotional; it read almost like a legal document, except for the clinical descriptions of the sexual acts Gerty had witnessed. Cole's secret finally sank in when she reached the exhibits marked A through H. The photographs depicted Michael Cole engaged in a variety of homosexual acts.

"So that's what she had on him," she mumbled to herself, ignoring Gerty's presence.

"Yes, she nailed him to the wall. The bastard didn't even use a condom. Good Lord, with AIDS and who knows what else running around out there, I figure this guy just took double portions of dumb when they passed out brains."

Roe closed the file and softened her stern, authoritative stance with Gerty. "Thank you. This is an immense help to our investigation."

Roe slipped the file into her briefcase.

"Say, aren't you supposed to leave a receipt for that?"

Whatever consideration Roe had shown Gerty a moment earlier was now replaced with a withering stare. "Only if I was *officially* here, which I am not. This conversation never took place, Mr. Gerty."

Gerty understood the implied threat in Roe's tone and nodded in agreement.

"You said it yourself, Mr. Gerty: According to the terms of the Coles' divorce settlement, all materials from your investigation were to be turned over to Michael Cole. Officially, this file doesn't exist, so there's nothing for me to sign for. Good day, Mr. Gerty."

Roe's visit left the grizzled private investigator seated behind his desk, speechless.

Chapter 8

Kilkenny checked his dive watch and punched a button on the global positioning satellite receiver mounted into the curved console of the swimmer delivery vehicle. He matched up the longitude/latitude figure from the GPS with the nautical map that he'd memorized over the last few weeks, then verified that they were on target, on schedule.

After launching from the submarine USS *Columbia*, Kilkenny led the SEALs on a six-mile submerged approach to Haiti's southern coast. When they reached the ditch point, the squad shut down the SDVs and set them on the seafloor half a mile from shore and under enough water that only a major storm could disturb them.

The squad NCO, Chief Max Gates, unhooked the roll of camouflage netting from his SDV and began unfolding it. The other SEALs each grabbed an edge and pulled the fabric over the two SDVs and staked the corners into the seafloor. After a quick check on equipment and air, Kilkenny led the squad on a half-mile swim to the beach.

Once ashore, the SEALs stripped off their scuba gear, wrapped the equipment in weatherproof bags, and buried it. Kilkenny recorded the location of the buried gear from the GPS.

Each man then checked his equipment and provisions for this leg of the mission. The satchel charges and food were stowed in backpacks, while the weapons and ammunition were placed on each man, close at hand.

Black and green camouflage paint was applied to their faces, making them virtually invisible in the dense jungle foliage. The devils with green faces had arrived in Haiti.

Kilkenny then took the headset from his communications specialist and flipped the switch on the satellite transmitter. "Trident is feet-dry," he announced, informing the mission planners in Washington that they had arrived.

"Message received, Trident," a distant voice responded. "Good hunting."

Chapter 9

Chicago, Illinois
December 11

In light of Gerty's report, Cole's one-sided divorce settlement made complete sense. Roe had found his deepest secret and, after five days of trailing Cole in Chicago, she was now prepared to use it in exactly the way the government feared—as a means of manipulating an employee of the CIA. While Gerty's report implied a certain level of promiscuity, Cole currently displayed no interest in any kind of social life. The divorce had left him emotionally, as well as financially, castrated. Cole lived a quiet, solitary existence that included few entertaining diversions.

The CIA rented an apartment for Cole a few blocks from Moy's headquarters. While he was at work, Roe entered the unit and found it to be a great improvement over his Washington home. The apartment was bright, open, and equipped with tasteful rented furniture. On the kitchen counter were several travel brochures for the Caribbean islands. The brochures all described the warm climate, friendly natives, sunny beaches, and excellent scuba diving.

Cole's been living like a monk since his divorce, Roe thought as she tried to get a sense of the man. Perhaps he's planning a long vacation once his project is finished.

That evening, Roe followed Cole as he emerged from Moy Electronics onto the cold Chicago street. Since his apartment was within walking distance, Cole didn't bother keeping a car. He didn't cook much at home, either, as Roe discovered when she looked into a nearly empty refrigerator. The CIA probably had a meal per diem, which Cole would use in local restaurants. Tonight, he picked up a late edition of the *Chicago Tribune* and stopped in for a bite at McGregor's Pub.

Roe waited about fifteen minutes before entering the bar. McGregor's was a throwback to a different era—a dark old neighborhood public house, like those found in every little town in Ireland. Established in 1905, McGregor's had weathered Prohibition, the Great Depression, and innumerable changes of time and fashion, yet it remained nearly untouched well into its third generation of ownership. The influx of young urban professionals had brought new economic vitality to the bar's bottom line, but the owner obviously had no intention of upscaling his working-class bar by adding ferns or trendy beers.

She sat on a stool beside the massive oak and brass bar that ran the length of the room. Steam rose from a pass-through window between the bar and the kitchen beyond; the scent of the grilled food filled the air. Roe ordered a draft beer and the fish and chips special. After looking over the bar, she located Cole tucked in a corner booth near the back.

Her food arrived quickly, the fish still sizzling from

the deep fryer. Roe gathered up her dinner and utensils in one hand and her beer in the other and walked over to the booth. Cole was halfway through a Reuben sandwich, his face buried in the paper's "Commentary" section.

Roe summoned her most disarming smile. "I thought I saw a familiar face in here. Mind if I join you?"

"I guess not," Cole replied, motioning to the bench opposite him as he folded his evening paper. The puzzled, blank look on Cole's face told Roe that he didn't quite remember her. "You're doing that story on Moy, right?"

"Yes, I'm Alex Roe, and don't worry about forgetting my name. You can't expect to remember everyone you meet."

Cole looked visibly relieved at being let off the hook. "I admit, I'm awful with names. It takes me weeks before I get them straight."

"Now, Michael, if I'm going to join you for dinner, I do have one ground rule: no shoptalk. I deal with computers and technology and business all day long, so I don't want to hear about anything along those lines. Is that all right?"

"Fine. I can't talk about work anyway. So what do you want to talk about?"

"I don't know," Roe mused. "Have you seen the new exhibit at the art museum, the Muromachi paintings from Japan?"

"No, I'm not really big on art," Cole replied, "just movies, books, and sports. I did finally go out to Oak Park to see the Frank Lloyd Wright houses. I never understood why so many people raved about him until I saw his houses next to all those Victorians."

"So what do you think of him now?"

"I guess I have to buy into the tour guide's party line: Wright was an architectural genius. All the houses in that neighborhood were built about the same time, but only his still look innovative."

"From what I know about Wright, that was true throughout most of his career. You mentioned books," Roe said, changing the subject. "What are you reading these days?"

"Would you believe a book about medieval France?"

Roe kept the conversation moving as they ate, bringing up light, unchallenging topics. Cole warmed up and actually seemed to appreciate the company. The waitress cleared away the plates and brought another round of drinks for them both—Roe's treat.

Cole was in a receptive mood and it was time for Roe to make her pitch. "So, I hear that your project is winding down. Are you back to Washington after that?"

"Eventually, but first I'm taking a much-needed vacation." Cole's persona outside the office was much more relaxed, and a few beers did wonders at easing the tension. "My wife and I busted up right when this job with Moy started going hot and heavy, which was good, because it didn't leave me much free time to wallow in self-pity. Now it's time for me to get my head back together, so I'm taking all the vacation days I've built up and heading for the islands."

"Where about?" Roe was playing the good listener, feeding Cole lines that would keep him talking.

"All over, Grand Cayman, the Bahamas." Cole was very enthusiastic about his upcoming vacation. "I'm even going to the Dominican Republic. I've never been there before, but I hear the diving is fantastic."

"You're a scuba diver, huh? I've done a little diving, but not as much as I'd like."

"There's nothing like it." Cole gushed with enthusiasm. "Shipwrecks are my personal favorite. I've been on some over four hundred years old. The sea life and scenery are unbelievable, too. There is nothing comparable to it on land. The only negative thing I can think about diving is that you have to come back up."

"That and the cost," Roe added.

"Yeah, that and the cost," Cole agreed, "but you gotta have some fun in life. I have most of it saved up, but I'll have to hit on my credit cards a little to get me over the top. It's a bit of a financial stretch for me right now, but I *have* to take some time off."

"I hear you," Roe said with a sympathetic voice, "and I'd like to help you out."

"What do you mean?" Cole's face suddenly looked tense and a little apprehensive as his mental defenses went up.

"I'll lay it all on the table." Roe was presenting her most honest, sincere self. "My presence here tonight is not an accident. I sought you out deliberately because I need your help, and I'm willing to pay you for your time and effort."

"Does this have something to do with that Moy article you're writing?" Cole asked suspiciously.

"Yes and no. The article is finished. What I'm referring to is a project for a *private* client, one whose information needs are very specific. This client has asked for a look at his major competitor's new product line before it hits the market."

"That competitor being Moy." Cole was following Roe's line of thought very carefully.

"Yes. My client produces computer and electronics components that are compatible with Moy equipment, at a lower cost. Their problem is that the reverse engineering time increases with each product generation, leaving Moy with longer and longer monopolies over the market while my client plays catch-up."

Cole shrugged his shoulders. "I don't work for Moy. How could I possibly help you?"

Roe leaned close across the table. "You can get me into Moy's computer network. Once inside, I'll find what I'm looking for. I'm offering you fifty grand for a onetime use of your password."

Cole blinked. He felt the adrenaline surge through his body while trying to remain outwardly calm. "That's a lot of money for a password. Why don't you just hack your way in?"

"I could, but that takes time."

"This sounds too easy. I get a bunch of money to let you use my password. The upside is great, but the down-side's a bitch."

"Those are the inherent risks of the game. You don't win big by hedging your bets."

"Up to now, all I've done is sit here and listen to your pitch. You approached me; I did nothing to initiate this conversation. What you've proposed amounts to a bribe, and my acceptance of that bribe would be unethical and illegal. As a government employee, it's my duty to report this incident."

"But you won't." Roe spoke with a bold certainty, as if she already knew the outcome.

"What makes you say that?" Cole replied, shocked by her confidence.

"The money." Roe then pulled out a brown envelope from her soft-sided briefcase and placed it on the table in front of him. "My offer is very generous, and you need it."

"What? How would you know if I needed money?"

"I checked you out very thoroughly, Michael. I'd be a fool not to know as much as I could about you before making an offer like this. I know all sorts of interesting things, including the real reason behind your divorce."

Cole's eyes lit up and a look of anger flashed across his face. He held his cool, but just barely, as Roe continued.

"Approaching you, as you astutely pointed out, is a significant risk for me. I have a report from a certain private detective that minimizes that risk greatly."

"Let me see that," Cole growled as he pulled the envelope from under Roe's hand.

Inside, he found a copy of the report that his ex-wife's lawyer had used against him; the photographs, times, and dates were all there. Cole found he could no longer control his anger.

"How the hell did you get this?" he shouted angrily as he slammed the document onto the table. A few other patrons of the bar looked over at the disturbance.

"Settle down and I'll tell you."

Cole eased back into his seat, still enraged by her revelation. Roe knew that she'd rattled him with the report. Cole was feeling backed into a corner and now she would help him make the *correct* decision.

"Your ex-wife's lawyer had her detective retain it as an insurance policy. If I recall correctly, that's a direct violation of your divorce agreement."

The news infuriated Cole, who was now livid. "That bitch! I should have known I couldn't trust her."

"Well, now you don't have to worry about her." Roe spoke calmly and clearly. "I am the only person who can expose your secret. I don't really care what you do in your private life, or with whom; that's none of my concern. What I do care about are my clients. My offer still stands: You get me into Moy's computer, and I'll pay you fifty grand. Do we have a deal?"

"What about this?" Cole asked, pointing at the report.

"I keep the originals until I feel that I can trust you.

This report has no value to me other than to buy your silence; I have no interest in seeing your career destroyed."

Cole's anger eased a little, but he was still visibly upset.

"Look, if I was a real bitch, I'd just blackmail you and save my money. No, I'm a businesswoman, and what I'm offering you is a win-win deal. I get the information I want and you get some badly needed cash. I saw your divorce settlement—you got *burned*."

"Got that right," Cole agreed bitterly.

"Fine," Roe replied, attempting to channel Cole's anger toward her goal. "Here's a chance for you to get financially back on your feet. At fifty grand, I'm paying you more per word than Schwarzenegger gets in the movies."

Cole's focus slowly shifted toward Roe's offer and the booth grew quiet as he weighed his decision.

"All right, I'm in."

Roe smiled at him warmly. "Do you have a dedicated data line into Moy?"

"Yeah. The project I'm on has a tight schedule, so I log a lot of system time in the off-hours."

"Then it won't be unusual for you to log in on a Friday night. Is tonight a problem for you?"

"No, I don't have any plans. What about the money?"

"I have it with me," Roe assured him. "Once I'm in and out, the cash is yours to do with as you see fit. I'll bet you can do a lot of scuba diving on fifty grand."

"I think I can put it to good use."

"Great." Roe stood and collected her coat from the hook while Cole remained seated in the booth. She fished a wallet out of her purse and paid the bill.

"Business meal," she said jokingly while collecting the receipt. "Let's go."

Chapter 10

To Roe's delight, Cole's project had provided him with a Silicon Graphics workstation equipped with a high-speed modem. Over a clean, dedicated line, this transfer would go about twice as fast as her last job at Pangen Research. The nature of Cole's project also granted him unusually high system access for an outside contractor, high enough that Roe was easily able to create a temporary superuser on the Moy network with unlimited access. In ten minutes, Roe was effectively in total control of the Moy Electronics computer network.

Once Roe began copying the information she wanted onto her optical disk drive, there wasn't much left to do but wait.

"Here," Cole said as he held out a cold can of Coors, "it's on the house."

"Thanks." Roe popped the top and took a swallow of the frosty liquid.

"As terribly *exciting* as copying files is, I think I'll go watch the Blackhawks–Red Wings game."

"Go ahead. I'll just sit here and baby-sit the machine."

The sounds of rabid Blackhawks fans filled Cole's living room as the television came to life with the game. It was still early in the first period, both teams scoreless, but the checks were flying hard and fast between the longtime NHL rivals. Roe wasn't much of a hockey fan, preferring college football since her days at Georgia, so she kept her attention on the file transfer. A small window on the monitor's graphical display indicated that data was pouring out of Moy Electronics at an incredible rate.

Bored, Roe moved the mouse and clicked open another window. She decided to indulge herself by cruising through Moy's project library, looking at anything that piqued her interest. The depth of the project library was a tribute to the productivity of the company's engineering and software staff.

Littered among the report icons were a few multimedia demonstrations of upcoming Moy products. She slipped on the headphones that were plugged into Cole's computer and began running the demos. The presentations were slick and professionally done, several of the minimovies incorporating special effects that the gurus at Industrial Light and Magic would love to add to their repertoire.

Scrolling further into the library, Roe discovered a directory icon labeled *U.S. Government Projects*. She clicked the directory open and found three more multimedia icons labeled *Gatekeeper*, *Crypto*, and *Spyder*.

"No!" Cole shouted with the groaning fans on the television as Detroit scored.

Roe ran the Gatekeeper demo and learned of the government's effort to eliminate unauthorized computer access with neural-network devices that could actually learn and adapt to changing conditions. Such a device could fend off a hacker attack, going so far as to track the intruder back to his own computer. An anxious moment, in which Roe wondered if she was being tracked by a Gatekeeper, passed when the narrator announced that the first devices were to be installed on the government's computers early next year.

"Good thing there are no plans for commercial sale of those things"—she sighed—"or I'd be out of business."

The Crypto demo briefly described a new method of encryption for voice and data transmission that the government had recently put into place.

Very impressive, Mr. Moy, Roe thought as the second demo ended. You've pushed both the hardware and software envelopes with these two secret projects. I wonder what you've dreamed up for Spyder.

Roe's request was answered as the jazz sound track for the Spyder demo filled her ears. The device, a small black cube, appeared identical to the Gatekeeper, and the first moments of narration confirmed the two devices' common lineage. The narrator, a sultry-voiced woman, then began describing the Spyder's unique talents for covert intelligence gathering.

"My God," Roe gasped as the demo ran through a simulated Spyder operation.

Once in place, the device quickly took over the host computer network. Users who logged into the infested network unknowingly lost their passwords, thus their electronic identities, to the Spyder. The simulation ended with the Spyder activating an outside line from the host network and transmitting the stolen information to its controller. The demo credits listed Bill Iverson and Michael Cole as coauthors of the Spyder's operating program.

Roe slipped the headphones off and turned toward Cole, who was engrossed in a Blackhawk power play. *That man has created an intelligence-gathering gold mine.*

She walked into the living room and sat in an overstuffed chair facing Cole. "Michael, I think I've found an opportunity for us to develop a long-term, highly profitable business relationship."

Cole muted the sound on the hockey game. "I'm listening."

"Good. First, I want you to tell me everything you know about the Spyder Project. Then you and I are going to have a chat with my partner. If this Spyder of yours is real, it could be worth millions."

Chapter 11

Haiti

The jungle march was just what they'd expected: slow. Keeping clear of villages to avoid any undesired contact with the natives meant moving through thick jungle growth. What might normally be a two-day hike became a five-day exercise in silent motion. The heaviness of the flora seemed to envelop them as tightly as the sea, cutting off all but a few rays of sunlight.

The six men probing the jungle with Kilkenny moved as one, silently advancing, with their senses reaching out in every direction. The SEALs operated under the assumption that Masson and his men were as well trained and disciplined as they were. Their opponents also had the defender's advantage of familiarity with the jungle, and booby traps were to be expected as they approached the enemy camp.

Gates was on point with Darvas, leading the squad during the night march, when he raised his hand and brought their approach to a stop. In the dark growth ahead, Gates saw the unmistakable silhouette of a person in a clearing of jungle growth. He motioned for Darvas to provide cover while he approached the darkened figure.

Crawling slowly across the moist ground on his stomach, Gates closed the distance to his target. Each motion he made, each breath he took was carefully controlled and measured. Like a jungle predator, Gates was calm and patient in stalking his prey.

On Kilkenny's order, the remaining SEALs took up defensive positions around the clearing. Should Gates and Darvas find themselves outgunned, they would have a place to fall back. Kilkenny waited quietly with the rest of his squad as Gates neared the clearing.

From the jungle's edge, Gates studied the figure but detected no sound, no motion coming from the man. Not even the sound of breathing. The figure was upright, but unnaturally so, with arms extended outward to each side. Crucified.

Gates moved up close and discovered that, whoever it was, he had been there awhile. The remains were in an advanced state of decay, with the clothing rotted and little flesh remaining on the bones. A garland of feathers and beads was hung around the corpse's neck, along with several other items that Gates couldn't readily identify.

"I'm coming up behind you, Max," a muffled voice crackled in Gates's ear. After years of working together, he knew Kilkenny's voice even through the distortion of a throat mike.

"What do you think?" Gates asked, his gaze still fixed on the grisly figure.

"Voodoo. Practically everyone on this island believes in the voodoo religion, and Masson is considered a powerful high priest. This is a warning." Kilkenny looked at the tattered remnants of the man's uniform and noticed the shoulder boards hanging loosely. "Looks like he was Haitian military. We must be getting close to Masson's camp."

Kilkenny raised his hand, then pointed the way. Slowly, they re-formed and melted back into the jungle, leaving the grisly sentry to his silent watch.

Chapter 12

Langley, Virginia
December 13

Cole's flight arrived in Washington on schedule and the bleary-eyed systems analyst entered Frank Villano's office casually dressed and slightly rumpled. He dropped his suitcase and coat by the door and poured a cup of coffee from the pot that his boss brewed for his personal use. Villano liked his coffee strong, which is just what Cole needed this morning.

Villano took one look at Cole's faded jeans and day-old stubble and groaned. "A little casual for the office, aren't we?"

Cole just glowered at the thin, bespectacled man behind the desk. "If you haven't checked your calendar, it's Sunday, the sacred day of football as the play-offs draw near. Anyway, I answered your summons and caught the first flight in. I even came directly here from the airport without stopping off at home."

"Ah, Saint Michael." Villano raised his hands in

benediction. "You are a dedicated man, and, for that, I will forgive your transgression against the office dress code."

"Thanks." Cole sat down and took a sip of the steaming brew from his mug. "Now tell me, what's so important that you have to call me in from Chicago to deal with it?"

"We've been given an interesting challenge, one that requires a person of your unique technical skills and high security clearance."

Cole was all too familiar with the look on Villano's face. Someone on the seventh floor wanted another miracle from the computer department. "Something *hot* that they want yesterday, I assume?"

"You are correct. What do you know about the former KGB's First Chief Directorate?"

Cole thought for a second, but he recalled only a few generic facts about the KGB from his CIA indoctrination classes. "Didn't they handle Soviet foreign intelligence operations?"

"Right. We recently acquired some files that are alleged to be the property of Andrei Yakushev, one of the top men in the FCD. Yakushev ran their Special Operations group for twenty years, right up to the failed coup in 1991." Villano could see that the name meant little to Cole, and he needed him to understand just how important any information on Yakushev was. "Did you ever hear about the CIA's witch-hunts for moles during the sixties?"

"Yeah, I heard some stories from the *old-timers*."

Villano bristled for a second, but let the "old-timers" crack slide. Cole knew that Villano was part of that long-tenured group of CIA staff.

"Well, if there *were* any moles in the CIA, Yakushev

was running them. He was their best. Yakushev was also a political rival of KGB chairman Nikitenko, the guy who tried to oust Gorbachev. Now that you know the basics, I'll explain our situation."

With his arms behind his head, Villano tilted back in his chair, his feet propped up on top of his desk. "We have a new defector, a junior KGB officer who went AWOL back in '91 and has been hiding in Latvia ever since. He claims that Chairman Nikitenko personally ordered him to secure Yakushev's dacha, which had *accidentally* burned, and to retrieve the late comrade's files. Our boy followed his orders and went to the dacha, only the fire didn't look so accidental once he got there. All the bullet holes in the bodies kind of looked suspicious to him. He found the fire safe that Nikitenko wanted and headed back for Moscow. On the way back to Lubyanka, he had a revelation."

"He found God?" Cole asked lightly.

"No, but he decided that if he went back to Moscow, he had a very good chance of meeting him. Yakushev's place was a long way out in the country, so this guy was listening to the radio on the way back. That's when he heard about Gorby catching the Kremlin flu—you know the bug that all the general secretaries get before they croak. Our defector used his head and decided that there was a good chance the accidental house fire might be connected with Nikitenko's attempted takeover of the government."

"The bullet holes ruled out the possibility of a coincidence for him, I take it?"

"They have a tendency to do that, especially over there," Villano said with a nod. "Our defector saw the storm clouds rising and ran for cover. He was born up in the Baltics, so he hightailed it back home until the whole mess blew over, taking Yakushev's safe with him."

"Why is this guy defecting now? The Soviet Union broke up years ago, and the Baltics are independent. I don't see the value."

"He'd been living quietly and never intended to defect, until last week, when his cover was blown. The locals in that part of the world are touchy about Russian nationals and KGB collaborators. Somehow, word got out that he worked for the KGB, and things went bad real quick. For his own safety, the local police spirited him to Riga, where he appeared at the front door of our consulate with a dusty old fire safe and a wild story about the coup."

"Okay, so what did we find inside the fire safe?"

"That's for you to find out, Michael. We got it open—no big trick there—but all we found was a stack of computer diskettes. We don't know yet what's on them, but we have a theory. Like us, the FCD didn't keep operational information inside their agents' personnel records. For deep-cover agents, like the ones Yakushev ran, the personnel files at Lubyanka might even be falsified to protect agents in the field. The true operational histories and aliases of deep-cover agents might be known only to a handful of high-ranking officers, and our sources tell us that Yakushev was *very protective* of his operational files. Now, you know that the KGB didn't just disappear when the Soviet Union collapsed; the Committee for State Security just changed their letterhead. The Security Ministry, or MB, is still run by the same people and still doing the same old thing. If these disks contain Yakushev's operations files, a good number of agents identified in there may still be active."

"And the disks that might hold these valuable operational files were in a safe in the middle of a burning building." The thought of trying to salvage anything from disks exposed to the heat of a fire made Cole wish he'd stayed in Chicago. "Ouch! Now I know why you called me."

"You got it," Villano replied with an enthusiastic grin. "We need your magic. See if there's anything that you can pull off those disks. If our defector is telling the truth—and his story has checked out so far—these may be the operations files of one of the most dangerous men in the KGB."

Cole felt as if he were being asked to perform the miracle of the loaves and fishes with a parched stalk of wheat and a fish bone. "Where are the disks now?"

"In the lab waiting for you. Like you said, the boss wants an answer on this one yesterday. Good luck. You need anything, just ask."

Cole finished the last of his coffee and stared for a moment into the empty cup. He resigned himself to the inevitable, stood up, and moved toward the door. "Thanks for the coffee. I'll be in the lab."

Cole slipped on his white lab coat and entered the climate-controlled environment of the electronics laboratory. He ran his ID card through the magnetic strip reader and waited for it to unlock the door to the storage vault where all recovered pieces of electronics equipment were kept during analysis. During the Reagan years, this room had been packed with gear from a Soviet missile sub that *officially* sank in the Atlantic. Nothing quite that large had come through since.

He found a small box on one of the gray metal shelves that lined the vault; the number matched the file Villano had given him. Cole walked back into the lab, set the box down on a workbench and extracted thirteen small plastic cases. One by one, he opened the cases and found each filled with ten three-and-a-half-inch diskettes.

"At least Yakushev used world-standard media," Cole muttered to himself. "Now I don't have to cobble anything together to read these."

The disks all appeared to be in relatively good condition, despite their presumed exposure to fire. Cole knew the old agency motto about trusting walk-in intelligence: It's Not Gold Unless You Can Prove It's Gold. Just because this defector told a credible story doesn't mean it should be taken at face value, he thought. This could be a disinformation operation, or an attempt to start up another mole hunt. This could also be everything this guy says it is. If there was enough heat inside the fire safe to damage the delicate Mylar inside the floppy disks, they would never know one way or the other.

Cole then donned an environmental suit and took the disks into the lab's clean room, where he spent the next few hours studying the disks under a microscope, checking the surface structure for damage from heat, dust, or smoke. He wasn't about to put a contaminated disk into a disk drive and try to read it. A particle of smoke is large enough to crash a disk head and gouge the disk's surface, making data recovery all but impossible. The painstaking process of cleaning the disks took the rest of the day, all while Villano kept checking in on him like an expectant father.

The next day, Cole was ready to attempt a disk read. Starting with the most common personal computer format, he slipped the disk into an IBM-style PC and crossed his fingers. The program he was running would scan the disk at many different levels in an attempt to identify the data-encoding format, if it could be read at all. The screen quickly filled with a pattern of ones and zeros; the first disk appeared readable. Now he had to determine whether the information was intelligible. After scanning 130 disks, he found only four with physical defects that would prevent them from being read.

Cole had kept the disks arranged in the same order he'd found them, and the Agency translators helped decipher the disk labels as he looked for clues about what he was dealing with. Most of the label names meant nothing to him, just names of birds and fish. They could possibly be code names, but they didn't tell Cole a thing about what information the disks held. Then he found it, buried deep in the list, the one labled *Disk Operating System, #1*. The next ten disks were all system- and program-related. They were the core of Yakushev's personal computer.

It was eleven o'clock at night, late into his second day, but Cole now saw light at the end of the tunnel. He grabbed one of the lab PCs and formatted a new hard disk. If the translated titles were correct, within the next hour he might be able to reactivate Yakushev's computer files.

Cole loaded the first operating-system diskette into the disk drive and restarted the machine. As with all personal computers, the machine ran through its diagnostic tests, followed by a search for its configuration files. The screen then filled with a Cyrillic version of the MS-DOS setup screen.

Cole knew that the translators were home for the night, so he scrounged up another PC and began to install an old U.S. version of the DOS beside the Russian one. Step by step, the programs were identical in execution. In the end, he had two machines sitting there, with a C:> prompt on their screens, waiting for him to do something.

Using an ethernet jack in the lab, he connected the English-language PC to the building's local-area network and tied into the Linguistic Section's on-line translation library. He loaded the Russian technical dictionary and queried for a translation of the Directory command. Plodding along, he was able to list out the operating-system commands and identify their English counterparts.

Cole was a man possessed by the thrill of solving a difficult puzzle. As everything began to fall into place, his adrenaline surged. At two o'clock in the morning, rather than fatigue, he felt a burning desire to unlock the secrets on Yakushev's disks.

He took the first of Yakushev's program disks and loaded it into the machine that he now called the "KGB-PC" and requested a listing of its file directory. The screen began to scroll, filling with the names of programs stored on the disk. On the normal PC, he requested the Russian translation for the Install command and scanned the file list for a program bearing that name.

He found a small file with the appropriate name and typed the command for the KGB-PC to execute the installation program. Cole hadn't seen many examples of Soviet computer programming, though he'd heard their skills were excellent.

It took over an hour to load all of Yakushev's software onto the KGB-PC. Cole laughed when he discovered several of the programs were simply Cyrillic versions of popular business software from the early nineties. Who would have thought a good Communist would keep track of his material wealth?

He looked over the list of translations for the disks and eliminated those with generic names, such as Account Data and Correspondence. Instead, Cole decided to concentrate on those with the bird names; either Yakushev was a naturalist or these disks carried something more interesting than personal correspondence and account balances.

Cole loaded the first program, whose Russian name loosely translated into the English word *Records*. The KGB-PC's screen cleared and a single title line of text appeared across the top, followed by three numbered lines of text in the center of the screen. The cursor flashed above an Underscore character at the bottom of the screen. Not the prettiest program he'd ever seen, but it was obviously offering one of three choices.

Cole typed the screen text into his translator and discovered that the program was unable to find any data files on the hard disk. He was now offered the choice of loading files onto the hard disk, reading files from the disk, or exiting the program. He grabbed one of the bird-named disks from the stack and sent the computer off to read it.

KGB-PC's disk-drive lights began to flash as the cpu, hard disk, and floppy disk began to converse with one another in response to Cole's command. The screen again went blank before filling with information from the disk. In the upper-right corner of the screen, a photograph of a man appeared; in the upper-left corner, the shield emblem of the KGB became evident. The middle of the screen then filled with an options menu.

He translated the information on the screen and discovered that this was a personnel file for a KGB deep-cover agent. The agent, code-named "Seagull," was a man named Vitali Farkas. The program now offered Cole a look at Farkas's personal information, career record, medical record, cover history, current

assignment, historical assignments, and commendations. It was the complete life of a KGB mole tied up in
a neat package.

Cole could barely contain his excitement. Using the
information encoded on these diskettes, the CIA might be
able to cripple an entire section of the MB's intelligence-
gathering operations. In a few hours, Frank Villano was
going to be one happy man.

Since it was already 3:30 in the morning, Cole decided to work straight through until 7:00 A.M., when Villano would arrive, and give him the good news
personally. In the meantime, he would just continue
loading diskettes and browsing through what might be
the Who's Who of Soviet deep-cover agents.

Two hours later, Cole still hadn't come down from the
initial rush of success. He'd previewed and printed out
the complete files on ten agents whose assignments, up
until 1991, had placed them in sensitive positions around
the world.

The next disk Cole slid into the KGB-PC's disk
drive was for an agent code-named "Cormorant." For the
first time, an error message appeared on the screen, interrupting the program. Cole translated the message: "File
not found."

The message puzzled Cole; after reading the disks on
several agents, why would one suddenly be blank? It was
tagged just like the others. Since he had nothing to lose
by trying, he pulled the disk out of the KGB-PC and
loaded it into the other computer. He then loaded a disk-
scanning utility to give the Cormorant disk a once-over.
Yakushev's disks had been formatted in a standard DOS
environment, Cole reasoned, which meant that there was

a good chance that a DOS file utility program might be able to identify and correct the problem.

Sector by sector, the utility program found that the disk was undamaged. Cole then asked the program to look for any unallocated program fragments still present on the disk. The program went back to work and quickly returned after locating eight deleted files on the disk. Someone had erased the disk, but they hadn't wiped it clean of information. Cormorant's files were still there; only the directory names had been deleted. Cole immediately set out to recover the lost information. Re-creating the disk directory and file-allocation table took no more than ten minutes.

After completing the file recovery, Cole placed the disk back into the KGB-PC and restarted Yakushev's program. He sat back in his chair, sipping on a can of soda, waiting for the next Soviet agent to be unveiled. Cole choked in midgulp when the digitized photo appeared in the corner of the screen. The picture, though taken several years ago, bore an uncanny resemblance to Alex Roe.

Cole selected the cover-history option from the menu and, word by word, fed the information into the translation program. What came back confirmed his initial reaction. According to the text, the photograph belonged to a KGB deep-cover agent named Anna Mironova. The agent Cormorant was assigned to the acquisition of scientific and technological information under the cover of a Western journalist, freelance writer Alexandra Roe. The disk left no doubt. Cole had aided a foreign agent in acquiring restricted technology. An overwhelming sense of nausea swept over him.

He sat for several minutes, stunned by the truth about Roe. Gradually, his brain began to thaw from its initial panic and he started sifting through the rest of the Cormorant file. The list of commendations was extensive and, even though Cole didn't bother to translate all of them, he quickly realized that Roe was a valuable agent.

The last entry in the file was dated August 1991, just a few weeks before the coup attempt. Unlike the other commendation entries, this one had no bold capitalized entry naming the decoration. Instead, it was just a single sentence. Cole typed the entry into the computer and waited for the translation. The entry read: "10 August, 1991 Capt. Anna Mironova was killed in an automobile accident while on assignment."

Cole reread the translation several times. He even retyped it into the computer to double-check it, and the computer returned with the obituary for Mironova.

Cole's thoughts raced. If Villano was right about KGB record keeping, then the files in Lubyanka might list Mironova's many honors, but they would say nothing about how she had earned them. Yakushev's operational files would hold the *only* detailed account of Mironova's activities under the alias of Alex Roe, and the only known copy of those files was on this disk. As far as Moscow is concerned, Cole thought, Mironova died over seven years ago. Case closed.

In the midst of his disbelief, Cole made an intuitive leap: If Roe had faked her death in order to escape Moscow's control, how would her former masters deal with her if they discovered this deception?

A wicked smile curled on his face; the tables had turned. He now possessed information as dangerous to Roe as the Gerty report was to him—information that vastly improved his bargaining position with Roe and her partner. Cole copied Yakushev's program diskettes and the Cormorant disk onto four blank diskettes of the type that the CIA bought in bulk, then placed the copies inside his briefcase. He then scratched the Mylar surface of the original Cormorant diskette with a paper clip, rendering it unreadable.

Chapter 13

Haiti
December 20

"Shift change," Gates's raspy voice whispered through Kilkenny's earpiece. Changing of the guards at Masson's base camp.

Kilkenny repositioned himself and looked through a pair of night-vision binoculars at the camp below. Since passing Masson's gory marker just over a week ago, the SEALs had tracked and studied the activities in the guerrilla camp. The satellite photos they had used in preparing for this mission showed elements of the compound but gave little feel for how the place worked. That kind of information could only be gathered firsthand. Several days of on-site observation gave the squad the familiarity they needed in order to succeed.

What they discovered about their opposition's security astounded them. No mines, no trip wires, no booby traps of any kind. The most formidable aspect of Masson's defenses was the fear he'd spread over the surrounding villages, a fear that the SEALs did not share. The only protective efforts they detected at the encampment amounted to a few bored men casually patrolling the perimeter. The safety of this remote jungle haven had made Masson's men lax on their home turf.

Kilkenny set the binoculars down and closed his eyes in a silent prayer. The plan was set and his squad had taken up their positions around the camp. Tonight, they would attack. Kilkenny prayed for the safety of his men.

Little Creek Naval Amphibious Base, Virginia

Dawson walked into the Operations Center and signed into one of the mission observation rooms. The rooms mirrored their larger counterparts in the Pentagon, where senior officers and mission planners watched missions unfold. During World War II, it took days before film footage and reports from the battlefield reached the Pentagon. Now, through the use of satellite imagery and the combat electronics worn by his men, Dawson could witness the drama played out live. The downside of all this advanced technology was the very real possibility of seeing some of his men die in action.

He snapped his headset into place and punched in his access code. The five-by-ten high-definition wall display changed color as the computer confirmed his code and tied him into the mission feed from the Pentagon. An image of southern Haiti, as seen by a reconnaissance satellite passing over two hundred miles above and enhanced by a bank of supercomputers at the National Reconnaissance Office near Dulles, filled the display.

With a few keystrokes, Dawson superimposed mission elements onto the screen. Offshore, the *Columbia* remained on-station, waiting for her rendezvous with his men. A cluster of man-shaped icons were lumped together, deep in the jungle northeast of Jacmel.

He zoomed in on the cluster and switched from real-time imaging to infrared. Now he could see what his SEALs were up against. Over the past week, he, too, had been studying Masson's camp from this room, taking a head count of the opposition. His men were outnumbered four to one, and Dawson hoped that this was Masson's only advantage tonight.

Just minutes from now, at zero hundred hours local time, Kilkenny and his men would attack. A brief message from the SEALs indicated that everything was ready and the mission was still on. The guerrilla camp looked quiet, with only a token force on patrol, as the SEALs started to move. The assault had begun.

Gates and Rodriguez stalked the young soldier patrolling the perimeter of the camp. His rifle was slung carelessly over his shoulder and a cigarette dangled from his lips, each drag illuminating his face and robbing him of his night vision.

That mistake will cost you dearly tonight, Gates thought.

The sentry kept looking back at the hut on the edge of the camp—the whorehouse. His mind was obviously on the women who languished there as sex slaves. A terrified scream from the hut, followed by a loud stream of violent cursing, brought a smile to the sentry's face as he leaned against a tree and smoked his cigarette.

Nothing fancy, Gates admonished himself, just take him out.

From a crouch, Gates sprang up in front of the sentry just as a plume of smoke billowed from the man's mouth. Before his tiger-striped face even registered in the sentry's eyes, Gates drove his fingers into the man's throat, crushing his windpipe.

The sentry gasped, eyes bulging as Gates grabbed him by the head and expertly snapped his neck. Gates cradled the man, slowly lowering his lifeless body into the underbrush. Around the camp, the maneuver was repeated until the entire night patrol had been eliminated.

Near the hut where their female captives were kept, several soldiers sat near a small fire, laughing and drinking.

"*Merde!*" a haggard soldier growled as he stumbled out of the hut, struggling to pull up his tattered pants.

"What's the problem, old man," one of the younger soldiers remarked, "couldn't get it up?"

"Hah!" the older soldier spat back. "Fucking has never been a problem. Watch yourself around that new bitch—she's got claws and teeth."

"I like a woman who fights," a tall, muscular soldier boasted proudly.

"She's waiting for you, Gano," the older soldier replied as he inspected a gash on his stomach.

Gano handed the older soldier his bottle of rum and walked slowly toward the hut. Inside, several women huddled in a darkened corner, hoping to make themselves invisible, to disappear from this hellish place. Gano studied the quivering mass of bruised and bloodied flesh. He saw women as nothing more than animals, like chickens or goats, something you breed, slaughter, and consume.

He reached down and grabbed one of the women by the hair. As she screamed and dug her fingernails into his forearm, Gano picked her up and threw her into the center of the hut. She was naked, and purplish welts marked what had once been an attractive body. She pulled herself up from the ground, crouching on all fours.

"So, you like blood," Gano said as the clawed flesh on his arm reddened. "I do, too."

Gano viciously kicked the woman in the chest. She rolled with the blow, but the impact still managed to break two ribs. The sharp pain almost caused her to black out, but she held on to her consciousness.

Kilkenny's first shot punched a hole the size of a quarter in one soldier's forehead. The bottle slipped from the man's hand as his head slumped back. The others thought their companion had passed out, until a second man collapsed in a bloody heap. Kilkenny and Darvas didn't waste a single round from their silenced H-K MP5s; each shot hammered into a kill zone. With Darvas covering him, Kilkenny followed the screams into the hut.

Gano looked down at the woman and smiled as she struggled against the pain. He knelt, grinding his knee into her right leg to pin the limb down. Wrapping his right arm around her left leg, he spread her legs apart. She tried to pull her leg back, but Gano locked her knee, and each twist felt as if the joint would break.

"I'll give you a choice, *vache*," Gano sneered. First, he loosened the rope that held his pants up; then he pulled a grimy pistol from his hip holster and held it between her legs. "You can have me or my gun. Which will it be?"

Before the woman could reply, Kilkenny fired. The near-silent blast shattered the man's shoulder. The impact twisted Gano at the waist, turning him toward the hut's entry. Kilkenny's second shot exploded in the man's heart and sent him sprawling backward to the ground.

The woman had been kicking her captor furiously as Kilkenny entered, a dark figure backlit by the fire outside. She shrank back when she saw him, not certain if Kilkenny would now take the dead man's place.

"*Va!*" Kilkenny shouted at the women as he pointed to the door.

The women needed little encouragement as they bolted for their freedom, fleeing with little regard for personal modesty as they vanished into the jungle. Kilkenny's stomach tightened as he stowed his revulsion at the thought of his mother or sister in the hands of these monsters.

Kilkenny switched on his throat mike. "Hep, talk to me."

"We had a little trouble on the back side," Hepburn replied, "but the camp is secure."

Kilkenny had heard a sporadic exchange of gunfire—on the far end of the compound—which seemed to end as quickly as it had started.

"Good. The women are heading into the jungle like the devil's after them. See if you and Gilgallon can't get 'em to safe ground and tend to their wounds."

"Will do."

Kilkenny then left the hut and turned to Darvas. "Let's move."

The camp was quiet, unnaturally so as Kilkenny and Darvas moved among the huts. Through a few open doors, Kilkenny saw the bodies of Masson's men scattered in heaps on the ground. Gates scurried across the compound to join him.

"Masson's holed up in his hut. Rodriguez and Detmer have him pinned down. Near as I can figure, he's got the place lined with sandbags."

"Smart man. How are we set for time?"

"The satchel charges are in place and the clock is running. We've got just under five minutes to get clear."

The SEALs had planted enough plastic explosives around the camp so that, in five minutes, there would be nothing left but a scorched crater. Normally, they would just toss a couple of grenades into the hut and call it a day, but the C-4 they'd planted had a nasty tendency to detonate in the proximity of an exploding grenade.

"If we back off now, this guy just might get away, and that is fucking unacceptable. Masson is a cancer and we're cutting him out. Gates, you're with me. Darvas, cover our backs. Rodriguez and Detmer, make sure he doesn't pop out the other side. Let's do it."

Gates and Kilkenny ran a zigzag pattern across the clearing in front of Masson's hut, dodging fire as they approached. Well-timed bursts from Darvas's MP5 kept Masson from getting a clean shot at them.

Kilkenny let loose a burst of gunfire that perforated the corrugated metal door, twisting and warping flimsy steel until it finally pulled free of its hinges and clattered to the ground. Masson's weapon replied on full automatic, emptying itself quickly, although failing to find a target.

Kilkenny dove through the open doorway, tuck-rolling across the dirt floor, with Gates following his lead. Masson had just snapped a new clip of ammunition into an Uzi when Kilkenny's boot struck his stomach and sent him sprawling against a pile of sandbags. The blow stunned him, but his grip on the weapon was firm. Still gasping for air, Masson aimed at Kilkenny.

Muzzle flashes filled the interior of the hut like a strobe, but Gates found his target first. Pain seared Masson's mind as a dozen blistering rounds riddled his body, breaking bones and tearing flesh. The crazed ex-soldier fell backward before collapsing on the ground.

Kilkenny got up, nodded to Gates, and turned to his fallen opponent. A fire still burned in Masson's eyes, but his breathing came in wheezing gasps as he clung to his last moments of life.

Dawson zoomed the satellite image back in order to show a larger area of southern Haiti as his men left the guerilla camp. Right on cue, a bright thermal plume lit up the infrared display.

Helicopters from Port-au-Prince were racing toward the scene of the explosion, the government having been quietly notified that several captives of the scavengers had been liberated and required assistance.

"Bravo Zulu, Trident," Dawson said quietly to himself. "Well done."

The SEALs melted into the jungle as the helicopters approached the smoldering crater. The women, clothed and cared for as well as the squad could provide, were quickly evacuated from the scene. Kilkenny bowed his head as the helicopters disappeared from view.

"What ya thinking about, Nolan?" Gates asked.

"Something my mother taught me, the Prayer of Contentment. 'Lord, grant me the courage to change what I can change, the strength to accept what I cannot change, and the wisdom to know the difference.'"

"Good prayer. I can see how the first part applies to our current situation, but what about the rest?"

Nolan paused to consider why these words would come to him at this time. "I guess this is the first time since this mission started that I let myself think about what's waiting for me when we get back."

"Getting cold feet, partner?" Gates asked in his smooth-as-molasses drawl. "You could just sign up for another hitch and take the easy way out. Dawson hasn't filled your slot yet."

"C'mon, Max," Nolan said with a laugh, "you, of all people, know I never do anything the easy way."

"No, son, you don't. But you do what has to be done. That's what made you a good leader and a hell of a SEAL."

Nolan smiled, accepting the compliment. He had been paired with Gates for almost five years, and he had come to value the master chief's experience and to respect his opinions.

"This," Gates said, cradling his submachine gun and smelling the cordite in the air, "this is my life. This is what I was meant to do. This life isn't for everybody, and we both know it's not for you. This is your send-off, Nolan. It's time to move on."

"So I should just accept the fact that change is inevitable?"

"Deal with it, Lieutenant."

Chapter 14

Santo Domingo, Dominican Republic
December 24

Parnell chuckled quietly to himself.

"Something funny, Ian?" Roe asked, looking up from her laptop. An hour ago, she'd given up on trying to work during the long flight from London to Santo Domingo. Her computer screen now displayed a half-played game of solitaire.

"I was just thinking that if one of us had acquired Mr. Cole's device a few years ago, we might never have met."

"Oh, I don't know, Ian. We move in the same circles. I'm sure we would have *bumped* into each other at some point or another."

"Quite right," Parnell replied, amused at her double entendre.

A smile crossed Roe's face as she thought about the first time she'd met British business consultant Ian Parnell. His light brown hair had been a little longer than it was now, and in place of the Savile Row suit and the Burberry shirt that was tailored so well to his lean five-ten body, he had worn a suit of black Gore-Tex then.

Five years ago, Alex Roe had been hired by a corporate client to acquire technology from a German competitor. The technology had to do with methods of very precise measurement, and the German competitor was apparently able to size very small things with greater accuracy than was her client. She'd entered the German firm's research facility late one night, with the cleaning crew, and set out to locate the design documents relating to this device. While carefully negotiating a darkened room to avoid a night guard, Roe quite literally bumped into Parnell. Both quickly realized that they were working on the same assignment and decided to pool their resources and charge the client double. Since then, they had worked together on a variety of interesting and profitable projects.

The flight attendant arrived with a small bottle of champagne and two glasses.

"A toast," Parnell offered, tapping the rim of Roe's glass with his. "To the Holy Grail."

"Why the Holy Grail, Ian?" Roe asked before sipping the effervescent beverage.

"It's what you've discovered, the Holy Grail of our profession. We are on the brink of acquiring a skeleton key, one that can unlock storehouses of information around the world."

Their flight arrived in Santo Domingo in the late afternoon and, after clearing Dominican Customs and Immigration, they boarded a private helicopter for a short flight to Barahona. Parnell worked hard and he liked to enjoy the fruits of his labor; being whisked over the Dominican capital was one of life's simple pleasures.

Roe soaked in the tropical atmosphere with delight as the helicopter raced westward over the sandy shoreline. Their destination was an exclusive resort that offered numerous amenities to its guests, including secluded beaches, all manner of water sports, five-star dining, and excellent accommodations. While these were enjoyable, the resort also met their far more crucial needs for privacy and flawless digital communication.

Bellhops collected their bags from the helicopter, hustling to beat the new guests to their rooms. The resort catered to wealthy tourists and the management frowned on anything less than impeccable service from its employees. Praise by a guest meant an additional bonus in the next pay envelope, and each employee worked hard to shine in front of the guests. Poor service—or worse, rude behavior—could result in disciplinary action ranging from a reprimand to job termination. With a long waiting list for job openings, the staff at Las Brisas rarely did anything to jeopardize their employment.

A woman in her mid-thirties with flowing black hair and a perfect figure stood waiting for them as they walked to the edge of the helipad.

"Señor Parnell, Señorita Roe," she said with a warm smile, "welcome to Las Brisas. I am Delisa Santiago, the resort manager. If there is anything we can do to make your stay here more pleasant, please let me know."

"Ms. Santiago," Parnell replied, "if Las Brisas lives up to its reputation, I'm certain that my associate and I will enjoy our holiday immensely."

The manager pointed out items of interest along the walk to their bungalows. The resort's lobby and walkways were decorated with various objets d'art, ranging from pre-Columbian to contemporary, gathered from around the Caribbean.

Mayan statuary was mixed in with islander masks and jewelry; artifacts of peace and war, of life and death, added a unique dimension to the resort. Objects that had once helped a community of people know the gods they worshiped and understand their place in creation had become decorations in a tropical playground for the wealthy.

Even though they'd made reservations only a week ago, Parnell had little trouble arranging two bungalows near the beach. Those holding the original reservations were provided accommodations elsewhere, with the management's sincere apologies for "double-booking" the room.

Both bungalows were identical in layout—each offering its occupant an entertaining area, a kitchenette and bar, a guest bedroom and bath, and a full master bedroom and bath with an ocean-view terrace. In looking about the rooms, Roe noticed that her luggage had already been delivered and set inside the walk-in closet. She found her toiletries and decided to cleanse the long flight from her body.

It seemed as if only seconds had passed when Roe heard a knock at the bathroom door. She turned the shower off and wrapped a hotel robe around her dripping body. Opening the door cautiously, she discovered Parnell standing at the bar, mixing a drink.

"Ready for dinner?" he asked lightly.

"Not quite, but give me a couple of minutes. How'd you get in, anyway?"

Parnell fingered the gray plastic card key in his hand. "The manager, a wonderful woman, configured the keys to work on both of our suites. I figured you wouldn't mind if I made a drink while I waited."

"Rather presumptuous of you, Ian. Make yourself at home. I'll be out in a bit."

Roe quickly blow-dried her shoulder-length brown hair. After she finished up in the bathroom, she selected a lightly colored cotton dress that appealed to her sense of style and tropical comfort.

"When is Cole due to arrive?" Parnell asked as he took another sip of his gin and tonic.

"Around six, which leaves us about a half hour to kill."

"We could have a drink here or head to the dining room."

"I cast my vote for the dining room. I'm starved." Roe adjusted her dress in the mirror and mentally declared herself presentable. "Not to knock British Air, but airline food is still airline food. We can leave word at the front desk for him to join us once he arrives."

"Very well," Parnell tossed back the remainder of his drink. "You know, I must admit that I'm rather excited to meet this Cole fellow. If everything you've told me is true, we may have found ourselves a golden goose."

"Hello, Michael," Roe said as Cole entered the restaurant lobby. Cole looked tan and rested. He wore a light cotton sweater over a golf shirt and a pair of khaki trousers. Slung from his shoulder was a small briefcase containing his laptop computer.

"Hello, Alex. This is a nice place."

"Yes, it is," Roe replied; then she turned to Parnell. "Ian, this is Michael Cole."

Parnell held his hand out and clasped Cole's. Cole's grip was firm, but not punishing. "It is a pleasure to meet you finally. Alex has spoken very highly of you and your work."

"Thank you. She's told me a little about you, but I'd like to hear more."

"Well, that's what tonight is about, a proper introduction."

The tuxedo-clad maître d' approached. "Your table is ready," he announced in lightly accented English. "If you will please follow me."

They were seated at a circular table near a large plate-glass window with a view of the bay. The spectacular panorama caused all three to pause for a moment to take it all in.

"If you think this is nice," Cole offered, "wait until you see the sunset."

They took their seats at the table; Cole and Parnell sat opposite each other, with Roe in between. She recognized that, as this was their first meeting, her dining companions were sizing each other up. A waiter took their drink orders while another server filled their water glasses.

"So, Michael, how has your holiday been?"

"Great. Yesterday, I dove on a wreck of the *Conde de Tolosa*, up near Samana Bay. It was indescribable."

"Alex and I both do a little diving, don't we?"

"I'm not in Michael's league, Ian," Roe added coyly. "I only dive in warm, tropical waters."

"Say," Parnell said brightly, "I've chartered a boat from the marina for the day after Christmas. Alex and I were going to do a little motoring about. Perhaps you'd like to join us and do a bit of diving?"

"Sure. I plan to spend a few more days in the DR before I move on. The dive master who took me out to the wreck told me about a nice reef just south of here, due east of the beach at Baoruca. Nice scenery, and the water isn't too cold."

Roe smiled pleasantly. "Looks like I'll have to rent some gear."

Conversation at the table throughout the evening remained purely social, avoiding the evening's real purpose. Parnell continued to play generous host, with Cole as his pleasant guest. A few hours later, they left very pleased with the chef's culinary skills; the restaurant's five-star rating was clearly an understatement.

When they entered Roe's bungalow, she noticed a magnum of Dom Pérignon cradled in a vat of ice sitting beside three champagne glasses on the bar counter.

"That's for later," Parnell said, reading the question in her expression. "First, we have some business to attend to. Michael, are you prepared to go to work?"

"Yes, I am." Cole walked over to the desk and pulled a notebook computer from his briefcase. "Alex, will you call the front desk and ask them to hold all your calls for the evening?"

"Certainly."

After Roe's call, Cole plugged his modem cable into the suite's data jack. He then powered up his computer and checked that everything was working properly.

"Per our discussion a few weeks ago, I have regularly checked my E-mail at both Langley and Moy Electronics," Cole explained. "Tonight's call will be a continuation of that pattern."

As Cole spoke, he set the computer connection in motion. Upon receiving his command, the computer opened a phone line and began dialing the international prefix and phone number for Moy Electronics' Chicago-based computer network. From the resort, Cole's call was directed to the main telephone switching station in Santo Domingo, where a routing computer began looking for an open connection with a communications satellite in geosynchronous orbit over the equator. From the satellite, Cole's call continued to a U.S. telephone relay station, which routed it to a switching station in Chicago. The switching station then located the unlisted business line and connected the call.

"Good evening, Moy Electronics," Cole said, responding to the computer's on-screen greeting.

Parnell and Roe watched as Cole passed through the network's security and successfully logged on to the system.

Once the Moy network screen came up on the laptop's monitor, Cole rose and offered Roe the chair. "Your turn."

Roe sat down, pulled a disk from her briefcase, and slipped it into the drive slot on the notebook's front edge. From the disk, she loaded two programs into the Moy network computer's memory. The first sent Cole's user ID off into a diagnostic loop, while the second created a superuser with systemwide access.

"Gentlemen," she announced, "we now have complete access to Moy Electronics and, since it's Christmas Eve, I'll bet we have the place to ourselves."

"'Twas the night before Christmas, when all through the house/ Not a creature was stirring—not even a mouse,'" Parnell recited, patting Roe on the shoulder. "'The stockings were hung by the chimney with care/ In hopes that Saint Alex soon would be there.'"

"I don't think I'm quite the Santa that Moy Electronics hoped would slide down their chimney," Roe replied.

"More like the Grinch Who Stole Christmas," Cole offered wryly.

"Now now, Michael, Alex isn't going to steal Moy's Christmas. She's just shopping for that *perfect gift*." The combination of jet lag, a few drinks, and the promise of untold riches propelled Parnell into a seasonably good mood. "Please proceed."

"The first thing we need to do is find a good home for our Spyder." Roe began probing the system for internal safeguards and found only a few layers of security among the different areas of Moy's operation. "Here we are, the order logs. Would anyone like a supercomputer?"

"That might be a bit too cheeky," Parnell replied. "What else have they got?"

Skimming through the main order directory, Roe located the log for Gatekeeper shipments. She clicked on the icon and a new window appeared, which contained a spreadsheet of orders, production dates, shipping dates, and product costs.

"Somewhere on here is our lucky winner," Roe said as she studied the list of Gatekeeper sites.

The first fifty orders were strictly government-agency retrofits—Gatekeepers specifically geared to provide an existing computer system with a new layer of protection. Early on, Parnell and Roe had decided that they would avoid planting a Spyder in a government computer. Parnell was adamant that his work remain exclusively in the private sector; he did not spy on governments and he would not work from inside a government computer. The private espionage business was dangerous enough without risking any unnecessary *official* entanglements.

"Michael," Roe asked as she studied the information on the laptop's screen. "I've just come across several

Gatekeeper orders for Moy Electronics. Have they installed any yet?"

"No, or you wouldn't be messing around inside their computer. The project called for the installation of Gatekeepers on computer networks as identified by NSA. Since the initial production run for the device is low, Moy Electronics pushed off upgrading in-house until late January."

"Keep looking," Parnell added while pouring another gin and tonic. "I don't believe one of Moy's computers would be suitable for our needs."

Roe continued paging through the log entries until one for the Michigan Applied Research Consortium caught her eye. "Hmm, this MARC installation looks interesting."

Parnell walked over from the bar. "Have you found something?"

"Maybe." Roe clicked on the file icon and pulled up the detailed information of the order. "It says here that MARC is a semi-public venture that serves as a conduit between basic research at the university level and industrial applications. According to this narrative, they're being backed by some major players in the Fortune One Hundred."

"How are they going to use their Gatekeeper?" Cole asked.

Roe paged through the narrative to the order specifications. "It appears that MARC will be using their Gatekeeper as a means to control the flow of information between their existing Cray supercomputer and a new type of processor they're testing. The new processor design is based on optics, rather than the conventional electronics used in standard computer chips."

"Sounds rather exotic," Parnell opined.

"Does it say what else that Cray is connected to?" Cole asked.

"Yes," Roe replied as she clicked on the icon for the MARC network. A new window opened with graphic depiction of the entire MARC's network, including the proposed placement from the Gatekeeper. "Will that do, Michael?"

Cole studied the image intently, imagining the flow of information over the network described on the screen in lines and symbols. "Yes, it'll have access to the outside world. Let's take a look at the external networks."

Paging down through a list of other computer systems that were considered part of the MARC network, Roe discovered a list of scientific and corporate entities with the privileges on the MARC computer network.

"Ian," Roe said, her voice quivering slightly, "I think you'll want to take a look at this."

Every major university, think tank, and corporate research center in the United States was tied into MARC. The thought of all that brainpower being accessible from one location brought a satisfied smile to Parnell's face; his avarice was nearly palpable.

Roe glanced at the two men peering over her shoulders and laughed. "I believe we've found a home for our Spyder. Let's find out when they want it."

Clicking over to the production schedule, Roe learned that MARC's Gatekeeper had already passed final testing and was scheduled for shipment in the first week in January. Roe made a note of the MARC Gatekeeper's serial number and exited the order system.

"Now that we have our site," Roe said, "it's Michael's turn to upgrade MARC's Gatekeeper."

*   *   *

Moy Electronics had spent a great deal of money during the last few years perfecting their automated production facility. The flexible factory was capable of switching product lines in a matter of days, where traditional factories might take weeks to retool for a new product. Dull, repetitive tasks had been handed over to industrial robots, allowing experienced factory workers to become the brains behind the tireless machines.

On Christmas Eve, only a skeleton crew of security officers and operations personnel were on duty; anyone who might be needed during an emergency was on call at home. The machines, which never slept, were in the middle of a preprogrammed production run when Cole and Roe loaded a new series of instructions into their memory.

Material-transport robot 43 had just finished delivering a pallet of components ready for shipment to the loading dock when it received new orders via the network of overlapping communication "cells" mounted throughout the factory. Robot 43, an industrial robot that bore a strong resemblance to a metal footlocker, glided along the smooth concrete floor on four high-density rubber rollers. Its long, squat form was designed specifically to roll underneath freestanding storage carts and to carry those carts on four internal hydraulic jacks.

Forty-three's new orders called for it to return to the warehouse and retrieve a package for the testing lab. As it stopped at the designated point in the warehouse, another robot fitted with a hydraulic double-jointed arm removed a box from a shelf twelve feet above the floor. With the package securely held by its fork-and-mandible collecting apparatus, the arm carefully lowered it onto 43's back.

The warehouse central computer then instructed 43

to proceed to the testing laboratory with the crate. Many people would find such a fully automated factory disturbingly dark and quiet, even more so on the night before Christmas, but these thoughts never bothered robot 43. It simply received and executed commands from the warehouse computer, interrupting its day only to recharge its batteries.

The testing lab's doors swung open as motion sensors detected 43's approach. The robot glided in and stopped at the laboratory's designated delivery station. An articulating robot arm swung around from the diagnostics bench and collected the package from 43's back. New commands flowed over the cellular network and 43 rolled from the lab toward its next objective.

Inside the lab, several robotic arms, mounted on a ceiling track system, moved into place above the box. They removed the protective packaging, revealing a black cube-shaped chip mated to a 256-pin receptacle. A thin articulating arm, fitted with a pair of hooked nose pliers, swung down from the ceiling and extracted the black cube from the receptacle. The arm then set the cube into the socket connection on the face of a chip encoder.

Prior to his vacation, Cole had customized the original Spyder program instructions to include the contact points where it could reach Parnell and Roe in the outside world. This revised program now resided in the internal memory of the chip encoder.

On Cole's command, the encoder ran a low-voltage signal across the chip's internal memory, wiping the old program away. Once the internal memory was purged of the Gatekeeper code, a second signal began to flow through it, this one carrying the Spyder program.

After five minutes of loading and another ten of

confirmation testing, the transfer was successfully completed. The articulating arm retrieved the chip and placed it back on the shipping receptacle. The other arms repacked the Gatekeeper and, right on cue, robot 43 returned to pick up the package.

"The Spyder is on its way to Michigan," Cole said as he issued the command that sent 43 back to the warehouse.

"Now we just need to tidy up a bit," Roe added. "Bring up the activity log for the lab robots."

Cole clicked on a few icons and a spreadsheet list of time intervals and activities scrolled out onto a new window. The lab had been quiet tonight, other than their little memory transplant. Cole modified the lab robots' work logs to list them as running self-diagnostic routines.

"That should make it look like those robots have been sleeping all night. Now let's see how forty-three is doing."

Robot 43 had completed its task and was heading back to a charging station in the warehouse.

"Michael, I think forty-three was feeling a little ill about the time we logged in," Roe suggested. "See if you can't send it over to the maintenance shop with a malfunction."

"I think I can handle that," Cole replied.

Cole brought up robot 43's maintenance history and noticed a recent failure of its hydraulic system. He copied the old entry into the current time slot, indicating that 43 had sensed a partial system failure and reported to the maintenance shop twenty minutes prior to their entry into the Moy computer system. Then he commanded the robot to report to the maintenance shop, where it would power down and wait for the day-shift mechanics to arrive.

"Robot 43 is down with the flu. What next?" Cole asked.

Roe ran through a list she'd compiled while Cole was manipulating the automated factory. "The testing reports for the MARC Gatekeeper order; make sure they're finalized and that the unit is listed as *ready to ship*."

Cole punched through the order log, checking off the quality-assurance checks. On Friday, when the lead shipping clerk ran a report of items ready to ship, MARC's Gatekeeper would be among the many items on the list.

"That's it," Roe commented. "All we can do now is cross our fingers and hope it works."

"It'll work," Cole said, proud of his creation.

"I believe that tonight's efforts deserve a toast," Parnell announced triumphantly as he uncorked the champagne.

Cole, too, felt the glow from successfully stealing a Spyder. As Parnell poured out three flutes of champagne, Cole retrieved from his briefcase an envelope containing a printout of the Cormorant file. From day one at the CIA, he was told that information is power; tonight, he felt that power as he accepted the glass from Parnell.

"To a prosperous New Year," Parnell offered.

Cole clinked his glass. "To the Spyder, may it make us all rich beyond our wildest dreams."

Parnell, Roe, and Cole drained their glasses in the spirit of the moment; then Cole laid the envelope on the bar.

"What's this?" Parnell asked as he refilled the glasses.

"Something I picked up from the CIA that may have some bearing on the structure of our business relationship. Alex, why don't you look it over first while I discuss profit sharing with Ian."

Chapter 15

December 26

Kilkenny scanned the deserted stretch of beach, looking for anything that might get in the way of his squad's departure from Haiti. After three weeks in the jungle, it was good to see the ocean again.

Gates and Darvas finished a last sweep of the surrounding jungle and flashed a thumbs-up to Kilkenny. The beach was secure. With a nod, the SEALs began exhuming their buried diving equipment. Kilkenny checked his watch; they were right on schedule. At the prearranged time earlier that day, they'd radioed the submarine to be prepared for tonight's pickup. A brief exchange of code words set in motion the plan that would take them home.

Each man carefully checked his dive gear for damage from the time it had spent interred. The dry-wrap bags had done their job, keeping everything free of water, dirt, and any of the tropical insects that might have tried to take up residence. Inhaling a beetle under sixty feet of water is not recommended.

Once their weapons were stowed and his squad was ready, Kilkenny ordered his men into the water. After three weeks in a tropical rain forest, none wasted any time plunging into the surf. Once they reached the calm water beneath the waves, the squad swam in a loose formation, with Gates taking the point. The digital locator on Gates's wrist zeroed in on the SVD's homing beacon, leading them straight back to where the camouflaged minisubs lay on the seafloor.

The SDVs displayed no ill-effects from their long rest on the bottom. Each started right up and the batteries showed no appreciable loss of charge. The homer in each of the SDVs found a strong signal coming from the *Columbia*, about eleven miles out to sea. Kilkenny rotated his finger, signaling that it was time to move out.

The ice rattled in Parnell's drink as the thirty-six-foot cabin cruiser bobbed in the light swells of the Caribbean. Parnell leaned back in the captain's chair and sipped on the iced gin, his mind on neither the sea nor his thirst.

Damn that Michael Cole! His thoughts raged. How dare he blackmail me into renegotiating our deal.

Two days earlier, on Christmas Eve, he had embarked on a promising new venture with the acquisition of a Spyder device. He had come to Santo Domingo believing that the arrangement with Cole had been finalized. Cole was to resign from the CIA and open a consulting business whose sole client would be one of Parnell's well-shielded corporations. As a consultant, Cole would earn generous fees for the services that he provided for this client—namely, running the Spyder.

But Cole had surprised him, and Ian Parnell didn't

like being surprised. The computer engineer had made a play for a greater share of the Spyder profits, backing his bid with the threat of blackmail. The leverage that Cole claimed to possess confirmed something Parnell had long suspected, that Alexandra Roe had once worked for the KGB.

Parnell really didn't care where Roe had learned her trade; as a freelance spy, she was one of the best. Unfortunately, Cole's threat posed a very real danger. Even if all of his consultation work was completely legitimate, Parnell knew that any hint of an espionage scandal would destroy his business. He took another sip of gin and ran the scene with Cole through his head for the hundredth time.

He was alone on the bridge, a solitude paid for by a small bribe to the Barahona harbormaster, who'd rented him the Hatteras. Eighty feet below the boat, Cole and Roe explored a spectacular reef that a local dive-shop owner had recommended. They'd spent the morning deep-sea fishing off the western shore of Pedernales, near the Haitian border, catching nothing, and Parnell now sat back and enjoyed the quiet as he decided what to do about Michael Cole.

"Ian, we're up!" Roe called out as she broke the water's surface behind the boat.

The shout interrupted Parnell's brooding. Cole and Roe were already climbing onto the jump deck when he opened the stern rail. The divers handed their gear up to him before climbing aboard.

"Alex, do you mind tending ship for a bit? I think it's time Michael and I discussed the revised terms of our deal."

Roe nodded and continued checking her scuba

equipment while Cole toweled off and accompanied Parnell below.

"I've laid out the revised proposal on the galley table. Why don't you have a look while I use the head?"

Cole leaned over the legal documents that Parnell had spread out for him, careful not to drip water on the papers. He skipped over the boilerplate defining the relationship between Cole's professional corporation and Parnell's corporate shell in the Caymans to the paragraph on fees and percentages. Cole's heart skipped a beat when he read the breakdown of profits; the sliding scale was definitely skewed in his favor. After eighteen years at a mediocre salary and a disastrous divorce that had left him all but bankrupt, Michael Cole saw himself poised to earn a small fortune. The structure of the agreement hid the money well enough that his ex-wife would never see a dime of it.

"Ian," Cole called out. "This looks—"

Parnell drove the three-pound rubber mallet down on Cole's skull like an ax, rendering the man unconscious. He grabbed Cole as he collapsed and dragged him to a hatch in the stern of the boat. Carefully, he hauled Cole down into the boat's engine compartment and placed him between the twin diesels, securing his arms and legs with duct tape. He then disconnected the exhaust pipe from one of the diesel engines. Satisfied that everything was ready, Parnell closed the hatch and returned to the bridge.

"How did it go with Cole?" Roe asked when Parnell appeared on deck.

"I think he found the revised terms agreeable. He's not feeling too well, though; he seems to have a bit of a headache. I left him below to rest while we head back to port."

Parnell primed the pumps and started the engines. After checking the compass heading and the charts, he turned the boat around and headed back to Barahona.

Both Parnell and Roe remained silent most of the way back, each deeply engrossed in their own thoughts. For Roe, memories of a past life, long buried, had resurfaced. The information that Cole had produced, details about her identity and her KGB career, could only have come from one source—her mentor, Andrei Yakushev. Yakushev alone had kept the files that linked his agents with their deep-cover assignments, but he was long dead.

Roe had been in Moscow when the hard-line Communists tried to overthrow the Gorbachev government. Fearing the worst, Yakushev had altered her records in Lubyanka, listing her as "killed on assignment," and destroyed the operations files that identified her as Anna Mironova. She had last seen Yakushev during the opening hours of the coup, when he freed her from the KGB. The Soviet power struggle was one that Yakushev did not expect to survive.

The sudden quiet brought Roe back to the present. They had been cruising at a leisurely pace for forty-five minutes when Parnell cut the engines and brought the boat to a stop.

"That ought to about do it."

"Ought to do *what?*" Roe had no idea what he was talking about.

"Cole. He's dead, or should be by now. I knocked him out and left him down beside the diesels. I estimate three-quarters of an hour should be enough to kill him. What do you think? Should I run it for another twenty minutes, just to make sure?"

Roe's mouth opened to form a question her mind

was still trying to assemble. Parnell talked about killing Cole as if it were some kind of recipe he was trying to follow. "What have you done with Cole?"

"I killed him." Parnell spoke in slow, measured tones, precisely delivering each word.

Roe bolted from her chair and ran belowdecks, hoping that this was just a sick example of British humor. Parnell wasn't laughing.

"I wouldn't go down there if I were you, fumes and all. Might get you, as well."

Cole was nowhere to be seen in the main cabin. Roe located the hatch panel to the engine room and opened it. It was just as Parnell had described; Cole lay prone and motionless along the beam of the boat, between the twin engines. The compartment was thick with heat and grimy diesel exhaust.

"Yes, he's dead," Parnell declared icily, looking over her shoulder.

Roe found it difficult to suppress the violent shiver running down her spine. "Why?"

"Don't give me that. It's not like I'm Jack the Ripper. We don't *need* him, and I won't have a bastard like Cole holding a sword over my head for the rest of my life. The way I see it, I did both of us a favor. Now go get your scuba tank on." Parnell's tone left no room for discussion.

After Roe suited up, Parnell instructed her to take Cole's scuba tanks into the engine room and, using a small electric compressor, dope them with monoxide-tainted air. Should Cole's body ever be recovered, Parnell reasoned, the fouled tanks would be the apparent cause of death. Once Roe finished with the tanks, she dragged Cole's body up on deck. By this time, the sun was gliding down to the horizon and twilight was upon them.

"Ian, if Cole just disappears like this, don't you think someone is going to report it to the police?"

"Yes. That's why his disappearance has to be very public and explainable. Michael was scheduled to dive with a tourist group out of Barahona tomorrow. I intend to take his place, and you are going to help me stage a tragic accident." Parnell eyed Roe carefully. "I realize that this alters our professional relationship. We are both going to have to trust each other if we are to succeed in our new venture. You are with me on this, aren't you?"

Sitting on the deck beside a dead man and his killer didn't encourage Roe to question Parnell's plans. There was no way she could explain any of this without going to jail. Worse yet, Cole's murder had occurred in a foreign country. She might well be in prison for years before she ever got to see the U.S. ambassador, who wouldn't visit at all if her former espionage activities came to light. She was trapped, trapped by her past, by Cole, and now, by Parnell.

Parnell and Roe struggled to place diving gear on Cole's lifeless body. If Roe hadn't still been in shock over her situation, she might have found the morbidly absurd scene amusing. As it was, she was not as careful inspecting the fittings as she had been when they dove earlier in the day.

"Good riddance, you sorry sod," Parnell said as he pushed Cole's body off the back of the boat.

The black form fell sideways and struck the calm water with a slap. It lay there on the surface for a moment; then, slowly, the blue water enveloped it.

Once the body disappeared, Parnell returned to the bridge to start the journey back to port. Roe remained on the aft deck, sensing that they both needed to be alone for a while.

*   *   *

Weighted down with a belt of lead weights and a nearly empty metal scuba tank, Michael Cole's body plummeted to the seafloor as quickly as the water would allow. The lifeless black form spiraled downward like a leaf, slowly tumbling over itself in the descent. The eighty-foot drop ended when Cole's fins struck a coral outcrop on the seafloor. It fell forward, facedown, expending its last bit of downward momentum.

A black rubber hose protruded from the left side of Cole's buoyancy-control device; the end containing the controls to inflate and deflate the device dangled freely. The purpose of the BCD, essentially an inflatable vest, was to allow a diver to achieve balance in the water, neither floating nor sinking. As Cole's body struck the coral, the BCD's black rubber hose was pinned against the reef.

A hissing sound began to emanate from the BCD, slowly at first; then bladders of the floatation vest began to fill with air. As the BCD inflated, the body slowly lifted off the reef. When the weight of Cole's body no longer pressed against the inflation control, the hissing stopped. Now buoyant in the seawater, Cole's body began to drift with the current.

Chapter 16

"*Cerveza, señor?*" Ponce Sebastian asked, offering a cold beverage to the heavyset man in the fighting chair.

"Sure, Ponce," the man replied, trading an empty bottle for a full one.

Ponce Sebastian was a short, wiry man and the captain of his own fishing boat. This boat, the *Alazna*, was also his home. Ponce chartered his boat out for day trips to tourists. Today, this overweight American from Alabama wanted to fish for sea bass. It was only nine in the morning and the man was already on his third beer. Ponce didn't mind; the man had paid in advance.

The reel on the man's rod jerked and began to spin. Then it stopped. The tourist wiped the sheen of perspiration off his brow and looked at the reel. As the boat bobbed with the next wave, it spun again, then stopped.

"Hey, Ponce, I think we got something on the line."

Ponce walked over just as the reel began to spin. It

turned slowly, nothing like a large fish fighting for its life. Again, it stopped.

"That's the third time it's done that."

"If that's a fish, señor, it's got no *cojones*. We must have snagged something. Let's reel it in."

The tourist put one hand on the rod while the other turned the reel. Judging by the way he tested the line as he drew it in, Ponce knew the man had some experience fishing. The man also wasn't afraid to work. Some of the tourists he had carried barely lifted a finger while at sea, leaving him to land the fish and take their picture with it.

"You're right, Ponce. Whatever it is, it sure ain't swimming."

The tourist wiped his brow and resumed his task of reeling in the line. Ponce watched the thin wake that broke where the heavy nylon line sliced the water's surface. Gradually, a dark form began to rise from the depths. The line started to slacken and the tourist was turning the reel as fast as he could. The black form emerged from the sea twenty feet behind the fishing boat. Both men stared, trying to divine what they'd brought up from the sea.

"Ponce, I think it's a body."

"I think you're right. Help me pull it in."

The tourist continued to work the reel, slowly now to ease the black form closer to the aft of the boat. Using a pole that resembled a long shepherd's crook, Ponce hooked the body and pulled it against the hull.

"Let me handle that hook, Ponce. You pull him up on the jump deck."

Ponce opened the aft gate and stepped onto the jump deck while the tourist strained to keep the body in place.

"On three, señor," Ponce instructed.

On the third count, both men heaved and the full weight of what they had caught became apparent. With a single burst of strength, they struggled the lifeless form through the gate and onto the deck.

"Señor, I don't think you should look. This person may have been in the water awhile."

"Don't worry about me, Ponce, I've been to war. There's not a lot I haven't seen."

Ponce carefully rolled the body onto its side. The body was rigid, like a mannequin. Both men looked at the diver's face, which, though ashen, was still intact.

"I don't think this guy's been dead too long, Ponce."

"Señor, I apologize, but we have to return to port. If you like, I will refund your money."

"No way, Ponce. You promised me a fishing trip I'd never forget and you delivered. Hell, no one back home is going to believe this."

Chapter 17

Little Creek, Virginia
January 1

The unassuming working-class bar known simply as Mike's was closed on the busiest drinking night of the year, as it was every New Year's Eve. Closed to the public, that is. Inside, the bar that was best described as "a dive" was standing room only with members of the nation's elite Special Warfare fraternity. Mike was one of the first SEALs, having signed on after President Kennedy authorized the formation of the teams in 1962. Before that, he'd been a frogman with the navy's Underwater Demolition Teams.

Mike's bar was a reflection of his personality; at first glance, it was gruff, surly, and intimidating, but to those who got to know it, like those here tonight, it was an old friend. The beer was cold and the drinks straightforward and unpretentious. The jukebox by the back wall blared out a new song that combined hyperactive guitars with an amped-up drumbeat in a mixture that the music mag-

azines described as "industrial jungle." This selection was
made by one of the younger revelers in attendance.

The front half of the bar held small circular tables
and chairs; four battered pool tables filled the back. At
the end of the bar, Jack Dawson and Max Gates sat with
Nolan Kilkenny.

"Another round?" Dawson asked rhetorically as he
held up his empty beer bottle and three fingers for the
bartender to see.

A moment later, three icy longnecks replaced the
empties.

"Thanks, Mike," Dawson said.

Mike nodded and returned to his post behind the bar,
where he was holding court for some of the younger men
who eagerly listened to his stories from the old days. Mike
Roark was an old navy enlisted man who topped out at five
feet even and was shaped like an anvil. He was thickset,
and the ten years since his retirement from the navy hadn't
softened his physique by much. Mike had never married,
and the men in his bar tonight were his sons and brothers-
in-arms.

"I spoke with Hopwood's widow a couple days ago,
about the time when you guys got back. She got word,
back-channeled through the flag wives' grapevine, that
the score regarding her husband's death has been settled.
She sends her thanks."

"To the admiral," Kilkenny offered.

"Here, here," Gates seconded before draining another inch from the longneck bottle.

"So, Nolan," Dawson asked, "did the Bureau of Personnel get all your paperwork taken care of?"

"Yeah, and at midnight I became something I
haven't been since I was eighteen years old."

"What, a virgin?" Gates asked jokingly, elbowing Kilkenny in the ribs.

"No, scarier than that. A civilian."

Dawson scratched at the paper label on his bottle. "Nolan, do you know what made you a good SEAL? It was your mind. You were able to cut through the bullshit and the chaos of battle and reach your objective. It was your mind that kept you alive. It's also the one thing that will keep you from being a great SEAL."

"What do you mean, Cap'n?" Gates said defensively. "Nolan's a hell of a SEAL."

"Stand down, Master Chief. It's not an insult, just a fact."

Kilkenny spoke up. "Max, what the captain means is, my heart's not it."

"You can only go so far on brainpower in this profession. Max, for guys like us, this is more than our job; it's our way of life." Dawson threw an arm around Kilkenny's shoulder. "Nolan's heart is elsewhere, and it's time for him to get out. For him to stay would be a waste of talent, like using a Porsche to haul trash."

"Well, it's true that this life ain't for everybody, but you made a hell of a go at it while you were here." Gates took a long draw from his bottle. "Shit, heart or no heart, I just hope the next officer I'm paired with is half as good as you."

"Last call!" Mike bellowed out from behind the bar. It was going on three in the morning and was well past the bar's normal closing time.

"Drink up, Nolan, and let's get the hell out of here," Dawson ordered. "I need my beauty rest, and you've got a long trip ahead of you. I just hope my wife hasn't locked me out of the house."

Chapter 18

Jackson Barnett finished glancing over the report prepared for him regarding the death of Michael Cole. He had been away on Christmas holiday in South Carolina when he was notified of the murder. The deputy director of Central Intelligence had briefed him on the situation and Agency people were already in the Dominican Republic investigating with the local authorities. The distillation of those efforts was the ten-page report that now sat on his desk.

Barnett was thinking about what he'd read and watching the snow fall outside his window when his speaker phone buzzed. "Yes, Sally?"

"Everyone has arrived for your ten o'clock meeting."

"I'm on my way."

Barnett gathered his file and entered the conference room adjacent to his office. He immediately recognized two of the men seated at the table: Frank Villano from

the CIA's Information Technology Group and Cal
Mosley, the CIA's in-house investigator. Mosley was
forty-eight and about Barnett's height, but he carried ten
inches more around his waist. The combination of a
balding pate, a pair of unkempt eyebrows, and a bushy
mustache that threatened to cover his entire mouth gave
the CIA investigator the appearance of a walrus.

The third man, Dan Harmon of the FBI, was pouring himself a cup of coffee. Barely thirty, Harmon looked
every bit like the handsome dark-haired quarterback he'd
once been in college. Harmon was a seven-year veteran
of the FBI's Counterintelligence and Surveillance Divi-
sion and came with his director's highest recommendation.

"Mr. Harmon," Barnett said as he extended his hand,
"a pleasure to meet you. I've heard good things about
you."

"Thank you, sir."

Barnett took his place at the head of the table and
pulled the Cole report from his file. "Gentlemen, thank
you for coming today. We're here to discuss the unusual
circumstances surrounding the death of one of our computer specialists, Michael Cole. We've got a lot of ground
to cover, so I'd like to start with you, Cal."

"Thank you, sir. On December fifteenth, Michael
Cole left Washington on an extended Caribbean vacation. On the twenty-fourth, he arrived in Santo Domingo
for a scheduled five-day stay. On the twenty-seventh, a
tourist dive ship reported Cole as missing and presumed
drowned. As yet, the body has not *officially* been found.
On the morning of the twenty-seventh, approximately
three hours before Cole allegedly disappeared from the
dive ship, a deep-sea fishing boat recovered the body of a
scuba diver. The body has been identified as that of

SPYDER WEB   141

Michael Cole. It's definitely a cover-up, but we don't know the motive behind it yet."

"Mr. Harmon," Barnett said, turning to the young FBI agent, "what is the status of the FBI's medical investigation?"

"Since we received the body, our forensics team has gone over every inch of it with a microscope." Harmon inched forward, sitting on the edge of his seat as he explained. "We have a theory about how Cole was murdered. Based upon the analysis of blood gasses and other fluids, they believe that Cole had been diving just prior to his death. Samples of tissue from his bronchia and lungs showed a massive short-term buildup of carbon and other by-products of combustion. Analysis of this material and the remaining air in his scuba tanks revealed the chemical signature of diesel exhaust."

Barnett jotted down a few notes on a legal pad as Harmon spoke. "Was Cole killed by the contaminated air in his tanks?"

"While it's possible for a person to become ill, or even die, from a scuba tank tainted with carbon monoxide, that's not what happened here. Not only were his lungs coated with traces of exhaust but so was his wet suit. The salt water washed off exhaust residue from his exposed skin, but not from inside his wet suit. Without going into detail, the forensics lab found minute traces of diesel exhaust all over the body."

"What is the FBI's theory on how the exhaust got there?" Barnett asked.

"The short version: Cole went scuba diving. After his dive, somebody put him in a sealed space and smoked him. Once he was dead, they dumped him back in the water. Neat and clean. Other than a small bump on the back of his head, there were no unusual marks on the body, but the forensics people believe that the wet suit would mask any sign of restraint. Traces of an adhesive were found around the ankles and wrists of the wet suit—the same kind of adhesive found on duct tape."

"Cal, could the ship that reported Cole missing be involved with the murder?"

"Not likely, sir. The boat that reported Cole's disappearance is a large commercial trimaran. We have solid reports that on the night Cole was killed, this boat was chartered for a party." Mosley doodled a sportfishing boat in the margin of his report; he had been on several during his initial investigation of Cole's death in the Dominican Republic. "That island is a tropical paradise with a lot of boats, and we haven't been able to place Cole on any of them."

Barnett added another note to his list. "Unfortunately, none of what we have, thus far, gives us a clue as to who murdered Cole, or why. That's why I've asked you to be here, Frank. What was Cole working on prior to his vacation?"

Villano cleared his throat. "Just one project, sir. It's classified."

Barnett cocked his head and glared at Villano. "Frank, both Cal and Mr. Harmon are cleared for any material deemed crucial to this investigation. They *have* to know what Cole was working on, since it might have some bearing as to why he was killed."

"Sorry, sir," Villano apologized, "but I'm used to being very quiet about projects like this."

"No explanation necessary, Frank," Mosley reassured him.

Villano relaxed a little and flicked back an errant strand of black hair. "For the past year, Cole acted as the

CIA's technical liaison with the Moy Electronics Corporation on the Spyder project."

"Spyder?" Mosley asked.

"In layman's terms," Barnett instructed, clarifying the request before Villano could respond.

"Basically, it's a programmable device that can capture and transmit information from inside a computer network." Villano could see that his description didn't help Mosley or Harmon. "Say you wanted to know how the North Koreans are doing in their nuclear weapons program. You know the North Koreans are hot for faster computers, so you let one *accidentally* fall into their hands. The trick is, you've planted a Spyder inside that computer. Once they get their stolen machine up and running, your Spyder is going to ferret out every little secret they put into it. As long as the Spyder can find a phone line, you'll get every piece of information that it comes into contact with."

Mosley could only imagine what it would be like to have a direct tap into the immense flow of information passing through the computers at Langley. The volume would be staggering. "Is this project finished?"

"Yes and no. Cole's work is complete, but the Spyder will remain under wraps until Operations works up a scenario for using it." Villano paused as something disrupted his train of thought. "Now that I think of it, Cole was involved with another project just before he went on vacation."

"What was this other project?" Mosley asked.

"It was more of an interesting puzzle than a project. A recent defector came over with an unusual gift: a box of old computer disks alleged to be the property of Andrei Yakushev, a former KGB Directorate chief who ran dozens of deep-cover agents in the West. Cole restored most of these disks and recovered the records of several previously unknown KGB agents. The files were very detailed, everything about the agents' personal and professional history, including photographs."

Mosley directed his next question to Barnett. "Sir, have we been able to judge if the files are real or not?"

"Mr. Harmon's associates are investigating the leads, and several of them look very promising. In some cases, the individuals named as deep-cover agents are living seemingly normal lives as U.S. citizens. It'll take some time to find any hard evidence to substantiate the files."

Harmon turned to Mosley. "Is there anything in Cole's background that makes him vulnerable?"

"Cole had recent marital difficulties that ended in a quiet divorce. The settlement left him with some financial problems. He does fit the profile of someone who might try to market something on the side."

"Michael Cole was a decent man and a top-notch computer scientist," Villano shot back in Cole's defense.

"Decent or not," Barnett interjected before Mosley could respond, "Michael Cole is dead, and he seems to have given someone ample reason to kill him. Robbery has already been ruled out, so there has to be something else in Cole's background that led to his death. Cal, please continue."

"Thank you, sir. If Cole was dealing house secrets, and I had to choose from his last two projects, I'd put my money on those old KGB files."

"Why is that?" Barnett asked.

"Simple—blackmail's an easy buck. Say Cole is restoring these files and he happens to come across someone he knows, maybe somebody here at Langley or up on the Hill. If Cole was the blackmailing type, he'd swipe the files and threaten his target with exposure. With his back to the wall, the target would either buy Cole's silence or kill him."

"Interesting speculation." Barnett leaned forward and rested his arms on his desk. "With that information in hand, I want you to take a look at Cole's records up here before heading back to the Dominican Republic. Maybe there's a name that we can match up with DR Customs and Immigration. There are still several large holes in the days that Cole spent in the Dominican Republic, and I want to know where he went and whom he saw. Also, find out who was on that dive ship. Somebody must have gotten a good look at the impostor, and that's our best lead to finding Cole's killer. I'm sure that most of those people were tourists, so feed us the names of everyone who's left the island and we'll track them down from here. Frank, I want you to go over the computer files that Cole decrypted and look for any irregularities. I realize that's a needle in a haystack, but it's all we have to go on right now."

Mosley spent the next few days wading through the life of the late Michael Cole. He'd spoken with Cole's ex-wife, a nice-enough lady who really didn't have much to say about her former husband other than that she hadn't seen him since their divorce became final. There weren't many friends, either, no one close who could tell you what the man was really like. Cole seemed to be a quiet loner, and that was exactly the type of person who always seemed to end up selling secrets to the other side.

Cole wasn't a wealthy man by any stretch of the imagination, but no one got rich working for the Agency. His bank statements showed a marginal balance in his checking and savings accounts, indicating that he was just getting by. The only financial surprise were his latest credit-card statements. After carrying a balance on his credit cards, he paid them off in full prior to his vacation. That sum increased by several thousand dollars when added to the cash and prepaid traveler's checks that he took with him on his vacation. Michael Cole had found a new source of money, but what had he done to get it?

Chapter 19

Ann Arbor, Michigan
January 8

After purchasing a staff parking sticker for his Mustang, Nolan drove through the university's North Campus to the new home of MARC, the Michigan Applied Research Consortium. He was amazed at how much the North Campus had changed, growing from a small collection of buildings on the university's fringe into a self-sufficient academic complex complete with its own bell tower.

MARC was the realization of an idea that Nolan's father, Sean Kilkenny, had nurtured during his long and successful career in international finance. As a player on the world market, the elder Kilkenny had observed a disturbing trend: Ideas and technologies created in American research labs found their way into foreign products well before reaching domestic manufacturers. During the seventies and eighties, this technology gap widened and

U.S. firms were no longer considered innovators in several key markets.

Sean Kilkenny had studied the situation and discovered that no direct linkage existed between American academia and American industry. Like the Fraunhofer Institutes in Germany, MARC would bridge that gap with a formal structure for joint business-university research projects. If MARC was successful in Ann Arbor, Sean Kilkenny hoped to transplant the idea at other research universities around the country.

The university's contribution to Sean Kilkenny's dream came in the way of a land grant for the MARC facility in the rolling hills of the North Campus. The difficult site contained two prominent ridges and a rocky swale in which a six-inch-deep creek flowed. MARC's architect responded to the terrain by designing a series of interlocking circular modules mounted on tall, slender *pilotis*.

Few of the trees or natural features of the site were disturbed, as most of the building rose well above steep grade, like a forest of interconnected tree houses. The modules formed a solid canopy, penetrated by light wells that allowed sunlight to reach the ground beneath the facility. In contrast to the earth-toned brick buildings owned by the university, the MARC building reflected the high-tech ambitions of its owners. A sleek curved skin of stainless steel and black glass tightly defined the nearly liquid form suspended in the densely wooded site.

Nolan walked in and greeted the receptionist before entering his father's office. The interior of the building was a palette of neutral finishes, whites and grays, accented with bright splashes of color and light. The effect was an image of calm efficiency of purpose.

"Come on in, son," Sean called out as Nolan peered

through the doorway. "I don't think you've seen the place since we finished construction last year."

"No, but it looks great." Nolan gazed out the window into the snow-covered woods. "Nice view, too."

"There's not a bad view in the building. Come on, I want to show you something."

Nolan followed as his father led him through the serpentine corridors; the interior seemed to ripple and flow as much as the exterior.

"Did your boxes arrive from Little Creek?"

"Yeah, Dad. The movers dropped everything off at the house. I'll finish unpacking this weekend."

"It's kind of funny, actually. Of all my children, you were the last one I would have picked to move back home."

"You always did like the others more."

Sean glared at his son. "That's not what I meant and you know it."

"Just kidding, Dad," Nolan said with a laugh. "Anyway, I won't be bivouacking with you for that long."

"Oh," Sean said, surprised at the announcement. "Where will you be going?"

"The barn—up in the loft, actually."

In the rolling hills, fifteen miles west of Ann Arbor, sat the twelve-hundred-acre Kilkenny Farm. From the early 1820s until Martin Kilkenny bought the land from his father-in-law in the 1950s, the property had been known as the Egan Farm. For over 150 years, the farm had produced corn and hay. These days, most of the acreage was leased out to farmers on adjoining parcels; a few acres around the house provided the family with fresh produce and flowers.

Three buildings had been constructed on the site. The newest, the house where Sean and Meghan

Kilkenny had raised their children, had been built in the 1960s. Next in age was the farmhouse, which, due to numerous renovations, could not be dated with any accuracy. The oldest and by far most dramatic was the Egan barn. Its massive stone foundations grew out of a hillside like the trunk of a great oak. From there, a skeleton of hand-hewn timbers rose like the arches of a Gothic cathedral. The barn was forty by one hundred, and nearly fifty feet tall at the ridge. It had been the first building erected on this site and the upper loft became home to the first generation of Egans who settled here after leaving Ireland.

"Is this your grandfather's idea?"

"How did he put it? 'Nolan, you're a grown man now, and living with your father, good as he is, is sure to put a damper on your love life.'"

Sean laughed. "Your brogue's pretty good. You sound just like him."

"My love life aside, I think he was really looking for an excuse to renovate the loft. He's finished off the lower areas for his shop and the garage for your car collection. I think he's just itchy for a new project."

"What the hell. Actually, it sounds like a good idea. You'll still stay with me until the loft's done?"

"I'm Grandpa's grunt labor, so I better be on-site."

After a few more turns, they arrived at the home of the MARC computer lab. Sean Kilkenny ran his magnetically coded ID card through the reader and the electronic lock immediately released the door. Inside, Nolan recognized the cylindrical form of a Cray supercomputer at one end of the lab, beside a bank of computer equipment. In the corner of the lab, a boom box played a Leonard Cohen–Jennifer Warren duet.

"Hey, Grin, are you in here?" Sean Kilkenny called out over the music.

"Yeah, I'm here," a disembodied voice replied to the summons. "Give me a sec. I'll be right up."

Nolan followed the voice to an open panel in the floor. Peering in, he saw a pair of blue jean–clad legs ending in two well-worn leather hiking boots. "I found him, Dad."

"Yeah, yeah, yeah, and I'm coming up for air," Grin called out from below as he slowly wiggled back to the opening.

A hand sprang out of the opening, which Nolan clasped firmly to aid in extracting Grin from the access floor. Rising disheveled from below, he stood about five foot eight and had a pointed goatee and shoulder-length brown hair drawn back in a ponytail. He wore a pair of round wire-rimmed glasses perched low on his nose and sported a wide smile that gave him a slightly mischievous appearance. This image was enhanced by a tattoo of a mythological Pan seated on a crescent moon, scattering pixie dust, that he sported on his left forearm.

Grin wiped a dusty hand on his faded blue jeans before offering it to Nolan. "Thanks for the assist, man. That's a nasty place to work in, unless you're a rat. By the by, I'm Bill Grinelli, but everyone just calls me Grin."

"Nolan Kilkenny. Pleased to meet you."

A smile of recognition appeared on Grin's face. "Are you the guy who wrote that wild imaging program at MIT?"

"Yeah," Nolan replied tentatively. "How'd you find out about it?"

"I gave it to him," Sean answered. "Grin is our resident computer genius."

"Naw." Grin smiled. "I just like to play with the toys.

Anyway, Nolan, that program was a nice piece of work. I was impressed by those nifty algorithms you used—elegant stuff."

Sean Kilkenny smiled proudly. "That's high praise, Nolan. This guy *knows* his way around computers. How's it going in here, Grin?"

Grin stroked his goatee. "Pretty well. The ITC data line is finally in, so Newton's lab should be operational by the end of the week."

"This is where Kelsey's lab is moving to?" Nolan asked as he looked through the glass partition into the adjacent room. The lab was square, with twenty-foot sides and a lay-in tile ceiling ten feet above the floor. The lighting was a mix of fluorescent tubes and recessed incandescent downlights, allowing the amount of light in the room to be varied. The center of the lab was dominated by an isolation table, a four-inch slab of stainless steel mounted on stainless-steel legs capped top and bottom with rubber cushioning pads. The mass of the table and the rubber pads helped to dampen, or isolate, the table from vibrations within the building. Numerous boxes of equipment were stored in the room and portions of the access floor were open.

"Yeah, and that's why I've been busting my tail to get all these data lines in so that you and the fair professor can plug her new toy into my Cray." Grin obviously felt territorial about everything inside the MARC computer lab; he was the overworked master of this domain. "Have you talked with Nolan yet about giving me a hand around here? I know it looks like everything's under control, but I really could use the help."

Sean shook his head, scowling. "No, I haven't had the chance to discuss it with him yet." Turning toward his son, he said, "I was planning to talk to you once you had a feel for your workload, but Grin's let the cat out of the bag."

"Why do I get the feeling I'm being set up?" Nolan asked.

"Nolan, let me give you some background," Sean began. "I hired Grin because he impressed the hell out of me with everything that he knew about computer technology. I respect his opinion on everything that goes on in here. As a personal favor, I asked him to look over your master's thesis and doctoral proposal, so I could understand better what you were doing."

Grin picked up the story. "I loaded your code and ran the programs. Like I said, it's cool stuff. It was my idea to get you working in here. I could really use somebody like you to help out with all the wild research we're going to be getting into. I figured since you and Kelsey will be working out of here anyway, maybe we could cut a deal. If it'll help you decide, you'll get doctoral credit for your efforts."

Nolan threw up his hands. "You two are shameless!"

"Playing you just like a Stradivarius, huh?" Grin asked, a devilish smile flashing through his goatee.

"Full concert and a couple of encores," Nolan replied. "Of course I'd love to work here; I'd be an idiot not to. Don't feel bad about spilling the secret, Grin. If you hadn't brought it up, I would have asked before we left anyway."

"Great. I've already worked up a brief for you on the system specs and our workload." Grin looked visibly relieved now that the lab's labor problem had been solved. "When can you start?"

"Right now. I've got some time before I meet with Kelsey. Why don't you show me around?"

Chapter 20

Chicago, Illinois

Following the holidays, maintenance technicians had performed a routine diagnostic check on robot 43's mechanical and electrical systems and found nothing that would have caused the machine to take itself out of service. The robot was a reliable workhorse in the automated factory and had logged very little downtime over its entire service life. Whatever had laid it low that night had, thus far, not reoccurred.

The shipping program, which coordinated customer orders with finished products, sent the material-transport robots scurrying about the warehouse in search of items ready to ship. The warehouse was always busy following the Christmas–New Year's holiday, filling orders that customers scheduled for delivery after the first of the year.

Robot 43 glided down the aisleways, finally coming to a stop over the flush stainless-steel sensor pads. From above, an articulating mechanical arm reached down and grasped a small package and placed it on 43's back. The arm retracted back to the ceiling and robot 43 rolled back into the main aisle and sped to the loading dock.

Six freight trucks sat at the opened bays, quickly being filled with electronics equipment. Though they still personally delivered and installed their large computer systems, Moy Electronics found it more cost-effective to ship smaller, user-installed components via commercial carrier.

The UPS truck at Bay 5 was nearly full when 43 stopped at the end of its run, waiting for the clerk to collect the package from its back. The shipping clerk scanned the package's bar-coded shipping label with a wand reader. Two seconds later, her handheld computer flashed back a confirmation that this package was to be sent to the Michigan Applied Research Consortium in Ann Arbor, Michigan.

Upon receiving confirmation from the dock, the computer logged the package as shipped and ordered robot 43 to return to the warehouse. The clerk took the package over to the UPS driver, who tagged it with their in-transit tracking bar code and loaded it on the truck. Within the hour, the Spyder would be processed at the UPS distribution center and loaded on the next truck to Ann Arbor.

Chapter 21

Hong Kong, PRC
February 11

It promised to be a good day indeed for Wu Zhusheng. From his office, he enjoyed a commanding view of Hong Kong. Freighters, junks, and tourist ships busily filled the waters with activity, like bees swarming around the great economic hive. Fortunes were made and lost each day in Hong Kong, and today Wu's gamble had paid a great return.

Four generations of the Wu family had lived in the former Crown Colony, and in that time none had been permitted to carry a British passport. That fact hadn't been a problem until the British lease expired. Without a British passport, Wu knew that neither he nor any member of his family could legally emigrate from Hong Kong.

Six years before, Wu had begun a quiet campaign to curry favor with the power brokers in Beijing. Unlike the West, where business relationships form and dissolve very quickly, trading relationships in Asia take years to nurture and are not hastily discarded. By the time Hong Kong reverted to Chinese rule, Wu had turned the focus of his computer-manufacturing corporation eastward.

Wu's company had blossomed during the early days of the computer revolution by manufacturing compatible components for many of the world's most powerful mainframe computer systems. He carved his place out of the market with aggressively priced clones of existing hardware systems. When the age of personal computers dawned, he rushed into the market with systems based on the Intel architecture. Wu subsidiaries, with manufacturing plants dotting the Pacific Rim, built PCs that several computer companies sold under their own name.

Over the last few years, Wu had increased his contacts with the Chinese Communist government, signing lucrative trade agreements and offering technical assistance. He had even secretly sold technologies to China that Western governments had forbidden. The Chinese, for their part, had assured Wu that both Hong Kong and his company would be left untouched when the Crown Colony reverted to Chinese rule.

As his relationship with the Red Chinese improved, they became more open to his assistance in acquiring forbidden hardware and software from the West. High-speed supercomputers were always in demand by Beijing, and Wu had been able to supply them with older Cray and Moy computers without arousing suspicion abroad.

The Red Chinese appreciated his efforts, but both parties knew the machines he acquired were not the same state-of-the-art computers used by the United States government and her allies. The Red Chinese wanted the best, and Wu knew that their lust for technology was the key to securing his future under their rule.

The intercom phone buzzed softly on Wu's ornate hand-carved desk. He lifted his eyes from the report that he was reading and answered.

"Yes, Yuying?"

"Kang Fa is here to see you," his secretary announced respectfully.

"Excellent. Please show him in."

The large black-lacquered door swung open silently as Wu's secretary led the man in. Kang was a frequent visitor, having become Wu's primary contact with the Red Chinese in Hong Kong. The two men met in the center of Wu's office. Both were dressed in finely tailored business suits, crisp white shirts, and silk ties. To an uninformed observer, Kang appeared more like a Hong Kong stockbroker than a Mao-suited Communist from Beijing.

Wu bowed respectfully to his guest. "Kang Fa, how are you today?"

"I am well," Kang replied politely. "And you?"

"I am also in good health. Thank you for coming on such short notice."

Kang sat opposite Wu in one of a pair of ornate chairs. "You expressed some urgency when you called. Is there a problem?"

"There is no problem, only an opportunity. Over the years, I have provided Beijing with significant assistance in acquiring various equipment and technologies."

"And you have been well compensated for your efforts."

Kang usually hid his emotions well, but the tone in

his voice expressed a hint of annoyance. He had developed Wu as a resource, using the man's access to the West to help China with its technological leap forward.

Agents such as Wu are like small children, Kang thought, always in need of constant reassurance that they are appreciated.

"Ah, but your needs were never fully met. That is about to change." Wu sat back comfortably in his chair, enjoying the puzzled look on Kang's face. "Would Beijing be interested in the next generation of supercomputer technology, a type of machine that even the government of the United States does not yet possess?"

Kang sat forward in his chair, his calm demeanor replaced by a heightened level of enthusiasm that he knew would flatter his host. "Of course! How would this be possible?"

"I recently acquired the technical designs for the new Moy Electronics supercomputer. This machine is not yet on the market, and the first units are not scheduled to ship until March. With the proper funding, I should be able to provide a comparable machine in a few months' time."

Kang knew well his government's desire for the latest supercomputers, machines whose sale to China was forbidden by the United States. "I do not think that you will find any difficulty in financing this venture. What will you require?"

"Here is a proposal, as well as the performance characteristics of the new machine." Wu handed over a manila envelope. "The new device incorporates some rather exotic technologies that will make the reverse engineering a little more difficult."

"How difficult?" Kang inquired as he picked up the proposal.

"Nothing insurmountable," We reassured him. "By late spring, Beijing will be in possession of a machine unlike anything they've ever worked with before."

Kang opened the envelope and thumbed through the proposal. He noticed several of the pages in the appendix were internal documents from Moy Electronics, describing the new supercomputer. This was indeed a coup for Wu.

In his previous efforts, Wu had obtained computers and software that already existed—items that he could legally purchase through his U.S. subsidiaries and secretly deliver to China. This information was different; it had been obtained directly from the source.

Wu must have an excellent contact inside Moy Electronics, Kang thought, a source that could be useful on another matter.

Kang placed the proposal into his briefcase and joined Wu for a cup of tea. The conversation turned away from business as he complimented Wu on his efforts. For his part, Wu modestly accepted the praise, hoping that he had ensured his family's security in China's Hong Kong.

Neville Axton watched the digital VU meters register the sound energy passing through them, checking for at least the tenth time that they were recording the conversation taking place inside Wu's office. British Intelligence had leased a small office in an older building across from Wu's suite. From there, they were able to mount an eavesdropping campaign against the Chinese industrialist.

Axton's associate snapped off several photographs using a long telephoto lens. "Terrible shame I can't make out what's on those papers Wu just handed off.

Those blinds half-open like that will just bugger any legibility on the enlargements."

"Don't worry about it," Axton said to the photographer. "I think Wu has already told us what's in those papers."

"Pity we can't just arrest him, sir."

Axton cast a withering glance at the young man. "Under the new Hong Kong rules, we're the ones who should worry about being arrested. Our job here is just to watch and see if we can figure out how Wu is getting the goods on his competitors. Somebody outside Hong Kong is selling restricted technology to Wu, and that's the bloke we're after." Axton smoothed back his thinning gray hair. "A security leak at Moy—the Yanks aren't going to like that one bit. I'll bet you a bottle of single malt that Sir Daniel Long will be on the hot line to the CIA once our report reaches London."

The photographer leaned up from his camera. "Well, sir, it looks like the show's over for today."

Axton observed the scene through a pair of field glasses, watching Kang exchange pleasantries with his smiling host. In his mind, another scene came into view, that of a young woman murdered on a dock not far from here. Lin Mei, her brother, and all the rest had been murdered by the man he was watching. It had taken him over six months to put a name and a face to the person responsible for the deaths of his agents and an innocent girl. Axton just wished this view was through the scope of a sniper's rifle.

"So, you finally crawled out from under your rock, you bastard," he whispered to himself. "I know who you are, Kang Fa, and I haven't forgotten what you did to Lin Mei."

Chapter 22

London
February 18

Wu Zhusheng waited in the London hotel room, just as Kang had ordered. A week had passed since he had made his proposal to Kang, and the response from Beijing was not what he'd expected. Instead of a lucrative contract, Kang had demanded to know how the Moy computer designs had been acquired.

The interrogation had lasted for over two hours, with Kang questioning him repeatedly on the details of his arrangement with the British business consultant Ian Parnell. Once satisfied that he'd wrung out every scrap of information from him, Kang demanded an introduction to Parnell.

At 9:10, Wu answered the knock at his door. It was Kang Fa. Without a word, Kang ushered him down to the hotel lobby and into a waiting car.

* * *

Axton's report from Hong Kong arrived just ahead of Wu's flight, giving the watchers barely enough time to set up their surveillance, not that their first ten hours of watching Wu had produced much. According to the report, Wu's departure from Hong Kong had been sudden and followed a meeting with the Chinese agent Kang Fa. Kang's appearance in the lobby of the Inter-Continental caught the hotel team completely off guard. This was the only glimpse of Kang that the watchers in London would get today. By 9:20, Kang's car had disappeared into the crowded streets of London, driven by someone who knew how to evade observation.

Kang's car pulled up to the contemporary mixed-use high-rise nestled among the old wharf buildings and tower cranes of London's Canary Wharf. Kang and Wu entered and took an elevator to the twelfth floor, where they reached the office bearing the brass nameplate PARNELL ASSOCIATES.

The receptionist greeted Wu and his guest and notified Parnell of their arrival. Both men took a seat in the tastefully decorated reception area, patiently awaiting their audience with the high-priced consultant. After a few minutes, she escorted them into his office.

"Zhusheng, it is good to see you again. I trust that there are no problems with our recent efforts on your behalf?"

Parnell stood as Kang and Wu entered, towering nearly a foot over his visitors. Wu had declined to tell him the purpose of this visit, other than that he wished to make an introduction for an associate in need of Parnell's special consulting services. Wu was a valued client and Parnell was always willing to assist him.

"None," Wu replied with a crisp bow. "Your work

was outstanding, and our reverse-engineering efforts are proceeding satisfactorily."

"I'm pleased to hear that," Parnell replied.

"It is in light of your work on that project that I would like to introduce my associate, Ba Xan." Parnell shook hands with Kang, who had created a new identity for this meeting. "He will be assisting me financially with the development of our products."

After everyone had taken a seat around the black granite conference table, Parnell again turned his attention to Wu. "To what do I owe the pleasure of your visit?"

"Ba Xan is a longtime associate of mine with varied interests throughout Asia. He has a project with very specific requirements that I believe you can assist him with."

Parnell basked in the glow of Wu's compliment before turning to Kang. "I am certain that Zhusheng has represented us fairly before bringing you here to London."

"He has indeed. Wu speaks very highly of you and the services you have provided for his corporation." Kang shifted from pleasantries to business. "Recently, you acquired very detailed technical information from Moy Electronics, information that could only have come from a source within that firm. I also have a need for information that can only be acquired from within Moy Electronics. You are the only person, whom I am aware of, with access to such information."

Parnell thought briefly about Moy Electronics and Michael Cole. "What do you require?"

"Moy Electronics has developed an advanced encryption technology that increases the security of data moving among computers. My firm is involved with projects across the Pacific Rim and we must ensure that our data traffic remains secure."

"Why don't you just buy this technology from Moy?"

"It is not that simple. The technology is restricted by the United States government and may not be sold outside that country. My firm does not qualify as a legal purchaser of that technology. Therefore, we must acquire it through *alternate* means."

If Ba turned out to be as high-paying a client as Wu, Parnell would be happy to do business with him. "It's possible that we may be able to assist you in this matter. How long will you be staying in London?"

"Only a few days."

"That should be long enough for us to make a determination. Zhusheng has informed you that our fees are nonnegotiable and final for services of this nature?"

"Yes, and I am certain that your fees reflect the full value of your services. So that you understand how serious my request is, I am prepared to offer you one million pounds for discreet acquisition of the cipher system's hardware design and programming." Kang pulled a business card bearing his alias from his wallet and wrote the name of his hotel on the back. "This is where I am staying while in London. Contact me when your proposal is ready, and I will draft a check for your retainer."

Parnell's eyes glittered, and then narrowed at the mention of such a fee. He reached over and accepted the card. "I look forward to doing business with you."

Following the meeting, Parnell lay down on his leather couch, kicked his shoes off onto the floor, and phoned Roe in New York with the news. What he didn't expect was her lukewarm response to Ba Xan's request.

"Alex, I don't understand you at all. Ba simply wants a data encryption system that's not for sale at his local shop. What's the problem?"

"Think about it. This guy wants encryption technology—that is, ciphering technology. We already know what kind of ciphering Moy has, and whom they made it for. This isn't business software; this is the kind of thing my *previous employer* might have sent me after."

Roe's reference to the KGB wasn't lost on Parnell. "So you think we should turn Ba down?"

"That's your call, but I don't have a good feeling about this. You don't know a thing about Ba, and I'll bet money that some intelligence service is pulling his strings. I think you should pass. Even if Ba is legitimate, he wants forbidden fruit from the U.S. government." Over the phone, Roe couldn't tell if she was making any headway with Parnell. "If it helps you decide, we don't have a secure way into Moy right now, and it's much too soon for me to do a follow-up interview."

Parnell was silent. Roe knew he was weighing a million-pound fee against his cardinal rule of avoiding governmental espionage. "I think you're right. This one is just too hot for us. Shame about the money, though."

"What good is a million pounds if you're rotting in some prison for espionage and treason? It's just not worth the risk."

That evening, just before Kang planned to go to dinner, a courier delivered a letter from Parnell *regretfully* declining his request for services. A deep anger filled him, and he walked for several hours that evening, working out how he would overcome this obstacle.

Parnell started his morning with an early workout, followed by a light breakfast. Once dressed for the day, he took the stairs from his fifteenth-floor flat to his suite of offices three floors below. This was his idea of a perfect commute to work. As usual, he was the first to arrive, which allowed him some quiet time at the start of the business day. When he unlocked the door to his private office, he found Ba Xan waiting for him.

"What are you doing in here? How did you get in?" Parnell demanded.

"Close the door and sit down." The request was delivered in a tone of voice that thinly disguised a threat. Parnell closed the door and took a seat opposite Kang.

"Can I assume that your presence here indicates that you received my letter?" Parnell asked sarcastically.

"I did indeed, and I must say that I am disappointed. May I inquire what prompted you to make such a rash decision?"

"Quite simply, I don't want this kind of business. Normally, a referral from a long-standing client such as Wu would be received with open arms. Your request enters into an area that I have made a strict practice of avoiding."

"Which area are you referring to?" Kang asked.

"I do not traffic government secrets. I will not work for, or against, any government." Parnell was adamant on this point and spoke with conviction. "That field is filled with professionals with whom I have no desire to compete."

"But my request is against no country," Kang assured him. "The technology I require from Moy Electronics is no different from that which you provided Wu."

"There is a clear difference. The information I acquired for Wu was commercial in nature. What you have requested is for the sole use of the United States government." Parnell was firm and direct. "The information is of no real value to anyone unless they're trying to decrypt that government's internal communications. I don't particularly care whom you are working for, but I will not get involved in this kind of business."

Kang seemed unmoved by Parnell's protests. "I appreciate your position but I would like to make something very clear to you. On several occasions, you have provided illegally obtained technology to Wu Zhusheng for use by his electronics firm. Some of that information was offered to the government of the People's Republic of China in exchange for considerations to Wu and his family. If you do not agree to obtain the technology that I require, the authorities in London will learn the true nature of your business dealings with Wu. I can assure you that Wu Zhusheng has kept meticulous records of his transactions with your firm."

Kang reached inside his pocket and pulled out Parnell's letter and held it for a moment before sliding it across the table. "Your refusal is unacceptable. Since money has failed to persuade, perhaps the future of everything you've built here will."

Parnell rose and began pacing. He thought best on his feet and needed to project a sense of control over the situation.

"You're wielding quite a stick against me. Therefore, I must insist that I be appropriately compensated for my efforts. I'll make an attempt to secure the cipher technology from Moy Electronics. I will *not* seek to obtain it from any other source, especially the American government. For this *attempt*," Parnell continued to define the terms of the deal, "you will pay me five hundred thousand pounds. This is a tremendous risk that I'm being forced to undertake, a risk that deserves its own reward. You will transfer that amount to my offshore accounts now, and another half a million pounds later, if I am able to deliver the ciphers. These are my terms for taking this assignment, and they are *not* negotiable; either accept them or leave. If you insist on pressing me into service for anything less, I will fold up my business and expose your operation to Her Majesty's government in exchange for immunity from prosecution. The Americans will, of course, be informed of your interest in their ciphers by the British government, making any future attempts even more difficult."

Parnell had made a daring play and hoped that his gamble would pay off. Ba Xan would either call Parnell's bluff and agree to these terms or he would decide that dealing with Parnell was too much trouble and walk out. Parnell preferred the latter option and hoped that his uninvited guest would also find it the more palatable of the two.

"I agree to your terms. I will authorize transfer of the first half of your fee this afternoon." Kang then handed Parnell a business card with a phone number written on the back. "Contact me at this number when you are ready to turn over the cipher information. I expect to hear from you soon."

After Ba departed, Parnell sat behind his desk, looking out the window at the Thames and thinking about the predicament he now found himself in. Everything he'd worked for was now at risk; everything depended on how he dealt with this man's request.

"Ian old boy," he said to himself, "I think it's time we began moving to safer ground."

Chapter 23

Ann Arbor, Michigan
March 1

Kilkenny watched as a graphic depiction of his program's performance unfolded on the computer screen before him. Every computer in existence was composed of two essential items, the physical hardware of the machine and the program, or operating system, which told the hardware how to function. Inside the MARC Cray supercomputer, the operating-system program that would one day earn him a doctorate battled to tame a computer simulation of Kelsey Newton's revolutionary optoelectronic processor. The data showed his program to be stable and capable of managing the intricate flow of information within Newton's radical design. Unfortunately, a simulation was all Nolan had to work with.

Kelsey had spent over two years designing her optical processor. Ten months of that time had been spent building this simulation, modeling in the computer how she believed her optical processor would behave. If her design worked, it would show chip manufacturers a way around the dead end that current computer processor designs were approaching. To date, each new generation of computer processor had been faster than the one that preceded it. This feat had been accomplished by increasing the number of circuits on the chip and decreasing the space between each of the circuits. As electronic circuits continued to get closer, the processors got faster and generated more heat, and heat destroys computer chips. If the current rate of circuit miniaturization continued, within two generations the cooling fans in personal computers would have to be replaced with refrigeration systems.

Kelsey's design avoided this problem entirely by replacing electrical circuits (standard electronics) with optical circuits (optoelectronics). Instead of electrons racing about on a flat two-dimensional freeway of transistors, beams of light fired by an array of millions of tiny semiconductor lasers would pulse with information within a three-dimensional space. The same technology allowing a CD player to read information from a disc would provide the framework for computer designs more powerful than any machine in existence.

At this point, though, this entire experiment was still all theory, and it would continue to be theory until the prototype of the optical processor was up and running in the lab next door.

Kelsey, who was on sabbatical from her teaching duties at the university this term, had spent the last six weeks at a chip-fabrication facility, overseeing the creation of her processor. The materials and methods required to build her processor pushed conventional production techniques to their limits. Then again, Kelsey Newton never did anything the easy way.

The phone by Nolan's workstation rang, calling him away from the colorful image cycling on the screen. "This is Nolan Kilkenny."

"Nolan, we've done it!" Kelsey shouted back at him excitedly. "We got the impurities out of the polymer!"

In the simplest terms, the processor inside a computer was nothing more than a vast collection of switches. Each switch was either on or off. The more switches, or circuits, a processor had, the more complex the information it could handle. The core of Kelsey's design rested on the use of a polymer, a chemically complex transparent plastic, to remember what position the processor's switches were in. The polymer was a storage vessel that Kelsey called "a holographic memory." What made this greenish lump of transparent plastic valuable was that its molecular structure reacted when hit by various frequencies, or intensities, of laser light. In Kelsey's design, if two beams of blue laser light intersected at any point within the polymer, that spot would react. This reaction was, in a sense, like turning a switch on. Different combinations of blue and red laser light on that same spot could either read the position of the switch or change the position of the switch. For this holographic memory to work reliably, the material had to be optically clear and free from any contamination or defects that would interfere with the laser beams. In eliminating the impurities in the polymer, Kelsey's processor could now be built.

"Fantastic! How soon before you can build the laser array?"

"It's in production as we speak. They're going to fabricate five test units for us and, at a hundred grand a piece, we better not break any of them. I'll be back the day after tomorrow with the prototypes."

"Everything will be ready and waiting. See you then."

Two days later, Nolan picked up Kelsey from Metro Airport and drove her straight to MARC with the first five Newton processors. Both Nolan's father and Grin stayed late, and they were waiting in Newton's lab when Kelsey and Nolan arrived.

"It's show time," Nolan announced as he placed a well-sealed box on the stainless-steel lab bench.

"You must be very excited, Kelsey," Sean Kilkenny commented enthusiastically.

"To be honest, this is better than winning a Big Ten Championship."

"Personally, I'm trying to keep my enthusiasm in check until we actually get one of these going." Nolan sliced through the heavy plastic with his Swiss Army knife and carefully pried open the box. "I've been running on a model for six weeks, and I'd kind of like to sink my teeth into the real thing."

"I'll just be glad to get you off the Cray," Grin said as he peered over Nolan's shoulder at the five carefully wrapped processors. "You've been hogging way too much time on my prime machine, time that I could have been selling to paying customers."

Nolan let the dig slide. Grin knew full well that all his project-related time was funded by Kelsey's very sizable grant for optoelectronic research. He pulled a black transparent bag from its foam packing and handed it to Newton. "This is your baby. Do the honors."

Nervous with excitement, Kelsey broke the seal of the bag and pulled out the two-inch greenish square that was nearly half an inch thick. The face of the processor seemed to reflect within itself, giving an illusion of infinite depth, and the perimeter was ringed with gold pins that would connect the device to Newton's experiment. The strange beauty of the optical processor silenced everyone as Kelsey held it in the light.

"Here goes nothing," Kelsey said as she carefully pressed the processor into place. It snapped in perfectly, and Sean Kilkenny recorded the auspicious moment with his video camera.

Proudly, Kelsey turned to Nolan with a relieved smile. "Now it's time for you to earn your doctorate."

"Damn, this is exciting, Kelsey!" Nolan turned to face her. "You've created something that could totally change the computer world. Thanks for asking me to be a part of it."

"Nolan, you are the best programmer I know. I need you on this project. Without your timely E-mails, I would never have completed my simulation program."

"I've always thought you two made a good team," Sean declared with fatherly pride. "It didn't matter whether it was a lemonade stand or a homecoming parade float, you two always got the job done and done well. I predict great things from this collaboration."

Kelsey moved next to Nolan and threw her arm around his shoulder. "What do you say, partner, are you ready to kick some butt?"

"Anything you say, Kelsey."

The next morning, Nolan began testing the ITC cable that ran between Kelsey's optoelectronic processor and the Cray computer. The ITC cable differed from normal types of wiring in that it was made of a very expensive superconducting material that, when chilled with liquid nitrogen, lost all electrical resistance and allowed greater amounts of information to flow across it. Given the

known speed of the Cray and the theoretical speed of
Kelsey's processor, the ITC cable was the only means of
handling communications between the two machines.
Nolan's tests involved sending a series of signals across
the cable to verify that it was functioning properly. Once
done, he could begin testing his operating system on the
new processor.

After checking the cable connections, Nolan logged
on to the Cray from his workstation in the lab and sent a
signal to Kelsey's processor. As the low-voltage signal
began to flow, the experimental processor came on-line
and the dormant Spyder became active.

Through the open ITC cable, the Spyder pieced together a picture of the electronic world it was now a part
of. It ignored the data flowing from Newton's experimental processor; the unusual patterns were unlike anything
it had been programmed to encounter. Instead, it focused
on searching through the Cray for a route to the outside
world.

The MARC Cray was one of only five supercomputers located in southeastern Michigan that leased time
to outside researchers. As part of Sean Kilkenny's
arrangement with the University of Michigan, this machine was part of the interuniversity very high speed
Backbone Network Service, or vBNS network, which
linked Michigan to several other research-oriented universities.

At 12:10, a graduate student from Michigan State University's College of Engineering logged on to the supercomputer. The Spyder monitored her progress from
inside the Cray's memory, watching as communication
protocols were confirmed, as passwords were verified,

and, finally, as information began to flow between East Lansing and Ann Arbor.

The successful connection between the Cray and the outside world allowed the Spyder to wander freely inside the interuniversity computer network, where it found exactly what it was looking for: the switchboard for the network's communications lines. Using the password pilfered from the MSU researcher, the Spyder logged on to the university's Internet server and sent an encoded message to Roe's E-mail address. The Spyder then logged off the network.

Chapter 24

Chicago, Illinois
March 5

It had been another long day at the office for Phillip Moy and, unfortunately, the duties were ones that he abhorred. Since receiving Barnett's warning about a security problem, Moy had his internal security staff searching for the leak. It made him feel as though he couldn't trust the very people who worked for him—the people who had made Moy Electronics an industry giant.

He had spent the better part of his afternoon with his director of Security, reviewing their in-house investigation. The findings were essentially inconclusive. None of the employees with access to the new supercomputer's design showed any of the warning signs that would make them receptive to an outside offer. Other than one troubled marriage, all of the potential candidates were in good health and their families were fine and financially untroubled. In short, no hardship motives that could make an employee sell out to a competitor were found.

The director of Security also looked at any outside contractors working with the firm over the time period covering the development of the stolen computer-system design. A cross-reference of network log-ins by outside contractors against the computer's internal logs revealed two curious discrepancies, both of which were attributed to Michael Cole.

The director of Security found part of her answer on the mainframe's internal activity logs. On both occasions when Cole was apparently running a diagnostic program, other areas of the computer system were engaged. All other users on the system at that time could be accounted for, yet the mainframe's internal register of processing time did not agree with the system administrator's logs for both nights. The internal register reset itself each day and was in agreement with the system administrator's logs until Cole accessed the system. After he logged off, the two records of processing time used no longer matched.

Admittedly, the evidence was circumstantial, but it pointed to some unusual activity by the CIA's liaison on their computer system. Unfortunately, Cole's death prevented them from talking with the one person who knew what he was doing on those nights.

Moy thanked the director of Security for her efforts and waited until she had left before conferring with the director of the CIA. He dialed the direct line to Barnett's office, bypassing Langley's main switchboard, and his call was received by Sally Kirsch.

As the call came through, a computer read the incoming caller's phone number and cross-referenced it against Kirsch's phone database. By the second ring, she knew that the caller was Phillip Moy.

"Good evening, Phillip," Kirsch answered, "working a little late, aren't we?"

"I could say the same for you," he replied.

"I'm just tidying up a few things before I leave. Jackson's still in his office, I'll buzz him for you."

The line clicked as Moy's call went on hold for the transfer. A few seconds later, the deep, rich southern voice of Jackson Barnett filled the receiver. "Phillip, what can I do for you tonight?"

"I just received the results of our in-house investigation, and we've turned up some interesting, and disturbing, information. The only questionable activity we've been able to locate has been attributed to an employee of yours who was working with us, Michael Cole."

Barnett glanced over at the Cole file on the corner of his desk. "What do you have on Cole?"

"Not much really, nothing that conclusively points to him as the leak." Moy skimmed the report summary for highlights. "All we actually have is some strange computer activity on his part, coupled with some possible computer-log tampering. It's coincidental, Jackson; there's *no* smoking gun. I just thought that I would pass our suspicions on to you."

Barnett made some notes about Cole for discussion with Cal Mosley. "I appreciate that. Could you send a copy of that report to me?"

"It's already on the way. Have you found out anything more regarding Cole's death?"

"Nothing solid. Cole was obviously involved with something that resulted in his death, but we haven't been able to determine just what that something was. If Cole was selling your secrets, he may have gotten greedy and paid a higher price than he bargained for. Your report may shed some light on the situation. Thank you for your help."

Like Barnett, Moy wanted to know how his secrets

had been stolen and who was responsible. "My pleasure, though I prefer working with you on more pleasant tasks."

"I completely agree. Say hello to Cynthia for me."

"I'll do that," Moy replied.

The line went dead and Barnett cradled the receiver. This new information gave him three possible scenarios for Michael Cole's death. A high-level source working for British Intelligence had verified that the Yakushev files were genuine; was Cole blackmailing one of the moles named inside those files? Phillip Moy believed that Michael Cole was doing something unusual on his computer system; was Cole committing industrial espionage? Cole had spent a year working on the Spyder; could that have something to do with his death? The circumstances of Cole's murder still posed more questions than answers.

As the director of Central Intelligence, Barnett knew that industrial espionage was a national problem that far exceeded the damage caused by spying against the U.S. government. Industrial espionage was part of the global economic war, where industries clashed instead of armies and victory was measured in terms of market share. If Cole was the leak at Moy, the next logical step would be to find the connection between him and the recipient of the information in Hong Kong.

Chapter 25

Ann Arbor, Michigan
March 18

Grin was in early, as always, caring for the computers that he referred to as "the toys." MARC might materially own the hardware that toiled under Grin's care, but no one ever questioned his dominion over the machines.

After an early-morning workout, Kilkenny arrived at MARC looking a little more tired than usual. He dropped his backpack and coat in the chair beside the Cray console and walked over to the computer lab's refrigerator, where he stored a large container of orange juice.

"Getting your vitamin C for the day, I see," Grin commented without even looking up from his monitor.

Kilkenny hoisted his glass in a toast before taking another drink. "Everyone has their vices, and mine could be a lot worse. How are we doing today?"

Grin scanned his systems monitors. "Everything this

side of your processor is working just fine. The Cray is happy as a clam and ready to go to work."

"Let's do it."

The program was to simulate nuclear fusion in a new reactor design. An accurate, real-time model of the problem required the Cray to process thousands of variables simultaneously in order to mimic the theoretical, man-made sun. Physicists from around the world had collaborated on the development of this model, hoping to one day solve the riddle of a sustainable, energy-efficient fusion reaction.

The graphic display on Grin's console showed two new signal lines, each representing a distinct electronic link between the MARC network and the outside world.

"Nolan," Grin called out from his console, "are you hooked into the university's mains?"

"Yeah, I'm downloading from the Engineering Library."

Grin studied the report from the network closely. "I can account for that. Are you doing anything else, like a network query or E-mail?"

"No, just a lengthy download off an old mainframe." The fusion problem's program and data set occupied several gigabytes of memory. "If it wasn't for the new vBNS cabling that campus recently installed, this would take all day."

"That *very high speed* Backbone Network Service has lived up to its name, for which I am truly thankful. I save many hours every week because of it." Grin turned his attention back to the strange signal. "I wonder what that is."

Kilkenny walked over to Grin's station and looked over his partner's shoulder. From this console, Grin could survey the performance of the mainframe computers and information network within MARC. He zoomed in on the window that monitored all of the Cray's network connections; only two lines were in use.

"That's odd," Kilkenny said, "I should be the only user connected to the Cray."

"Got that right. Your physicists aren't scheduled to log on until this afternoon." Grin tried to bring up a listing for the second signal, but each time the program told him it didn't exist. "I wonder what that is."

The signal they were tracking was strong and steady, but neither of them could identify it. Kilkenny was just as puzzled as Grin. "Well, wherever that signal is coming from, it doesn't appear to be affecting the Cray. Do you think it's a hacker cruising in over the network?"

Grin considered Kilkenny's suggestion for a moment. "It could be, but it would have to be a damn good one to bury his tracks like this. I'm lucky to have found this signal at all. It's times like this I wish we'd picked up a Gatekeeper for our net when we got that one for your project."

"A Gatekeeper?" Kilkenny asked.

"Yeah, a Gatekeeper," Grin repeated. "It's a tricked-out neural-net chip that was specifically designed to manage high-speed signal traffic and to secure computer networks. The government began installing 'em on their computer networks a couple months ago. We managed to snag one of these babies because of the high priority the government places on Kelsey's project. It's line-management capabilities were the important thing for us, but the government's using them to keep hackers off their systems."

"Well, I've always believed in safe computing. We wouldn't want to catch a computer virus."

Grin rolled his eyes but politely refrained from further comment. "From here, all I can tell is that we have an open line to campus. I'll call up my buddy down there and see if he can find out who is holding a door open to our Cray."

For the Spyder, the MARC installation was not ideal. Instead of being housed completely within a machine, where it could mask its activities as part of the host computer, it sat as an independent switch gear on a high-speed data-transmission line. It could still perform its covert duties, but it could not conceal itself completely. Per its built-in programming, the Spyder waited until system activity picked up before seeking a connection to the outside world—that way, its signals might be masked by the other users on the network.

The Spyder passed through the Cray to a campus mainframe and, from there, opened a line from the interuniversity network to Central Michigan University. A tap into CMU's Internet server allowed the Spyder to access its E-mail and receive instructions from Parnell and Roe.

Chapter 26

London, England
April 1

"Alex, I closed on those stock options you identified. We're looking at a three-million-dollar profit." Parnell sounded almost giddy over the phone.

"It's always nice to see an investment pay off," Roe agreed as she checked the stock's final quote for the day.

The Spyder's first weeks of service had started with a slow trickle of information about the different computer systems that interacted with the MARC network. As the Spyder became more adept at manipulating its electronic environment, the quality and quantity of its product increased. Under Roe's control, the Spyder unlocked a fortune in corporate secrets that Parnell had turned into a series of very profitable short-term gains.

"On a less pleasant matter, Ian, I can't solve the problem we were discussing earlier; there is simply no way around it."

"Well, then that's the answer, and Ba Xan will have

to accept it. Bring the details to our meeting this afternoon, and we'll spell it out for him."

Kang's flight in from Taiwan was a daylong ordeal that left his back aching. During the last trip, he knew that British Intelligence had observed him collecting Wu from the Inter-Continental. By now, photographs of him had been cross-referenced against customs tapes and the alias of Ba Xan had been rendered useless. If he dared to enter Great Britain under that name again, MI5 would have surveillance forces lined up in the airport to accompany him during his visit.

Today, he traveled under new documents, which identified him as Deng Cho-Nam, a Taiwanese national. With any luck, he would pass through British Customs with little more than the cursory once-over given to ordinary tourists.

"Look sharp, people," Axton ordered. "Kang's flight has arrived at the gate."

Across from the line of arriving visitors at Heathrow's customs area, behind a one-way mirror, Neville Axton watched the travelers as they passed, waiting for Kang Fa to appear. The day before, watchers from Hong Kong had followed Kang to the airport in Taipei, where the Chinese agent boarded a direct flight to London. As luck would have it, Axton was in London for debriefing and reassignment to the Kang Fa surveillance. It was Axton's long-standing interest in Kang Fa that led the decision makers in London to select him. His sole duty now was to track Kang and uncover what he was up to.

Kang entered customs with the second group of passengers, not too close to the front of the line, nor too near to the end. He was a professional, an adversary worthy of Axton's respect and, on occasion, grudging admiration.

As Axton watched, his miniature earpiece crackled with the voices of the watchers who had assembled there to shadow Kang Fa. Several of the tourists milling about the concourse and a janitor wearing a Walkman were part of Axton's team.

The customs agents, having been forewarned by Axton to look harried, passed Kang through with minimum difficulty. He then stopped at a newsstand, scanning the crowd while purchasing a copy of *The Times*, before walking toward Heathrow's Underground station.

"He's headed toward the Tube station," the janitor whispered into his Walkman after Kang was out of earshot.

"This is team five," a woman's voice responded. "We have the target."

Axton listened as his teams began converging on the platform of the station. London had spared no expense in mounting this surveillance operation. They had provided Axton with a small army of professional watchers, allowing him to blanket Heathrow for Kang's arrival.

Sir Daniel Long's directive to Axton had been simple: "Every minute of every day that Kang spends on British soil must be accounted for, including everyone he talks to, everything he sees, and everything that he does."

If Kang Fa so much as broke wind, it would be in Axton's surveillance report.

"This is team five. Target is bracketed by five and six. Next train is pulling up."

Over his headset, Axton heard the train coming to a stop. The squeal and hissing of the brakes was quickly replaced by the commotion of arriving passengers wading through those waiting to board.

"Five and six, maintain visual contact with the target. Don't let him give you the slip and double back," Axton advised his watchers.

"Target has boarded the train. Six is following."

The team five lead ceased reporting momentarily, waiting to see what Kang would do. Kang found an empty seat and sat down.

"Target is staying on the train. Team six is in the car with the target. Team five is taking up position in next car forward. Train is Piccadilly line number four, direct to Hyde Park Corner."

"Confirmed, team five. Keep visual contact with target. You'll hand off contact at Hyde Park Corner."

"Understood," the voice replied while the transmission crackled with noise and interference from the tunnel surrounding the accelerating train.

Axton spoke clearly into his microphone to the other watchers assembled around the concourse. "All right, boys and girls, our target is on his way to Hyde Park. That gives us approximately a half hour to regroup our welcoming party. Let's get moving, shall we?"

Axton exited the airport and met a black Austin cab as it pulled up to the curb. The driver, part of Axton's surveillance team, was one of three cabs queued up, waiting to ferry or follow Kang. "Hyde Park Corner, sir?"

"Yes, Jack, and hurry," Axton replied as he slouched in the rear seat. "We want everything to look natural when our guest arrives."

Axton's team reached Hyde Park Corner five minutes ahead of Kang's train, thanks to the relatively light traffic and a judicious use of portable police sirens. The train stopped at the platform, and its passengers began exiting the cars. True to form, Kang waited until over half the car had emptied before making a move to the exit, hoping to pick up on anyone shadowing him. Team six walked past him without notice, looking very much like a young couple in love. Team five held its position in the next car forward, taking time to gather up their luggage.

The male half of team six, now locked in a passionate kiss on the platform with his partner, motioned for a handoff as Kang exited the car. A new pair of watchers, team three, acquired the target for the next leg of his journey. Team five, also relieved of responsibility for the target, departed, paying no attention to the man who had dominated their thoughts for the last forty minutes. After a change of clothes, and perhaps partners, the watchers would be recycled in a randomly changing pattern of surveillance designed to evade detection by Kang.

Kang emerged from the Underground station onto the bustling streets of downtown London, and luck was on Axton's side today. Kang looked exhausted from his journey as he flagged down a taxi, one driven by a member of the surveillance team. Axton listened closely to the exchange over his radio between the Cockney cab driver and the Chinese spy. Kang gave the address for a building in Canary Wharf, downriver from London proper. Axton ordered the mobile watchers to maintain a loose pursuit of Kang in case he decided to stop along the way. The watchers on foot regrouped and boarded vans that were to shuttle them to Canary Wharf.

Axton smiled with devilish delight as Kang's taxi slipped into the afternoon traffic with five different vehicles taking up position ahead or behind. Today, Kang was traveling with the finest government escort in all of London, with the possible exception of the queen.

*   *   *

The taxi arrived at the building and Kang paid the fare, plus a reasonable tip. Along the way, he had directed the driver to take less direct routes, under the premise of a little sight-seeing. This tactic, which Kang was using to shake loose any unwanted surveillance, allowed Axton to get part of his team in place before the spy arrived.

Axton hoped that this modern high-rise was Kang's true destination; otherwise, his forces would be spread perilously thin. He found himself holding his breath, waiting to see if Kang would hail another cab or proceed on foot.

"Twelfth floor—the lift has stopped on the twelfth floor," the watcher in the lobby announced.

"I read you," the second watcher replied. "I'll be there in a second."

"Don't jump out too quickly," Axton said cautiously. "We don't want to startle him this early in the game."

The watcher slowly exited the stairwell, which was around the corner from the elevator lobby, next to the lavatories. Kang rounded the corner just as the watcher feigned an exit from the men's room. Kang passed by, taking little notice of the young man hunched over the water fountain. Using his peripheral vision, the watcher, who was truly thirsty after bounding up twelve flights of stairs, observed Kang enter a suite at the end of the hall.

"He's gone in," the watcher whispered into his microphone. "The doorplate reads PARNELL ASSOCIATES."

"Good work," Axton responded. "Hold position on twelve; your relief is on the way up."

Axton then turned to the radioman in the van. "Get the Home Office on the line. I want to find out who Parnell is and what kind of shop he's running."

*   *   *

"Good day," Kang greeted Parnell's assistant as he entered the suite. "My name is Ba Xan. I have an appointment with Ian Parnell."

"Yes," Paulette replied coolly. "I'll let him know you've arrived. Please have a seat."

Kang seated himself on the black leather sofa, but his eyes never left Parnell's executive secretary. The hairs on the back of her neck stood on end, as she was self-consciously aware of his unwanted attention.

"You may go right in, sir."

Kang nodded and walked into Parnell's office. Inside, both Parnell and Roe were waiting at the conference table. Kang sat in a chair opposite them. "I received your message. What have you discovered?"

"The information that you are seeking is available through the Moy Electronics computer network, but only under a very restricted set of circumstances. It is impossible for our source to obtain this information without alerting Moy and the American government." Parnell slid a synopsis of the Spyder's latest report across the table. "This outlines the structure of the Moy computer network and identifies the barriers to the files you want. Moy Electronics maintains complete documentation on every project. The high-security projects that they develop for the U.S. government are kept on a separate computer and only Phillip Moy himself can authorize a tie-in for file transfers. We cannot imitate that authorization."

Kang scanned the report, stopping when he reached the section describing the computer that held the cipher files. The only time that this computer was brought online with the Moy network was for transmission of software upgrades to the U.S. government. "Can you access this computer during one of these transfers?"

"In theory, yes," Roe answered, "but only if we knew precisely when such a transfer would take place. We would need to access the computer just as the U.S. government does, with all the correct passwords and protocol, in order to download any information. The problem is, we don't know when the next transfer will occur or what authorization codes they'll use."

"We have pushed our source inside Moy Electronics as far as we dare," Parnell concluded. "The information you've requested is simply beyond our grasp."

Kang sat quietly, his face displaying nothing other than deep contemplation of the information just presented. He said nothing for what seemed an eternity to Parnell and Roe—Westerners with no sense of patience. Roe held her composure well, but Parnell's anxiety telegraphed from his face and hands.

"Your work is not yet complete."

Parnell's manner turned to ice. "We have a deal—"

"Yes, we do," Kang agreed, interrupting Parnell in midsentence. "And the conditions for terminating that agreement have not been met. You have told me nothing about Moy's security that I didn't already know. If you knew when Moy's next transfer would occur and you were provided with the access codes, could you then obtain what I want?"

Parnell deferred to Roe for the answer.

"Maybe. If we had that information ahead of time, we might be able to simulate a legitimate government access into Moy's computer."

Kang smiled. "Good. Then once you have acquired the ciphers, the final payment will be transferred into your account."

"We still have no way of knowing when the next

transfer will take place," Parnell objected, "or what the access codes will be."

"Those details aren't your concern anymore. Just make sure that you're ready when the time comes."

Axton pressed his luck once more, placing two taxis with fresh drivers around the corner from the high-rise. New watchers inside the building informed him when Kang left Parnell's office and boarded the lift. Kang made no other stops in the building. He hailed a taxi as he walked out to the curb. One of Axton's cars picked up the fare. The driver almost choked when Kang directed him to a hotel; it was a serious statement about the man's confidence that he wasn't being followed.

Kang remained at his hotel for the rest of the day, ordering room service for an evening meal before retiring. He rose early the next morning, checked out of the hotel, and hired a taxi to Heathrow Airport, where he caught a flight to New York.

Within an hour of Kang's departure, Axton found himself summoned before Sir Daniel Long, the head of British Intelligence.

"Good afternoon, Axton. Do sit down." Long ignored Axton's disheveled appearance. Having once been a field agent, he understood completely. "I believe some congratulations are in order. Bravo to you and your team on the Kang surveillance."

Axton acknowledged Long's praise with a curt nod. "We know where he went, sir, but we haven't discovered what he was up to. Why did he visit this consultant, Parnell? Skimming off a few pounds from his operational fund, perhaps? No, he's running some kind of operation, but I'll be damned if I can figure out what it is."

"Actually, your surveillance has shed some light on one aspect of this mystery." Long opened a file folder on his desk and pulled out a report that Axton had filed from Hong Kong. "A few months back, you observed a meeting between Kang and a Hong Kong national."

"Wu Zhusheng," Axton recalled.

"Precisely. The transcripts from your report indicated that Wu had acquired some new technology from the Moy Electronics Corporation. I think that you've uncovered Wu's source."

"Parnell is selling industrial secrets?"

Long nodded and closed the file. "We've got no proof of that charge, but we have heard Parnell's name before. It seems he's a rather capable fellow who provides his clients with a wide range of services."

"Some of which might not be legal, I presume."

"That implication has been made," Long replied. "This is the first real evidence that Parnell might be stealing fire."

Axton, too, knew the ancient Greek legend of Prometheus, the titan who stole fire from the gods and illuminated the world. He paid the ultimate price for that technology transfer.

"Where do we go from here, sir?"

"We expand your surveillance operation to include the home and offices of Ian Parnell. He's been positively linked with a known agent of a foreign country, which is enough to justify the warrants. Get me a list of what you'll need to do the job."

After his meeting with Axton ended, Long placed a call to Jackson Barnett, his counterpart at the CIA.

"Hello, Daniel," Barnett said with a slow drawl, "to what do I owe the pleasure of your call this morning?"

"We've had an interesting development in the technology-transfer case. I believe that we've discovered who provided Moy's designs to the gentleman in Hong Kong. The seller is a business consultant here in London."

"Very interesting."

"There's more. The Chinese agent working with Moy's competitor, a fellow by the name of Kang Fa, just spent the day in London and he met with this consultant. We don't know the substance of their conversation, but I find the connection unsavory. Kang is currently en route to your side of the pond. Your staff should have his flight and passport information shortly."

"If I recall your dossier on Kang, he's a man of considerable talent."

"He's no choirboy. If he's involved, then the Chinese are after something big, and it appears that they're using industrial spies to do the job."

"I would appreciate your sending me what you can on this consultant. I'd like to pass it on to the FBI for their part of the investigation. Maybe they can find the link between Chicago and London and tie these pirates up. I'll notify the FBI about Kang's arrival so they can roll out the welcome mat. Thanks for the help, Daniel."

Long scribbled a note of the request for his secretary. "All part of our agreement. The report on Parnell will be in your hands by the end of the day."

Chapter 27

Spring's arrival was not only apparent in the weather, but in the attitude of Ann Arbor's inhabitants. The student body let out a collective howl and took to the outdoors for recreation and a change of study venue from the libraries and dorm rooms they'd occupied for the last seven months. The academic year was nearing an end and a sense of new beginnings filled the air.

Nolan Kilkenny guided his freshly washed and waxed 1968 Mustang into the parking lot of the MARC building. The Acapulco blue pony car glistened with a finish that seemed almost liquid. It still had the magic for turning heads on the street and garnering whistles from passersby. Kilkenny parked next to the Grin's faded yellow VW microbus.

"Morning," Grin called out from the VW.

Kilkenny switched off the Mustang's engine and set

the parking brake. "Having a little morning tailgate, I see."

Grin sat in the open door of his van with his legs dangling out. Kilkenny could see a thin layer of mud covering his hiking boots. With one hand, Grin held out a well-worn canvas tote bag. "Nothing but Mother Nature's finest. Have a taste."

Grin's harvest contained a variety of nuts, wildflowers, and berries, some of which Kilkenny had a difficult time identifying. "Did you get all this tromping around in the Arb this morning?"

"Naw, it's still early in the season, though I did find a few goodies out there. Most of this comes from my favorite bulk munchy store. My little nature walks are pretty much for the soul until mid-May."

Kilkenny dug into the bag and pulled out a handful of dried fruit and nuts. "I'm looking forward to harvesting that strawberry patch near my grandfather's barn."

"Just remember me when that crop comes in."

"Will do," Kilkenny agreed as he bit into a dried apricot.

Grin and Kilkenny ate quietly, enjoying the early-morning calm before the working world forced them indoors. Kilkenny pulled out a thermos of juice from his workout bag, splitting the last two cups with his friend.

As the clock approached eight, the MARC parking lot began to fill with other employees, including Nolan's father. The elder Kilkenny parked his red Ford Explorer nearby and walked over. "Morning, boys, I see you're enjoying the sun on this glorious day."

"You bet. Care for some organic munchies?"

Sean peered into Grin's bag and, finding nothing that he could identify as food, returned it. "No thanks. When you have your heart set on a chocolate cream-filled doughnut, granola just won't do. Actually, to change the subject, have you had much luck tracking those strange signals on the network?"

Nolan shook his head. "Not much, but Grin and I have a few theories about what's causing it."

Grin picked up on Nolan's lead. "It's really a strange phenomenon. For the past few weeks, we've been picking up this intermittent signal traffic. It's like someone's on the line, running *inside* our own transmissions. It might just be some signal rebounding that we're getting over Nolan's high-speed data line, but I haven't been able to nail it down yet."

Nolan drained the last of his juice and snapped the cup back on the thermos bottle. "Fortunately, when Kelsey designed this experiment, she anticipated that we might want to monitor performance at various points in the process for troubleshooting and fine-tuning. Grin and I plan to check the signal traffic at several different points to see if we can isolate the source of the anomaly."

"Sounds like a reasonable plan," Sean agreed. "Are these signals dangerous to any of the other equipment?"

Grin shook his head. "No, not that I can see. The signals are low-voltage ones, like the rest of our communications traffic, so we're not dealing with a power spike that could do some real damage. Nolan's processor seems to be fine, same with the Cray. I'd write something like this off as an open data connection to the network, but there aren't any that I can find, and campus sure hasn't billed us for any time. It's just one of those strange puzzles that drives you to solve them just for the sake of solving them."

"Well, you boys can keep chasing these anomalies as long as it doesn't interfere with our project schedules."

"It shouldn't, Dad. Grin and I are going to spend a

couple hours this morning jury-rigging a laptop to act as
signal filter on our network lines. When it pops up again,
we should be able to isolate it."

"Sounds like a good plan, just don't let it turn into a
sacred quest. I'm speaking from experience in dealing
with obsessive problems," Sean Kilkenny admitted with
an embarrassed smile. "I recall once that Nolan and I
nearly tore down my Jaguar because of this annoying rat-
tle. It turns out that I took the car out only on sunny days,
when I'd wear sunglasses and set my regular ones on the
dashboard. My own glasses were rattling right there in
front of me, in plain view. I couldn't believe it."

Kilkenny and Grin spent the first few hours of the morning jury-rigging a laptop computer to act as a signal filter
for monitoring the network lines inside the MARC lab.
When they finished, a bundle of thin wires fed out from
a port in the rear of the laptop to the network switchboard at the base of the Cray. The duo then returned to
their regular duties, waiting to see if the anomaly resurfaced.

"Nolan, you got a second?"

Kilkenny saved the file he was working on and
turned toward Grin's station. "Yeah, what's up?"

Grin tapped on the network diagnostics monitor.
"Our anomaly has returned, and I'm up to my eyeballs
with something over here. Can you try to pinpoint it?"

"Sure thing, boss."

Kilkenny tapped the space bar on the laptop and
brought the portable computer out of its energy-saving
hibernation. The laptop passively scanned each of the
network lines, much like picking up a second phone to
listen in on a conversation. The first signal Kilkenny

locked into was the internal communications line between the Cray and the optical processor. A window
popped up in one corner of the flat active-matrix color
screen displaying the same information currently shown
on the Cray's monitor.

"Well, that one's my project."

Kilkenny instructed the monitoring program to filter
out the first signal and to continue scanning the remaining lines. The next few lines were either unused or carrying network updates, which appeared as intermittent
signal traffic, but not the type of anomalies that they
were experiencing. Kilkenny moved on to the next line,
which displayed a system log-in screen for an underground Ann Arbor Web server.

Kilkenny just shook his head in disbelief. "Guess
what, Grin? It looks like some hotshot is using the university's network to surf the Net."

"You're kidding me. I wonder how that got bounced
all the way up here."

"Well, I'm going to isolate the line so we can trace it
back." Kilkenny filtered the line from the network bundle.

"Hey, Nolan. That squirrelly signal we're chasing
just disappeared. You want to check that line again?"

Kilkenny switched the line filter off and on several
times, and each time the mysterious signal reappeared
and then disappeared.

"Well, it looks like this is our anomaly," Kilkenny
agreed. "I thought for sure we'd find something echoing
across the line from the optical processor. Still, it seems
strange that campus would route a signal up here; we are
a little out of the way. In any event, Kelsey will be happy
that her processor isn't causing the problem."

Grin walked over and sat beside Kilkenny. "I'll be damned. How'd he tickle an outside line from campus?"

"I take it that that's not supposed to happen very easily?"

"Hell no, or we'd have every student with a modem logging into the network and making long-distance calls for free." Grin leaned back in his chair and grabbed the phone off the lab bench. "Outside lines are accessible only to the system administrator. All other communications are regulated within the network. If this isn't Carl, the people down on campus are going to be very annoyed."

Grin dialed the number of his counterpart at the university's Main Computing Center, Carl Moynes. The phone rang several times before Moynes's deep voice filled the receiver. "Computing Center."

"Yo, Carl. Grin here up at MARC. We've got a little problem you might be able to help us out with. You got a few minutes?"

"I'll make the time," Moynes agreed cheerfully. "What can I do for you, old buddy?"

Grin punched a button and switched the phone into speaker mode. "Carl, I'm putting you on the speaker so my compadre Nolan Kilkenny can listen in."

"Fine by me," Moynes replied.

Grin smiled; Carl Moynes was a good man. "We've been tracking a peculiar signal on the network lines for the past few weeks, a real squirrel. We originally thought it was something rebounding from that new processor we're testing."

"I've been reading about that, a very radical piece of hardware. How's that going anyway?"

"The processor?" The question caught Grin off guard. "It's fine, but back to our problem. We wired up a signal skimmer so we could take a look at what's passing over the lines, and we've found something that might interest you."

"Do tell, old friend, do tell."

Grin interlocked his fingers and cracked his knuckles. "Carl, are you or any of your fellow computer gurus currently logged into the Warlocks of Doom?"

"I'm surprised that you would make such an accusation." Moynes's denial was deeply sarcastic. "You don't think that our fine upstanding group of computer scientists would utilize the university's property for their own personal amusement, do you?"

"Never in a million years," Grin responded flippantly, "but seriously, we're sitting here watching someone log into the Warlock server over one of your outside lines."

"Give me a second and I'll bring up the system status on that end of the network."

As Grin waited for Moynes to check his system, Kilkenny leaned over and tapped him on the shoulder. "What's up?"

Kilkenny angled the laptop toward Grin. "See for yourself."

The hacker had broken into the Warlock server and was using it to access another phone line. They couldn't hear the modem dialing tones, but the screen told them that the intruder was passing to yet another computer system.

The Spyder had successfully navigated through the U of M's network hardware, where it opened an outside phone. A week earlier, it had observed a hacker intrusion, via the Warlock server, into the university's network. That experience taught it a new means of reaching the outside world. The hacker's intrusion was successfully blocked by an observant system administrator. Unlike the hacker's attempt, each of the outside connections made by the Spyder was virtually undetectable. The Spyder also left no trace of its presence on the network's system logs.

Late the previous night, the Spyder had uploaded its latest acquisitions to Roe's E-mail address and downloaded its new instructions. Its current target was the Chrysler Corporation. An automotive engineer, currently pursuing an MBA at the university, had unknowingly taught the Spyder how to access Chrysler's computer network when she logged on from her office at the Auburn Hills Tech Center. Recent news indicated that Chrysler was poised for a major push into alternative powered vehicles, and Parnell wanted inside information on the automaker's financial structure, suppliers, and engineering data on their electric-vehicle systems.

Kilkenny watched as the hacker's phone call was received by the next computer. The laptop's screen cleared and the main log-in screen for the number-three automaker appeared in vivid color.

"This guy's busting into Chrysler," Kilkenny announced. "Carl, can you cut him off?"

"I hear you," Moynes's voice answered through the phone's speaker. "I'm looking into it from our end, but I'm not showing anything active. Which line is he running through from your Cray?"

"I'll check." Grin ran back to the Cray's operator station and began furiously issuing commands to the supercomputer. In a few seconds, the machine responded with a full report on current system activities. Everything appeared normal, with no network lines currently accessed.

Grin ran back to Kelsey's lab. "Carl, I know somebody's out there, but the Cray's telling me that we don't have any user lines open between your system and mine."

"This is very weird." Moynes sounded puzzled.

Kilkenny was checking all the diagnostic points from the laptop when he found something. "Hey, guys, the hacker is physically on line five leading out of the Cray. Carl, how's that match up with your switchboard?"

"Give me a second and I'll check."

Grin and Kilkenny could hear Moynes flipping through pages of a systems manual, looking for the physical addresses of his network connections. Normally, he would be able to track any network connection through his system-administration programs, but this intruder forced him to doubt what his computer was telling him.

"I got it," Moynes's voice boomed over the speaker. "Let's say we bounce this guy off the system."

"Easy, Carl," Kilkenny replied. "We can't just blast this guy. We've got to be a little more subtle."

"Fuck subtle," Moynes growled back. "I say we kick his sorry ass off my computer."

Moynes was justifiably angry, but Grin knew that Kilkenny was right.

"Hold on, Carl. I think I see what Nolan's getting at. If we blast him, he'll know he's been tagged."

"And what's wrong with that?"

"Nothing, unless you want to catch the bastard," Grin explained. "This guy's not one of our harmless student types, exploring the system. He's a pro who's just entered the Chrysler Engineering Projects Library."

"If you don't want me to pull the plug, what do you suggest?" Moynes replied bitterly, taking his system's violation personally.

"Cut him loose," Kilkenny explained, "but make it

look like a maintenance shutdown. Issue a warning that the network's integrity has degraded or something."

Grin nodded. "Yeah, make it look like there's a system failure that requires a full shutdown. That way, our hacker won't know he's been spotted."

"I can do that," Moynes agreed, "but taking down the whole network will tick off a lot of people."

"Carl"—Grin's voice was calm and steady—"it's your call, but consider this: Whoever this hacker is, he's good enough to punch through our network without either of us ever seeing him. Hell, it was dumb luck that we stumbled onto him at all. We have an obligation to try to catch this bastard, but we can't do that unless we're ready the next time he passes through. If we spook him now, he may never come back."

Moynes relented. "That'd be just fine with me, but I see your point. I'll start crashing the network. The boss is going to have a stroke when she hears about this."

The intruder rapidly passed through the file indices of Chrysler's engineering mainframe. A moment later, a message from Carl appeared across the bottom of the screen, warning of an imminent network shutdown.

"Message received, Carl," Kilkenny said. "Our hacker is shutting down."

The Chrysler screen vanished after the intruder logged off. A few more quick keystrokes and he was out of the Warlock server. Grin's jaw dropped when the screen filled with the live image of Moynes's system-administration screen.

"Our unwelcome friend is in your sys-ad program. It looks like he's playing around with the logs."

They could hear Moynes punching keys to bring up the information on his computer. "I don't see a thing from my side. You sure?"

"It's right here in front of me," Grin assured his colleague. "He's going after the network accounting logs."

"Shit! What the hell is he doing in my computer?" Moynes was furious as he scrambled through his network files looking for the hacker. "He's locked me out of the logs. I am not a happy camper!"

The laptop screen went blank and Grin slumped back in his chair, disappointed. "He's off the network."

"I don't know about you guys, but I'm pissed! In five seconds, I'm going to have an office full of angry users, topped off by a short-fused boss who's going to wonder why I brought the whole network down."

Grin understood his friend's anger—the situation was a lot like finding a burglar in one's home. "Carl, it had to be done. We've got a dangerous player out there who's running fast and loose through our network. That's bad business for all of us, and I'm sure your boss will understand. We'll back you up all the way."

"I'd hope so, since I have no proof that any of this happened." Moynes sounded a little calmer, but not much.

"Actually, you do have proof. The laptop we're using recorded most of this hack, including your heroic system shutdown."

"Grin, I feel like I just threw myself on a grenade." Moynes's anger seemed to be dissipating, but his mood was still foul. "Speaking of grenades, my boss is coming down the corridor, and she doesn't look happy. Gotta go, guys."

"Call if you need us, Carl."

"Thanks, Grin."

Moynes's line went dead and Grin switched the humming speaker off. "Well, that was fun. What do we do for an encore?"

Kilkenny pulled the optical-disk cartridge from the laptop's external drive. "I think it's time we reported this incident. It may not seem like much, but we've just witnessed a crime."

Later that afternoon, Nolan and Grin sat in Sean Kilkenny's office with two agents from the FBI's Detroit office. The agents took their statements and toured the computer lab. Despite the fact that computer crime was a serious offense, it didn't always get the same treatment from the law-enforcement community as bank robbery and drug trafficking. The FBI agents were polite but noncommittal until Nolan replayed the intruder's penetration of Chrysler's computer network.

"Do you have any questions?" Nolan asked as the computer screen went blank.

"Can we have a copy of that disk?" Special Agent Ullrich replied. "I'm sure our computer lab techs would love to watch this guy in action."

"Already done, Agent Ullrich," Grin said as he handed over a duplicate diskette.

Ullrich slipped the diskette into her briefcase with her notes. "Thank you."

"I appreciate your coming out here," Sean told the agents, "but what should we do about this situation?"

"There's not much that can be done, sir," Ullrich replied. Her answer wasn't a dismissal of their complaint, simply a matter of fact. "Our only hope is to catch this individual in the act. Special Agent Harbke and I are experienced in dealing with these types of criminals, and, believe me, it takes time to build a case against them."

"Most of our successful prosecutions are the result of turning a hacker against his own ring," added Harbke. "Unless there is some physical evidence of the crime, we're stuck. Your disk is a start, but it doesn't mean a thing until we can tie it to somebody. I think you handled this situation correctly. This hacker is using the university's network to cover his tracks. Since he doesn't know you spotted him, odds are he'll be back. What I'm going to suggest to my superiors is that we obtain the necessary warrants to trace your network lines during one of these intrusions."

"I don't think that you'll have any problem with MARC or the university with regard to the line taps, Agent Harbke," Sean assured her.

"We usually don't in situations like this." Harbke smiled. She knew from experience that high-profile victims of this type of crime were normally very helpful. "In the meantime, please keep monitoring the network for any further intrusions. The more information we have about this hacker's methods, the better chance we have of catching him. Thank you for your time today, gentlemen. I'll contact you as soon as we get the warrants."

After escorting the FBI agents out, Sean Kilkenny returned to the lab with Grin and his son. "When I got up this morning, I had no idea that I would spend the better part of my afternoon with the FBI. I still can't believe that somebody just waltzed through our network so easily. If this hacker is behind the anomalous signal you've been chasing for the past month, I don't even want to think about what he's gotten away with already."

"At least we're onto him, Dad."

"Actually, we'd still be in the dark if you and Kelsey weren't studying every little burp that processor of hers makes," Grin admitted frankly. "If it was just little old me in here, I very much doubt I would have spotted this guy. Our hacker's got a real nice touch."

"Grin's right—we were lucky to have discovered this guy at all. Whoever it is doesn't know that we're onto him yet, and that's the only advantage we have right now."

Sean moved to the next item on his mental list of concerns. "Is Kelsey's processor secure from tampering by this hacker?"

Nolan thought about his father's question for a minute, going over in his head the optical processor's linkages to the MARC network. "The processor itself is well insulated from the network, so this guy can't get a direct feed into it, but all of our project data is stored on the mainframe. Good thing Grin is religious about backing up the system. I don't know what I fear more, though—having this guy steal our work or vandalizing it."

"So much for a victimless crime." Sean sighed. "Boys, I want you to cooperate with the FBI fully on this matter. Stopping this hacker is now your number-one priority. We are an information-based concern, so we can't afford to have some criminal punching holes in our security. Do what it takes to nail this person."

Chapter 28

Chicago, Illinois
April 15

Traffic was never clear and easy in downtown Chicago, but Moy drove as quickly as Lake Shore Drive allowed and pulled into the parking garage beneath the twin black towers overlooking Lake Michigan.

Following a disturbing call from his wife, Phillip Moy had canceled the rest of his afternoon appointments and left for the day. Cynthia Moy had sounded frantic over the phone, pleading with him to come home immediately. Although she couldn't explain what had happened, Moy knew his wife wasn't one to raise an alarm unnecessarily.

As he entered his condominium, Moy was met by his wife, who wore an expression of deep concern. She was normally a pleasant, happy soul possessed of great inner strength. When she looked this way, he knew to expect bad news. Moy embraced his wife, sensing her concern. "Cynthia, what's wrong?"

Her voice was a quiet, dull whisper. "Your father has come to visit, and he has brought a guest."

Moy's wife had always gotten along well with her father-in-law. The aging physicist often joked that if they ever divorced, he would keep Cynthia. Inside the living room, which faced Lake Michigan, was Moy's father and a man he didn't recognize. The elder Moy sat on the couch, deep in thought, as the visitor turned from the window to face him.

"Good afternoon. I'm Phillip Moy."

Kang Fa smiled and introduced himself under his current alias. "My name is Deng Cho-Nam. I have come from Hong Kong with news of your uncle, Moy Huian."

The mention of his uncle's name stunned Moy momentarily as memories of a man he hadn't seen since he was a small boy flashed across his mind. He now understood his wife's distress. Moy Huian had served over four decades in a Chinese reeducation camp, a surrogate prisoner for Phillip Moy's father. The hairs on the back of Moy's neck bristled.

"What is the purpose of your visit, Mr. Deng?" Moy asked with cool suspicion.

Kang unbuttoned his double-breasted blazer and sat in a black leather chair. Moy sat opposite him on the couch, next to his father, who looked unusually old tonight.

"I am here for *humanitarian* purposes." Kang spoke like a diplomat. "I've brought word from Guangdong Province regarding Moy Huian. The Chinese government is preparing to release certain political prisoners to appease the West. I have well-placed contacts in Beijing that can ensure Moy Huian's name is on the list of those to be released."

"Here is a letter from my brother," his father said,

offering several pages of Chinese characters with a black-and-white photograph; it was the first direct communication they'd received from Huian in over forty years.

Moy scanned the letter, which told briefly of the years following his father's escape to Hong Kong. Moy Huian had stayed behind with his parents, who were too old and sick to make the journey to the West with their eldest son. Two months after his father's defection, Moy's grandparents had died and Moy Huian was imprisoned. For the past forty years, Moy's father had carried the guilt of abandoning his family and leaving his brother to face the punishment for his defection.

The letter showed no sign of censorship, and the characters told of Huian's longing to see his brother again. The photograph showed a man who had aged well beyond his years while imprisoned.

Moy was still skeptical. He had heard of con men selling promises to the families of those trapped in China, men who would disappear once the required bribes and fees had been paid by the family.

"Father, are you certain that this letter is from Huian?"

"This *is* my brother." Moy's father pointed to the photograph. "The handwriting in the letter is his, and he refers to things that only he and I would know."

Moy accepted his father's confirmation and turned back to Kang. "What is your interest in this matter?"

Kang looked directly into Moy's eyes and spoke sincerely. "I enjoy helping people."

Moy's eyes narrowed slightly as he took his measure of the man. "Thank you for bringing my father some measure of happiness in his old age. I do hope that it is not a *false* happiness."

Kang picked up on the wariness in Moy's voice, a distrust that was understandable. "It is no *false hope*," he replied confidently. "My contacts inside the PRC can get your uncle out, but the price will be very high."

"Let us talk in private." Moy motioned toward a pair of French doors off the living room. "I wouldn't want my father to think that I would haggle over his brother's freedom."

Moy's study was furnished in an eclectic mixture of traditional Oriental furnishings and artwork combined with pieces from the Arts and Crafts movement. Strangely enough, the chairs by Charles Rennie Mackintosh worked quite well with the sixth-century urn. Moy's wife brought in tea before returning to the living room.

Both men studied each other for a few moments and Moy found Deng's expression unreadable. The man appeared totally unconcerned about the deal he was brokering.

"You come here tonight in a position of strength. If you truly have the ability to extract my uncle from the PRC, please tell me how this feat will be accomplished and what it will cost me."

Kang took a long sip from his teacup, swirling the brew lightly in his mouth before quietly swallowing. He wiped his mouth clean with his napkin in an effort calculated to intensify Moy's anxiety. "My fee is nominal, a mere one hundred thousand dollars for arranging this exchange. The people who control your uncle's fate require something more."

"Bribes for the officials, I presume," Moy replied.

"In most cases, that would be true. But not in this case." Kang set his teacup down on the side table and leaned forward in his chair, resting his elbows on his

knees and drawing closer to Moy. "You know as well as
I that the Chinese are a patient people who remember
disturbing events for a long time. Beijing still remembers
the sting of your father's defection, and they do not forgive such actions quickly or easily. Moy Huian has
served as a surrogate in your father's place. To win his
freedom, I must deal with the Chinese security apparatus directly. They have agreed to your uncle's release,
conditionally."

The last word hung in the air like a sword waiting
to fall. "And what are their conditions?"

"What your father stole from them, they were able
to replace many years ago. There is nothing that he
could now offer that has any interest to them. Beijing
wants you to provide them with something of equal
value to the knowledge they lost when your father de-
fected; they want information. Your company developed the ciphering system currently in use by the
American government. They want the keys to break
this system."

Moy felt his blood pressure rise twenty points in a
single heartbeat. His father had been branded a traitor
for following his conscience and defecting. Now he was
being asked to betray the country that had welcomed
his family, the country that he'd called home for most of
his life, to repay the crime of his father's defection.
Phillip Moy fought back the urge to remove this man
bodily from his home for making such a request. He had
no doubt that Deng Cho-Nam worked with PRC Intelligence to prey on the guilt of Chinese émigrés who'd
left family members behind.

Moy maintained a calm, receptive expression in
spite of the troubling and violent emotions that boiled
within him. "Your contacts in Beijing are correct; I did

develop the ciphering system now in use by the American government. Unfortunately, I no longer have access to the specific details of that project." Moy was bluffing, hoping that Deng would counter with a cash offer. "It is common practice for all materials relating to a highly classified government project to be turned over once the project is complete."

Kang topped off his teacup and eased back in his chair. "That may be a common practice for most government projects, but not in this case. The hardware, engineering data, and the ciphering programs are maintained on a special-projects computer housed at your Chicago facility. Access to this computer is strictly limited, but the information can be retrieved on your personal authority. The ciphers are the price of your uncle's release; anything less would be unacceptable to my clients."

Everything this man had said was true. The thought of an informer inside his company, a spy supplying the PRC with classified information, caused Moy's anger to swell even further. Moy fought hard to keep his head clear of emotion.

"Assuming that you are correct and I still have access to the ciphering information, how could I turn it over to you? I am subject to the same security measures as my employees. I can't simply make a copy of the files and walk out of my office with them."

"I am surprised at you." A thin smile curled on Kang's face, the look of a cat toying with its prey. "Is this not the information age? There is no need for you to risk yourself in this exchange. All that my clients require is the exact date and time of your next data transfer to the government. That information, and the access codes to your computer, will allow them to retrieve what they desire. Once they have the ciphers, your uncle will be turned over to you."

The smile then disappeared and Kang changed his expression to one of deadly earnest. "There are two other points that I must make very clear to you. First, if you do not accept these terms, your uncle will be killed. Second, if the Chinese are unable to break the American codes with the information from your computer, they will assume that you have betrayed them. For that betrayal, your family will be killed. You see, the factor that determines whether a piece of information is priceless or worthless is time. Beijing must have the time to make use of the cipher information; otherwise, this effort is futile. Once the American government discovers that their codes have been broken, they will immediately alter their method of encryption. For you and your family's sake, that event must be pushed as far into the future as possible. Do as I have instructed and you have nothing to fear."

Nothing but a lifetime of looking over my shoulder, waiting for the next time your clients in Beijing want something from me, Moy thought. As in many difficult negotiations, Moy's poker face held. Deng was equally calm and unreadable.

"Since you leave me with no alternative, I accept your conditions." Moy looked Deng directly in the eyes. "But I do have one condition of my own."

The thin, knowing smile returned. "You wish to meet with your uncle before the exchange is made."

"Yes," Moy replied with a nod.

"This request was anticipated. Prior to your next data transfer with the American government, you will contact me with the date and the access codes. In return, I will instruct you where to go, to meet your uncle, on the day of the exchange. You will both be held until the cipher information is acquired. If my clients are not successful in acquiring the information they desire, you both will be killed. When you call, give yourself plenty of time; you will be meeting your uncle outside this country."

"Not in the PRC, I hope?" Moy asked.

"No, for you to travel there would rouse the suspicions of the American government." Kang deliberately took a sip of his tea, leaving Moy waiting uncomfortably. "You will meet your uncle in a country that shares unrestricted travel with the United States. At that time, you will also bring a cashier's check in the amount of one hundred thousand dollars, my fee for brokering this transaction. When U.S. Immigration asks how your uncle obtained an exit visa from the PRC, you can explain that you *greased* a few palms. I am certain that you will have no trouble getting Moy Huian admitted into the United States on humanitarian grounds."

Kang reached into the breast pocket of his blazer and pulled out a business card, which he handed to Moy. "The phone number on the back is where you can reach me. We will not meet again until the day of the exchange. Follow these instructions fully and we will have no problems. Are you clear on the conditions of this transaction, Mr. Moy?"

"I understand you perfectly," Moy said, thinking to himself, you son of a bitch.

Kang stood up and straightened his double-breasted blazer. "Then let us inform the others of the good news. Moy Huian will soon be reunited with his family."

Moy followed Deng out from the study, choking down the foul taste that this meeting left in his mouth.

Long ago, Moy had vowed never to work with Beijing until the Communists were thrown out of power. I won't trade freely with your masters, Deng Cho-Nam, Moy thought while smiling politely, and I most certainly won't commit treason for them.

Langley, Virginia

Jackson Barnett was working late again, one of the many tireless servants of the state. Two of the former Soviet republics seemed poised to go to war with each other and the White House needed answers, not that they'd read any of the previous briefings he'd sent over the past few months, when this situation first appeared on the horizon. None of that mattered, though, and the information Barnett's people assembled would aid the President in deciding how to deal with the crisis. The world was a different place from ten years ago, but intelligence work was still the same.

Sally Kirsch had left him with a stack of intelligence assessments and a fresh pot of coffee, knowing that he would be putting in another long day. Barnett had just kicked his shoes off and loosened his tie when the phone rang. The double ring told him it was a direct call on his private line. "Barnett here," he answered, cradling the receiver against his shoulder as he sat down.

"Jackson, it's Phillip Moy. We need to talk."

The strained sound in Moy's voice told Barnett that this wasn't a social call. "What can I do for you?"

"I just received a visit from a man who claimed that he could get my uncle out of China."

"Another charlatan no doubt."

"I don't think so. He brought a letter and a recent photograph that my father positively identified. This material came out of a Chinese labor camp. He also delivered Beijing's conditions for the release. Are you sitting down?"

Barnett listened, taking notes as Moy described the scene and answered Barnett's more detailed questions. Barnett knew the story of Moy's father, and the brother who had stayed behind.

"Did he ever come out and admit that he was Chinese Intelligence?"

"No, he seemed to be trying very hard to distance himself from the PRC government. He tried to leave me with the impression that he was nothing more than a well-connected broker who could reunite my family for a fee. At the conclusion of our meeting, he gave his card and a number to call once the next file transfer is scheduled. He used the name Deng Cho-Nam."

"Phillip, could you repeat that name for me again?"

"Certainly, Deng Cho-Nam. You've heard of this man?"

"I'm afraid I have. I received word recently that a Chinese agent was traveling to the United States under the alias of Deng Cho-Nam. The FBI lost him up in New York, and we had no idea where he went. It looks like he went to visit you."

Chapter 29

Frankfurt, Germany
April 19

The Northwest flight into Frankfurt landed in the early morning, which meant that it was still sometime the previous night by Cal Mosley's watch, but months of following leads had finally paid off. Cross-referencing the sketchy records from the dive ship with Dominican Immigration's tourist data, Mosley finally located the woman who dove with the Cole impostor.

Petra Spanhaur taught art history at a secondary school just outside of Frankfurt. She lived in a modest apartment with her husband and a pair of cats. They welcomed Mosley into their home, though they seemed wary of him. Mosley took a chair while Spanhaur and her husband sat on the couch.

"Thank you for seeing me on such short notice," Mosley said in fluent German.

"It was no trouble, Herr Mosley. How can I help you in your investigation?"

Mosley could see from the look on her face that the
incident still troubled her. "As I said on the phone, I'm
investigating the death of Michael Cole. We have reason
to believe that it was not accidental."

"You don't think my wife killed this man?" Spanhaur's husband objected.

"Absolutely not," Mosley replied. "No one believes
that your wife had any responsibility for this man's death.
She is, however, a witness to what happened. Frau Spanhaur, could you please describe to me the events surrounding that day?"

"*Ja*. Last Christmas, my husband and I were on holiday in the Dominican Republic. It was beautiful."

As Spanhaur began her narrative, Mosley could tell
that she'd relived it every day since. He felt sympathy for
the woman, who was still visibly shaken by her experience. Holding her husband's hand, she spoke of the wonderful time they had had in the Caribbean.

"On the night before the dive, my husband ate
something that made him quite ill. The next morning, he
felt better, but not well enough to dive with me. I had just
earned my dive card and he encouraged me to go on
without him. The dive master was very helpful, and he
paired me up with Herr Cole. The reef was spectacular—
I had never seen such colors before, and the light was indescribable. I was having a wonderful time, but then I
noticed that Cole was acting strange."

"How so?" Mosley asked.

"He was swimming erratically, bumping into things,
turning abruptly for no reason. When I tried to assist him,
he lashed out at me. The look in his eyes was crazy—he
was a madman. He tore my mask off, and that was the last
I saw of him. I was unable to find my mask, so I made a
controlled ascent to the surface. I told the dive master

what had happened, and the rest of the divers searched for Cole, but they never found the poor man."

"My wife did everything she could. For a novice diver, she performed admirably. I have been diving for many years, and I have seen what she's described happen to other divers. It could have been nitrogen narcosis or drugs or any number of things."

"Could you describe the man you dove with?"

"I can do better than that, I have a picture." Spanhaur retrieved a photo album from the bookshelf and flipped through the last few pages. "Here it is. My husband took this just before we dove."

Mosley accepted the album and studied the candid photo of Spanhaur and the impostor on the trimaran's jump deck. A woman, dressed for sunning on the main deck, was handing the man his fins. He looked at the photo for several minutes before setting it on the coffee table and opening his briefcase.

"Frau Spanhaur, are you certain that this is the man you dove with, the man who attacked you before disappearing?"

"*Ja,*" she replied, a little confused to be asked such a question, "this man is Michael Cole."

Mosley then handed a photograph to the Spanhaurs. "Actually, *this* gentleman is Michael Cole."

"This is not the man I dove with." Spanhaur gasped.

"No, it isn't," Mosley agreed. "This Michael Cole was murdered at least twelve hours before your dive." Mosley explained this slowly, letting the Spanhaurs grasp what he was saying.

Spanhaur's husband held her close for several minutes as a tangled flood of emotion welled up inside her. She was shocked, angry, relieved, happy, and confused all at the same time. Mosley turned away until she had time to compose herself.

"Is there anything else, Herr Mosley?" she asked daubing away at a few errant tears.

"If you don't mind, I would like to borrow your photo. It's the first solid clue we have in this investigation."

Spanhaur tore the print from her album and handed it to Mosley. "This man used me to hide his crimes. I hope you find him and bring him to justice for what he has done."

Mosley placed the photograph in his file. "That's why I'm here. Thank you both for your help."

Chapter 30

Mosley's short trip to Germany had produced his best lead in the four months since Cole's body had been pulled from the sea. Computer analysis of the man in Petra Spanhaur's photograph quickly turned up a match, British business consultant Ian Parnell. Dominican Immigration verified that Parnell had arrived in Santo Domingo a few days prior to Cole's death.

Mosley wasn't back in his office thirty minutes when a security guard escorted Dan Harmon to his doorway.

"Mr. Harmon," Mosley said with a warm smile, "what brings you all the way out to Virginia?"

Harmon pulled out an enlarged copy of the Spanhaur photograph. "You have to warn me before sending over stuff like this. The Spanhaur photo has blown part of this case wide open."

Mosley leaned back and propped his feet up on the desk. "How so?"

"Fundamentals, Cal. I wired a copy of the photo to our Chicago office and had an agent run it past Cole's team at Moy Electronics."

"I hate to put a damper on your story, but we already ID'd the guy."

"I'm not talking about the guy—I got a name for the woman handing him the fins. Like I said, we ran the picture past the people at Moy, and they all had lunch with her, including Cole. She's a freelance journalist named Alexandra Roe and we can definitely place her in the DR at the time of Cole's murder."

Mosley scrawled Roe's name beneath a copy of the photo pinned to his wall. The large tackboard was covered with items related to this investigation. "Nice work, Dan. I'm impressed."

"But wait, there's more." Harmon turned his head and motioned for someone to join them. A man of medium height and stocky build entered Mosley's cramped office, taking the guest chair indicated by Harmon.

"Cal, I would like to introduce Lou Gerty. Lou here is a kindred spirit in the investigative world, though his work lacks the luxury of our federal positions."

"This guy talks an awful lot." Gerty pointed a thumb in Harmon's direction.

"Yeah, well he's FBI. What can I say?" Mosley held out a hand to Gerty. "Pleased to meet you, Mr. Gerty."

Gerty quickly shook Mosley's hand. "Call me Lou. Dan asked me to come down and tell you my story, so here I am. I'm a private investigator, mostly domestic stuff, custody, that kind of thing. A couple of years ago, I handled a case for a young lady who works for one of the congressmen up on the Hill. She had her suspicions about her husband and wanted them checked out."

"The husband in question is Michael Cole," Harmon added.

"I was getting to that!" Gerty turned his attention back to Mosley, a little perturbed at the interruption. "Yeah, the guy I was watching was Michael Cole. I'm sorry to say that his wife's fears were justified. It's bad enough when a guy's cheating on his wife for kicks, but this guy Cole was leading some kind of double life."

The term *double life* had a specific meaning for career intelligence officers, and Gerty's offhand comment grabbed Mosley's attention. "Could you elaborate on that, please?"

"Certainly. Michael Cole was a practicing homosexual with wide and varied tastes. His liaisons were, to put it mildly, inventive." The look of disgust on Gerty's face told Mosley that he didn't approve of alternative lifestyles. "I photographed Cole in several encounters with different partners over the course of several weeks. All were male and some may have bordered on the age of consent. I performed my investigation for an attorney, who used my report to back a divorce suit against Cole. She crucified him. Afterward, she asked me to stash a copy of everything I'd dug up, just in case her client needed to protect herself in the future. I had my copy until last December."

"What happened last December?" Mosley asked.

"I was in my office on a Friday afternoon, just working on some paperwork, when I was visited by this woman who said she was FBI. She had proper ID and I had no reason to doubt her. She told me that Cole was a suspect in an espionage investigation. She knew I'd tailed Cole and that I had something on him strong enough to make him walk away from his divorce empty-handed. In the end, she walked out of my office with my entire file, including the negatives. I decided to let it go at that, figuring that Cole deserved whatever he got."

"That's where I can pick up the story," Harmon announced. "Cole's ex-wife didn't tell us anything about the reason for their divorce, at first. Their settlement called for both parties to remain silent and she was honoring that agreement. Once she realized the seriousness of the situation surrounding her ex-husband's death, she offered up Gerty's investigation into Cole's life. Unfortunately, by then almost everything Gerty had on Cole was already gone."

Gerty sat back in his chair, smiling proudly. "Everything but my memory."

Harmon threw a supportive arm around Gerty's shoulder. "This guy has a near-photographic memory. When he described the woman in his office, I figured it was probably one of Cole's friends helping him out. At least that's what I thought until you found Petra Spanhaur. Lou, will you tell Cal what you told me this morning?"

Gerty pointed at the Spanhaur photo on Mosley's wall. "That's the woman who took my files."

Mosley didn't respond for a moment, digesting the new discoveries. Without saying a word, he stood up and walked over to the dry marker board on his office wall that bore a bubble diagram of the investigation. The bubbles held the names of people and activities surrounding the death of Michael Cole; dashed or full lines indicated respectively weak or strong connections in the investigation. Mosley picked up a bold red marker and drew a line connecting Michael Cole, Ian Parnell, and a new bubble with the name of Alex Roe.

Chapter 31

Ann Arbor, Michigan
April 28

Kelsey, Nolan, and Grin quickly made their way through the corridors of the MARC complex to Sean Kilkenny's office. Nolan's father had called them down to review the FBI's findings regarding their hacker. From the tone of his voice, the MARC director was not happy with what he had heard.

"Good morning, ladies," Nolan greeted the FBI agents as he entered the office with Grin.

"Take a seat," Sean Kilkenny ordered, "I want you three to hear what the FBI just told me." Sean Kilkenny's body language signaled loud and clear that the news was not good.

"We appreciate your cooperation on this investigation," Ullrich began. "Without your efforts, we wouldn't have been able to follow this hacker at all."

So far so good, Nolan thought to himself.

"In each of the telephone traces we initiated, we

were unsuccessful in locating any unusual communications entering your network. Your monitoring made it easy for us to find out where he was going, but we still don't know how he's getting in. The lack of any incoming traffic to this building has led Agent Harbke and myself to believe that our suspect is operating from inside your computer network."

Boom! The other shoe dropped with a resounding thud in Nolan's mind. "You think our hacker is someone inside MARC?"

Ullrich didn't appear the least bit defensive toward Nolan's challenge. "Yes, it's the only theory that fits the evidence thus far. We're dealing with a very sophisticated computer penetration by a highly skilled individual. This is a person with advanced knowledge of networks and operating systems, a person capable of altering system records to hide his or her presence."

"Frankly speaking," Harbke added, "Agent Ullrich and I are very impressed by this individual. In our years of dealing with these types of crimes, we've never come across anyone quite this good."

"Son, they've requested a list of our employees and researchers with system access." Sean obviously didn't like the idea that a member of his staff was a criminal hacker. "I want you and Grin to assemble the information they need."

"That list will be easy, but the two most likely suspects are sitting right here," Grin said, indicating Nolan and himself.

The possibility that they could be considered suspects had never dawned on Nolan until this moment. "True, nobody else around here knows the system like we do. There's got to be someone else, though. . . ."

Nolan's line of thought was cut short by his beeper.

He looked down to the device clipped to his waist to read off the number. "It's the lab. Our hacker is making another run through the system. Ladies, you're just in time for another live performance."

Everyone bolted from the office and double-timed it to the MARC computer lab. Grin took up his station at the Cray, and Nolan sat in front of the laptop. The FBI agents and Nolan's father watched over Nolan's shoulder as the hacker began punching his way through computer systems.

"Grin," Nolan called out, "can you bring up the internal network status?"

Grin was scanning rapidly through the network's status screens. "One step ahead of you. Other than a couple of researchers, no one else is tied into the mainframe."

"Damn, how is this guy getting into the Cray?" The situation didn't make any sense at all to Nolan; the intruder had to be on one of the incoming communication lines. "Let's drop those two off the system and see if that has any effect."

"I'm cutting them loose. Hope they're not too mad at me." Grin sent out a "Thirty seconds to shutdown" warning, which caused the MARC researchers to scramble to close their files before the network cut them off. Both were off the system with a second and a half to spare.

"We're all alone now," Grin announced. "Is our friend still there?"

"Happily hacking away, but from where?" There was puzzled disappointment in Nolan's voice.

Special Agent Harbke wandered away from the rest, looking over the jury-rigged wiring connections behind the Cray. She followed the bundle of network fiber-optic cables as they emerged from the raised access floor like an orange tentacle reaching into the back of the Cray. Another bundle of thickly wrapped cables ran from the Cray into the floor and emerged in a glass-enclosed portion of the lab. Through the glass, she saw a metallic cube and two cylinders of liquid nitrogen.

"I'm going to bring down the internal network, leaving only our line from here to campus up. If he's inside MARC, we'll know it real soon." Grin typed furiously, entering the commands that would sever the communication links between the mainframe and every PC inside the MARC complex. With MARC's internal network down, the hacker could only be coming from the outside.

"Is he gone yet?" Grin asked as MARC's internal network shut down.

The hacker was still cycling through their computer down to the university's Main Computing Center. "Nope, he's still there."

"Excuse me, Mr. Grinelli," Harbke called out from across the lab, "but could you explain something to me?"

Grin turned to face Harbke, who stood in front of the MARC network connections. "Sure, but only if you call me Grin. What's your question?"

"The network line you're tapped into is part of that bundle feeding into the back of the mainframe"—Harbke pointed to the orange-coated fiber-optic cables—"and from there you can access campus or the outside world, correct?"

Grin's eyes followed the cable bundle from the end connected to the mainframe until it disappeared into a floor tray. "Yeah, that's right."

Harbke then crouched down and pointed to a well-insulated cable bundle that emerged from the floor. "Then what's this super-cooled connection used for?"

"You want to field that one, Kelsey?" Grin asked.

Kelsey walked over to where Harbke stood looking at a spaghetti tangle of cables. "That's an ITC cable, which we use to carry—"

"Huge amounts of data," Harbke completed the sentence. "But what's it doing here? These are still experimental, and the fiber lines should be more than adequate to service this equipment."

"Adequate for what's inside *this* room." Kelsey then turned toward the glass wall separating the main lab from her own. "Our ITC cable connects the Cray to an experiment of mine in the next room."

"Where are you coming from?" Grin's frustrated shout drew everyone's attention.

Nolan walked over and stood behind Grin's chair to watch the screens over his shoulder. "What's up?"

"This guy is really good. I don't have a clue how he's getting over the network and through the Cray. I've isolated every communications feed I can find and he's still out there. If I didn't know any better, I'd say he was here in the lab."

"That's what I'm getting at," Harbke answered from beside the ITC line. "You've isolated the outside phone lines and campus network ties and come up empty. Grin has shut down the building, and we still have nothing. Your laptop is wired into this line, and it still says that the hacker is out there. If I read your wiring correctly, I'd say the only cable we haven't looked at is this one."

"It can't be the ITC cable," Kelsey argued. "It only goes from here to there. We can see the entire thing."

Harbke didn't look convinced, and she continued playing devil's advocate. "Maybe, and maybe not. Did you put that cable in yourselves, or was it contracted out?"

"We had the professionals install that cable," Grin

replied. "I went to school for two weeks on it, but I wouldn't want to try and put one in."

Harbke knew she was grasping at straws and could sense the doubt in the others' minds. "I know it's a long shot, but we have to eliminate every possibility, no matter how remote."

"All right, we'll give it a shot." Nolan slapped Grin on the shoulder. "Let's get to it."

Grin and Nolan spent the next ten minutes tapping into the ITC cable.

"Here goes nothing," Nolan said.

The laptop displayed two windows, side by side. One depicted the information flowing through the Cray; the other reported on the ITC cable.

"Nolan," Kelsey said with a touch of concern, "this shows the hacker's on our ITC cable."

"Can't be," Nolan said, "I must have gotten the wiring ass-backward."

Nolan rechecked the laptop; he'd programmed everything correctly. "This is weird. The laptop thinks that it's picking up our hacker on the ITC cable, but that's impossible. I must have screwed this program up somehow."

"Well, let's prove it once and for all." Grin reached down and yanked the monitor wires from the Cray's network.

The first window on the laptop suddenly went blank and an error message appeared, indicating that the signal had been lost. To Nolan and Kelsey's surprise, the remaining window still showed the hacker hard at work.

"I feel sick," Kelsey said, massaging her temples.

"I'm seeing, but I still don't believe."

"Believe it, Nolan," Grin replied, the other cable

dangling from his hand. "The laptop is taking only one feed, and it's coming off the ITC cable."

Kelsey just shook her head in disgust. "Only one thing we can do now, Nolan. Let's open the floor."

Grin slipped a toolbox out from under his desk and pulled out a small flat pry bar and a pair of suction cups.

"What are you going to do?" Ullrich asked.

"Open the access floor," Nolan replied. "Like Kelsey said earlier, the ITC cable only goes from here to there. By physically inspecting the line, we can see where our hacker made his tie-in."

Tile by tile, the access floor came up, revealing a tangle of wiring that serviced all the equipment in the computer lab. In five minutes, they'd exposed the entire length of the ITC cable. They searched the thick umbilical from one end to the other and found it intact and uninterrupted.

"This guy's some kind of magician."

"I hear you, Grin," Nolan replied. "I don't know how he's doing it, but he's getting on this line. Kelsey, could you please disconnect the laptop and bring it over here with the cables?"

Kelsey gathered up the small computer and handed it to Nolan.

"What are you going to do now?" Ullrich asked.

"We know this guy's on our line somewhere, right? I'm going to eliminate where he's not. Kelsey built in a lot of checkpoints for this prototype, so that we could gather data anywhere in the experiment. By moving from point to point, we should be able to isolate any breach in the cable."

"That still leaves Kelsey, you, and me as the prime suspects," Grin commented dryly.

"First things first. Let's find out how our hacker got in here."

Nolan clipped the monitor cables at another point of the ITC line; the monitor showed the intruder was still there. When he tapped into the next two points along the line, both showed the presence of the intruder.

Nolan then lay flat on his stomach, resting his chin on his arms, which were folded flat against the floor. His eyes followed the ITC line in the open floor duct below him.

"That's interesting. I was half-expecting to find some kind of transmitter embedded in the line somewhere, hidden by all the insulation, but we're at the end of the line, so to speak." Nolan stood up and brushed the dust from his clothes. "Time to take a look at the equipment on the lab bench."

Nolan unplugged the laptop and carried it into Kelsey's lab. "Here's where the ITC cable ends and the processor begins."

Grin and Kelsey watched the laptop as Nolan snapped the monitor cables into place. Before Nolan could even ask, Kelsey just shook her head; the hacker was still on-line.

Grin scratched his goatee as he looked at the lab bench. "Kelsey, you don't suppose that this brilliant experiment of yours is the hacker?"

"Not for a minute—it's just a machine."

Nolan knew the hacker had to be tying into the system from somewhere. "Let's move to the next point." He clipped the cable to a receptacle placed between the Gatekeeper device and the optical processor.

"He's gone," Grin announced as the signal disappeared from the laptop screen.

"Quick," Nolan barked, "the other set of cables. Let's see if he's still down-line."

Grin clipped the second set of cables to the last point they'd checked; the hacker was still on-line. The wires leading from the laptop were fitted into connectors on either side of the Moy Gatekeeper, effectively watching everything that went in and out of the device. Nolan had already isolated the optical processors' signal traffic to the Cray, leaving only the hacker's signal unaccounted for.

"It would appear that this small black box bearing the name Moy Electronics is our culprit."

"What is that?" Harbke asked.

"Special Agent Harbke," Kelsey announced, "I would like to introduce you to our Gatekeeper."

Nolan and Grin both stifled a laugh.

Sean Kilkenny glowered at the pair; he found nothing amusing about this situation. "Mind letting the rest of us in on your joke."

"Sure, Dad. This little black cube was designed to be a security guard of sorts for the government's computer systems—something to keep people like our hacker out."

"Which it seems to be doing just fine. Our hacker hasn't reached the optical processor," Grin added.

"Not that a hacker could do much once he got there," Kelsey added.

"This device is strictly for governmental use. Why do you have one?" Ullrich asked.

"Moy Electronics is a substantial backer of MARC, with a strong interest in this project," Kelsey explained. "They've provided me with aid on a variety of levels. This device is one of their contributions, and it's here with the government's blessing."

Harbke studied the device closely. "I remember reading about this thing in a memo back at the office. The government is installing them everywhere. Word is that it can track hackers back to their own systems and nail them in the act."

"Unfortunately," Nolan offered, "it appears that our Gatekeeper is part of the problem, rather than the solution."

"He's gone, everybody," Grin announced as the signal disappeared. "I guess that concludes our broadcast day."

"Well, gentlemen, I'm baffled," Ullrich admitted. "Agent Harbke and I need to take this latest bit of information back to the office for a consult. This Gatekeeper is new territory for us."

After the FBI agents departed, Kelsey, Nolan, and Grin began poring over every piece of documentation they had on their Gatekeeper. Several hours, a vegetarian pizza, and a large dose of diet Coke later, they were no closer to determining the magic that Moy Electronics had packaged inside their little black cube.

"Well, guys, I've had enough," Kelsey announced, her frustration shared by all. "I'm heading back to my apartment to take a hot shower and get packed."

Kelsey slowly stood up and stretched her arms upward; she was exhausted. She placed her hand on Nolan's head and ruffled his hair. "See you in about an hour?"

"I'll be there."

As Kelsey picked up her briefcase and walked out of the lab, Grin glanced over at Nolan.

"What?" Nolan asked, questioning the look on Grin's face.

"Nothing."

"Back to business, Grin. Bottom line, this thing is

programmable," Nolan concluded after reading a dense listing of the Gatekeeper's specifications, "so I guess the trick now is to find out what that program is. Chicago's an hour behind us, so it's only forty-thirty there. Let's get somebody from Moy on the phone."

Nolan made the call to Moy Electronics in Chicago, and after describing his problem, he was connected with software engineer Bill Iverson.

"Bill, this is Nolan Kilkenny at MARC in Ann Arbor."

"What can I do for you, Nolan?" Iverson sounded friendly and helpful.

"I'm having a little trouble with one of your I/O controllers; it's a Gatekeeper. Are you familiar with it?"

"A little," Iverson answered modestly, "I wrote most of its code. What seems to be the problem?"

Nolan explained the situation, how the device was installed, and their problem with the hacker.

Iverson's voice went from helpful to surprised. "Let me get this straight—you've isolated the Gatekeeper as the *source* of a hacker problem you're experiencing?"

Nolan sat beside the lab bench, looking at the wire clips connected to either side of the Gatekeeper. "That's the way it looks from here. What do you think?"

"I'm stumped," Iverson admitted honestly. "What you describe is possible, if you knew how to program a Gatekeeper. There's only a handful of people who know how to do that and they all work here. I agree with you— we should dump the sucker's core program and see what's driving it."

Iverson talked Nolan through the procedures for downloading the Gatekeeper's program. From the Cray, Nolan brought up the Gatekeeper control software and gained direct access to the device. A moment later, the Gatekeeper's program began scrolling up Nolan's screen.

"It's dumping, but I don't have a clue as to what I'm looking at. Did you guys come up with a new programming language for this thing?"

"Yes, it's true, we're gluttons for punishment here at Moy." A perverse sense of masochistic pride seemed to run through computer programmers and engineers, a character trait evident in Iverson. "Once you've finished the dump, I want you to load the file into a text editor and check a few things for me."

The download finished and Nolan brought the program file up on the screen. Iverson walked him through a few key areas of the program, looking for any changes that would account for this Gatekeeper's deviant behavior. Each of the major points matched the program Iverson was looking at in Chicago. Everything in the incredibly long file seemed to be in order, leaving them with no further clues. Nolan hit the Home key and the file jumped back to the beginning.

"What you just ran past me checks out." Iverson sounded as puzzled as Nolan was. "I don't know what to tell you."

"Looks like I'm back to square one." Nolan was disappointed that they'd come up empty-handed. Absent-mindedly, he skimmed over the credits in the header of the Gatekeeper program. "Thanks for your help, Bill. I see your name's listed here with the other programmers for version one point one. It's nice that your company lets you sign your work."

"We're proud of what we do and—" Iverson stopped abruptly. "Can you read me that version number again?"

"Sure, version one point one."

"That's weird. One point one was just a beta test. I

didn't think we released any units with that batch of code. It still had a couple of nasty bugs."

"Could those bugs explain our problems?" Nolan's question was a shot in the dark, but they had long since exhausted the questions that made any sense.

"No," Iverson replied quickly, "the bad code would have caused the Gatekeeper to lock up on you every now and then, but nothing that would have sent it off hacking."

"I thought as much, but at least this one hasn't bombed out on us." Something else about the version number bothered Iverson, but Nolan didn't know why.

"That surprises me even more," Iverson admitted. "Can you send me a copy of that code? I'd like to run it past some other people on that project."

"I can do better than that. Professor Newton and I are leaving for Chicago in an hour for a long weekend. We can meet at your office and have a closer look."

"Great, I'll make arrangements here." Iverson sounded relieved, since some problems just weren't diagnosed well over the phone. "I think there'll be a few people here interested in hearing about your experience."

Nolan hung up the phone and transferred the Gatekeeper file to an optical disk, which he tossed into his Eddie Bauer briefcase. He also gathered up some real-time copies of the hacker in action, to demonstrate to the people at Moy what they were all up against.

"Are you out of here?" Grin asked.

"Yeah, I got to pick up Kelsey and drive to Chicago. She didn't need this hacker nonsense, not with all the time she's been putting in with the chip fabricators. She's wiped. My sister-in-law is taking her out for a little shopping therapy while I help my brother renovate that old house of his. Hey, keep an eye on our *friend* while I'm gone."

Grin caught the pager Nolan tossed his way and clipped it to his belt. "Will do. Just have a good time. Say, if you don't mind my asking, when are you going to do something about Kelsey? She's too good to let get away."

"I thought you didn't believe in marriage, something about it being an archaic ritual that diminishes women to the level of property."

"I didn't say anything about marriage; it's just that I've gotten to know the two of you pretty well over the last few months, and you make a great team. Just something to think about during a long drive to Chicago with a pretty lady."

"You're right on one count—Kelsey Newton is a *very special lady*."

Chapter 32

London, England
April 29

"Ian, I've something you ought to take a look at," Roe announced as she entered Parnell's office.

Parnell looked at his watch and saved the document that he was working on. "You're a bit early—we're not scheduled to meet until noon. What's so urgent?"

Roe sat in the leather chair in front of Parnell's glass-and-steel desk. "We've made a little headway at Chrysler, but only a piece of what you wanted is there."

Parnell thumbed through the report; the financial data he had requested was listed as "Inaccessible" from that system. "It was a long shot, trying to punch through from the engineering side to finance, but worth a try anyway."

"There is some troubling news at the end of the report."

Parnell flipped through to the last page and read the Spyder's status report. The device was operating nominally, as always. Parnell's brow furrowed when he reached the item regarding an attempt to dump the Spyder's operating program. "What does this mean?"

"Someone is taking a close look at the device, closer than we'd like. Unfortunately, it can't tell us who or why, so we don't know if it has to do with that experimental processor it's attached to or something else." Roe didn't have to elaborate on what "something else" might be.

"Any thoughts on what we might do about it?"

"Unfortunately, we're not going to get anything more detailed about this situation without going there. Actually"—Roe mused for a moment—"that might not be a bad idea. They've gotten a fair amount of press regarding that optical processor. Perhaps I could arrange an interview to see how things are progressing. That might get me close enough to see what they're doing."

"Excellent idea," Parnell agreed. "I'll have Paulette make arrangements for you to fly out this afternoon. After all, we wouldn't want our source to disappear suddenly."

In the building across the riverfront park from the late-modern tower that housed Parnell's office, two watchers from Axton's team sat armed with cameras and laser-driven sound amplifiers. From their vantage point in the unleased space, they had a clear shot at Parnell's corner office. Teams had been staked out here around the clock since Kang Fa's last visit to London, without much success. If Parnell was involved in something illegal, he was doing a good job of not discussing it during business hours. This afternoon, Neville Axton sat in with the watchers, taking his measure of the man in the other building.

"Interesting, lads—that's the first time I recall Parnell mentioning an outside source for his information. Interesting, but strange," Axton mused.

"How so?" one of the watchers asked.

"Well, it's their language," Axton explained, still not clear himself about this train of thought. "They never come out and say who their source is, but Roe mentioned that someone was looking 'at the device.' I wonder what she meant by that. Very odd."

Chapter 33

Ann Arbor, Michigan
April 30

Roe arrived at the MARC building and parked her rented car in a visitor's space next to a beige sedan bearing government plates. As she walked into the building's lobby, she quickly checked her notes on the research project tied to the Spyder.

"Good morning. I'm Alex Roe," she announced as she reached the reception desk. "I would like to speak with Professor Kelsey Newton, if she's available."

The receptionist checked Newton's calendar. "I'm sorry, but she's out of the office. Was she expecting you?"

"No, I'm afraid I don't have an appointment. I was in the area doing research for another story, and I decided to stop by and see how her project was going. I read about her work in the *New York Times*, and I was thinking about writing a detailed piece for magazine publication."

The door to the left of the reception desk opened,

through which two conservatively dressed women passed, followed by Sean Kilkenny.

"That gentleman is our director," the receptionist offered politely. "Perhaps he can help you."

Roe waited until Kilkenny had escorted his guests out the door and over to the government sedan. She studied the women as they left and noticed the unmistakable bulge of pistol holsters on both. They were armed and, undoubtedly, federal agents.

The receptionist flagged Sean Kilkenny down as he returned from the vestibule. "Mr. Kilkenny, this is Alex Roe. She came to interview Professor Newton about the processor."

Roe offered her hand to Kilkenny. "A pleasure to meet you, and no, I didn't have an appointment. As I told your receptionist, I was in the area and I thought I'd stop by and see how things are progressing. Unfortunately, I seem to have picked a bad day."

"Very true. Both Professor Newton and my son are in Chicago doing a little troubleshooting."

"Troubleshooting?" Roe feigned a journalist's detached interest. "Nothing wrong with the processor, I hope."

Kilkenny shook his head. "No, just visiting one of our vendors. I can furnish you with some publicity information about the project, but, unfortunately, we don't have anyone else here who is technically qualified to speak with you about it."

A slight tremor of panic shuddered through Roe. Perhaps they were closer to discovering the Spyder than she'd imagined. "When are they expected back?"

"It's just a weekend trip; they'll both be back Monday morning. If you like, our receptionist can schedule an interview with them early next week."

"Unfortunately, I'm flying out this evening." Roe finished jotting down a few notes and closed her pad. "As soon as I finish up my current project, I'll try to get back out this way. And next time, I'll call ahead."

Roe handed Kilkenny a business card and left the MARC building. She was amazed at how well she'd held her composure while speaking with Sean Kilkenny. The researchers at MARC might be very close to unmasking the Spyder. In all her years as a spy, Roe had never felt so close to discovery.

After driving around town to get her thoughts in order, Roe returned to her hotel. The information she had was circumstantial; what she needed was verification.

"Moy Electronics," the receptionist answered enthusiastically. "This is Debra. How may I direct your call?"

Roe smiled at the sound of a human voice. Moy Electronics might be one of the premier high-technology companies in the world, but its owner was a firm believer that a human voice was better than an electronic voice-mail system for communicating with his customers.

"Hello, Debra. This is Rena from the Michigan Applied Research Consortium in Ann Arbor," Roe lied with ease, "and I need your help. Two of our people are in Chicago, and they've misplaced their itinerary. I don't have a copy of it here, and I'm desperate. I need to re-confirm their meeting schedule. Do you have that information available?"

Roe knew from her previous visit to Moy that all staff schedules and on-site meetings were accessible by computer. The only snag would be if Debra didn't take pity on her and refused to pass that information over the phone.

"Normally, I wouldn't do this," Debra replied, "but I guess I can help you out. What are your people's names?"

"Kelsey Newton and Nolan Kilkenny," Roe answered, her voice showing just the right amount of relief and gratitude.

Roe could hear the receptionist clicking away at her computer to locate the information. "I show only one meeting for them—today at two-thirty, with Bill Iverson. No other information is listed in the entry."

"Today at two-thirty, Bill Iverson," Roe repeated. "Thanks, Debra, you're a lifesaver. I just hope the other companies I have to call are as helpful."

"It was no trouble," the receptionist replied cheerfully, responding to the compliment. "You have a good day."

The line went dead and Roe held the phone for a moment as it buzzed. Kilkenny and Newton were going to meet with Iverson, the brain behind the Spyder project. Things were definitely getting too hot. The wailing of the phone in her hand brought Roe back to the present. She depressed the phone cradle to clear the line and dialed Parnell in London.

"Paulette, it's Alex. Is Ian in? I need to talk with him."

"He's in, but he's with Ba Xan." The distaste Paulette felt for the man was evident in the sound of her voice.

"That's fine," Roe assured her. "This has to do with him, as well. Put me through."

The line went silent for a moment as Paulette transferred her call.

"Alex, I've got you on the speaker with Mr. Ba. I've informed our client that you are in the States looking into a problem with our source. What seems to be the difficulty?"

"Discovery, or damn close to it. They've identified our device as part of a communications problem they're experiencing. Two of their people are in Chicago to talk with the engineer who designed it. This supply line looks like it's going to dry up very quickly. I suggest we download the suicide program and cut our losses."

"Sorry," Parnell apologized, "but we're going to have to hang on a little longer. Our client has some news for us."

"Miss Roe, this is Ba Xan." Even with the Atlantic separating them, Ba still sounded dangerous. "Your partner has graciously taken me into his confidence regarding the source of your information. I must insist that you keep it available for the next few weeks."

"Ian, can I assume that our client's position is not negotiable?"

Parnell correctly took Roe's question to mean that they had no choice in the matter. "Precisely."

"Mr. Ba, Ian and I would love to keep our source in place for another few weeks, just for you," Roe said sarcastically, "but forces outside of our control are moving to shut it down as we speak. I doubt that it will last much past Monday."

"Please describe your situation and the people involved," Kang said calmly. "I might be able to assist in keeping your source in place."

While Roe explained what she knew about the unraveling situation at MARC, Neville Axton and his watchers were having fits with their equipment across the way.

"Damn, all we're getting is static!" Axton growled. "I

can't believe our luck! Kang pops up, and now this. What's going on?"

"Sir, the equipment's fine," a frustrated engineer replied. "Kang's got a white-noise generator of some kind that's feeding us all this static. It's even affecting the phone tap. Sorry, sir, but I'm not picking up enough of what's being said to make any sense at all."

Axton slumped in his chair, still staring at the obscured window in the building across the park. Inside that office, a foreign agent was executing an intelligence operation on British soil. Part of him wanted to break in and arrest the bastards, but he knew better. Like any good hunter, he had to study his quarry, understand it, before he could move against it. Kang was dangerous, and very clever—not the sort of man you went after unprepared.

Chapter 34

Chicago, Illinois

Their journey to Chicago had been a quiet one, with Nolan driving and an overworked Kelsey sleeping the entire way there. Sensing Kelsey's weary state, Nolan's sister-in-law, Maureen, immediately made plans for the physicist's recovery. Unfortunately, John Kilkenny felt no such compassion toward his younger brother and immediately put him to work. While Kelsey and Maureen spent most of Thursday being pampered at a luxurious spa, Nolan and John demolished the old garage to make room for a new addition.

By Friday morning, with two full nights of sleep in her system, Kelsey had returned to her normal self. As she entered the kitchen, she found Nolan and his brother seated at the table, eating breakfast and reading the newspaper.

"Good morning," Kelsey said with a lilt in her voice.

"You ready to head downtown for our meeting?" Nolan asked.

"I guess so. After yesterday, I'd put that part of my brain on hiatus. I think that masseur removed my bones. I feel like I'm made out of Jell-O."

Nolan slowly turned his head, rotating it from side to side. There was an audible snap as he leaned forward. "I could use a little of that right now."

"Allow me."

Kelsey stood behind Nolan's chair and began kneading his neck and shoulders. Nolan let his head sag forward as she released the tightness from his sore muscles.

"Hey, Mo," John called out as his wife entered the kitchen, "how about doing me?"

"No way. The last time I did that, I ended up pregnant."

"Can't blame me for trying," John replied while studying the National League box scores.

"Did you tell Nolan about the dress you bought?" Maureen asked, prompting Kelsey.

Kelsey hesitated for a minute. "Maureen took me to this fabulous dress shop down on Michigan Avenue and I found this stunning blue silk dress."

"It's the same color as her eyes." Maureen was many things, but subtle wasn't one of them. "Our next project is to find some accessories."

"Now all I need is a reason to wear it."

"Kelsey, when was the last time you had a date?" Nolan asked.

"That would be Scott, so about seven months ago."

Nolan closed his eyes, enjoying the healing magic Kelsey was performing on his neck. "We might have to do something about that."

Kelsey glanced over at Maureen, who stood grinning by the refrigerator. Maureen gave her a thumbs-up before reaching in for the orange juice.

*   *   *

Nolan and Kelsey arrived at the Moy Electronics complex, both hoping to find an answer to the Gatekeeper
problems they were experiencing by talking with the man
who had designed it. Tall and rumpled, Bill Iverson met
them in the main lobby and proceeded to give Kelsey and
Nolan what he called "the nickel tour" of the facility.
Iverson showed them nothing classified, but the public
spaces, research labs, and the automated production facility were enough to make Kilkenny consider updating
his résumé. After the abbreviated tour, they settled down
in a conference room to discuss their situation.

"So, this is the dump you ran Wednesday?" Iverson
asked rhetorically as he slipped Kilkenny's disk into the
computer. "You got me thinking about something that I
need to check."

Iverson loaded a split-screen editor onto the conference room's computer. He then loaded the current generation of the Gatekeeper code on the left side and placed
Kilkenny's code on the right.

"I'm going to run a simple text comparison of these
two versions of the Gatekeeper program," Iverson explained. "This one on the left is the one our computer
claims it installed on your device before it was shipped
last January. I can understand someone goofing and forgetting to update the header, but let's see what we've really got here."

Iverson issued the commands and the computer
began a line-by-line comparison of the two programs.
Four hundred lines into the comparison, Iverson halted
the procedure. "I think I've seen enough to know that the
program you got wasn't what our computer says it sent
you. Excuse me while I make a phone call."

Iverson dialed an inside line and asked the person on the other end to come over to the conference room.

Kilkenny looked over the comparison with Newton while Iverson finished his phone call. "Bill, does this version of the program have any bearing on my hacker problem?"

"This program by itself? No, not at all." Iverson joined Kilkenny at the wall monitor. "In fact, if your Gatekeeper was running this program, I expect you would have called us months ago to ask for your money back."

"What do you mean 'if'?" Newton asked. "This *is* the program our Gatekeeper is running, isn't it?"

Iverson shook his head. "I don't think so. This version was flawed, prone to crashing the system two or three times a day at the data-transfer rates you're using. I checked around, and the only current use we have for the beta version is as a decoy to protect a similar device."

Before Iverson could elaborate, the conference room door opened and a heavyset older man in a gray suit entered, followed by a younger man in a dark blue suit.

"Good morning, Professor Newton, Mr. Kilkenny. My name is Cal Mosley and I'm with the CIA. My associate here is Dan Harmon of the FBI. The fact that Mr. Iverson has asked us to join you means that your problem has just gotten a lot worse." Mosley then turned to Iverson. "Before we go any further, I think I should brief them on security with regard to the device."

"Now is as good a time as any," Iverson agreed.

"It's an understatement for me to say that everything you're about to hear is classified." Mosley then pulled out a copy of Kilkenny's service record from his briefcase. "Actually, I was quite surprised to discover that you hold a security clearance almost as high as mine."

"I held a fairly high clearance as a SEAL," Kilkenny admitted modestly, "but I'm a civilian now."

"Nolan"—Mosley thumped the cover of the service record—"your clearance, with all its privileges and responsibilities, has been reinstated to allow you to assist us in this investigation. Professor, your DOD security clearance has been upgraded, as well. We're going to tell you only what you need to know about the Spyder Project, and you are both bound by law not to reveal any of this information."

Security clearances, particularly high ones, weren't the easiest credentials to come by. Kilkenny and Newton nodded to each other. "We understand our obligations," Newton replied, speaking for them both. "What does this Spyder Project have to do with our hacker problem?"

Iverson slid two color product brochures across the table. Each bore a nearly identical photograph of a black cube; one was titled *Gatekeeper*, while the other read *Spyder*.

"Think of the Gatekeeper and the Spyder as opposite sides of the same coin. Both devices operate from the same basic kit of parts, but they use those parts a little differently. The Gatekeeper was designed to maintain a clean flow of information through a computer network, for legitimate users, while keeping undesirables off the system. For that latter aim, we built in a variety of tools the Gatekeeper could use to track and identify unauthorized users."

"I selected the Gatekeeper for its I/O handling capabilities," Kelsey added. "It was the only thing that could keep up with my processor."

"And that part seems to be working fine," Nolan agreed.

Iverson nodded and continued his explanation.

"The Spyder takes this scenario one step further. The CIA is concerned with illegal technology transfers to nations considered unfriendly to the United States. Every once in awhile, a high-end computer mysteriously finds its way across the borders of one of these nations. A Spyder placed inside one of these computers would do everything the Gatekeeper is programmed to do, and more. Using the same algorithms, the Spyder could track its way out of the hostile computer network, looking for a way to call home and tell us what its host computer is up to. Once the Spyder made contact, it could be programmed to do all sorts of *interesting* things."

Kilkenny took in everything Iverson had said while studying the pictures of the two sibling devices; the black boxes were outwardly identical. "And you believe that one of these Spyders is sitting on our lab bench, hacking through the university network?"

"After looking at this file you brought in, I'm sure of it."

"Just great." Disbelief rushed through Kilkenny's mind as he massaged his forehead. The whole situation had given him several headaches over the past few weeks, and today's revelation wasn't helping matters.

"Gentlemen," Kelsey said with just a touch of annoyance, "how is it that a highly classified piece of hardware can just be shipped out of here?"

"Well, Ms. Newton, that has become a long and interesting story," Mosley replied. "One that has occupied much of Dan's and my attention over the past few months."

"We're investigating the murder of a CIA technician that occurred last December. This technician's involvement in several classified projects, including the Spyder"—Harmon pointed to the brochure—"left us wondering just what he was up to. We've been able to link him to a pair of suspected industrial spies, and your discovery strengthens the likelihood that he helped these people acquire control of a Spyder."

"This just keeps gettin' better and better," Nolan said in disgust.

"You can say that again," Kelsey agreed.

"We understand your frustration, but I think we've reached the point where we can go on the offensive." Mosley had read Kilkenny's service record and guessed that he didn't like being limited only to reacting against an opponent. "Bill is already hard at work on a couple of little toys for us."

Iverson sat up in his seat, resting his forearms on the conference table. "The program dump you ran told us a lot, but it also told our opposition that we're looking at the Spyder. Before you two head back to Ann Arbor, I'm going to provide you with another little black box that'll let you bypass the Spyder's internal security. This will give us a clear picture of what they're doing without tipping our hand. Once you get it in place, we'll dump the real operating program to see what's what."

"What's the second little toy?" Newton asked.

"Before we knew that we were dealing with a Spyder operation, Harmon's associates in Detroit were trying to trace your hacker the old-fashioned way." Iverson took some measure of pride in the success his creation had enjoyed to date, even if the Spyder was being run by criminals. "Now that Cal and Dan are tying their investigation to your problem, you can use some of *our* techniques. I've read the Detroit office's report. The Spyder's using anonymous E-mail addresses as dead-letter drops, which prevents us from making a direct connection to the people controlling the device. That's standard operating procedure for the Spyder. The FBI has gotten permission to install a Gatekeeper at each of the known Internet servers being used as Spyder drops. With a few modifications, we'll be able to track these guys right back to where they live."

"I'd appreciate it if the two of you would clear your calendars for next week, from Wednesday on." Mosley's suggestion was polite but emphatic. "The DCI is holding court at Langley with all the key players on this investigation. Due to your unusual involvement, you've been invited."

"We'll be there," Kelsey replied for them both.

Kilkenny felt good about the direction things were heading and that they would finally start to track down the thieves who'd invaded his computer.

Chapter 35

"That's Kilkenny's car, and Newton is with him," Kang announced as the deep blue Mustang drove away from the old Hinsdale farmhouse.

Behind the smoked glass of the van, Vince Falk studied the car as it turned the corner and headed toward the tollway. The car and its passengers matched the information that had come with the retainer for his services.

When asked, Falk described himself as an independent contractor, a freelance troubleshooter of sorts. The kind of trouble he shot was exclusively human.

"Let's go," Falk said to his driver.

The van and a battered pickup truck pulled out of the parking lot, where they had waited most of the morning, and began following Kilkenny's car.

Falk leaned back in his seat with a map, looking over the route between Chicago and Ann Arbor. Two days earlier, a valued client had contacted him with an urgent assignment. The client, an Asian with strong ties to the Far East drug trade, tripled his usual fee. He didn't like rush jobs, preferring to set his own schedules, but the man was willing to pay and the assignment didn't look too difficult. The only unusual aspect of this job was the observer, a man he knew only as Mr. Deng, who sat quietly in the front passenger seat, watching the Mustang. Falk hoped that he would stay quiet and out of the way for the remainder of their trip.

The target was a young couple who were in Chicago at the time of the call and would be returning to Ann Arbor today. The client refrained from giving any reason for wanting the couple eliminated, and Falk knew enough not to pry into the man's business affairs.

The drive east had been pleasant, with fair weather and light traffic easing the four-hour journey. Between Jackson and Ann Arbor, Nolan's Mustang approached a stretch of road under repair on I-94. A temporary road sign warned that the construction zone would start in four miles and that all vehicles should merge into the left lane.

Kent Smith and Joe Hooks were making good time today. The pair of short-haul truckers were ferrying another load of premium blended fuel to the gas stations along the Kalamazoo–Ann Arbor corridor. At this rate, they'd be done early today and on their way home while it was still light. A few weeks from now, during the Memorial Day weekend, they both knew they'd be lucky to finish this run by midnight. Hooks was riding in the passenger's seat as he gazed at the deep blue Mustang.

"Sharp car, huh?" Hooks asked as their truck pulled ahead of the pony car.

Smith took another quick glance at the car in the truck's right-side mirror. "I had one from the same year, but mine never looked that good."

Hooks leaned out his window to study the car, and the stunning blonde in the passenger seat, as they passed. When he noticed the Mustang's occupants looking back at him, he pointed at the car and nodded with respect. The Mustang's driver threw a short, friendly wave. "Cute girl in there, too."

"Hadn't noticed," Smith lied.

"Oh, to be young again." Hooks sighed as he settled back into his seat.

Falk switched on his radio headset and called out to the driver of the pickup. "Jack, you awake back there?"

"I'm up," the crackling voice answered Falk's summons.

"Good, we're approaching the construction zone. Time to isolate the target."

"I'm in position."

Falk watched the Mustang merge left, behind the fuel truck, as they approached the construction zone. His driver punched the accelerator, passing the Mustang on the inside. Falk's van pulled up just beyond the Mustang's front end and began jockeying to merge.

"I don't believe this guy," Nolan growled. "He comes flying up from behind, trying to beat everyone into the merging lane, and he expects me just to let him in when he cuts it too close."

"Aren't you going to let him in?" Kelsey asked nervously as she watched the van trying to nudge itself into their lane. "It looks like he's trying to squeeze over."

"He's a jerk, so he can wait."

Nolan gave the accelerator pedal a slight nudge and the gap between the Mustang and the truck closed to three feet. The van's driver flipped Nolan the finger and roared ahead.

Kelsey sighed with relief when the van passed. "That guy is one serious asshole."

"Yeah, it's a shame they don't test for that when you get your license."

"Sorry, Vince," Falk's driver apologized.

"Not your fault. We'll just have to improvise. Merge in front of this truck and slow down once the road narrows to one lane." The van roared ahead and cut over with only fifty feet remaining in the merging lane.

"Jack, are you still in position?"

The pickup driver's voice crackled back in Falk's headset: "I'm right behind him."

The two eastbound lanes of the highway narrowed to one that was then channeled across the median and onto the westbound side of the road. A temporary concrete barrier was all that separated the two single lanes of opposing traffic. With a concrete wall to the left and a construction zone to the right, most drivers on the twelve-foot-wide strip of road felt like they were running a gauntlet. Nolan eased back on his accelerator, widening the gap between the truck and his beloved pony car. A beat-up red pickup truck closed in from behind, its grille filling the Mustang's rearview mirror.

Nolan glanced in his mirror at the tailgating pickup

truck. "I wonder if that guy is related to that jerk who passed us."

Kelsey eased her seat back. "Why?"

"No reason. He's just riding my rear close enough to kiss me, and I'd hate to see him mess up my chrome."

The freeway wasn't very busy, which provided Falk with the best possible conditions for the hit.

The driver in the red pickup responded to Falk's request by reaching out through his rear window to locate the quick-release fittings that held a set of cables tightly over the load of hay bales in the pickup's flatbed. He twisted the fittings and the cables sprang loose. Almost immediately, the bales began bouncing and shifting freely. The driver then ran the pickup over a few nasty potholes, and his load of bales tumbled onto the highway.

"We're all set back here," Jack reported once the lane of traffic behind him screeched to a halt.

"Good work," Falk replied. "Watch for your cue to bump and grind."

Falk nodded to his driver, who slowed the van to forty miles per hour. In minutes, a quarter-mile-long gap opened between the van and the next car on the road ahead; the four-vehicle procession was completely isolated on the one-lane stretch of highway.

Falk fed a clip into his silenced semiautomatic pistol and flipped the safety off. "Keep the van steady while I take out this truck."

"I wonder what that bonehead's problem is," Hooks muttered bitterly. "First he races up to cut us off and now he's slowing to a crawl. See if you can get him back up to the speed limit."

Smith narrowed the gap between his rig and the van

and flashed the high beams. "Maybe I can encourage him to pick up the pace."

As the van drew close to the truck's front bumper, the rear doors swung open and the truckers saw the gunman.

"Holy shit!" Hooks yelled. "Back off, Kent!"

The truck's gears ground in protest as Smith downshifted and braked. "You don't have to tell me twice. I just hope the bastard doesn't shoot."

Falk balanced himself carefully on the van's rear deck and took aim. His first burst ripped into the front wheel on the driver's side of the truck. The tire disintegrated into a hundred pieces of rubber. The truck's cab shuddered and lurched into the concrete barrier, sending a shower of sparks onto a car in the westbound lane. Falk watched as the wide-eyed driver fought furiously to bring his rig under control. He then aimed at the truck's remaining front wheel, shredding it as easily as the first.

"Nolan, watch out!" Kelsey screamed as the first pieces of the shredded tires pelted the Mustang like blackened hail.

"I see it," Nolan replied with a focused calm. "He must have had a blowout. Hang on!"

Kilkenny's white-knuckled hands were locked on the wheel as he tried to avoid the flying debris and distance himself from the damaged truck. He braked, only to feel his car suddenly lurch forward. Kelsey jerked in her seat again as the pickup struck from behind a second time.

As the semi's trailer bounced off the barrier and ricocheted to the open side of the road, the pickup rammed the Mustang from behind at full speed. The car's taillights

shattered and the deck lid crumpled from the impact with
the pickup's concrete-filled steel-pipe bumper. The rear
window of the Mustang exploded in a spray of glass fragments.

The pickup backed off and then accelerated again,
ramming the pony car into the gap between the flailing
semi's trailer and the concrete barrier. The Mustang's
metal skin howled as the trailer's rear bumper tore into
the passenger door, dragging the car against the concrete
barricade.

Back and forth Smith fought, trying to bring his crippled
rig under control. He was down to thirty miles per hour,
but it felt more like three hundred. He didn't know what
kind of nut would do something like this, but he planned
to kill the one directly in front of him. His trailer started
to swing again and Smith compensated, struggling to
keep his rig upright and on the road. Behind, he felt a
strange tugging, as if his trailer had gotten caught in
something.

"Nolan!"

Kelsey's frantic scream was cut short by a second collision between the semi's rear wheel carriage and the passenger side of the Mustang. The Mustang's passenger
door caved in, showering her with glass from the wind-
shield and door. The trailer's rear bumper speared
through the Mustang's left side, just behind the door, and
locked the two vehicles together. Nolan and Kelsey were
nearly jarred from their seats when the semi's trailer
pounded the car against the construction barriers.

Kilkenny's shoulder burned with pain after bouncing
off his door. Kelsey was flung forward with the impact,
her head connecting with the dashboard before she

snapped back into her seat, unconscious. Were it not for her seat belt, she would have been thrown across the hood to her death. Kilkenny held on to the wheel, but he had no control over where his car was going.

"Shit! Shit! Shit!" Hooks screamed as the entire rig shuddered and nearly jackknifed.

The semi's nose skipped off the concrete roadway and dug itself into the soft sand of the shoulder. As the front bumper burrowed deep into the ground, the trailer snapped outward like a whip into the median. The semi's sudden stop sent the fuel inside the tanker rushing forward in a violent swirl that shifted the trailer's weight off its wheels and into a roll.

As the trailer rolled right, its rear bumper lifted the right side of the Mustang off the road. Nolan leaned inward as the roof of his car scraped along the concrete barrier. Halfway into the roll, the trailer's bumper pulled loose, leaving the Mustang upended on the driver's side.

The fuel trailer, still three-quarters' full, continued to roll as the liquid inside shifted with the momentum of the turn. Hooks and Smith didn't have time to recover from the jarring stop when their rig rolled onto the gravel bed created for the highway's refurbished eastbound lanes. Sand and gravel flew into the air as the semi's nose was pulled free from the ground by the roll. The cylindrical fuel tank ruptured when it struck the ground, pouring hundreds of gallons of fuel into the median.

Gasoline flowed like a waterfall from the broken tanker and soaked into the ground surrounding the overturned rig. A wave of fuel rushed down toward the cab, where it splashed against the semi's hot, twisted exhaust stacks. Flames flashed instantly across the surface of the growing pond of gasoline, until they reached the fumes contained inside the ruptured tanker. The explosion sent a billowing yellow-black fireball into the sky. Hooks and Smith died instantly in the blast—their bodies trapped and incinerated inside the overturned rig.

The Mustang rocked from the blast, shaken enough that it fell back onto its wheels. Kelsey slumped lifelessly in the seat beside Nolan, blood visible from the cuts on her face and arms. Nolan was still groggy from the crash, but he didn't need to move to feel the bruises that covered his entire body. The pain in his head told him that his skull had bounced off something hard, but at least he was still alive.

He tried to survey the scene outside his car, but his eyes were watery and his vision blurred by the salty blood that flowed from his forehead. Flames and smoke billowed from the fuel truck and he could feel the intense heat of the blaze. Both doors were jammed, and he hoped that his car was far enough away from the inferno. A van stopped on the road ahead and a person got out and started walking toward them. Help was on the way.

Falk didn't bother to check on the two truckers trapped inside the burning rig; they were already dead. All that remained was to verify that the couple was dead and leave before the police arrived. If they were still alive, he'd finish the job. The hay bales they'd dropped had stopped traffic several miles back from the accident scene, and he figured that he had about two minutes to escape unobserved.

Kilkenny watched the man's approach—it was cautious, but pointed directly at the battered Mustang. Nolan was ready to call out when he noticed the elongated pistol in the man's left hand. Even in his battered state, he knew that Good Samaritans didn't carry silenced weapons. Kilkenny remained motionless, watching through the slits of his eyes as the stranger advanced.

Falk studied the two forms inside the Mustang carefully as he approached. The passenger was slumped forward, almost on her knees. The driver lay back against his seat, with one arm hanging out the battered door. Both looked dead from where he stood, but he needed to confirm the kill before he could collect the rest of his fee.

He walked over to the driver's side, shuffling sideways in the narrow space between the car and the barrier, and placed two fingers on Kilkenny's neck.

With a swift motion, Kilkenny's left arm shot up from the door and hammered a pressure point in Falk's forearm just below the elbow. The nerves in Falk's arm flared with pain for a moment before going completely numb from the blow. Before Falk could react, Kilkenny flipped his fist over and drove it upward into the assassin's jaw. Kilkenny's fist glanced off Falk's chin and continued upward, where it connected solidly with his nose. Blood and tears flowed around Falk's eyes as the fragile bones shattered.

Falk rocked back, dizzy and partially blinded by the blow to his face. Blood hammered around his skull, which throbbed with pain. Kilkenny reached out with his right arm and grabbed Falk's weapon hand, pulling the killer against the car with a quick, violent motion. Falk's chest and abdomen bounced off the door, the air bursting from his lungs on impact. Despite the blow, Falk still held on to his weapon.

Gasping for breath, Falk threw his right forearm across Kilkenny's face and drew back his weapon to fire.

Kilkenny slammed both of Falk's arms up violently into the car's roof; the blow knocked the pistol from the killer's hand and into the Mustang's rear seat. Falk's belt buckle glistened with the fire's reflection, a glowing target through the shattered window of Kilkenny's door. Pinning Falk's arms with his left forearm, Kilkenny struck just above the killer's groin with the flat palm of his right hand. The angle and force of Kilkenny's attack lifted Falk several inches off the ground, jamming him against the concrete barrier. Falk's pelvis made an audible snap as it cracked in two and twisted against the tail of his spine.

Falk staggered as his body lost all its strength. Shock would soon give way to unconsciousness and finally death from internal bleeding. Kilkenny locked eyes with the killer as the last flickers of understanding died out and the penetrating stare glazed over. Falk's body went limp and Kilkenny released his hold, letting the unconscious form slide to the ground.

The wind shifted and sent a black curl of oily smoke over the Mustang and across Kilkenny's face. The eddies and whorls seemed to drift with an unnatural sluggishness to Kilkenny, who was in a deeply focused mind-set, his warrior one. All his senses were charged.

He'd eliminated one threat and was searching for any others through the haze. His search stopped on what he thought was a person in the road ahead. The figure stood motionless, fading in and out of Kilkenny's vision as the billowing clouds of blackened smoke passed between them. He tried hard to focus clearly on the figure, but the air around him seemed to thicken as the smoke mixed with steam from the Mustang's cracked radiator.

Kilkenny's eyes burned as he tried to stare through the smoke and blood that obscured his vision. He began to suspect what he saw was simply a mirage, when the wind shifted and the smoke began to clear. Not ten feet from Kilkenny stood an Asian man staring directly back at him. The man made no move toward him, but Kilkenny felt an intense rage, as if they were sworn enemies. He'd never seen the man before, but, like Etienne Masson, the man's hatred filled the space between them.

He wiped his bloodied face with his sleeve to get a better look, but, as soon as he cleared his eyes, the man was gone. Kilkenny looked around quickly, but he found no sign of the man.

The driver of the pickup rushed past the battered Mustang and fled in the killer's van. Nolan was unable to make out the van's license number as it sped away. Seeing no other dangers, he turned and cradled Kelsey in his arms.

Chapter 36

Michigan state trooper Jean Gordon was approaching the area where several bales of hay had stopped traffic, when she saw the fireball rise over the crest in the road ahead. She pulled onto the shoulder, to drive around the growing line of cars stopped there, and sped toward the explosion.

"This is car forty-one–five. I have a large explosion on I-Ninety-four near mile marker one forty-nine, and I am moving to investigate. We're going to need fire and medical teams and additional units to block off the highway in both directions. Do you copy, base? Over."

"We copy, forty-one–five," the dispatcher at the Jackson State Police post responded. "Additional units are en route to your position. Please advise when you reach the scene."

"Roger, base. Forty-one–five, out."

Gordon slowed as she approached the accident. She

could make out three vehicles in the cloud of swirling smoke: a battered car, a pickup truck, and an overturned tanker that was engulfed in flames.

"Forty-one–five to base, over," Gordon called out on her radio.

"Go ahead, forty-one–five."

"I have a multivehicle accident blocking eastbound I-Ninety-four. One vehicle is a gasoline tanker that is burning. We're going to need a *lot* of help out here."

"Understood, forty-one–five. Additional support is on the way."

Survival Flight lead pilot Dean Waters had just rescued the POWs from the enemy prison camp and was racing his helicopter across the desert sands of the Middle East when his pager began beeping furiously. He paused the game on his computer, grabbed his flight bag, and sprinted out of the basement-level offices housing the University of Michigan's Survival Flight Service. Waters ran past the elevators, bounded up four flights of stairs, and quickly emerged on the rooftop lobby of the Taubman Center, next to the helipad.

"What do we have?" he asked as he reached the dispatcher.

"MVA out on I-Ninety-four, a nasty one," the dispatcher replied. "Two passenger vehicles and a fuel truck. We've got two injured and the truck is burning. Here are your maps with possible landing zones. Your contact on the scene is a state trooper named Gordon. You can reach her on this frequency. Byrd and Landis are already on the pad."

Waters nodded. "Our patients are in good hands today. Let's get to it."

Waters walked out to the Bell 230 medical helicopter, where the two flight nurses were loading supplies. "A lovely day to fly, don't you think?"

"We're ready when you are," Landis replied as Byrd climbed aboard.

Waters boarded the helicopter and strapped in. Landis and Byrd took positions in the rear, linking up with the on-call physician in the emergency room. After running through the preflight check, Waters powered up the helicopter and opened the throttles on the Bell's engines. The helicopter responded with a near-deafening roar as the rotors chopped through the air. Waters increased the angle on the main rotor blades and lifted the helicopter off the helipad.

As soon as the helicopter reached its cruising altitude, Waters saw where they were headed. A plume of black smoke smeared the horizon, creating a hazy filter over the late-day sun. The winds were light, out of the south, with visibility that was measured in miles. Waters estimated this would be a fifteen-minute trip to the accident scene. In the seat behind him, Landis made contact with the state police officer on the scene.

Five miles east of the crash, Waters flew over the start of a long traffic jam. I-94 would be closed for a while and everyone parked below would be better off finding an alternate route. He banked the helicopter into a wide circle around the smoke plume as he looked for a place to land that was free of fuel. A smooth patch of gravel, just upwind of the burning truck, met his needs nicely. Below, paramedics fed Byrd and Landis status reports on the survivors.

Once on the ground, the flight nurses bolted from the helicopter. Two firemen met them at the door to help with their medical gear. Waters kept the chopper warmed up and ready to move once the patients were on board.

"How are they?" Landis asked a paramedic by the car.

"One's unconscious, with possible internal injuries. The other one's banged up, but not too badly. The doors on the car are a mess, so we'll have to tear them off. Both of these people have been bounced around a lot, but the woman took the worst of it."

The firemen were working their Jaws of Life on the passenger-side door of the Mustang. The car's steel skin and frame groaned as the hydraulic pressure increased inside the device, tearing away at the crumpled metal of the car. Landis quickly glanced at the black body bag on the ground, a few feet away from the Mustang, before squeezing into the narrow space beside the driver's door. The driver was bruised and bloodied as he held the unconscious woman beneath a protective cover that the firemen had placed over her.

"Sir," Landis said as she placed her hand on Kilkenny's shoulder, "my name is Michelle. I'm here to help you. Can you tell me how you're feeling?"

Kilkenny turned toward the voice and saw a woman in a dark blue flight suit. "To be honest, I feel like shit, but I'm alive, so I guess that's a start. I'm Nolan Kilkenny and this is Kelsey Newton. I can't say for sure how she's doing, but Kelsey's been out for a while, and she doesn't look too good. We took a hell of a shot from that semi before it rolled."

Byrd was now on the Mustang's hood, assessing Newton's condition while Landis checked Kilkenny's vital signs and kept him talking. The metal of the car's door groaned loudly before releasing its hold and pulling free from the car. Byrd moved over to the opened side and began treating Newton. Kilkenny eased away to give Byrd room to work, but his hand remained firmly wrapped around Newton's.

Landis gently wiped away the blood from Kilkenny's face to inspect the gash across his forehead. "Can you tell me what happened?"

"The fuel truck blew a tire and started jumping all over the road. A pickup rammed us from behind, and we got hit by the back end of that burning hunk of junk."

Landis placed a dressing on his forehead. "Sounds awful."

"It got worse," Kilkenny replied.

The EMTs cut Newton out of her safety belt and eased her gently onto a backboard. Her slender neck was already wrapped in a cervical collar and a breathing tube was inserted down her throat. Byrd rolled out a pair of MAST pants and zipped them up around Newton's legs; the inflatable device acting as both a splint for any broken bones and as an antishock aid for the trip back to Ann Arbor. After setting an IV, Byrd and an EMT hustled Newton to the waiting helicopter.

"All things considered, you're looking pretty good," Landis commented as she packed up her kit. "I'm going to leave you with the EMTs; they'll get you to Ann Arbor. I've got a flight to catch with your lady friend."

"Take good care of her," Kilkenny asked as he squeezed Landis's hand. "She means a lot to me."

"We'll do our best for her," she assured him. "See you soon." A moment later, the helicopter bearing Newton lifted off into the sky.

Kilkenny's condition, though more stable than Newton's, was still considered serious. The paramedics gingerly extracted him from the driver's seat and strapped him to a backboard. A waiting ambulance rushed Kilkenny away from the hellish scene.

Chapter 37

Kilkenny awoke several hours after his arrival at University Hospital. The EMTs had given him a painkiller in the ambulance, and after that, everything seemed just a blur. Gradually, memories of the accident came back to him: the truck, the fire, and the man with the gun. And Kelsey.

He remembered Kelsey lying there beside him in the mangled car, covered in blood. He tried to sit up, but he was still sore and his eyes were swollen to narrow slits.

"Easy, Nolan. Save your strength," his father said quietly to him. He felt a firm hand on his shoulder. "You've had a rough ride, but you'll be fine."

"Dad, how's Kelsey?" Nolan asked with a raspy throat that felt parched.

"She's hurt pretty badly, but the doctors think she'll pull through. They finished up with her about an hour ago." Sean Kilkenny couldn't hide the concern he felt over the seriousness of Kelsey's condition.

Nolan took several short sips from a glass of ice water; the first few seemed to evaporate halfway down his throat. "Can I see her?"

"Tomorrow," his father advised, patting him on the leg for reassurance. "You both need your rest. Everything will be fine."

Exhausted from the effort, Nolan closed his eyes as the painkillers took hold once more and he drifted into an uneasy sleep.

It was almost two in the morning when he awoke again. His face still throbbed from the bruises, but the swelling around his eyes seemed to have receded a little. Slowly, Nolan eased himself off the hospital bed, carefully testing his strength. He found a gym bag that his father had left for him and with only a few muffled groans managed to change into a pair of sweats. He remembered only a handful of missions where he'd felt this bad afterward, and those pains were the result of self-inflicted hangovers.

At this hour of the night, most patients were asleep and the medical staff was at a minimum. Kilkenny quietly made his way down the empty hallway. He could hear one of the nurses attending to a patient as he passed, but he didn't know how many others would be on duty at this hour. Kilkenny quietly walked down the hallway, following the signs to the Intensive Care Unit.

Once inside the ICU, he found Kelsey's name written in bold black letters on the bed-assignment chart. He slid the curtain open slowly and only wide enough to squeeze inside before closing it again. If she was asleep, he didn't want the bright lights of the nurses' station to wake her.

Kelsey lay in the hospital bed with her upper body slightly elevated. Several tubes flowed to and from her body and one of the machines beside her bed made an ungodly hissing sound. Under the faint glow of the room's indirect lights, she looked so fragile.

Memories of his mother's final days returned in a painful flood of emotion. No, he thought, pushing the memories of that loss back, this is different. Kelsey will survive.

He approached the bed slowly, moving as quietly as he could, hoping not to disturb her. At her side, he grasped her hand and felt the warmth of the life still within her. Kelsey's face, now framed with sterile dressings instead of a flowing mane of blond hair, still radiated beauty and peace in her sleep. The guilt and responsibility Nolan felt over her injuries subsided as he memorized every detail of her exquisite face.

A sudden flash of light nearly blinded him, ending his quiet meditation. As his eyes adjusted to the light, he saw a woman silhouetted in a fluorescent halo.

"All right, Mr. Kilkenny," a hushed but stern voice called out to him like an arresting officer, "it's time for you to get back to bed."

The nurse was right, of course, but that still wouldn't have kept him from Kelsey's side tonight.

"You caught me, warden," Kilkenny said with his most charming smile. "I'll go peacefully. How's she doing?"

"They ran some tests on her, but the results won't be back until morning." The nurse closed the curtain around Kelsey's bed and escorted Kilkenny back to his room.

"Your parents warned us about you two. They said if either of you was missing, just go looking for the other."

"How's she doing?" Nolan asked more emphatically.

"She's in pretty rough shape," the nurse said gravely, "but I've seen cases much worse than hers make a full recovery. Only time will tell if there will be any lasting effect from her injuries. Now, if I catch you out of your room again tonight, I'm going to have to give you an icewater sponge bath."

"Don't worry, I'll be good," Kilkenny replied in surrender. "I haven't been treated like this since boot camp."

The nurse saw Kilkenny to his door, where he bid her a good night and walked back to his bed. The room was dark, as he had left it, but something seemed out of place. Throughout his years of martial arts and military training, Kilkenny had learned to use all his senses to protect himself, and those instincts were warning him that something was amiss. He slowly panned the room to see if he could detect whatever was triggering his defenses.

"I'm in the back corner," a familiar voice called out. It was Cal Mosley of the CIA. "Is the nurse back at her station?"

"Yeah, she's gone."

"Good, then turn on some lights in here so we can see each other. I gave up this skulking-around-in-the-dark shit years ago. Sorry if I startled you, but it is after normal visiting hours. I got here as soon as I could. How are you feeling?"

Kilkenny eased himself into his hospital bed and flipped on the reading light. "I've been better."

"I don't doubt that." Mosley looked Kilkenny square in the eyes. "I was quite relieved to hear that you and Ms. Newton survived. This business of ours is getting ugly, which is why I'm here in the middle of the night arranging security for you and the professor. Your 'accident' was anything but. You were set up. The state police ran the shooter's fingerprints against the FBI database and they found a match. The guy you took out was a high-priced hit man, the kind crime bosses like to use when they want a neat job with no questions."

"Somebody paid to have Kelsey and me killed?"

"Looks that way. The FBI is assisting the state police regarding your accident and we consider it officially part of our investigation. We've found the getaway van near the airport, completely burned out. Not much left of the two guys who were in it, either. The van was stolen, of course, but we've got a few other leads to follow up on. We're getting warm, Nolan—I can feel it. I'm just sorry you and Kelsey had to prove our theories the hard way."

Kilkenny took in everything Mosley was telling him. It bothered him to know that there were people willing to kill to prevent the loss of the Spyder. "Is your director's meeting still on for Wednesday?"

"If you're up to it, but don't push yourself." Mosley handed Nolan a business card. "Here's my number while I'm in town. If you need anything, just call. Take it easy, Nolan. I'll be in touch."

Chapter 38

Throbbing knots of pain that seemed to fill every muscle in his body roused Kilkenny from a restless sleep. It was early in the evening, about half past six. A nurse, noticing that he was awake, took his vitals and changed his dressings. Once cleaned up and fed, he picked up the bedside call button and rang the nurses' station.

"Mr. Kilkenny, how can I help you?" asked a petite young nurse, who didn't look old enough to be out of high school, as she entered his room.

"You can start by calling me Nolan. My father is Mr. Kilkenny, and I'm not old enough to deserve such formality."

"All right, *Nolan*." She giggled. "What do you need?"

"I'd like to see Kelsey Newton. Is she up for visitors?"

"I'll go find out."

The nurse returned a few minutes later and parked a wheelchair beside Kilkenny's bed.

"I take it that permission has been granted?"

The nurse laughed at her eager passenger as he sat in the chair. "Her exact words were, 'Get that lousy driver over here so I can give him a piece of my mind.'"

Nolan ran his hand across the stubble on his chin. "Maybe I ought to rethink this. . . ."

"It's too late to back out now. Her parents just left for dinner and you're next in line." The nurse spun the wheelchair around and whisked Kilkenny down the corridor.

When Nolan had last visited her, Kelsey had been in the Intensive Care Unit following her surgery. Her condition had improved enough to warrant a transfer to a private bed in the step-down unit. The nurse rolled Nolan into Kelsey's room and parked him beside her bed. Kelsey smiled as he arrived and held out her hand.

"Hey, gorgeous," Nolan said as he cupped her soft hand in his and gently kissed it, "how are you feeling?"

Kelsey's eyes stayed locked with his. "Not so good, but better now that you've come down to see me."

Nolan stroked her hand gently, almost unconsciously. "They couldn't keep me away."

"So I heard. One of the nurses told me about your visit last night. I thought I'd dreamt it, but I'm glad you came."

Nolan couldn't hold the smile any longer. He still felt responsible for her injuries. "Kelsey, I'm sorry about this."

"I don't blame you for the accident. It wasn't your fault. You were doing fine until that jerk rear-ended us. It was just an accident, one of those things."

"No, it wasn't," Nolan admitted quietly.

Kelsey just stared at him as he softly explained what had happened after she was knocked out, and as he related his conversation the previous night with Mosley. She could find no words to express what she was feeling. A random accident was tough enough to understand, but premeditated murder was unimaginable.

They'd had long talks like this before, after missions when he'd been forced to kill, when he needed someone to help sort it all out. When those conversations turned too morose, she always found humor to be a good way to get Nolan to snap back.

"I should have known you couldn't keep out of trouble after you left the navy," Kelsey said, shaking her finger at him. "Next time you decide to be heroic, let me know so I won't get in the car with you."

Nolan just looked blankly at her for a moment, then smiled. "If I start looking heroic again, let me know." Nolan paused; his smile was suddenly replaced by a look of panic. "Oh no!"

"What's the matter?" she asked, fearing something terrible.

"My car! I forgot all about it." Nolan grabbed the phone and dialed the number Mosley had given him.

"I don't believe you!" If she'd had the strength, she would have hit him. "We barely survived that crash, and you're worried about your damn car!"

"I don't love my Mustang nearly as much as I love you, but that's not what I'm thinking about."

Kelsey studied Nolan as he dialed, her hopes balanced less on what he was thinking and more on how he was apparently feeling toward her.

The phone rang several times before the line clicked, forwarding the call to another number.

"This is Cal Mosley."

"Cal, it's Nolan Kilkenny. Do you know if they recovered my gear from the car?"

"I'm not sure. Why?" Mosley then picked up on
Kilkenny's train of thought. "That's right, the Spyder bypass. I'll check with the police post in Jackson. The car's
still on their lot. Whatever you left in the car will be in
your father's office by morning."

"Thanks, Cal." Nolan's gaze didn't leave Kelsey, who
looked a little embarrassed for her assumption. "The
sooner we get that bypass in, the sooner we nail the bastards responsible for this."

"Sounds like you've got a reason to live. That's a
very healthy sign, Kilkenny. I think you'll pull through.
By the way, my boss sends his best wishes to you and the
professor for a speedy recovery and says he hopes that
you'll be in attendance on Wednesday."

"Barring armed guards at my door, I'll be there."
Nolan sounded like a man committed to a goal.

"Great, I'll call you tomorrow with the flight information." Mosley hung up and Nolan cradled the receiver.

"Excuse me," the nurse who had caught Nolan the
night before sternly announced from the doorway, "but
this patient is on *restricted* visiting hours. I'm afraid that
she's done for the day. Please say your good-byes."

Nolan started to turn his wheelchair when Kelsey
shook her head. "Nurse, I'd like another few minutes."

The nurse checked her watch and nodded. "Very
well, you have two minutes and not a second more. I'll be
back to escort Mr. Kilkenny to his room."

"Nolan," Kelsey asked, her voice low and uncertain,
"did you mean it?"

"Mean what?" He felt like an idiot for not knowing
what she was talking about.

"When you said that you loved me? I've never heard you say it before, not like that."

"I've always loved you. The worst part of our accident was seeing you lying there and fearing that you were dead."

Kelsey held out her hand, which Nolan grasped tightly. Tears glistened in both their eyes. "The doctors say I was probably unconscious right after the crash, but I would swear that I felt you holding me, protecting me."

"I did the best I could. I'm sorry it wasn't enough."

"We're both still alive. I think you did great." She took hold of his hand as he stared into her iridescent blue eyes. "I've never had the courage to say anything before. I've just been so afraid that if I tried to change our relationship, to make it into something more than it is, I'd lose what we already have." Kelsey blushed at her own honesty.

Nolan agreed with what she'd said about their relationship. He'd grown up with Kelsey, and he had a difficult time thinking of her romantically, thinking of her as something other than family. It now became clear to him that there was nothing wrong with thinking of Kelsey in a different sense, as family.

"Kelsey, I don't want you to be afraid to love me. I'm not afraid to love you."

Nolan rose from the wheelchair, leaned over, and kissed her gently. She turned her head slightly and returned his kiss, full on the lips. The kiss was gentle, slow, and passionate. It was not the kiss of old friends; it was the kiss of new lovers.

A forced cough from the impatient nurse brought an end to the kiss. "That's enough, you two. Scat, Mr. Kilkenny, or I'll have to hose you off. This is a hospital, not Club Med. Ms. Newton needs her beauty sleep, and, Lord knows, you could use some, too."

"I guess I am a sight for sore eyes."

"And I've got the sore eyes for looking at you, Kelsey. I'll see you in the morning. Sweet dreams." Nolan sat down in the wheelchair and rolled toward the nurse standing guard at the door. "Have you ever considered a career in the military? I know some people who could use a tough drill instructor."

The nurse laughed as she grabbed the back of the wheelchair and rolled him out of the room. Their banter trailed down the corridor as Kelsey closed her eyes. She was still shaking, not believing her sudden bravery at exposing her feelings to Nolan. Since January, they'd spent more time with each other than anyone else, and, in recent months, that time had become the highlight of her day. Nolan was a kind, thoughtful, and intelligent man, and in him she found something she'd never found in anyone else: love. A smile lingered on her still-moist lips as she drifted into sleep.

Chapter 39

May 4

Sean Kilkenny picked up his son at the hospital's main entrance, which overlooked the Huron River Valley. Spring was in full bloom and the view of the river, as it flowed along the Nichols Arboretum, was spectacular.

"Ready to go home?" he asked as he tossed Nolan's overnight bag in the back of his Explorer.

Nolan thanked the orderly who had wheeled him down and then climbed in the passenger side. "I'm ready to get out of here, if that's what you mean."

"I understand. After my recent experiences with your mother, I'm not too fond of hospitals, either. Are you interested in stopping by MARC before we head home? I've got a few things I'd like to take care of, if you feel up to it."

"Sure, I want to check in with Grin anyway. Say, did Mosley get my gear out of the wreck?"

"Yes, right after he swore Grin and me to secrecy over this whole mess."

"Good, he got you both in the loop. I hope the bypass is still in one piece. I don't want to make another trip to Chicago just yet."

"I wouldn't think so," Sean agreed. "I've been meaning to ask you about that, Nolan. Grin is a brilliant young man and a very hard worker, but when I asked him to explain what you and Kelsey were after, I got a dissertation about ten levels higher than I could comprehend."

Nolan could easily picture Grin soaring way past his father with the intricate details of neural-network systems—not a topic for the faint of heart. "Grin's a little wired about the whole thing. I admit, it's a very interesting situation we've found ourselves in, and that little black box in Kelsey's lab is an exciting topic of discussion all on its own."

Nolan filled the remainder of the ten-minute ride with a layman's tour of Spyder technology, which was everything he'd gleaned from Iverson during his visit to Moy Electronics. The narrative continued with the CIA's current theory on how this Spyder had come to Ann Arbor and who was now controlling it. Sean Kilkenny pulled his truck into the MARC parking lot, stopped in his usual space, and sat behind the wheel, digesting what he'd heard.

"So we're not dealing with some kid joyriding a PC through our computer; we're up against some damned industrial spies."

"Sure looks that way, Dad."

As they entered the MARC building, the receptionist flagged them down. "Nolan, Cal Mosley just called for you."

"I'll phone him from the lab." Nolan then looked over his other message slips and stuffed them in his pocket. "Where's my stuff, Dad?"

"In my office."

Kilkenny searched through his dark blue Eddie Bauer bag for the box that Iverson had given him on Sunday. His soft-sided bag didn't look all that bad, considering the rough ride it had been through in the Mustang's trunk. He found the box still well protected by his clothing and completely intact.

"It takes a licking; let's hope it keeps on ticking. I'll be down in the lab."

"Just let me know when you're ready to go home, son."

In the MARC computer lab, Grin was hard at work running a system diagnostic. It was a tedious procedure that more often bored the system administrator to death while it ran. True to form, Grin sat back, his feet propped up on the main console, reading a book on the mythologies of early man. The cover illustration of a ceramic Earth Mother caught Kilkenny's eye.

"What are you reading there, Grin, a five-thousand-year-old *Playboy*?"

Grin's focus shifted upward from his book to cast a look of disdain in Kilkenny's direction. "Thank you for that commentary from the culturally illiterate. You may now crawl back into your dark corner and warm yourself by the glow of your television." His stern look broke into a wide smile as he got up to greet Kilkenny. "Good to see you back, man, but geez, you look terrible."

"Really, I hadn't noticed. But enough of this pleasant chitchat. Are you ready to go to work?" Kilkenny held up the box of Iverson's special hardware.

"You bet." Grin shared Kilkenny's enthusiasm for taking on their unwanted intruder. "Mosley briefed me about that thing in your lab, and you'll be happy to know that it's been very quiet all weekend."

Kilkenny was looking forward to putting a computerized noose around the stainless-steel rat that had infested his lab, though he would have preferred putting the real thing around the necks of those responsible for it being there. "Let's see what we can discover about our friendly little Spyder."

Like the Spyder, Iverson's bypass was a simple black cube equipped with connector ports for external communications lines. Grin brought the Cray off-line while Kilkenny powered down the experimental optical processor. They followed the standard procedure so the Spyder would be unaware of a sudden severing of its communication link to the university network. Grin joined Kilkenny in the latter's lab after the system successfully shut down.

"Well, Dr. Grin, the patient is under. Shall we perform surgery?"

"I'd prefer to use a hammer, Dr. Kilkenny, but I'll be happy to assist you."

"Excellent." Kilkenny held out an open hand. "Phillips screwdriver, please."

The procedure took only fifteen minutes, in which Kilkenny mated the bypass to the Spyder. Once connected, the bypass would provide complete access to the Spyder's program and a view on everything that the device was doing. The bypass tied in exactly as Iverson had promised and, after double-checking all the connections, they brought the optical processor back on-line.

Grin returned to the main lab and scanned the MARC network screens and his message file. "The network is up and running again, with only a few users bitching about the downtime."

"If they don't like our service," Nolan replied, "they can just take their business elsewhere."

Grin laughed hard enough that Kilkenny didn't need the speaker phone to hear him. Both men knew that the MARC computer lab was one of the finest supercomputer facilities in the country, and one of only a few in the Midwest that was available to outside researchers.

"Don't let your old man hear you talking that unbusinesslike trash. After all, we exist to serve our customers."

"Thank you for that 'total quality' reminder, Mr. Demming. Now let's see what our unwelcome guest is really made of."

Kilkenny unwound a patch cable and connected his laptop computer to the interface connection on the bypass module. After loading the communications software that Iverson had provided, he accessed the joint memory of the two black cubes. A menu of options appeared on the laptop's monochrome screen.

"Hmm, what to do first," Kilkenny mused while looking over his options. "I think I'll request a listing of the Spyder's operating code."

"Hold on," Grin's voice called out from the speaker. "Let me get over there and pull up a chair. I'd love to see what makes this thing tick."

Grin perched himself on the lab bench as Nolan made the request. Almost at once, the drive light on the laptop flashed on to indicate that information was flowing down the portable computer's hard disk. A few minutes later, the download finished and Nolan checked the size of the file.

"Boy, that program is a hog!"

Grin glanced down to the bottom of the screen, where a status line showed only twenty-two megabytes of disk space remaining on the laptop. "Good thing you had some room to spare. What now?"

"If you'd be so kind as to bring that phone line over here, I'm going to transmit this file to Bill Iverson at Moy."

Grin disconnected the phone and handed the line to Kilkenny. "Why not use the network? We've got a line into Moy, and it'll go a lot faster than your modem."

"This is why," Kilkenny replied, pointing at the Spyder. "Big Brother is watching us. Here, call the number on this business card; it's Iverson's direct line. He knows your name; just tell him you're with me and that we're sending him the Spyder program."

Grin slipped the card into his shirt pocket and began walking back to the main lab. "I'll be sure to tell him to have plenty of disk space free."

"I think he'll know what to expect."

Grin made the call and, once Iverson was ready, Kilkenny began transmitting the file. Even with high-speed modems, the transfer took almost twenty minutes. Iverson signaled Kilkenny over the modem line that the download was successful. With that program in hand, Iverson could dissect the instructions that the Spyder's controllers used to manipulate the device.

Grin returned to the lab as Kilkenny was reconnecting the phone. "What now?"

"Wait and watch. This bypass will allow us to keep a closer eye on the Spyder than our jury-rigged laptop, and I'll find out more about what happens next when I go to D.C. That reminds me—I'd better give Mosley a call."

A mischievous smile appeared beneath Grin's pointed goatee as he sat down in front of Kilkenny's laptop. "Well, while I'm just sitting around, maybe I'll just take a little peek at that thing's fancy hacker program."

"Grin, the Spyder is classified *so high* that no one in the government will even acknowledge that it exists."

The tone in Kilkenny's voice caused Grin to pause and turn in his swivel chair toward him. Kilkenny stood with his arms folded across his chest and a look of dead earnest on his face.

"Let me give you a little fair warning, as one who knows firsthand about government secrets. Don't let so much as one byte of that program out of this room or you and I might both find ourselves living in some dark hole in the ground."

"I know, I know." Grin pressed his hands against his heart with false sincerity. "Mosley read me the riot act yesterday. Rest assured, not one government secret will pass from my lips."

Kilkenny accepted Grin's word. "That said, let's take a crack at it; I'm just as curious as you are about how they accomplished this. Also, see if you can stash a copy somewhere for future reference. I expect that once this is all over, we'll be asked to turn over all materials related to the Spyder."

Grin's jaw dropped slightly before curling back into a smile. "Nolan Kilkenny, you sneaky devil! You read my mind."

"Great minds think alike, as they say."

Kilkenny picked up the phone and dialed the number that Mosley had left with the MARC receptionist. After two rings, a receptionist answered and informed him that he'd reached the Detroit office of the FBI.

"Nolan Kilkenny calling for Cal Mosley, please."

The operator put Kilkenny on hold as she made the connection.

"How are you feeling, Nolan?" Mosley asked, his gravelly voice booming over the phone.

"Been better, but I can't complain. What are you doing at the FBI?"

"The kind folks at the Bureau loaned me a little desk in the corner while I was in town. It's not as cozy as my rabbit hole at Langley, but it beats working out of a hotel room."

"Very true. I've got two things I wanted to talk to you about. First, Iverson's bypass is in place and working as advertised. I've already dumped the Spyder's operating program and sent it off to Chicago."

"Good work. The FBI agents you were working with are out making the installations at the Internet servers. They should be back in Detroit on Thursday to monitor the situation with the Spyder."

"Grin will like that. I think he's kind of sweet on Harbke."

"I heard that, Nolan!" Grin shouted back, loudly enough for Mosley to hear. "My relationship with Special Agent Harbke is strictly professional."

"I stand corrected. Grin is interested only in Agent Harbke's mind and has taken no notice of her other attributes."

Mosley's laugh roared through the receiver as a wadded-up ball of computer printouts struck Kilkenny's chest.

"I may be a gentleman, but I am not blind."

Kilkenny threw his hands up for a cease-fire. "All right, Grin. I won't speculate about your love life anymore."

"Thank you very much." With a curt nod, Grin accepted Kilkenny's surrender and sat down. "Now I can get back to work."

"That's a strange guy you're working with, Kilkenny," Mosley observed.

"Grin is definitely a book you shouldn't judge by its cover. The man is brilliant, but not without his eccentricities."

"So I've noticed," Mosley agreed. "What was the second thing you wanted to discuss?"

"The Washington trip. What's the plan?"

"We're booked on Northwest flight one oh two two, a nonstop from Detroit to Washington leaving tomorrow morning at seven-forty-five. Bring any notes or material that you might think helpful. The DCI is a very inquisitive man, and he's been known to grill guests at meetings like these. I expect that he'll want to hear about your experience with the Spyder."

"I'll see what I can scrounge up," Kilkenny promised. "See you in the morning."

Chapter 40

Washington, D.C.
May 5

The flight arrived at Dulles on schedule, and Mosley and Kilkenny were met outside the arrival area by a CIA driver, who then collected their bags and drove them out into the Virginia countryside. After clearing security and outfitting Kilkenny with visitor's credentials, Mosley guided him through the CIA's labyrinth. The office building was packed like a beehive, with every inch of available space occupied by a desk or work surface. Mosley explained that most of this wing's activities revolved around information analysis, the molding of raw data into something intelligible. The James Bond side of the business, Operations, was located elsewhere in the sprawling campus.

After an elevator ride to the seventh floor, they entered a conference room that was nearly full of guests and sat down near FBI agents Harbke, Ullrich, and Harmon.

The conference room buzzed with the sound of several conversations going on simultaneously—a sense of urgency building among the participants. A well-dressed man with graying hair entered the room, flanked by a woman furiously scribbling notes, and they took their places at the head of the table.

"Let me run down the list of players for you," Mosley offered, starting with the two who had just arrived. "That's the DCI, Jackson Barnett, and his right hand, Sally Kirsch. Next to Kirsch is Phillip Moy, the founder of Moy Electronics, and Bill Iverson, whom you met last week. Seated on Barnett's left is Kyle Lewis, the President's national security adviser, and FBI director Bob Metcalf."

"A room full of heavy hitters. I guess I'd better watch my step."

"You got that right. It's on my recommendation that Barnett asked you to be here, so don't make me look stupid. It might mess up my next raise." The strained smile on Mosley's face left Kilkenny wondering if he was serious.

Barnett stood and waited for the conversations in the room to die down. Under his steady gaze, the meeting quickly came to order. "Thank you all for coming. The topic, as most of you already know, is a serious breach of national security by an employee of this agency. Now we'll discuss the steps that need to be taken to rectify the situation. The first slide, please."

The lights dimmed and Barnett walked over to a lighted podium in the corner, where he could reference his notes as he spoke. The image that appeared on the large-screen wall monitor was a photograph of Michael Cole.

"This is the late CIA computer specialist Michael Cole. During his Caribbean vacation last Christmas, Cole was the victim of an apparent diving accident."

Barnett's next slide showed a nautical map detailing the southern coast of Hispaniola. Scrawled on the map was a circle and an exact latitude and longitude. "A sportfishing boat recovered Cole's body approximately three hours before he allegedly disappeared. Since that time, we have discovered that the circumstances surrounding his death pose a serious threat to our nation's security."

Barnett's delivery carried all the presence of his days as a prosecutor. With a little imagination, Kilkenny could easily envision Barnett making his case before a jury in a court of law.

"Two things immediately troubled us about Cole's death. First, he acquired a large sum of money shortly before his death from a source as yet unknown. The second quandary revolves around Cole's murder and the subsequent cover-up of that murder. What was Cole involved in that led to his death? To answer those questions, Cal Mosley of the CIA and Daniel Harmon of the FBI have been assigned to trace Cole's activities in the weeks prior to his death. Cal, would you please continue?"

Mosley handed some slides to the technician running the projector, then took Barnett's place at the podium. He quickly checked his notes while waiting for the next slide. "I believe that everyone in this room now has some familiarity with this device, the Moy Gatekeeper. Last year, the CIA assigned Michael Cole to work with Moy engineers in developing a modified version of this device for the CIA's use in future covert operations. This new device is called the Spyder."

Mosley asked for the next slide, and the new image showed a Gatekeeper and a Spyder side by side. "As you can see, the Gatekeeper and the Spyder are outwardly identical. Each device offers the same defensive capabilities to its host computer, but that's where the similarity ends. The Spyder is an intelligence-gathering device designed to be planted inside the computer networks of a hostile nation."

"I would like to add something, Cal," Barnett interjected. "The Spyder device is still considered experimental and the Agency currently has no plans to deploy one."

The DCI nodded and Mosley continued his presentation. "Until his death last December, Michael Cole was an integral part of the Spyder development team. His responsibilities included designing how the Spyder would operate once in place, the methods by which it would protect itself, and how it would deliver information to its controllers. Following the completion of this work, Cole went on vacation and was killed."

Mosley took a drink of water. The next slide that came up was the Spanhaur photograph. "In piecing together the last months of Cole's life, we found a connection to the two people highlighted on this picture, which was taken on the morning following Cole's murder. The woman is a freelance writer named Alex Roe. We know very little about her, other than that she's a highly respected journalist. The other person, British business consultant Ian Parnell, is another matter.

"Now at this point in the investigation, we've uncovered a pair of suspects, but no clear motive. Help in establishing motive arrived on two separate fronts. Last February, we received information indicating the latest supercomputer designs from Moy Electronics had found

their way to the People's Republic of China via Hong
Kong. Further investigation by British Intelligence has
traced the illegal technology transfer back to Ian Parnell.
Based on the evidence uncovered thus far, we believe
that Cole was engaged in industrial espionage with Parnell and Roe against Moy Electronics. Somewhere along
the way, their arrangement soured and Cole was killed. It
was at this point that our investigation took an unexpected turn and Nolan Kilkenny entered the picture."

Kilkenny nodded to the others at the table as Barnett made the introduction. "Nolan Kilkenny is a remarkable young man who recently left the navy to pursue
a doctorate at the University of Michigan. Mr. Kilkenny,
the floor is yours."

Nolan rose and walked to the podium. He asked for
the previous slide, that of the Gatekeeper and the Spyder. The twinge of nervousness in the pit of his stomach
surprised him. He'd given mission briefings before, but
never one where half the audience reported directly to
the President.

"Earlier this year, the Michigan Applied Research
Consortium received a Moy Gatekeeper for use with the
optical processor that we are developing. Shortly after we
connected the processor to our computer network, we
discovered some unusual signals on our communication
lines. Since we're using a lot of new equipment, we didn't
know quite what to make of the signals until we isolated
one and discovered that a hacker was working through
our network. When we discovered that the hacker was
trying to steal information from companies tied into our
network, we called in the FBI. With the help of Special
Agents Ullrich and Harbke, we tracked the hacker back
to our own facility. Our search ended when we reached

this device." Kilkenny held his hand up against the image on the screen. "Last Friday, engineers from Moy Electronics verified that our Gatekeeper is, in reality, a Spyder."

Barnett returned to the podium and thanked Kilkenny. He waited until Kilkenny seated himself beside Mosley before continuing. "Mr. Kilkenny's discovery has added yet another element to the mystery surrounding Michael Cole's death. Cole was our resident expert on this device. If anyone could have made use of a Spyder for illegal purposes, it would have been Cole. Now, unlike our human spies, who can operate on their own, a Spyder is completely lost without a controller. If it receives no new instructions from a controller, it will just sit there and operate like a Gatekeeper. As Mr. Kilkenny has pointed out, the Spyder inside his computer was installed after Cole's death and it is very active. Someone else is directing this Spyder's actions. We are now certain that the MARC Spyder is being run by Parnell and Roe."

Barnett paused for a moment while the slides were being changed. Kilkenny refilled his cup of coffee from one of the pots on the conference table. A large cloud of steam rolled from his cup as he poured; the brew was hot and black. On the screen was a grainy photograph that had been taken with a telephoto lens through an office window. The picture showed two men and a woman seated around a conference table; one of the men was seated with his back to the camera.

"Two of the people seated here are Parnell and Roe. A new concern has arisen regarding this third person, a Chinese intelligence officer named Kang Fa."

Kilkenny's coffee was still hot and the steam floated around his eyes as he sipped from the cup. The flash of the changing slide caught his attention, and he looked over the rim of his cup to the screen. The new image, clouded by a thin veil of steam from the coffee, was somehow familiar.

"This photograph of Kang was taken by British Intelligence at Heathrow Airport. Background assessments on Kang indicate that he is highly intelligent, skillful, and ruthless. The British have attributed the deaths of several operatives, both in China and Hong Kong, directly to Kang Fa."

Kilkenny sipped at his coffee again, still puzzling over why this man looked familiar. Once again, the steam from the coffee formed a light haze against his eyes. Kilkenny wiped the mist from his eyes and suddenly remembered. What he had thought was a shadowy illusion in the smoke and haze of the highway attack had been real. Kilkenny slammed his fist down on the table and brought the conference to a stunned halt.

Barnett glared over at the source of the disturbance. "Mr. Kilkenny, do you have something to offer?"

"Nolan," Mosley whispered out in a low growl. "What the hell do you think you're doing? This is the top brass here."

Mosley's reprimand and firm hand on his shoulder brought Kilkenny out of his anger and back to what was going on in the conference room.

"I'm okay, Cal." Kilkenny stood at ease and faced Barnett. "Sir, I'd like to apologize to everyone for my outburst. It was unacceptable behavior on my part. I would like to add, however, that I have recently seen this man. He was there last Sunday, when I was attacked."

"You didn't say anything about this before," Mosley said, questioning the revelation.

"That's because I didn't believe what I'd seen was real. Right after I killed the assassin, I thought I saw a man standing in the road, glaring at me. The look of hate I saw in his eyes was something I've seen only once before. I didn't mention it because I honestly thought I was hallucinating. My face was smeared with blood and sweat at the time, and, after he disappeared, I had more important things to worry about."

"You sure about this?" Mosley asked.

"Absolutely. That man was there."

"Cal, I'm inclined to believe him," Barnett announced from the podium. "For Kang Fa to be present during a wet operation is completely consistent with his psych profile. It is also very likely that Kang is responsible for the bodies you found in the burned-out van. This further confirms our theory that Kang, Parnell, and Roe are in control of the stolen Spyder. Parnell and Roe originally planned to use the Spyder for industrial espionage, but now we've finally discovered what Kang Fa has in mind."

Barnett then described Kang Fa's visit to Phillip Moy and the price that he had demanded for the release of Moy's uncle. As with most computer crimes, this one still lacked the evidence needed to arrest anyone. Even Cole's murder and the attack on Kilkenny lacked enough physical evidence to prove a conspiracy. The only crime they could prove was attempted extortion by Kang Fa, and his arrest now would endanger the life of Moy's uncle.

"Jackson, I appreciate how difficult an investigation like this is to pursue," the President's national security adviser began, "but, other than a lot of theory and circumstantial evidence, we've got nothing we can use legally to shut these people down. This situation has to be terminated, and I am willing to run any suggestions you may have to reach that goal past the President for his approval."

"Thank you, Kyle, but I think I have a solution that is both legal and expedient."

Chapter 41

Kilkenny returned from Washington late on Thursday evening, after a day and a half of meetings with representatives from the agencies involved in Barnett's sting operation. Iverson and Kilkenny were the prized speakers at these briefings, providing both theory and real-world experience in dealing with the Spyder.

Kilkenny's wounds were healing quickly, and five days after the accident, the soreness had eased greatly. He was still worried about Kelsey, despite the favorable reports his father had passed on about her condition. He'd spoken with her only once while he was in Washington. The sound of her voice eased his concerns a little, but it did nothing for the anger he felt toward those responsible for her injuries. The people who did this to you, Kelsey, Nolan thought, are no better than those monsters I killed in Haiti.

Since his Mustang was impounded and undrivable,

Kilkenny borrowed his father's Explorer and returned to MARC. In the computer lab, he found Grin hard at work on deciphering the Spyder program.

"Ahem." Kilkenny coughed over Grin's shoulder. "Whatcha working on there, big guy?"

"Geez, Nolan!" Grin yelped as he bolted up in his chair. "Don't do that."

"Sorry, just an old habit, I guess."

Grin's anxious expression quickly melted back into an elfish smirk. "So how was your trip to Washington? Meet any powerful movers and shakers?"

"Nothing quite so glorious." Kilkenny took a seat next to his friend. "The President was out of town and things were quiet on the Hill."

"Too bad. I hear those state dinners are real nice. What did you find out about our problem?"

"There are some very dangerous people on the other end of this Spyder, people who don't mind killing anyone who gets in their way."

"So when are they going to arrest the bad guys?"

"As soon as they get enough evidence to hang 'em. To paraphrase the head of the CIA, we have to catch these guys in the act to build any kind of case against them. That, my friend, is where you and I fit in."

It wasn't quite the answer Grin was hoping for, but it would do for the moment. "What's the plan?"

"Sit, wait, and watch the Spyder do its thing. Speaking of which, has there been any action since I left?"

Grin shook his head. "It's taken a couple of peeks outside, but it's not playing around like it used to. Maybe it's pouting."

"I don't think so." Kilkenny laughed.

An audible fast-paced beeping began to emanate from the laptop computer connected to the Spyder. Grin clicked a mouse button and brought the monitor out of its screen-saver mode to display the Spyder's status.

"What's with the alarm?" Kilkenny asked.

"You like it?" Grin asked proudly as he scanned the laptop computer's report. "It's my Spyder early warning system. I wrote a little piece of code that ties into the by-pass you brought back from Chicago. Every time the Spyder goes to work, the program signals me that something's happening. Looks like it works."

On the laptop's screen, a graphic depiction of the Spyder's penetration began to unfold. The first box on the screen was labeled *Spyder*. A line ran from it that con-nected to a box labeled MARC-*Cray*. From there, the Spyder passed through several other systems as the route grew across the screen. Eventually, the Spyder passed through sixteen networks, creating an electronic maze that would be difficult, if not impossible, to trace without Iverson's bypass.

Grin moved the cursor onto the last box in the series and double-clicked the mouse on it. The box expanded, filling the screen with what the Spyder was seeing and doing.

"The bypass program not only does everything we were doing before," Grin said excitedly, "but also lets us see what's going on inside the Spyder's twisted little brain. Check this out."

Grin clicked on one of the icons that ran across the top of the screen. The screen split into two windows: one that showed a server's user screen and one that illustrated a graphic depiction of the Spyder's internal program calls.

"That looks like a debugging tool," Kilkenny sur-mised.

"Right. It's what Iverson used to check the Spyder program's stability. Good piece of coding, too—I was impressed. This tool's helping me quite a bit in deciphering what's going on in there. Very radical stuff."

"I'm pleased that you're enjoying yourself."

The lab's phone rang twice, indicating an outside call coming directly to the lab. "MARC computer lab."

"Nolan, Kathy Ullrich from the FBI. Is the Spyder on-line?"

"Yes, it is. Oh, wait a minute, Kathy. Grin's shaking his head. I guess it's finished and has closed the connection. Let me put you on the speaker."

"Grin," Ullrich's voice called out over the phone, "did you get a list of penetrated systems?"

"Yes, and I'm printing it out right now. What do you want to know?"

"We know that the Spyder is using a handful of E-mail addresses as dead-letter drops. As soon as it accessed one of the drops, we began backtracking the connection. Here's what we got."

In reverse order, Ullrich read back the names of each network that the Spyder had passed through. Her list stopped three systems short of MARC.

"It looks like we got a good match," Kilkenny announced.

"This is good, gentlemen. We just need to keep the connection open a little longer to get a positive trace. Grin, have you and Iverson been able to figure out any pattern to its transmissions?"

"According to Iverson, it's completely random," Grin replied. "There's no rhyme or reason governing when the Spyder opens a line or which route it takes to get wherever it's going. The only thing it seems to like is having other traffic on the system. I guess it doesn't want to be the only user on the network. Regardless, when it decides to jump, and how many computer systems it decides to pass through, is totally arbitrary."

"I guess that means we just wait until it moves again." Kilkenny sounded a little discouraged. "Are you having any luck with the other side of the drops?"

"No, they haven't stayed on long enough for us to trace it all the way back. We lost the last one at a Comsat over the Atlantic, so our hackers could still be anywhere. British Intelligence just got their Gatekeepers this morning, so they won't be up and running until later today. Once they're in place, we should have enough overlap to cover the whole trail from London to Ann Arbor. I have to go, so keep in touch if anything develops."

"You got it," Kilkenny replied.

Chapter 42

London, England

Kang had returned to London early on Monday morning, following the disastrous attack on Newton and Kilkenny. The papers said three people were killed in the tragic accident with a fuel truck; his intended victims were listed among the survivors. Kang was bitter about that failure, but he could not make another attempt on the MARC researchers.

He thought about an exquisite tapestry that hung in his home in Beijing and the one flawed thread that marred its perfection. He dared not pull on this thread, or trim it, for fear of destroying the entire tapestry. Kilkenny and Newton were like that thread, marring the intricate weave of his current operation and threatening to unravel it.

Shortly after his arrival at Heathrow, Kang had caught a glimpse of an old adversary, Neville Axton. Axton was a formidable opponent, one who deserved Kang's utmost respect. Kang had no operational intelligence on Axton's current assignment, but he didn't believe in pure coincidence, either. Seeing his rival in the airport had added another level of challenge to this operation.

Kang had run a wild chase through London that afternoon, making chaotic changes in direction to flush out the agents shadowing him. He'd been successful in uncovering two pairs of watchers, which were enough to confirm that Axton was now managing his surveillance. Once clear of the watchers, Kang had made his way to a safe house that the Chinese embassy maintained just outside London, and he hadn't left since. He had kept his contact with the embassy at a minimum and had no contact at all with Parnell. With Axton in the area, it was foolish to take any unnecessary risks.

Four days had passed and the streets outside the safe house still appeared clear of any unwanted observation. While there, Kang altered his appearance by cropping his hair short and coloring the silver-gray strands black. The effect removed several years from his appearance, enough to fool a careless observer.

As he ate his lunch, the phone in the safe house range twice, then stopped. A moment later, it repeated the pattern of two rings before stopping; it was the embassy. He picked up the phone and placed a direct call to the embassy resident over the secure line.

"This is Kang."

"You have a call from Phillip Moy," a voice whispered back. There was no need for the man to whisper; their conversation was filtered through a scrambler at the embassy switchboard.

"Put him through," Kang demanded.

The phone made a buzzing sound as the connection switched to Moy. Kang turned on the cassette recorder attached to the phone. "This is Deng Cho-Nam. Do you have the information that my clients requested?"

"Yes." Moy's voice was calm and deliberate. "We will be transferring the cipher upgrades next Friday at eleven-thirty A.M. Chicago time."

"And the access codes to your computer system?"

"There are two sets, the first of which I will give to you now. These codes will provide access into our computer network. The second set of codes are the passwords to access the secure mainframe. I will turn these codes over to you when I have seen my uncle."

"Very well," Kang replied. Moy was performing as ordered. "The first codes, please."

Moy dictated specific instructions on penetrating his network without triggering the recently installed Gate-keepers. "Everything must be done correctly or the system will shut you out."

"Very good." Kang kept his voice flat and unemotional. He found that such detachment often unnerved his opponents, leaving him at an advantage. "Here are my instructions for you. Arrive in London no later than Thursday evening. Make arrangements to stay at the Hilton. We will contact you Friday morning for the final exchange. Do you understand?"

"Yes," Moy answered obediently.

"If the PRC representatives detect any sign of British or American security forces, your uncle will be killed. Do I make myself clear?" The question held a lingering threat for Moy and his family.

"Perfectly, Mr. Deng."

Kang detected a slight quiver in Moy's voice. The man is a docile sheep, he thought, despising Moy for his weakness. "Good. Then I will see you next Friday for the exchange."

Kang cradled the handset and smiled. The final pieces of this operation were falling into place. If he could remain out of Axton's view for one more week, he would succeed. He pulled the cassette from the recorder and placed it in a clear plastic shell. He had a lot of work to do in only a week's time.

Chicago, Illinois

Moy hung up the phone. He still felt awkward about handing the access codes to his computer network over to the Chinese spy. The codes were legitimate and, for the next week, this foreign agent would have nearly unlimited access to his electronic empire. It was a gamble, but his father often told him that much of life was a gamble. Moy hoped that Barnett's hand was good enough to win.

Chapter 43

London, England
May 8

Kang found no difficulty moving about London this afternoon, but he didn't allow a false sense of security to
develop around his apparent good fortune. He met the
PRC resident in a public park, where he gave the man detailed instructions for bringing the hostage to London.
Security for that part of the operation was critical and
Beijing would have to make the necessary arrangements.

After that meeting, Kang kept moving about the city
until evening, when he arrived at Canary Wharf. The
late-afternoon rain finally dissipated around sunset, when
Kang joined several other people out for an evening stroll
on the river walk. The Thames shimmered with the
lights from the buildings that lined its shores.

Kang already assumed that Axton and British Intelligence were aware of his contact with Parnell and would
be taking steps to determine why. If he was in Axton's
place, he would keep his teams loose, but well placed

around Parnell's building. He would also have taps on Parnell's phones and listening devices planted in Parnell's office and home. That was why he risked a surprise, direct contact with Parnell.

Kang carefully studied the other strollers, looking for anything that would signal a surveillance team. He found none. He waited until the river walk cleared in both directions before closing in on Parnell's building. When the walk was deserted, he slipped over the railing and dropped down onto the dock jutting out from the marina beneath the building where Parnell lived and worked. He passed by several boats tied up in the protected marina on his way to the stairs. Kang easily defeated the door lock and moved inside.

He didn't see any surveillance teams working within Parnell's building, nor did he expect to. Surveillance that's too tight runs the risk of alerting the subject before you're ready, he thought. Fifteen flights of stairs later and he was on the level of Parnell's flat. Peering out of the stairwell, he saw nothing but an empty corridor. Parnell's flat was on the other side of the elevator core, facing the river.

Parnell had just served dessert to his attractive dining companion when he heard the knock at his door.

"Bloody hell." Parnell hissed with disgust at the interruption. "Pardon me, Vanessa. It's probably a neighbor wanting to borrow some coffee."

"Do hurry back," she cooed in a sultry voice.

Vanessa was fantastic in bed, an acrobat between the sheets, and he often fantasized about her long wavy black hair cascading down on him as they made love. Tonight, her tan, provocative figure was clad only in a shimmering red dress that hugged the contours of her body as it descended from the thin straps on her shoulders to a hem some eight inches above her knees. Her ample cleavage was displayed like an invitation and, with each breath, her breasts challenged the tensile strength of the cloth that contained them. No undergarment telegraphed its presence through the fabric of her dress, and that thought excited him greatly.

Thus aroused, Parnell felt an intense annoyance at the disturbance that now took him away from her company. He'd even toyed with the idea of taking her to the islands once he'd closed up shop in London. He opened the door and, at first, didn't recognize his visitor.

"Parnell, are you just going to stand there, or will you invite me in?"

The voice made the connection for Parnell instantly—the forceful tones belonged to Ba Xan. The man's medium-length gray hair was now cropped short and colored black as India ink. The look was severe and disturbing.

"I am entertaining a guest right now. Could we talk at a more appropriate time, perhaps?"

"No, we must talk now," Kang demanded. "Give your apologies to your guest, as I require a *private* conversation with you—immediately."

Parnell did as he was told, leaving Vanessa with another glass of champagne and his sincerest apology for the interruption. It would only be a moment, he promised. With Vanessa barely suppressing her annoyance, he joined Kang in the study. Kang had tuned the stereo to a BBC broadcast of the London Philharmonic and aimed the speakers toward the windows.

"I hope you like classical music. I find that it soothes my nerves."

"What do you want?" Parnell, who had always

prided himself on his emotional control, bit back on the irritation that was beginning to seep through his well-built facade.

"You know what I want," Kang replied, enjoying Parnell's discomfort. "I'm here to provide you with the tools to get it for me. Next Friday, the computer containing the cipher files will be connected to Moy's network for a software transfer to the U.S. government. Several electronic file transfers will take place that day. One will be ours."

Kang reached into his coat pocket and handed Parnell a cassette tape. "These instructions will allow you to access Moy's network safely during the transfer window."

"If you have the codes to Moy's computer, why do you need me at all? You can buy a computer with a modem down the street and do it yourself."

"True, but I lack your experience with Moy's network. You are familiar with that environment and have penetrated it successfully in the past. I want that measure of security for this project." Kang had no intention of letting Parnell off the hook so close to the end. "The instructions on that tape will only get you into the network. Once there, you will require an additional set of passwords to authorize the transfer of the cipher files."

It seemed strange to Parnell that Ba would have everything but the passwords required to get the ciphers. What kind of game was he playing? "Where are the passwords?"

"I will have them when the time comes," Kang assured him. "We will meet in your office, next Friday at five o'clock."

"I'll see that all the necessary preparations are made. What about my money?"

"Once I have the ciphers, I will authorize the final payment to your Cayman account. When we have concluded our business, destroy that tape," Kang advised. "After Friday, it will be little more than a dangerous souvenir."

Parnell studied the microcassette warily. In the hands of a prosecutor, it would be more than enough to convict him of espionage.

Kang rose and straightened his jacket. "You will not hear from me again until Friday. Do you have any questions before I leave?"

"No," Parnell replied, pleased that this impromptu meeting was at an end.

"Good. Until Friday, then." Kang walked out of the study, gave a polite nod of apology to Parnell's dinner guest, and left.

"What was that all about, Ian," Vanessa asked, "that odd Chinese fellow and the loud music?"

"He's a client, dear, and a bit of an eccentric," Parnell lied, though his exasperation with the visit was genuine. "He wanted to talk some business, and everything is urgent in his mind. He pays well, so I put up with his quirks. With his needs addressed, I can now focus my attention on more important matters. More champagne, love?"

"Afterward," she murmured as she slipped into his waiting embrace.

Chapter 44

Ann Arbor, Michigan
May 10

Grin and Kilkenny were attending to their regular duties, the ones that they had occasionally neglected while tinkering with the Spyder, when Harbke and Ullrich arrived with two uniformed officers from the Ann Arbor Police Department.

"Afternoon, ladies," Grin offered warmly.

"William Grinelli and Nolan Kilkenny, I have warrants for your arrest," Ullrich announced in a clear, official voice. "You have the right to remain silent. Anything you say can, and will, be used against you in a court of law. You have the right to an attorney. If you cannot afford an attorney, one will be provided for you. Do you understand these rights as I have explained them to you?"

"Yes," Kilkenny replied. "What I don't understand is *why*. What are we being charged with?"

"In light of some new evidence, you are both being

charged with twenty-four counts of computer and telephone fraud," Ullrich replied.

The police officers handcuffed an angry Kilkenny
and a bewildered Grin and led them to a waiting squad
car. The FBI held a press conference in Detroit to an-
nounce the arrests as the result of an ongoing investigation. The FBI estimated the damage caused by Grinelli
and Kilkenny in the millions of dollars. News of their arrests shocked the research and academic community
around the country, and denunciations followed quickly
on news broadcasts and in the papers.

Chapter 45

Harmon pulled the case files for the Cole investigation and set them on his desk. Four months of investigative work lay summarized in the stack of paper sitting before him. Somewhere inside that stack, Harmon hoped to find an answer that had eluded him thus far.

When he had first started this investigation, Cole was an enigma to him. Over the past months, he'd become so familiar with the details of Michael Cole's life that he had begun to understand the kind of person this man had been. This understanding caused new questions to arise in Harmon's mind.

From what he had seen of Cole's record keeping, the man was fanatical. Cole had kept every receipt, every bill, and every financial statement that he'd ever received. If the IRS had ever decided to audit this man, he would have buried them in documentation.

Other aspects of Cole's life were much the same—

compartmentalized and rigidly ordered. The term his ex-wife used was *control freak*. This habitual need for organization raised a serious question for Harmon: If Cole had maintained records for everything, where were his notes on the money?

Someone with Cole's compulsiveness about record keeping couldn't possibly leave such a significant sum of money off his books completely. It had to be recorded somewhere.

After another pass through the file, which he had practically memorized, Harmon got up from his desk for a stretch. Cole must have hidden the secret of his new-found wealth; Harmon could feel it. He also knew that he needed a fresh perspective.

"I'll be down in the evidence lockup," he informed the department receptionist as he left.

After the FBI was assigned the domestic side of the investigation, Cole's personal records had been seized as evidence and placed in the basement storage area. There were three full-height file cabinets, as well as several boxes containing Cole's computer equipment, disks, and miscellaneous items that had been cataloged and stored. Mail from both of Cole's apartments was still being collected and forwarded to the FBI, several boxes of which sat on a shelf near the file cabinets. The catalog sheet noted that a box of new mail had been added since Harmon's last visit.

Harmon thumbed through the stack; most of it was junk mail, along with a few computer magazines and flyers. At the bottom of the box, he found a bundle of envelopes held together with a rubber band. Harmon pulled the bundle out and began sorting through the letters.

The bundle contained miscellaneous bills and recent bank statements. Harmon had pored over Cole's financial picture with a magnifying glass, trying to pinpoint the circumstances surrounding the new money, with no results.

A letter from a suburban Virginia bank caught his eye as he thumbed through the stack of new mail. Cole had accounts in Washington and Chicago, but Harmon didn't recall any activity with this bank. He slit open the top of the envelope and found a bank notice regarding the rental of a safety-deposit box. The box had been rented the previous December, just ten days before Cole's death.

He quickly scanned over the pile of labeled boxes and located the one marked *Bank Records*. Inside, he found the warrant and evidence tags for the safety-deposit box that he'd seized last January, and now he confirmed that the new letter identified a different box. Harmon signed out the letter and returned to his office to make a call for another search warrant.

The branch manager of the bank carefully scrutinized Harmon's warrant to verify its authenticity. The young man was obviously new on the job and was following bank procedures to the letter. Harmon had called ahead and requested that the manager have the bank's locksmith on hand when he arrived.

The young manager handed back the search warrant. "Your warrant appears in order, Agent Harmon. If you'll follow me, I'll have the box opened for you. I do expect an inventory of its contents before you leave."

"Of course," Harmon assured the manager. "I have all the necessary documentation for this seizure."

The manager's curiosity finally got the best of him. It was the first official dealing he'd had with the FBI, and visions of drug dealers or Mafia conspiracies were playing in his imagination. "If you don't mind my asking, what do you expect to find in the box?"

Harmon deflected the inquiry. "I can't comment on that right now."

"What about the owner, Michael Cole?" the manager asked.

"Recently deceased." The abrupt manner in which Harmon replied left no doubt in the manager's mind that Cole's passing was not from natural causes. He asked no further questions.

A high-pitched whine filled the concrete-and-steel-walled vault as the locksmith bored through the lock. Metal filings trickled out from the carbide-tipped drill bit as it sank deeper into the brass core. The drill groaned in protest as the core grabbed at the spiraling bit. Finally, the core broke free. The locksmith extracted the bit and punched the lock. The door of the safety-deposit box opened slightly.

The bank manager pulled the long plastic box from the wall and escorted Harmon back to his office with one of the bank's guards as a witness. He closed the door and set the box on his desk; a look of curious anticipation filled the manager's face. This was obviously the most exciting event he'd witnessed since starting work at the suburban bank branch.

When Harmon flipped the lid open, the box appeared to be empty. He then shook the box and dislodged a brown envelope from the rear of it. Harmon pulled the envelope out and rechecked the box. It now was empty.

"Contents of safety-deposit box five oh four, one envelope," Harmon announced as he unfastened the metal clasp and opened it, "containing four three-and-

a-half-inch high-density floppy disks, three sequen-
tially numbered and one labeled *Cormorant*." Harmon
studied the disk, wondering what information Cole had
placed on it.

"Is that what you expected to find?" the manager
asked.

"I won't know until I find out what's on them. I'll
be taking these disks back to FBI headquarters as evidence. Once the case is completed, all personal effects
of the deceased will be turned over to his family. This
clears your bank's obligation regarding this box. Thank
you for your help."

Harmon walked out to his car and picked up his cellular phone. After dialing Mosley's direct number, he
waited for the connection to be made.

A gruff voice rumbled through the earpiece: "This
is Cal Mosley."

"Afternoon, Cal. Dan Harmon. You got a minute?"

Mosley's voice warmed. "For my favorite FBI man,
you bet."

Harmon picked up one of the disks and looked at
the label. "Michael Cole had a safety-deposit box we
didn't know about. He rented it ten days before his
death and tucked four diskettes inside. Got a question
for you?"

"Shoot."

"Does the word *Cormorant* mean anything to you?"

"Not really. Hold on while I look it up." The
phone clunked as Mosley set it on his desk. Harmon
heard Mosley get up from his swivel chair and rustle
through his books.

"I'm back. Let's see what *Webster's* has to say. Cormorant, cormorant," Mosley repeated absently while

searching through the dictionary. "Ah, here it is. 'Cormorant: any of several widely distributed aquatic birds of genus *Phalacrocorax*, having dark plumage, webbed feet, a hooked bill, and a distensible pouch.' The second definition says a cormorant is 'a greedy or rapacious person.' Take your pick."

"Knowing Cole the way we do, I'd lean toward the second one. You say the main definition is a *bird*?"

"Yes." The illustration in the dictionary didn't show the cormorant to be a remarkably graceful or majestic creature.

"Didn't Cole work on a project involving a defector that had to do with birds?"

There was a stunned silence on the other end of the phone. "Son of a bitch! You're right. I completely forgot about that. Cole salvaged a bunch of old KGB computer disks. The agents listed on those disks all had bird code names. Where are you at?"

"Out in Virginia, about twenty minutes from Langley."

"Well, get over here with that disk. I'll have our computer people up and ready to take a look at it when you get here."

Harmon's drive to Langley went quickly in the midafternoon traffic; maybe things were going his way today. Mosley met him at the main reception desk, where Harmon was fitted with visitor's credentials. The bright orange-and-black badge clipped to his lapel singled him out as a guest with limited access to the facility.

"I'm taking you down to see Frank Villano. You'll remember him from our meeting with the DCI. When

I told him what you'd found, he just about jumped out of his skin."

After a dozen turns in the look-alike corridors of the main office building, Harmon was thoroughly disoriented. Occasional glimpses through office windows allowed him to reestablish his bearings in terms of direction. Mosley ran his ID badge through a magnetic strip reader, which confirmed his access code and released the lock.

Harmon looked over the banks of computers lined up within a glass-enclosed space that filled the interior of the Computer Department. Offices and support spaces lined the perimeter of the glass core, each space dependent on the powerful machines in the center.

They stopped at a corner office on the perimeter, where Villano's assistant waved them through. "He's waiting for you."

"Thanks," Mosely replied.

Villano's large office was filled with the typical debris found in the office of any manager of information systems: piles of printouts, odd software products, and the occasional piece of hardware. Villano was pounding away at his keyboard when Mosley and Harmon entered.

"Have a seat, gentlemen," Villano offered over his shoulder. "I'll be right with you."

Harmon hung his coat on the wall rack and pulled up a chair beside Mosley while Villano tapped out a few more keystrokes.

"There, that did it." Villano sighed with relief as he finished. He then turned around to face his guests. "Thanks for coming down. I understand that you've found some disks that Cole stashed away, one with the name Cormorant on it."

"Yes." Harmon fished the disks out of his shirt pocket and handed them to Villano.

Villano looked over the floppy disk. It was the same make as those purchased en masse by his department, and Villano easily recognized the distinctive handwriting. "This is Cole's all right. Let's find out what he was up to."

Villano inserted the disk into his desktop computer and directed the program to work with the files found on the disk. The drive light flashed as the computer read the disk and filled its internal memory with information. In a few seconds, the operation was complete and the program asked Villano what he wished to do next.

"You'll have to pardon me, but my Russian is not quite what it used to be."

Harmon and Mosley peered over Villano's shoulder and saw a screen filled with Cyrillic characters. It looked like any other computer program, except it was a language neither of them could read.

"What is that?" Harmon asked.

"This is a gift from a defector," Villano replied while trying to decipher the menu offered by the program. "Recovering this program and its related data files was Michael Cole's final assignment before going on vacation. The program seems to have found some data files on your disk that it recognizes. I'd say that you've found the files of another Soviet spy."

"Another spy?" Mosley asked. "Weren't all the original disks and data files accounted for last January when we started looking through Cole's work?"

"Yes, but a few of the original disks were damaged and the data was unrecoverable, including one labeled *Cormorant*."

"Frank, I suggest we find out who the hell this Cormorant is," Mosley offered. "That might just tell us why Cole squirreled away a copy of this disk."

Villano followed the menu instructions that guided him into the late Soviet spymaster's database. From the list of agent code names, he selected the Russian version of the word *Cormorant*. Villano's computer began churning away at the data until the screen cleared and a new image filled the nineteen-inch monitor. A grainy photograph appeared in the upper-right-hand corner of the screen. The face was that of a young woman.

Mosley walked around and crouched beside Villano to get a closer look at the photograph. "What's the text say?"

"The woman pictured is Anna Mironova. Born in the Russian Republic. Parents deceased. Educated in various preparatory schools and trained by the KGB at the First Chief Directorate Institute. She got in there very young, about high school age, if these dates are correct. Let's see what she's currently up to."

Villano selected one of the menu options that appeared in a status bar along the bottom of the screen. "Current assignment: First Chief Directorate, Directorate T, deep-cover agent in the United States."

"What's Directorate T?" Harmon asked.

"I believe that was the KGB's Science and Technology Group," Villano replied. "Some parts of the FCD were geared toward political or military information. Directorate T officers used to comb the outside world for any technology or scientific information that the Kremlin wanted."

"What's that part on the bottom of the screen?"

Mosley asked, pointing at a block of text. "That part right there."

"Hmm, says that she works as a writer—more precisely, a journalist, by the name of Alexandra Roe."

"Damn!" Mosley growled. "Get me back to that picture."

Villano tapped a couple of keys and the photograph of a young Soviet agent filled the screen.

"She look familiar to you, Dan?" Mosley asked, testing Harmon's imagination. "Add a couple of years, style the hair, and who do you have?"

Harmon studied the image, mentally altering it as Mosley suggested until his mind made the transformation. "It's her all right."

Mosley and Harmon had raced well beyond Villano at this point. "Who's her? Who is she?"

"Someone Cole met just before he was killed. Dan and I have been checking into her background, and so far, we've come up empty."

"Roe's background always seemed too clean to be real. She's got all the right documentation, but there's no depth, no personal history. It's like she existed only on paper before starting college."

Mosley had seen the signs of a deep-cover agent before. "It sure smells like a legend. If Roe really is a Russian agent and Cole tried to put the squeeze on her, it's no wonder he wound up dead. Frank, can you punch me out some hard copy? I want to take this to the DCI."

As Villano worked his way through the menus to request a printout, Mosley then sat back in his chair, shook his head, and laughed.

"What's so funny?" Harmon asked.

"Do you remember our little powwow last week, when we thought we had this whole thing figured out?"

"Yes, so?"

"We've already got the FBI, the CIA, British Intelligence, and the Chinese knee-deep in this little mess and now we discover that our old friends, the KGB, may have a player on the field, too. Who's next, the Mossad?"

Chapter 46

London, England

Two hours ago, Sir Daniel Long finished a phone call with Jackson Barnett of the CIA. His counterpart in the American intelligence community had just forwarded some startling news that one of the industrial spies, currently under surveillance, might also be a former Soviet agent. Barnett had asked that the new information about Alexandra Roe be verified by British Intelligence's high-level source. What disturbed Long most about Barnett's call was that if the information that the CIA had uncovered about Roe was genuine, then he should have already known about it. After the call, Long requested a driver for a trip out to the cottage—a country estate that British Intelligence used as a safe house.

The ninety-minute trip into the English countryside was uneventful, if not downright depressing. The past two days had seen nothing but rain and clouds over the British Isles and the weather didn't help Long's mood. A sense of betrayal burned inside of him as he looked over the pages that Barnett had sent, wondering what else he hadn't been told by the former mole.

The two black Austins that formed Long's entourage cleared the cottage's security and pulled into the circle drive by the main entrance. Long could make out the shapes of security officers, their collars turned up against the driving rain, patrolling the estate's perimeter. A guard with a large umbrella met Long at the car and escorted him into the main house. Long took off his wet mackintosh and handed it to the guard.

"Where is he?" Long asked the duty officer curtly.

The duty officer knew instantly that Long was not here to exchange pleasantries. "In the library, sir. Through there."

Long moved quickly across the foyer and through the archway that marked the entrance to the library. A fire roared in the mammoth stone hearth, fighting back the chill in the damp air. In an ornately carved wing-back chair sat an old man deeply engrossed in a book. The man didn't look up from his reading; he simply gestured for Long to take a seat in the adjacent chair.

After a brief moment, Yakushev marked his spot and closed the book, turning his attention toward Long. "I don't know how many times I have read Homer's *Odyssey*, and yet I never tire of it. This is an especially good translation. Sir Daniel, to what do I owe the pleasure of your company on such a dreary day?"

"I want to know about your deep-cover agents in the West, all of them," Long demanded.

"I have given you everything there is to know. You and your predecessors were aware of all operatives under my control."

Long could feel the folded pages of Barnett's fax in his suit pocket. "Are you absolutely sure of that?"

Yakushev's cordial manner melted into a scowl. "I worked for British Intelligence for over thirty years, inside the Soviet Union. Decades of service that nearly cost me my life on more than one occasion. I cannot believe that you would question my integrity now."

"Andrei," Long said, trying to smooth Yakushev's ruffled feathers, "you are still considered our most prized asset of the Cold War, and your honor remains intact. What I am questioning is the completeness of your disclosure. Do you recall the files that were recovered from your dacha after it burned to the ground, the ones that the Americans now possess?"

"Yes, we've gone over this material already."

"Yes, we have," Long said, reiterating the point. "You positively identified those named in the files as operatives under your personal direction. We sanitized your confirmations and reported back to the CIA that the files were genuine. Another file has turned up under highly suspicious circumstances."

Long handed Yakushev the pages of Barnett's fax. "Is this woman one of your agents?"

Yakushev scanned the report and, slowly, the fire of indignation faded from his eyes. After a silence, Long pressed again for an answer. "Do you know her?"

"I know Anya," Yakushev admitted nostalgically, "and yes, she worked for me."

"Then why didn't you tell us about her?" Long barely kept the anger out of his voice. "We have no report from you of her activities. According to this fax, she's been in place for almost twenty years."

"You were not told because it was not important for you to know," Yakushev shot back.

Long couldn't guess what hold Roe had on Yakushev, but the former spymaster was obviously trying to shield his agent. "Tell me about Roe, and why you are so keen to protect her. It's important."

"Please have the recorders turned on, Sir Daniel. Anya's story is a long one."

A security officer nodded to Long a few minutes later, indicating that the estate's tape-recording systems were on. The house cook brought out a tea service for Long and Yakushev before leaving quietly.

Long started the debriefing. "Tell me about Anna Mironova."

Yakushev went into the long story of how he had met the young girl with criminal tendencies during a training exercise; how he took her under his wing, trained her, groomed her for life in the West. Long realized quickly that Yakushev's relationship with Mironova was far different from the usual bond between agent and controller. Long listened quietly as Yakushev described young Mironova's evolution into a deep-cover agent. Yakushev drew his narrative to a close with the story of their last meeting, during the attempted Soviet coup, when he had set Mironova free.

"Why did you hold this information back?"

"I thought that I had destroyed all records relating to the Cormorant that night and that Anya would be free to live her own life. I have given you every agent who ever worked for me, all but Anya. Anya was different, and more than just an agent to me. She was like me, or-phaned in a hostile world, with only her wits to keep her alive. She had the natural talents to make a great spy, and she succeeded only because I sheltered her from the ide-ological nonsense that they force-fed recruits at the An-dropov Institute. Anya was special; she was like a daughter to me. That is why I set her free and why I didn't tell you about her."

After many interviews with the former KGB spy-master, Long thought that he had developed an understanding of the man. Yakushev's strong personal feelings toward Mironova added a new dimension to that understanding. "Are you aware of what she is doing now?"

"No. I have not seen or spoken with her since August of 1991." Yakushev thought about the night the coup started; about Anya killing the KGB assassin that had been sent for him. "If she followed the news accounts from Moscow during those days, she probably believes that I am dead."

Long believed that Yakushev was telling him the complete truth. Moscow had been in chaos in the days after the coup. His people spirited Yakushev out of the Soviet Union with a combination of false papers and hefty bribes. Since that time, Yakushev had been a quiet guest of the British people.

"Sir Daniel, what has aroused your interest in Anya?"

"It appears that your pupil has become an industrial spy."

"A good use of her skills. She's probably making a handsome living in the private sector, more so than her meager wages as a servant of the Soviet state." Yakushev laughed.

"This isn't a joke. Mironova is tied up with a British business consultant and suspected dealer of stolen technology named Ian Parnell. The two of them are currently providing services to a certain Chinese intelligence officer who once caused some of *your* people a bit of trouble."

Yakushev felt his stomach tighten. "Kang Fa?"

"Yes. Kang is in London right now, working with

Parnell and Roe to steal ciphering technology from an American computer corporation."

Yakushev's hands clenched the soft leather armrests of his chair. Even though they had never met, Yakushev knew that Kang Fa had been personally responsible for the deaths of several KGB agents over a fifteen-year period. In Moscow Center, Kang was regarded as a ruthless, but effective, agent who completed his operations by eliminating any loose ends. Unless something drastic was done quickly, Anya would be killed once her usefulness to Kang had ended.

"Would you find it helpful to have an agent *inside* Kang's operation?"

"Roe?" Long questioned.

"Yes. I think if I contacted Anya, I could persuade her to assist you. Anya is very intelligent. I'm certain that she has some sense of the gravity of her situation, and a familiar face, at the right time, might be just what she needs to extricate herself."

Long massaged his graying temples, weighing Yakushev's offer. Roe would provide the significant edge, but only if she could be trusted. "You've given me a lot to think about."

"Then you'll consider my offer?"

"Yes, but that's not a promise that I'll act on it." Long stood and smoothed out the wrinkles in his suit coat. "I'm going to have to mull this one over, but I'll leave a copy of the case file for you to review. I'd also appreciate it very much if you would check your memory again to see if there's anyone else you might have neglected to tell me about."

"Thank you. I'm certain that you'll do what's necessary."

Chapter 47

Since their arrest, Kilkenny and Grin languished in a cell at the Ann Arbor Police Station. They were neither questioned nor arraigned. They had received a visit from their lawyer, who didn't have much to say except that she was still waiting for the brief on the charges from the district attorney. Other than their three square meals a day, they were simply ignored.

"Room service, jailbirds," Mosley announced as the guard let him into the cell. "I spoke with Kelsey yesterday and she mentioned that you two like this Angelo's place for breakfast, so I got them to do up something special. Hope you don't mind."

Grin and Kilkenny remained on their cots, suspicious of Mosley. "The only thing we mind," Kilkenny said, "is being cooped up in here without any explanation. I hope you brought one of those along with the raisin toast."

"All in good time." Mosley wasn't about to be rushed and he dismissed their rude behavior as a product of their circumstances. In their place, he would probably feel the same. "Oh, here, Nolan. This is from Kelsey."

Nolan accepted the gift, wondering how Kelsey had accomplished such a feat from her hospital bed. He smiled as he read the gift card that was taped to the package; it was signed "With love, Kelsey." He removed the wrapping paper. Inside, he found a copy of Clive Cussler's latest Dirk Pitt adventure.

"Way to go, Kelsey," Nolan said as he looked at the classic car on the dust jacket.

"She thought you'd like something good to read during your incarceration." Mosley passed around the carryout containers and sat on the cot next to Grin, who brusquely shifted away from him. "Hey, I'm a friend."

"If you were our friend, you'd get us out of here."

"Grin's right. You, of all people, know that we're not responsible for those computer crimes."

"Yeah! My folks always thought that their hippie son would end up in jail, and here I am. We didn't do anything."

"Gentlemen, this is what we call 'a ruse.' Barnett and the FBI came up with it as a way to protect you against any further attacks. My boss does not want a repeat of that incident on the freeway. With the two of you in jail and Kelsey still in the hospital, we think Kang and the others will relax and proceed with their plans."

"Do you think you might have let us in on the secret?" Grin asked sarcastically.

"I apologize for that, but it was Barnett's call. He wanted your arrest to look as real as possible. As far as the bad guys know, you two are out of the picture. I'm here to spring you both, so you can get back to work. Grin, you're

going to hole up at MARC, with Agents Harbke and Ullrich, and watch the Spyder. Iverson and some of Moy's
people will cover the Chicago end."

"What about me?" Nolan asked.

"You and I are going to London."

Once their meal was finished, Mosley tossed his
empty carryout box in the trash and brushed a few stray
crumbs off his lap. "Get your things together. It's time to
go."

Five minutes later, a guard led Mosley and the prisoners down the back stairs, to the parking garage. Grin
and Kilkenny ducked in the backseat as Mosley's car was
waved through security and rode away.

Once clear of the police station, Mosley allowed the
escaped prisoners to come up for air. Their first stop was
the loading dock of the MARC building, where they
dropped Grin off to assist Agents Ullrich and Harbke in
operating the MARC computers and monitoring the
Spyder. Grin was to hole up in the computer lab until further notice. Mosley then took Kilkenny home to pack.

Chapter 48

London, England

From her hotel room, Roe finished coding a new set of instructions for the Spyder. Just working out the parameters for the complex program had taken the better part of the weekend. Unlike the earlier instruction sets that she'd downloaded to the device, this one defined a live on-line connection with the Spyder. That extra step forced Roe to modify her normal programming to increase security for the connection; everything had to be perfect if she was to execute a live data transfer from Moy Electronics safely.

After thoroughly debugging the program, removing any errors that might cripple the execution of her complex instructions, she encrypted the text and prepared to send the message.

As before, Roe started by accessing a local Internet server, one that happened to host one of her favorite Web sites, the Piccadilly Gardener. From there, she accessed the British National Telephone Exchange and jumped a few electronic circuits to cover her trail. Then she linked into their satellite communications lines and made her way to North America, where she passed through several other computer systems before finally sending her E-mail message to the Spyder.

Then, with a flurry of rapid keystrokes, Roe back-pedaled through the systems she'd penetrated. After downloading a few tips on spring planting, she logged off the Net. Roe smiled as she read over the gardening tips, hoping that the seed she just planted would successfully take root.

An hour after posting the latest instructions to the Spyder, Roe arrived at Parnell's office for a noon meeting.

"Still hard at it, Alex?"

"Just finished, and everything looks fine. I've sent off the new program, which should be picked up by the end of business today. Once it loads this file, it will go dormant until Friday."

Parnell leaned back and mentally ran over the checklist. "Excellent. We don't want to draw any suspicion away from the current suspects, now do we?"

"A remarkable stroke of luck, I admit," Roe replied dubiously. "I checked the Detroit newspapers' Web sites and it appears that Kilkenny and another fellow have been charged with several computer-related crimes, including ours. It's like Cole said—who would believe that the computer itself was capable of doing something like this? Unfortunately, with all the attention over there, someone still might figure out what's really going on."

"Perhaps, but by then, you and I will be safely out of reach, basking in the warm Caribbean sun. What do you say we step out for a bit of lunch?"

*   *   *

From their perch across the park, Axton was again sitting in with the watchers. Parnell's days seemed filled
with the mundane tasks that every businessperson deals
with. Most of the man's business operations were perfectly legal and, for the most part, ethical. Axton's crew
of watchers just sat and watched and listened for those
little details that they would use to build their case.

"Did you catch any of that, sir?" the sound engineer
asked as he adjusted the filtering levels on his equipment.

The conversation in Parnell's office had ended and
Axton pulled the headset off and rubbed his ears. "Just
two little pieces of interest, a mention of Cole and
Kilkenny. That confirms that they know about both of
them."

"Who's Kilkenny?"

"He's a Yank on the other end of this mess, lad,
someone for whom those two reptiles have caused more
than a bit of grief. Well, it looks like they're breaking for
lunch."

Axton switched on his radio headset and flagged a
warning to his ground crews. "Look lively, boys and girls.
Tweedledee and Tweedledum are coming down for a
snack."

"Roger, sir," the response came back over the radio.

Before real code names could be issued for this surveillance operation, the watchers started referring to
Parnell and Roe as "Tweedledee" and "Tweedledum,"
from Lewis Carroll's *Alice in Wonderland*. Following the
same logic, their base of observation was christened
"Looking Glass" and Kang Fa had been dubbed "the Mad
Hatter."

"Can you make me a copy of that last bit? Maybe

the lab boys can filter out some of that background noise."

"Consider it done, sir," the sound engineer replied as he handed Axton a cassette tape. "Figured you'd be wanting it for the folks at HQ."

Chapter 49

Ann Arbor, Michigan

In the MARC computer lab, an alarm sounded, announcing that the Spyder was once again active. Harbke and Ullrich gathered around Grin's station to watch the action unfold. The Spyder had just passed through the university network into another computer system. Grin punched a couple of keys and the alarm went silent.

"Liz," Ullrich said, turning to her partner, "let our monitoring teams know that the Spyder is on-line."

Harbke dialed out and passed the word while Grin and Ullrich watched the Spyder traverse several private networks.

"This thing still amazes me," Ullrich commented as she watched the Spyder punch through one computer system after another.

"It's a slick piece of work all right." While despising the people who controlled the Spyder, Grin still respected the technology behind the device.

Harbke returned after making the calls. "The CompuServe team reports that someone recently sent a file to the Spyder's E-mail box."

"Maybe that's where it's headed," Ullrich replied.

Fifteen minutes passed as the Spyder penetrated system after system, finally stopping at CompuServe.

"Looks like this is it," Grin announced. "Let's see what they want the Spyder to do today."

Grin split the laptop screen to display the CompuServe screen in one window and what the Spyder was seeing internally in another.

"All right, he's logged on and he's checking the mail," Grin said, announcing the play-by-play. "Bingo, it's found the message. The message is blank, but there's a file attached to it. He's downloading the file; everything's fine. He's logging off; he's done and closing up the connections."

The laptop's active-matrix screen flashed quickly as the Spyder logged off the computer networks that had covered its electronic tracks. Once the Spyder had returned to a dormant state, Grin loaded up the diagnostic program from Moy Electronics.

"Now let's find out what our friends in London are planning."

Grin switched off the monitoring program and enlarged the bypass window to full screen.

"Grin, what's all that gibberish?" Harbke asked.

Grin checked the program status bar at the bottom of his screen. "That file it downloaded was encrypted. What we're watching is an on-the-fly translation."

The odd-looking characters were rapidly converted into a new instruction set for the Spyder.

"Can you hand me that blank optical-disk cartridge?"

"Sure thing," Ullrich replied.

Grin fed the cartridge into the laptop's external drive and directed the bypass to copy the new instruction file. Unlike their initial attempt to dump the Spyder's core program, an effort that had almost cost Nolan and Kelsey their lives, the Spyder's internal security was completely oblivious to the information flowing out through the bypass.

After a few minutes, Grin ejected the cartridge and labeled it. "Now let's see if we can get Iverson on the phone. I assume that the FBI is interested in knowing what the Spyder has just been told to do?"

"Hell yes," Ullrich replied.

Chapter 50

London, England

Alex Roe spent the rest of the day at Parnell's office, attending to the details of a few of the legitimate assignments that she was working on. After locking up, she left the building and decided to have dinner in a quiet pub in a less developed part of the wharf district.

She'd walked about half the distance there when she began to feel like she was being followed. Roe looked around but failed to detect any of the telltale signs of surveillance. Still, she sensed something out of the ordinary. To ease her fears, she began running a varied pattern of movement through the area in hopes of shaking any pursuit out into the open. She made abrupt turns at random locations, ducked in and out of stores, and crisscrossed the street at random intervals. If anyone was mapping her movements, they would make no sense at all.

* * *

Just behind Roe as she made another turn, the team currently tracking her movements was having great difficulty keeping pace while remaining undetected.

"Team two to Looking Glass, over," the young officer whispered into a miniature microphone.

"Looking Glass here, team two, over."

"Tweedledum is running about like a rabbit. She's all over the place. I think she's onto us. Over."

"Pull back a little, and give her some room," the Looking Glass leader advised. "We don't want to alarm her."

"Roger, team two, out."

The British surveillance teams watching Roe pulled back, maintaining only the lightest contact. After a few more minutes of Roe's chaotic trailblazing, they lost her completely. The watchers reconvened at various points in the area, hoping to reestablish contact.

Roe kept her random movements up for another ten minutes, searching the thinning crowds for any sign of pursuit; she found none.

"Probably just imagining things," she reprimanded herself.

Roe's meandering course had pulled her nearly a mile away from her original destination. Halfway there, the hairs on her neck bristled in response to a regular pattern of footsteps that had maintained a constant beat several strides behind her. Turning quickly into an empty alleyway, she heard the footsteps slow and finally stop.

Roe flattened herself against the alley wall, out of the line of sight from her pursuer. Her heart raced as she tried to rein in her imagination and focus on the situation at hand. She had to assume the worst-case scenario: Her pursuer was either official or criminal. She'd ruled out coincidence, since whoever was following her had stopped when she had turned the corner, and was now waiting at the alley entrance.

Soft footsteps echoed from the mouth of the alley, measured and confident. The footsteps didn't rush in, but moved with patience, closing the distance between them. About ten feet from her position, the footsteps stopped. Backlit from the adjacent street, the silhouette of a slightly built man wearing a hat became visible; the figure threw a long shadow across the alley floor. The head of the shadow fell in line with Roe's concealed position. For what seemed like hours, neither one of them moved.

The man casting the shadow finally spoke. "Anya, it is your old friend, Andrei. I am alone. You may come out now."

A sudden shock swept through Alex at the sound of Yakushev's familiar voice. She'd prepared herself to fight or run, but not to face a ghost. Her mind froze and she found that she couldn't move.

The shadow drew closer, until the man stood before her. Half in light, he turned to face her. The harshly shadowed face was that of her mentor, Andrei Yakushev. Alex's mouth opened, but no words formed to express the jumble of thoughts that filled her mind.

Yakushev smiled at the sight of his protégée. "I see that you are full of questions. I understand. Come. I believe that you were on your way to dinner. If you don't mind, I would like to join you and get reacquainted."

Yakushev threw his arms around the still-shocked Roe in a warm Russian greeting. Alex returned the embrace feebly, still waiting for her mind to reconnect with her body.

"You look as though you've seen a ghost," Yakushev said jokingly. "I assure you that I am very much alive. Let us go now—there is much to discuss and little time before your British surveillance relocates you."

The firmness of her mentor's voice finally brought Alex out of confusion. Yakushev turned away and began moving back toward the street. Roe collected herself and followed. She watched Yakushev practice the expert tradecraft that had made him one of the Soviet Union's greatest spymasters. Not since she had been in training had the two of them prowled the streets of a Western city together.

Sir Daniel Long was dining at 10 Downing Street with the prime minister when an urgent call came through for him. Excusing himself from the table, he took the call in a private study near the dining room.

"This is Sir Daniel Long. What seems to be the problem?"

"Eldridge, at the cottage, sir. Sorry about the intrusion, but Yakushev's gone. We've searched, but he's not anywhere on the grounds."

Yakushev's disappearance caused a whole host of problems to emerge in Long's mind. "How long since he was last seen?"

"Near as we can estimate, sometime early this afternoon," the man explained. "Staff at the cottage say he was feeling a bit tired and went upstairs for a rest. That's the last they saw of him. We still haven't figured out how he got off the grounds or where he's gone to."

"I have an idea where he might be headed. Continue your search of the grounds and surrounding area and see what you can find. Call in whatever resources you feel necessary, but try to use some discretion."

"Right, sir," Eldridge replied.

Long broke the connection and dialed up the

evening duty officer of the surveillance section. The line rang only once before it was answered. "Surveillance, Duty Officer Cain speaking."

"Cain, this is Sir Daniel Long."

"Yes, sir." Cain's voice jumped to attention.

"Cain, I need to speak with Neville Axton. See if you can ring him up."

"He's off duty, sir, but I think I can reach him. Will you hold, sir?"

"Yes," Long replied with some annoyance, "just get Axton on the line."

Long waited as the phone went quiet. On the other end, Cain brought up Axton's directory listing on the computer and dialed the pager number. Two minutes later, Axton called in and Cain patched him through. The line buzzed for a second and then became clear as the electronic scrambling devices adjusted themselves to the new connection.

"Axton, we have a potential problem that you need to be made aware of. An aging defector, one that we've had under wraps for several years, is missing. I suspect he's making his way toward London, if he's not already here."

"Do you think he's heading for the airport?" Axton tried to be helpful, but he didn't see what place he had in dealing with an AWOL defector.

"No, I don't expect that he's trying to leave the country at all. I do think he may make some trouble with the Kang Fa investigation. I assume you read the notice I sent you regarding Roe's background?"

"Of course, sir." Axton remembered reading the sanitized report that blandly stated that Roe had once been a KGB deep-cover agent.

"The missing man is Yakushev, the chap who mentored Alexandra Roe back in Russia. I confirmed the connection between the two of them yesterday. Yakushev was very close with Roe, so I expect that he'll try to warn her. Meet me down at the office in half an hour and I'll fill you in on the details. In the meantime, inform your teams to be watchful for an elderly man trying to make contact with Roe. I don't know what he's up to, but it could be a problem for our operation. If your people spot Yakushev, bring him in immediately. Oh, and Axton?"

"Yes, sir?"

"Take care with him," Long advised. "He's very dangerous when he wants to be, but I don't expect that to be the case here. Try to get him to come back in willingly, before he reaches Roe."

"I'll see what I can do, sir."

Long hung up the phone and made his apologies to the prime minister and the other guests. After collecting his briefcase and mackintosh, Long left number 10 and took his chauffeured car back to the office.

Damn, he thought, what does Yakushev hope to accomplish?

Yakushev had become visibly upset when he learned of Kang Fa's involvement with Roe and Parnell. If Axton's people were lucky, they'd find him before he reached Roe and brought the entire operation crashing down.

Chapter 51

London, England
May 14

The British Air Concorde flight from New York landed just before noon at Heathrow Airport. Phillip Moy had traveled alone on this flight, but he prayed that he would have a passenger with him when he returned. In the next seven hours, Moy would both betray his country and his life's work in hopes of freeing his uncle.

A few hours earlier, another British Air flight had arrived at Heathrow. This one, from Hong Kong, carried several men bearing diplomatic passports from the People's Republic of China. All of the new arrivals passed quickly through British Customs and Immigration, bearing the credentials of trade representatives. In the midst of this group of travelers was an elderly man who appeared very frail and tired.

*   *   *

Moy checked into the Hilton, as directed, and began his vigil. Jackson Barnett had promised him security immediately upon his arrival in London. So far, he'd seen none. He knew that the promised security was out there, and hidden for obvious reasons, but he couldn't shake the feeling that he was naked and alone.

At 3:30, Moy heard a knock at his door. He answered and found a smartly dressed Asian with a firm, muscular build.

"It is time, Mr. Moy," the man announced.

Understanding the summons, Moy grabbed his jacket and followed the man to the elevator. Once inside, the man pressed a button for a higher floor. They exited the car and walked down the long corridor toward a suite where two men stood guard beside the door. Moy saw Kang Fa's security and wondered again about his own.

One of the sentries frisked Moy while the others watched. The sentry nodded that Moy was clean of weapons and listening devices, and the lead guard allowed him to enter the suite. Inside, he found three other men who looked much like the one who had come to get him. None of them spoke or even acknowledged his existence; their attentions seemed to be focused elsewhere. Another man walked out of the bedroom, and at first, Moy didn't recognize him. As soon as he turned to face him, Moy realized that it was Kang Fa.

"You have finally arrived. Good." Kang played the role of gracious host. "I assume that you will want to inspect the merchandise before completing our transaction?"

The merchandise Kang referred to was a human being, and Moy resisted the urge to strike the man for such a disgusting remark. How dare he refer to my uncle like a commodity to be bought and sold! Moy quietly raged.

"Yes, I would like to see my uncle."

Kang motioned with his hand. "He is in the other room. You have thirty minutes to hand over the codes."

Moy entered the bedroom and found a frail old man sitting on the edge of the bed. The man was gaunt, tired, and aged beyond his years by hard labor. Moy studied the man closely. His head was slightly bowed and he seemed not to notice Moy's arrival. But the man's face drew Moy in closer. His skin was like a faded parchment, but the features were so similar to Moy's father's.

"Uncle? Uncle Huian? It is your nephew, Guanhua. Can you hear me?" Moy spoke softly in his father's native dialect.

The old man looked up at Moy, and for the first time in many years, he tried to look outside of himself. Guanhua was a name he hadn't heard in a lifetime, not since his nephew was a child. Before him, he saw the face of the man that his young nephew had grown to become.

"Guanhua, is that really you?" Moy Huian asked in a soft whisper. "I did not believe them when they said I was going to meet you. I thought it was just another of their tricks."

"It is no trick," Moy assured him. "You and I are here in London. I am taking you home with me."

Moy's half hour with his uncle passed quickly and both momentarily forgot about armed men in the adjacent room. At the appointed time, Kang entered the bedroom, interrupting the old man's quiet whispers.

"Are you satisfied that this man is your uncle?"

"Yes, and I am ready to complete our transaction.

Here is the key to my hotel room and another for the safe inside the closet. Send one of your men down to retrieve a computer diskette and a cashier's check from the safe. You will find all the passwords required to complete the file transfer on that disk. The disk also contains a list of all the files that you will need to duplicate the ciphering system. The list is written as a batch command, so once you log on to the secure computer, execute that file and the computer will do the rest. It should take no more than thirty minutes to download everything you've asked for."

Kang accepted the keys and turned them over to one of his men with a quick order to retrieve the disk. He poured himself a drink and offered one to Moy—which was declined. Five minutes later, the guard returned from Moy's room.

"Show me how to use the disk," Kang demanded.

Moy sat down in front of the laptop computer on the desk and inserted the diskette into the drive. Switching over the diskette, he requested a listing of the file directory; only two files appeared. Moy pointed at the first file on the screen.

"This one contains all the access codes to the computer. Just enter the codes in the order listed, and you will pass right through the machine's security. The other file is a batch program that automates your file retrieval. This is everything you requested."

"Excellent." Kang pocketed the diskette. "I must leave you now. You will remain here with your uncle until the file transfer is complete. If everything is as you say, I will order my men to release you both. If not . . ." Kang shrugged his shoulders.

"I understand," Moy replied, studying his aged uncle.

Kang barked out some orders to his men and left with two of them. The other three remained to guard Moy and his uncle. Moy hoped that Barnett's forces weren't too far away if anything went wrong.

Chapter 52

Kang left his men with strict orders regarding their guests. Moy and his uncle were to remain in the bedroom with two guards in the suite and one posted in the corridor. When the call came, they were to be eliminated quietly. A cache of opium in the suite would cast the suspicion that the two dead men were involved in a failed drug deal. The Chinese embassy would denounce Moy Huian's diplomatic papers as forgeries and provide documentation identifying him as an Asian drug smuggler. Phillip Moy's reputation as a dynamic entrepreneur would be stained by an alleged link to organized crime and drug trafficking.

Kang and his men took the elevator down to the hotel's parking level and retrieved their rented car for the trip to Parnell's office in Canary Wharf. Teams of agents, posted throughout the Hilton, monitored Kang's depar-

ture, each seamlessly handing responsibility for tracking the Chinese agent to the next person.

From a maintenance scaffold in the hotel's parking
garage, one of Axton's watchers picked up Kang and
his men as they left the elevator and located their car,
a black Mercedes-Benz.

"Team one to team two, Mad Hatter is moving,"
the watcher announced over his radio. Kang's men paid
no attention to the maintenance worker as they passed.
"Black Benz pulling onto Park Lane."

"Roger, team one," team two's lead answered. "We
have him."

Axton and Mosley listened to the radio traffic of
the watcher teams as they followed Kang Fa. Officially,
Mosley was there to observe the British side of the operation, but, with the large number of CIA personnel
assisting MI5 with the technical aspects of the sting,
the two senior agents treated it as a joint venture.

Axton's people kept track of all the players moving about, while Mosley's staff monitored the computer
linkup between Chicago and London. If everything
went well, British SAS officers would be making the arrests in a few hours.

From Looking Glass, they could clearly see Parnell's office. Below, thirty agents composing fifteen
teams formed a net that would draw close around Parnell's building. Mosley checked in with his line-
monitoring crews while Axton followed the status of
his watchers.

On the streets below, Nolan Kilkenny and British agent
Peter Stone were returning to Looking Glass after making a final check of the team monitoring the district's
telephone switching station. All the phone lines ser-

vicing Parnell's office and flat were tapped by British Intelligence with equipment from Moy Electronics.

Kilkenny and Stone blended in with the crowds of people milling about the street. As they approached Parnell's building, Kilkenny noticed a work crew by a manhole, several delivery vehicles, and assorted cars. Looking closely at the crowds as they roamed, he began to pick out people who weren't what they seemed. Despite the use of scarves and hats, he spotted the lightweight communications gear favored by the surveillance teams. A young lady in a pair of brightly colored running shorts and a tank top skated by on Rollerblades. Beneath her helmet, Kilkenny spotted a thin wire.

Kilkenny identified twelve teams of agents stationed around the building. The path that Stone and he followed was circular, randomly doubling back on itself in case Kang had any of his own people in the area. The last circular sweep ended behind the office building where British Intelligence had set up their base of operations. They were about to enter when Stone got a call over his headset. Kilkenny waited while Stone received new orders and signed off.

"Do you know anything about boats?" Stone asked.

Kilkenny smiled. After six years in the navy and a lifetime of sailing on the Great Lakes, he knew more than most people. "I can find my way around one if I have to. Why?"

"No reason really." Stone chuckled at the absurdity of the story he'd just been told. "A few days back, we managed to 'borrow' a slip in the marina underneath Parnell's building. Parnell has a boat down there, and we want to make sure that every exit is covered.

Our boat was supposed to be on-station by now, but its motor is running foul. They're puttering a ways upriver, but they're not going to be of much help to anybody. I've been ordered to suit up and take two men down to cover the marina. Axton has graciously asked if you'd be willing to give our boys on the boat a hand when they finally get here. There's a small dock alongside the park where they'll tie up."

"Sure, I'll see what I can do," Kilkenny said, accepting the assignment. "Beats waiting upstairs anyway. I don't think your boss likes having strangers hanging around his command post."

"Axton's a strange one all right," Stone agreed, "but he knows his business."

Stone walked Kilkenny over to the edge of the park where he was to wait, then bought him a newspaper. It was a pleasantly warm, overcast May afternoon with less than an hour to go before the file transfer was scheduled to occur. Kilkenny sat down on a park bench and began flipping through *The Times* while waiting for the troubled boat.

Several boats moved along the river: a couple of tourist ships and a small barge. When Kilkenny was younger, his uncle had often taken him out to Belle Isle or the Saint Clair River to watch the great ships on days like this. He'd spent many afternoons along the shore, hoping to catch a glimpse of a thousand-foot freighter.

An older man with a bag of bird feed strolled along the river walk and sat beside him on the bench. Soon a small congregation of pigeons flocked at his feet, waiting for the next handful of seed to be dispensed.

"A lovely day, is it not?" the man asked in thickly accented English.

"Yes," Kilkenny replied, "though I wouldn't mind a little more sun."

"Young man," the stranger's tone became more serious, "why are you here?"

Kilkenny feigned innocence. "I'm just sitting in the park, enjoying the day."

"That is not true." The stranger's rebuke was firm, but not angry. "I have been watching you since you arrived. You are involved with a surveillance operation, but only as an observer. Officers of the British government are stationed all around *that* building." The old man nodded his head in the direction of several teams visible from where they sat. "I also believe the base of this operation is located on the twelfth floor of this building. Don't bother to deny these facts or feign ignorance of them. I know them to be true. I also know that you are Nolan Kilkenny, from the United States. So I ask you again: Why are you here?"

Everything the stranger had said was true, but Kilkenny couldn't guess where this man's interest lay. The power and confidence with which the man spoke reminded him of Jackson Barnett. Like Barnett, the man's complete grasp of the situation made Nolan feel like a pawn in this game. Kilkenny also sensed that any denials he made would be a waste of breath.

"Are you with British Intelligence?"

"Yes and no," the stranger replied cryptically. "It depends upon your point of view. I am very interested in what is about to happen inside that building. For a close friend of mine, it's a matter of life and death. I believe that you know about such things already. Did you not face death recently?"

There was no threat in the man's voice, nothing that roused Kilkenny's defenses. The man *knew* about the attack on the interstate and appeared to sympathize with him. "Yes."

"Did you know that the death you faced has a name? I have lost others to this practitioner of death, good people who did not deserve to die. You and your companion were fortunate when you faced him. I hope that my Anya will fare as well."

Kilkenny knew whom the man was talking about. "Kang Fa."

"Yes. I could tell you many stories about Kang Fa, but I will summarize his career with this one fact: Kang Fa leaves nothing behind. He is a perfectionist who eliminates all loose ends."

The man took a glance at his watch. "My time grows short. Beneath that building lies a marina. It is the one weak point in Axton's defenses, weak because I have made it so."

"The engine trouble on the boat?" Nolan guessed.

"Very perceptive. If Kang Fa remains true to his past, once he has acquired the ciphers, he will kill Parnell and my Anya. That is his way. They will remain alive only as long as Kang Fa needs them, which brings us back to the marina. Once the net begins to draw tight, Kang will need a way out."

Kilkenny began to see the strategy that the old man was laying out for him. "Stone told me that Parnell keeps a boat down in the marina."

"You grasp the situation quickly. I expected no less from a former commando. When it becomes clear to Kang that he is trapped, Anya will offer him this way out. It is my hope that she will be able to free herself during the escape attempt."

"And if Kang escapes?"

"That is a risk I am willing to take for my friend.

With your help, I can minimize that risk. Come with me. We both have our own scores to settle with Kang Fa."

Kilkenny thought about what the man had said, and everything was true. Mosley had briefed him on Kang Fa, and the Chinese agent was as ruthless as they came. While his mind urged caution, his gut told him to trust the old man. Six years in the SEALs had taught Kilkenny to listen to both.

"Sir, what is your name?"

The old man grinned, knowing that he had an ally. "Yakushev, Andrei Yakushev."

Twelve stories above the riverside park, Axton and Mosley awaited the arrival of Kang Fa. Mosley picked up a pair of binoculars and began surveying the grounds around Parnell's building. A helicopter, code-named *Eagle*, maintained a safe distance, holding its position upriver. All of Axton's teams were in place and everything seemed ready.

Axton joined Mosley, who stood at the window studying the scene below. "Kang's making good time in traffic, ETA of ten minutes."

"Excellent. I checked in with the computer teams; they're all ready for the linkup. The ground teams are all in position and . . ." Mosley paused. Something on the ground near Parnell's building suddenly caught his attention. "Wait a minute?"

"What is it?" Axton tried to find what Mosley had spotted.

"Damn! What's Kilkenny doing down there?"

"What are you looking at? Where?"

Mosley handed the binoculars to Axton in disgust. "Down in the park, those two people on the river walk.

The redhead is Nolan Kilkenny; he's supposed to be waiting to assist your boat. Is that one of your people with him?"

Axton focused in on the two men. Unfortunately, their backs were turned toward him. "I can't tell if it's one of ours or not. Kilkenny seems to be following the other man. Wait—they've slipped over the railing onto the dock. I can't see them now, but they're headed for the marina."

Axton switched on his headset microphone. "Team five, this is Looking Glass, over."

"Team five here," Stone replied from the marina lobby.

"Stone, we have a possible security breach near the marina. Kilkenny and another person are headed down to the river entrance. See if you can find out what the hell he's doing."

"Will do, sir." Stone signed off and flagged one of the other officers over. "Williams, do a perimeter sweep of the marina for a pair of civilians. See if you can find them. One is that Yank—Kilkenny."

As Williams went off to search for the intruders, Stone and the remaining officer took their positions near the marina lobby.

Kilkenny and Yakushev slipped into the marina and hid themselves near the entrance. A large sailboat screened their position from the three officers posted in the lobby. Shortly after they arrived, one of the officers split off from the other two and began checking the boat slips.

"Andrei, those men are the replacements for the crew of the boat you disabled. One of them is starting to sniff around—looks like someone noticed us heading over here."

"It's of little matter. This is a large marina with ample room for concealment. We must remain in a position to aid Roe when the time comes."

Chapter 53

It was 5:00 P.M., the end of the business day, and the building's professional tenants were leaving their offices for the weekend. Kang and his men were waiting quietly in Parnell's office as the staff filed out. By 5:15, only Parnell, Roe, and the Chinese agents remained inside the suite. Parnell locked the doors and returned to his office.

"Can we hear anything?" Axton asked the sound engineer.

"No, sir. I can't filter them out from the noisemaker that Kang's running. None of their speech is intelligible."

"Keep trying," Axton urged. "We need to know what's going on in there, and I'm a terrible lip-reader."

Inside Parnell's office, the mood was tense. Only Kang appeared confident and unaffected by anticipation.

"It's time," Parnell announced.

Roe sat down at Parnell's computer and accessed the communications program. After cruising through a few local computer networks, Roe logged into the Piccadilly Gardener's server. Then she sat back and began to wait.

"What is she doing, Parnell? Why did she stop?"

Roe answered Kang directly. "The final connection to Moy's computer will be made through a remote system. I'm waiting for that connection to be made before I continue."

Too bad the screen faces away from the window, Mosley thought as he watched through the binoculars. I'd love to see what Roe is doing.

"Gatekeeper one, this is Looking Glass. Over," Mosley called out.

"This is Gatekeeper one. Over, Looking Glass."

"Are you monitoring an outgoing signal?"

"Yes, sir. We've got a clean signal from the Tea Party. They're holding at a local server."

"Keep on it, Gatekeeper one," Mosley advised. "Looking Glass out." Mosley turned to Axton, who was talking with the sound engineers. "So far so good. Roe's right where she's supposed to be. It's five-twenty now, so in five minutes, the Spyder should be going on-line."

Grin watched the clock in Newton's lab with Harbke and Ullrich, the second hand sweeping out each minute as it closed in on 12:25. Right on schedule, the Spyder logged on to the university network. Using separate lines, it burrowed two pathways out of Ann Arbor. The Spyder bounced through ten computer networks in each direction, crisscrossing the country before making its final connections.

Grin had brought in a large-screen color monitor,

which he attached to the laptop so they could watch the action unfold. Harbke was on a conference call with Washington, relaying status reports to the staff there. At 12:27, the Spyder logged into the Moy Electronics Corporation. At 12:28, it passed through that system security and was poised to strike once Moy's secure computer came on-line.

The Moy computer network appeared in a window on the right side of Grin's large monitor. On the left side, contrasting the superb graphics and professional design of the Moy screen, was the bland text-based menu of the Piccadilly Gardener. After logging on to the server as user Woodrow, the Spyder requested a private chat session with user Iris.

Roe's computer beeped as the server notified her that Woodrow was requesting a private chat session with Iris. She agreed to chat and a direct link was made to the Spyder.

"I believe we're ready for the codes," Parnell announced.

Kang retrieved the diskette from his inside coat pocket and handed it over, repeating Phillip Moy's explanation on how the information was to be used. Parnell inserted the disk into a notebook computer on his desk and brought up the instructions. Roe issued a series of control codes that gave her direct access to Moy's computer network. The chat screen disappeared and was replaced by a colorful display from Moy Electronics.

Mosley had Gatekeeper teams on both sides of the Atlantic reporting in on the link between Parnell's office and the Moy network. "She's connected to Chicago, Neville. All stations are reporting in."

"That's it, you buggers. Take the bait," Axton whispered, urging the people across the park to commit their crime.

At 5:30 London time, Roe requested access to Moy Electronics' secure computer. Normally, the network would issue a reply that the requested computer was unavailable, but today the network granted her request. She followed Phillip Moy's instructions to the letter. The Moy computer responded favorably and granted her access to the cipher files.

"We're in," Roe announced. The relief in her voice was apparent. "Now I need that batch program."

Parnell handed over the diskette and Roe executed the program. Within seconds, the Moy computer began disgorging millions of bytes of information across the electronic connection. The read-write optical disk drive attached to Parnell's computer hummed as the platter inside reached the desired rate of revolution. Bit by bit, the semiconductor lasers modified the optical disk's surface, inscribing the data flowing out of the computer in Chicago.

On monitors from Chicago to London, agents from three different governmental services watched as computer files detailing the latest United States ciphers passed illegally out of the country. More than one of those who were watching the transaction wondered, If protected files like Moy's were so easy to obtain, how well defended were the rest of the nation's secrets from brilliant, dedicated, and ruthless thieves?

Roe got up to stretch her legs and walked over to the window. The file transfer had been running for thirty minutes, no doubt slowed by some of the systems that they were using to hide their entry into the Moy network. From Parnell's corner office, she looked down the river and over at the adjacent park. Across the Thames, a new office tower rose from the dilapidated warehouses of the old empire.

Kang joined Roe at the window. "It's quite a view. On a clear day, you might even be able to see the Houses of Parliament." Kang waved his hand upriver.

"Actually, it's more to the left," Roe corrected him. "The Thames snakes around quite a bit down here, but its general direction is that way."

Kang looked off into the distance, but the overcast haze blurred the horizon into a blotchy abstraction. A helicopter passed across his field of vision, drawing his attention as it moved along the skyline.

Unusual for it to be flying so low, he thought. Perhaps it is just riding beneath the low cloud cover.

He watched it circle the area again, making a low, lazy circle east of the building. He briefly considered what purpose the helicopter might serve, then dismissed it.

Parnell's computer beeped; the transfer from Moy was complete. Roe returned to the computer and verified that the optical disk had recorded the ciphering information. All the files were there, as Moy had promised. Roe logged out of the Moy network and ordered the Spyder to sever its connections. Like a cascade of falling dominoes, the screens of those watching the file transfer went blank as the Spyder went off-line.

Parnell retrieved the optical disk and handed it to Kang. "Here is everything you requested."

Kang inspected the sealed disk cartridge for a moment before sliding it into his coat pocket. "Thank you. Now I must make a phone call."

Kang picked up the phone and dialed a local number. It rang only once before being answered. The guard who answered the phone didn't speak, per Kang's orders. In his native tongue, Kang spoke just one word to the man: "Go."

No reply was required for the order. The guard cradled the handset and nodded to his compatriot. Each man pulled a silenced pistol from his shoulder holster and checked his weapon.

Chapter 54

"Hilton teams," Axton called out over the radio. "This is Looking Glass. Over."

The leader of the Special Air Service strike team surrounding the Hilton responded to Axton's call. "Hilton team leader here. Over, Looking Glass."

Axton spoke slowly and clearly, as if he was dictating a letter. "All clear. Move in on the suite."

"Understood, Looking Glass," the leader replied. "We're moving in."

The SAS teams were stationed at several points inside the twenty-eight-story hotel, positioned to choke off all egress from the building on a moment's notice. After Kang departed, two teams moved up the tower and took up position on the twenty-sixth floor, at opposite ends of the corridor leading to Kang Fa's suite. Most of the rooms on that floor were held empty today, by official request. The rest held plainclothes British police posing as guests.

Black-garbed officers emerged from the stair towers, two on each end of the long corridor. Earlier reconnaissance of the floor by an officer dressed as a hotel waiter informed the teams that only one guard was posted outside the suite. Subtracting the two that accompanied Kang to Canary Wharf left two inside with the hostages.

The team leader issued his orders via a throat mike, which made his voice sound a little like Donald Duck in his team members' headsets. The first pair sprang from the stairway alcove into the main corridor, the sudden motion attracting the guard's attention. As he drew his weapon, the lead officer took aim and fired a round through the man's throat. It was an easy shot, less than fifty yards with no wind. The single bullet obliterated the man's larynx and shattered the base of his skull. A quiet, one-shot stop. The guard slumped to the hallway floor, dead before he hit the ground.

Inside the suite, the two remaining guards froze when they heard a muffled thump outside the door. The one in charge motioned for the other to check on the sentry outside while he dealt with the hostages.

The lead guard entered the bedroom quietly, pistol drawn but concealed behind him. The old man they'd escorted from China remained seated on the bed, head down in a permanent bow. A gurgling sound in the bathroom told him the American nephew was indisposed. Killing them one at a time greatly simplified the job.

He smiled politely at the elder Moy, pulled his weapon, and aimed it toward the man's head, both hands clasped around the grip. He started to pull back on the trigger when the old man, using every last ounce of adrenaline in his body, lunged, springing toward him from the bed.

This moment was an opportunity that Moy Huian had dreamed about in the deepest recesses of his mind, an ember of his desire to live that he now fanned into flame. Despite the frailty of age and past abuse, he struck, knowing full well that he would either win his life back or die trying.

Moy Huian landed a crushing blow, grinding his heel into the top of the assassin's shoe. A snapping sound confirmed that several of the long, thin bones running the length of the man's foot had shattered. The guard's instant of surprise turned to pain. Huian's second blow sent a mind-numbing shock through the man's forearm, and as it turned him around, his weapon fell to the floor.

Phillip Moy emerged from behind the door only seconds after Huian had begun his attack. He drove his fist into the guard's floating ribs, breaking three more of the man's bones. His next strike, a blow to the man's head, was hardly necessary following his uncle's attack. The guard fell to the floor, battered and unconscious. Moy retrieved the guard's pistol and moved into the other room.

Just as Moy Huian had landed his first blows, the remaining guard opened the suite door. A black-suited SAS officer charged and drove him backward into the suite with a vicious kick to the groin. The guard crashed into a chair before tumbling to the floor. The officer checked the room, then crouched over the fallen man and pressed his assault rifle against the man's face. No words were exchanged. The guard laid his weapon down and surrendered.

"Drop the weapon!" the SAS team leader shouted as two more men emerged from the bedroom, one holding a pistol.

Moy dropped the pistol and raised his hands as one of the soldiers frisked him. He knew not to make any sudden moves until the assault team had verified his identity. "Officer, my uncle and I are very happy to see you."

"You're Phillip Moy?" the officer asked, taking a closer look at him.

"Yes, and this is my uncle, Moy Huian. My identification is in my coat pocket." His uncle bowed for the introduction.

The team leader found the wallet and verified Moy's identity. "We counted three guards earlier. Where's the other one?"

Moy brought his hands back down to his sides and relaxed a little. "He's in the bedroom. I think he's still alive, but I didn't stop to check."

One of the other officers emerged from the bedroom and nodded to the team leader that he'd found the other guard. "Holster your weapons; this area is secure." The strike team's leader switched his headset mike on. "Hilton team to Looking Glass, over."

"Report, Hilton team," Axton answered, eager for news.

"The hostages are secure. I repeat, the hostages are secure."

Mosley and Axton both smiled at the good news. "Understood, Hilton team, well done. Wharf teams— crash the Tea Party!"

On the ground, several teams began to close around Parnell's building. All roads leading to the building were barricaded and uniformed traffic police began ushering all pedestrians and vehicles away from the area. The helicopter moved out of its holding pattern and took up position over the building. The net was drawing tight.

Chapter 55

After completing his call, Kang walked over to the bar where Parnell was fixing himself a drink. Roe, who had been unusually pensive throughout the exchange, stood at the window, staring blankly at the hazy London skyline. Yakushev had warned her about Kang, and now Roe wondered if this ruthless PRC agent would live up to his reputation for violence. Roe's question was answered by the metallic sound of an Uzi being readied to fire.

"There is just one more item of business before I leave. It is regrettable, but I cannot permit either of you to live with knowledge of this operation. Such a breach of security would be unacceptable."

Parnell's drink fell to the floor as the threat of Kang's betrayal became clear to him. "This is outrageous! We have an agreement, and we have fulfilled our end. You have my word as a gentleman that this transaction will remain in our strictest confidence."

"Your word as a *gentleman*, Parnell?" Kang parroted back with a laugh. "The days of honor and chivalry in England, and China, are long past. This is business, nothing more."

Kang placed his briefcase on Parnell's conference table and opened it. From inside, he retrieved a thick file folder. Parnell recognized it as one of his "special" reports.

"This is a copy of the information that you supplied to our mutual acquaintance, Wu Zhusheng." Kang fanned the report dramatically, showing extensive red marks on several sheets of the document. "Unfortunately for Wu, the information in this report contains significant errors. These errors were discovered too late for Wu to salvage his considerable investment in this project. My government has also withdrawn its support for several of Wu's ventures, leaving his company financially ruined. Wu arrived in London this morning to face those he feels responsible for his losses. After 'murdering' the two of you, Wu will return to his hotel room and 'commit suicide.' We've left Wu where he will be found in a day or two."

Kang tossed the sheaf of paper in an arc around the floor. "These documents, found in this office with your bodies, will provide a plausible explanation for your deaths."

"I don't think it'll be quite that simple, Kang," Roe announced calmly as she stared out the window.

Kang was momentarily stunned by the use of his real name, but he quickly regained his composure. "What problem do you see with my plan?"

"Actually, I see several problems surrounding this building right now. Correct me if I'm wrong, but I believe the authorities have closed off the area." Roe spoke in deliberate, measured tones to emphasize the gravity of Kang's plight. "If you kill us, you kill any real chance of escaping with the ciphers."

For the first time, Kang's stony composure cracked, revealing a sense of fear and uncertainty. Roe was telling him the truth: The streets below the office tower were empty, barricaded by police. The helicopter he'd seen earlier took up a new position near the tower. A net was being cast and Kang could feel it drawing closed around him.

"What are you offering in return for your life?"

"A way out," Roe replied. "We all need to get out of the country as quickly as possible, but first we need to get out of this building. There's one route that doesn't appear to be blocked: the marina. Ian's got a fast boat that should buy us some time and distance. We can figure out our next steps later, but right now, I think we should get moving."

Mosley watched the scene in Parnell's office unfold through his binoculars. "Something's happening over there. The Chinese have just pulled their weapons. Kang's at the window; I think he's spotted the ground teams."

"Probably sensing a double cross." It was a risk bringing in the police, but they had to be sure that the area was completely sealed off. "Looking Glass to all teams. Proceed with caution. Subjects are armed and aware of your approach."

One by one, the teams acknowledged Axton's directive. They'd lost the element of surprise. Hopefully, their superior numbers would be enough.

Kang turned to Parnell. "Is what she says true? Can you get us out of here?"

"Let me check the river," Parnell replied. He joined Roe and Kang at the window and studied the winding Thames below. Kang's men kept their weapons trained on Parnell and Roe, awaiting their orders. "Alex is right. It's clear as far as I can see, nothing but barge traffic and a couple tour boats. If they don't block the river between here and the coast, I can get us out to international waters. Can you do anything from there?"

Kang knew that at any time there were several Chinese freighters near European ports. "It's possible. Let's go."

On Kang's orders, his men lowered their weapons against Parnell and Roe but kept them ready. As they exited the suite, they saw two SAS soldiers in the corridor rushing toward them.

"Back inside!" Kang ordered as his men opened fire.

The corridor began to fill with the smoky scent of gunfire. The SAS soldiers drove Kang's men back into the suite with short bursts from their submachine guns. Exposed as they were in the wide corridor, the soldiers pressed their attack, knowing it was the only way for them to stay alive.

Kang also quickly grasped the tactical situation. "You"—he pointed to one of his men—"open fire down the corridor. Shoot wildly to keep those soldiers pinned down."

The man did as he was told and, exposing only the barrel of his weapon, began spraying bullets in the direction of their pursuers.

"Those soldiers are pinned down with no protection. Finish them," Kang ordered his other man.

The two Asians leapt into the corridor, each picking a target and firing their weapons on full automatic. Hot brass casings spiraled through the air as they emptied their clips of ammunition into the prone soldiers, who had closed within twelve feet of the suite door. One of the soldiers managed to fire a short burst, grazing one of the Asians, before several bullets transformed his face into a bloody pulp.

When the Asians' weapons were empty, the corridor became eerily quiet. Parnell and the others felt a slight ringing in their ears from the loud bursts of sound that had accompanied the violent exchange.

"Good work," Kang congratulated his men as they snapped fresh clips of ammunition into their weapons.

Kang turned from the carnage and noticed the counters on the elevators increasing toward their floor. "More soldiers are coming. Which way out?"

"Upstairs," Parnell replied, stepping over bloodied bodies in the stairwell. "We'll use the residents' express elevator."

"Move!" Kang barked, and his men complied.

The condominium level above Parnell's office had six elevators instead of the five available on the office floors. The elevator must have been nearby, because the doors opened almost immediately after Parnell hit the button. The fugitives boarded the elevator car as Parnell punched in the access code for the marina level. The second team of SAS soldiers reached the twelfth floor just as Parnell's elevator car sped past.

Chapter 56

After listening to the first team's disastrous encounter with Kang's men over their headsets, the second team emerged from the elevator ready for a firefight. Team two's leader expected the worst, but he found the elevator lobby empty. The soldiers fanned out from the lobby, moving from doorway to doorway down the corridor. They reached the stairwell, where the other team had been ambushed. The team leader left two men there while the rest searched Parnell's office; it was empty.

"Team two leader to Looking Glass. The office is secure. No sign of them. Three men are down. We'll have to do a floor-by-floor search."

Axton felt as if his luck had just run out. "Understood, team two leader. Keep us advised of your progress. Looking Glass out."

"Damn it!" Mosley growled.

"Looking Glass to all teams," Axton announced.

"The subjects are on the move. Don't take any chances with them."

Kilkenny and Yakushev successfully evaded detection by the lone officer searching for them. They moved quietly along the docks, hiding behind and occasionally inside the boats berthed there. They'd doubled back on their pursuer and were now concealed by a sleek green offshore racing boat.

"Do you see that dark blue vessel over there?" Yakushev asked as they knelt out of view.

Kilkenny scanned the slips on the opposite side of the marina until he found a metallic blue racing boat. "The Cigarette named *Merlin*?"

"That's Parnell's boat. If Anya is convincing, she will draw Kang Fa down to it for his escape."

"They'll have to get past Stone and his men first. As long as Kang doesn't kill your friend once they get here, she might make it." Kilkenny studied the path between *Merlin*'s slip and the marina entrance, trying to picture how the action would unfold.

"Yes, and we must be ready to assist her when the time comes."

On the far side of the marina, Kilkenny could see the elevator lobby and the door to the stair tower. Roe and the others would be coming from that direction. The layout of the marina provided Kilkenny and Yakushev with good cover for when the shooting started.

In the marina lobby, he watched as Stone and another officer shifted position. Stone entered the stairwell, with the other officer covering his back.

"Something's happening, Andrei. They've moved off their points."

Kilkenny had lost track of the third officer and was

trying to locate him when the man stepped around the bow of the boat that they were hiding behind.

"All right, gentlemen. The game's over."

Before the officer could say another word, a bell in the marina lobby signaled the arrival of an elevator car. As the car door slid open, Stone's partner turned from the stair tower, drawn out by the sound. The elevator lobby was partially shielded from the stairwell opening, enough so that Kang and his men saw the SAS soldier first.

Kang fired immediately; his first burst hammered into Stone's partner, ripping through the side of the man's head. A second burst pounded into the man's protective body armor, flinging him backward into Stone. The impact knocked Stone's weapon from his hands and sent him staggering back behind the protective wall, unarmed.

The soldier on the docks turned and rushed to Stone's aid, firing into the elevator to cover his partner's retreat. Kang responded with a deadly salvo down the long, straight dock and killed the man.

"Kill the other one," Kang ordered, dispatching one of his men to deal with Stone. "Parnell, where is your boat?"

"Right over there," Parnell replied, leading the way.

Stealthily, Kilkenny retrieved the fallen officer's pistol and took careful aim at Kang's man. He clustered three shots in the man's chest and dropped him at Stone's feet.

The sound of Kilkenny's shots echoed in the marina, instantly drawing fire from Kang and his lieutenant. Bullets riddled the dock and the boats around Kilkenny, pinning him down while Parnell readied his boat. Ignoring the

"No wake" rule, Parnell shot *Merlin* out of her slip like a racehorse.

Kang emptied his weapon in a vain attempt to kill Stone, whose sprint from the stairwell was screened by a row of boats. Parnell's quick turns and the jarring bumps from the rebounding wake prevented Kang from getting a clean shot off.

Roe crouched on *Merlin's* stern, still clutching the line she'd cleared as the boat thundered toward the river opening. As *Merlin* reached the entrance of the enclosed marina, she jumped. Instead of cool water, she felt a sudden jolt as Kang's watchful lieutenant tackled her in midair and slammed her down on the fiberglass hull. Her arms dangled in *Merlin's* frothy wake. Grinning at her contemptuously, he pulled her harshly into the boat.

"We wouldn't want you falling overboard," Kang said with a sneer as he held the barrel of his weapon under Roe's chin. "At least not until I've had a chance to review your role in this betrayal." Kang turned to his man. "Lash her to the chair."

Merlin cleared the marina with a deafening roar as Parnell opened up the boat's engines. Kang's lieutenant grabbed a length of the ship's line and secured Roe to the captain's chair beside Parnell. Kilkenny and Yakushev watched as the Cigarette boat sped out into the Thames with Roe still on board.

Chapter 57

Stone reached the open slip, winded but uninjured. "I don't know what the hell you're doing down here, Kilkenny, but I'm very thankful just the same."

Kilkenny accepted Stone's hand, which trembled a little as they shook. "I've been there a few times myself, Pete."

"So, Nolan, who's your friend?"

"Andrei Yakushev," the retired spymaster replied, "at your service."

Stone arched an eyebrow at Yakushev. "We've been looking for you all week."

Kilkenny looked at Stone's bullet-torn uniform. "You okay?"

Stone's chest felt sore where several rounds had hammered against his Kevlar vest. "I guess I'm okay, thanks to you. I'd just like to take another crack at those bastards. They've taken out five of our men today."

Kilkenny eyed the Heckler-Koch MP5-K Stone was cradling. "Would you *really* like another shot at them?"

"Damn right I would!" Stone replied. "What do you have in mind?"

Kilkenny thumped the side of the green offshore racer berthed beside them. "Simple. We go after 'em."

"If that's the case, we're going to need some more firepower. Here," Stone said as he tossed his rifle to Kilkenny, "I'll be back in a minute."

While Stone sprinted back to collect arms and ammunition from his fallen men, Kilkenny and Yakushev prepared to commandeer the offshore racing boat. Kilkenny's luck held out as he discovered the keys in a bin beside the wheel. Stone returned and leapt on board as Kilkenny fired up the boat's engines and familiarized himself with its controls. The boat was obviously the toy of a very wealthy man; it had been custom-fitted for its owner and bore an unusual paint scheme. The needle-pointed bow was emblazoned with the same tooth-filled shark's mouth design found on RAF fighter planes. The boat's markings finally made sense to him as he pulled it out of the slip and noticed the name painted across the foredeck: *Spitfire*.

"Well, girl," Nolan muttered to himself, "I hope your owner named you well, because I'm about to see what you're made of."

Kilkenny took a little more care than Parnell in navigating the *Spitfire* out of the marina, but the wake radiating behind him still sent the docked ships clattering in their berths. When he last saw *Merlin*, the Cigarette boat had turned downriver toward the sea. Slamming the throttle forward, even Kilkenny was surprised by the boat's response. Backing up the boat's name were a pair of jet-turbine helicopter engines refitted for marine use.

The owner had named his ocean racer after the RAF Spitfires he watched as a youth, battling over Britain against the Luftwaffe. The marine incarnation of the Spitfire was a fifty-foot-long hull of honeycombed Kevlar hurtling down the Thames.

"Pete," Nolan shouted over the engine's thunderous roar, "see if you can raise Axton and Mosley on your headset. Let them know what's happened, and tell them we'll try to slow Parnell down until help arrives. We don't want them thinking we're part of Kang's team."

"I'm on it." Covering both ears to block out the engine noise, Stone tried to connect with Looking Glass.

"I'd hate to have both sides shooting at us," Kilkenny muttered under his breath.

Stone contacted Axton and gave a concise report on his situation, starting from the ambush at the marina elevator to their current boat pursuit. Axton was pleased with Stone's initiative, until he learned who was with him.

"Say again, Stone!" Axton demanded. "Who's in that boat with you?"

Stone shouted his answer slowly and clearly. "Nolan Kilkenny and Andrei Yakushev. They saved my life, sir."

One side of the conversation was enough for Yakushev to figure out what was being said. He leaned close to Kilkenny. "I don't think Stone's superiors approve of his current choice of company."

"They damn well better, or their spies are going out to sea." Kilkenny turned his head and shouted over the engine noise. "How far to the coast?"

Stone took a quick look at the shoreline to get his bearings. "It's about forty-five or fifty kilometers to the Thames estuary and another thirty to the open sea."

Kilkenny ran through the math in his head. "Our

best chance of catching these guys is if we can keep them bottled up in the river. Once they hit the ocean, your people will never be able to catch them. See if Axton agrees with me on that. If he can block the river before it widens too much, we can run them down. At this speed, we've got about twenty minutes before they hit the estuary."

Axton and Mosley concurred with Kilkenny's assessment and issued a frantic series of calls from Looking Glass. Below, strike teams broke from their positions and began moving downriver by land.

Axton studied the map closely, then called out to the helicopter for a visual report. "*Eagle*, has Parnell cleared the flood barrier at Silvertown?"

"Yes, sir," the pilot reported, "about two minutes ago. Kilkenny and Stone are passing through right now and closing. The two boats should be in sight of each other in another minute."

"That gives them another ten kilometers before the next barrier." Axton switched his microphone back on. "This is Looking Glass to Home Office, do you copy?"

"Home Office here, Looking Glass. We've been monitoring your situation. What assistance do you require?"

Axton marked the stretch of river where they would trap Parnell's boat. "I need the Thames flood barriers closed down between Silvertown and Tilbury and I need it done now!"

Spitfire was approaching the turn in the river near North Woolwich when the automated gates began to close. Up ahead, Kilkenny saw the white-water rooster tail of *Merlin*. The Thames had opened up into a relatively straight passage of water, allowing Kilkenny to push his engines full throttle. *Spitfire*'s screws bit into the calm river water, bringing it to a boil behind her blades. The bow of the boat rose high in the water, baring her teeth to those in her way.

A thundering sound reverberated off the river, echoing with an explosion of power behind them. Parnell and his passengers looked upriver and saw a man-made shark flying across the water in their direction. The pursuing ship's vicious image was not lost on any of them.

"Faster, Parnell!" Kang ordered. "They're gaining on us!"

"She's at full throttle now, but it won't do much good," Parnell replied. "I know that boat. They'll run us down before we can reach the sea."

Kang slammed a fresh clip into his weapon. "Then we'll have to deal with them here."

Merlin's bow rode high, as if the boat was trying to break free of the water. Kang and his lieutenant positioned themselves in the stern of the boat. Both men crouched into a squat position that provided adequate cover and additional support for their arms as they trained their weapons on the approaching craft.

Parnell was right—even with his boat pushed to the limit, the monstrous green vessel kept closing the distance. Kang crouched by the rear deck and waited until *Spitfire* loomed large enough to provide clear targets.

A voice from above crackled in Stone's headset. "*Spitfire*, this is *Eagle*. Do you read me?"

Stone began scanning the skies for the surveillance helicopter. He was unable to hear *Eagle*'s thumping rotors over *Spitfire*'s engines. "*Eagle*, where the hell are you?"

"Ahead of you," the pilot answered. "I'm skirting the shore parallel to the boat you're chasing."

Kilkenny noticed that Stone was talking over his headset and looking around for something. "What are you looking for?"

Stone looked ahead over the port side. He found *Eagle* darting in and out of the low cloud cover ahead of their boat. He pointed at the helicopter and Kilkenny nodded. Stone then crawled into the bow cabin, where he could hear more clearly.

On the basis of Stone's first signal, Looking Glass had ordered the helicopter downriver to keep pace with *Merlin*. At full speed and traveling as the crow flies, the helicopter had easily caught up with her. Unfortunately, *Eagle* wasn't a gunship, or it could have done more than just watch the action from above. Stone finished the update with the helicopter pilot and emerged from the cabin.

"What's the word?" Kilkenny asked.

"It seems that the chaps up ahead of us have noticed our approach."

"I can't imagine why," Kilkenny commented sarcastically; *Spitfire* was loud and fast. "What are they doing?"

"*Eagle* reports that they're running flat out, but we're closing quickly. Two of them have taken up position on the stern with weapons ready."

"And they'll be firing once we're in range." Kilkenny studied the shortening distance of water that separated the two speeding boats. "All right, everybody, hang tight. I'm going to throw this green beast through some moves."

The Thames began widening as they approached the sea, the river stretching nearly five hundred meters across as Kilkenny turned the boat on a sharp diagonal course.

Spitfire reveled in the challenge, sending foaming white sheets of water into the air.

Kilkenny's evasive maneuvers slowed their approach toward *Merlin* somewhat, but it successfully kept the spies from taking an easy shot at them. Kilkenny cut wide toward shore before sharply turning to port again, bringing his side of the boat close in for their first strafing pass. With his left hand on the wheel, Kilkenny raised the MP5 with his right and strafed the metallic blue craft. Stone and Yakushev followed his lead and fired over the starboard side.

Bullets tore into *Merlin*'s hull, splintering the fiberglass and ripping through the cushioned seating. Stone took careful aim and clustered three rounds in a tight circle on the forehead of Kang's lieutenant, killing him instantly. Kilkenny pulled the boat away, holding his course toward the north shore before swinging back for another pass.

"How are you two doing back there?"

"Nothing more than a few scratches to the hull," Stone replied.

"I am also uninjured," answered Yakushev.

"Great! We got one of theirs, but the next pass won't be so easy. Are you both ready for another run?"

Stone and Yakushev replied by slipping fresh clips of ammunition into their weapons. Kilkenny brought *Spitfire* about, turning back in the direction of *Merlin*. He drew an imaginary arc across the water, aiming the boat not for where *Merlin* was but where it would soon be. Yakushev and Stone crouched on the port side as *Spitfire* made her next approach.

The dual-opposed engines showed no signs of strain with the grueling paces Kilkenny was running them through. The needle on the engine temperature gauge was centered in the middle of the normal range and the rpms were only three-quarters to the redline. *Spitfire* was a well-engineered, well-crafted machine.

Kang took aim and fired as the menacing green ship closed upon them. He emptied twenty rounds into *Spitfire*, raking the bow and shattering the windscreen in front of Kilkenny. Stone and Yakushev popped up briefly just as Kilkenny drove *Spitfire* over *Merlin*'s wake. Both fired wildly, their aim disrupted by the hammering of their ship's hull in the wake behind *Merlin*. Before Stone could adjust his aim, Kang peppered his chest and arm with several rounds. Stone collapsed backward, landing beside Yakushev as the skirmish ended.

Kilkenny looked over his shoulder and saw Yakushev and the wounded Stone. "Andrei, how bad is it?"

"Difficult to say. He is bleeding extensively, but—"

"I'm okay," Stone said with a start, his head shaking as if he'd just awakened from a bad dream. "Just busted up my arm, that's all."

Yakushev helped Stone sit up, an effort that caused obvious pain. "I am definitely alive—being dead wouldn't hurt this much."

"Sure as hell beats the alternative," Kilkenny added, knowing from personal experience. "Andrei, there should be a first-aid kit in the bow. See what you can find to patch him up. Hang in there, Stone. You'll be fine."

Stone grimaced at Kilkenny, then cupped the hand from his good arm over his ear. "Could you ease up on the engines? I'm getting a signal from Looking Glass. They want us to back off."

"Back off? All right, but I hope they've got something in mind." Kilkenny brought *Spitfire* to a stop while *Merlin* continued its drive toward the sea. "Let me borrow that headset while Andrei cleans you up."

Kilkenny helped Stone remove his communication gear and body armor. The chest plate had stopped several potentially lethal rounds, leaving only deep bruises on Stone's chest. His arm, on the other hand, had been torn open. Stone would be fine as long as they could stop the bleeding. Yakushev returned with the first-aid kit and began tending Stone's injuries.

"All right, Mosley, what the hell is going on?" Kilkenny shouted into the microphone.

"Kilkenny, you dumb son of a bitch," Mosley growled back. "You really got yourself into it this time. How's your crew doing?"

"Stone took a couple rounds on the last pass." Kilkenny saw Stone grimace as Yakushev cleaned his wounds. "Other than that, we're fine. The opposition is down to three. What's the story? Why'd you pull us off?"

"The river's blocked about four kilometers ahead of your current position. Parnell's not getting out that way. Axton's people are set up to pounce on them as soon as they approach. We also closed the flood barrier you passed through about six kilometers upriver, in case they try to double back."

Merlin was now a white foaming speck downriver from where Kilkenny stood. "Ten kilometers of river is still a lot of area to cover. He may head for shore."

"We'll take our chances," Mosley replied, acknowledging the risk. "Axton orders you to sit tight and wait for his people to come and get you. You can't return the boat you stole until they open the floodgates anyway."

"I'm deeply offended by your accusation. This vessel was officially commandeered by a legitimate representative of the British government. I merely came along for the ride."

"I'll bet you did, smart-ass. Tell Stone to hang in

there; help's on the way. You guys did real good out there."

"Thanks."

Kilkenny helped Yakushev dress Stone's wounds. One bullet had left a deep gouge in his forearm, while another had passed through his biceps. Stone was in good spirits despite his pain, keeping a stiff upper lip in proper British fashion.

Chapter 58

Downriver, Kang relaxed a little as *Spitfire* faded from view. He knew that he'd hit one of the snipers. Perhaps a lucky shot had found the driver of that devil boat. In any case, they had broken the pursuit and were now moving unopposed toward the ocean. Kang was just about to ask for *Merlin*'s ship-to-shore phone when Parnell eased back on the throttle.

"Why are you slowing down?"

"I'm not sure," Parnell replied as he looked downriver, "but it appears that the floodgates have been closed."

Both sides of the shore were illuminated by scores of police lights. Parnell could only imagine that many of the small figures lining the embankments had weapons trained on them as they approached. A pair of river patrol boats began moving toward *Merlin*. Before anyone said a word, he turned the wheel around and pushed the accelerator forward, leaving the ambush behind.

"What are you doing?" Kang shouted as Parnell turned his boat around.

"They've closed the river," Parnell shouted back, stifling Kang's complaint. "I can outrun their patrol boats, but we have to get ashore before it's too late. There's an abandoned dockyard a few kilometers back that we can use. With any luck, the police are spread so thin that we can escape by land."

The closure represented by the wall of concrete and steel that tamed the river's floodwaters caused a brief sensation of panic that Kang quickly suppressed. Parnell was right: It was time to get off the river. "Go. If we can evade our pursuers, my people will get us out of the country."

"What about Roe? We can't leave her behind."

"I agree," Kang replied icily.

Upriver from Parnell's boat lay the idle *Spitfire*. Stone's wounds were tended as well as Kilkenny's training and the onboard supplies would allow, and the three men waited for further assistance.

Kilkenny was still wearing Stone's headset, monitoring the British radio traffic, when Mosley called out, "Kilkenny, you still there?"

Kilkenny switched the headset back into the send/receive mode. "Yeah, Cal. What's up?"

"Parnell caught a whiff of us and turned tail; he's heading back in your direction. The British have a chopper and a pair of patrol boats keeping an eye on him. I want you guys to lay low and let him pass. We've got him bottled up, Kilkenny, so no more heroics. Understand?"

"Loud and clear." Kilkenny flipped the microphone

off and slammed his fist into the ship's deck in frustration.

"What did you find out?" Stone asked.

"They reached the blockade and have turned back. They're heading our way, and Axton wants us to stand aside while his people try to chase them down. If Kang and Parnell are as smart as everyone thinks, they'll dump that boat and disappear onshore."

"Where are we?" Stone asked as he tried to peer, uncomfortably, over the ship's side.

Kilkenny stood up but found no landmarks that meant anything to him. "Hell if I know—I'm not from around here."

"I'm afraid I won't be much help, either," Yakushev added.

With Yakushev and Kilkenny's aid, Stone stood up and studied the shoreline carefully, trying to get his bearings. "We're in Essex, east of London proper. There are some old docks about a kilometer back. Parnell's a local lad, like me, so he's probably familiar with the area. If he's going to abandon ship, he's going to do it there."

"And he'll make land before your people can run them down," Kilkenny concluded. Other than *Spitfire*, Parnell had the fastest boat on the Thames. The spies would be safely inland before the authorities could put anything near them by land or river.

Over the short period of time they'd spent together, Stone had taken his measure of Nolan Kilkenny and he already knew what thoughts were going through his mind. "Orders or not, we can't let that happen."

"I agree with him," Yakushev said in defiance of Axton's order. "We must intervene."

"I hate sitting around anyway." Kilkenny surveyed

the river for Parnell's boat. "We don't have much time. Let's get into position."

Kilkenny piloted *Spitfire* to the center of the river before turning her perpendicular to the river's flow, with the port side facing downriver toward the approaching boat.

"How's your shooting arm?"

Stone stretched and flexed his right arm; it felt weak. "It's a bit wobbly, but otherwise fine."

"Good, because we'll need all the firepower we can muster if we're going to offer effective harassment. The plan is the same as before. We're not going to try to stop them, just slow them down and keep them on the river until help arrives. I hope everyone's ready, because here they come."

Merlin rounded the slight turn in the river and came into view with a prominent fan of water issuing from the speeding boat's tail. Yakushev and Stone crouched and took aim on the approaching ship while Kilkenny eased the throttle into low gear. As *Merlin* approached, Kilkenny hoped his opponents would assume that the drifting craft offered them no threat.

Merlin left the patrol boats far behind, and only the police helicopter kept up with the blue craft. Parnell showed no sign of veering his boat out of the main channel as it approached *Spitfire*.

"He's going to pass close, probably thinks we're out of commission," Kilkenny whispered to his crew. "Let's draw him in before we open up. On my mark, gentlemen."

Merlin was almost upon them when Kilkenny shouted, "Now!"

All three opened fire on *Merlin*—bullets shattering

the blue fiberglass hull as they struck. Kilkenny concentrated his fire on Parnell, strafing the bow deck and windscreen. Both Kang and Parnell ducked, but Parnell didn't move fast enough for Kilkenny's deadly aim. Three rounds caught Parnell in the right shoulder, shattering his collarbone and upper arm. The blow turned Parnell halfway around and nearly cast him overboard. His left hand, still clutching the wheel, pulled *Merlin* into a sharp starboard turn toward *Spitfire*.

Kilkenny dropped his weapon and slammed *Spitfire*'s throttles forward. Too late. *Merlin*'s upturned bow surged forward and struck them broadside, her keel driving deeply into the grinning shark's mouth on *Spitfire*'s tapered bow. The high-tech composite hulls of both ships exploded into a million tiny pieces. Kilkenny and his shipmates were flung overboard as *Merlin* plowed deeper into *Spitfire*, trying to capsize her. *Merlin*'s hull, now locked into *Spitfire*, broke in two as the green ship's reinforced keel rolled up from below and, like an ax, struck it amidships. The stern half of Parnell's vessel, carried forward by the engine's momentum, catapulted over the capsized boat into the river.

The captain's chair that Roe was lashed to broke free from its base, ejecting her into the water, seat and all. Kang hit the water clear of the largest pieces of the broken vessel.

Merlin's stern crashed down on Parnell and the fractured fiberglass hull tore into his clothing and skin. Parnell's pain gave way to sudden panic as the back half of his precious *Merlin* grabbed hold and dragged him down. He flailed vainly to free himself from the wreckage, clawing hopelessly at the water, but each second that passed found him another foot beneath the surface.

At ten feet, Parnell could hold his breath no longer

and he coughed the oxygen-depleted air from his lungs.
He gagged on the first trickles of water that ran down his
throat as he inhaled the river. Each involuntary spasm,
his body's frantic search for air, sent another mouthful of
the river into his rapidly flooding lungs. Twenty feet
down, he was no longer aware of the brown-black world
that surrounded him. Parnell's mind had closed in upon
itself in the final moments of consciousness.

The broken stern of *Merlin* spiraled silently downward into the silty river with the body of Ian Parnell im-
paled upon its fractured end. A few scattered bubbles
sprang loose when the wreckage struck bottom, tumbling
upward to the surface. The weight of the stern pushed
Parnell's body down into the soft river bottom.

Chapter 59

Kilkenny grabbed hold of Stone's jacket as *Spitfire* capsized and they were flung into the river. Once in the water, he threw his free arm across the injured man's chest and pulled him clear of the wreck. Yakushev broke the water's surface nearby, still shaken from the crash as he seized hold of the *Spitfire*'s hull.

With Stone in tow, Kilkenny swam over and joined Yakushev beside the wreckage. "You okay?"

"I'm a little bruised," Yakushev replied, "but otherwise fine. What about Kang and Parnell?"

"You're right. One or both of them might still be able to cause us some trouble. Can you hang on here with Andrei?" he asked Stone.

"I think so—I've still got one good arm."

Kilkenny left Stone by the hull and began treading water. "I'm going to take a look around and see if anyone from Parnell's boat survived. Holler if you guys see any trouble."

Kilkenny glided away from his comrades, propelling himself silently beneath the water with only his head above the choppy surface. Steam and exhaust poured out of *Spitfire*'s engine compartment. The boat's propeller finally sputtered to a stop as the engine choked on river water. Rounding the stern, Kilkenny discovered a widespread field of flotsam littering the surface.

About five meters away, he found someone struggling in the water. Kilkenny fought off the vindictive urge to let one of the conspirators drown; instead, he moved in to help. Kilkenny recognized Roe in the brief instant that her face was above the water. She was lashed to a captain's chair and the seat's foam cushions were buoyant enough that they held her facedown in the water. Kilkenny's muscled forearm wrapped around the chest of the frantically choking woman and pulled her head out of the water.

"I've got you," Kilkenny reassured her. "You're going to be fine. Just relax and I'll take care of everything." Kilkenny pulled her through the water and Roe calmed down once she stopped choking and caught her breath. "By the way, I'm Nolan Kilkenny."

"Kilkenny!" Roe's eyes grew wide when she repeated the name. "I thought you were in jail!"

"A simple misunderstanding that a Russian friend of yours claims you can explain."

Looking at the wreckage, Roe wondered how her mentor had fared in the violent exchange. "Is Andrei all right?"

"Yeah, he's a tough old guy." Kilkenny pulled Roe back to where the others clung to *Spitfire*'s hull.

A fatherly smile came to Yakushev when he recognized the person in Kilkenny's grasp. "Anya, are you hurt?"

"I'm fine, Andrei, just a bit handicapped by these ropes."

"I'll get those off as soon as I can get a few more hands on you," Kilkenny promised. "Andrei, take hold of her for a minute."

Yakushev grasped the chair with his free arm, struggling to keep Roe from flipping facedown into the river. Kilkenny let go and treaded water while untying the knotted ropes.

"Nolan, did you see anyone else over there?" Stone asked.

"No."

"Kang, Parnell, and I were the only ones left," Roe offered.

"Well, it looks like you're the lucky one," Kilkenny replied. "I'm surprised that any of us survived that crash."

The pilot of the police helicopter *Eagle* witnessed the collision in horror from above the river. He had maintained a safe distance from the speeding boats earlier to avoid drawing any gunfire; now he held his distance for fear of swamping the survivors before help arrived. He hovered as close as he dared and counted four figures in the water, clinging to an overturned hull. One of the survivors waved to him. It appeared that they were all right.

Chapter 60

Kang had dived deep after striking the water and his effort paid off when the rest of Parnell's boat landed where he'd just been. He opened his eyes only for a moment, but the brownish murk in the Thames diminished underwater visibility to nothing. He stayed under as long as he could, holding his breath as the distorted sounds of twisting wreckage and rumbling engines filled his ears. After what seemed like hours, he moved toward the surface, hands forward as he rose blindly in the water.

He broke the surface with a stale gasp of air bursting from his lungs. Kang hyperventilated for several minutes before his breathing returned to normal. He opened his eyes, to find that he was not out in the open water, but in the large air pocket formed by the capsized hull of *Spitfire*. He was also alone. The question in his mind about other survivors was quickly answered by the thumping sounds he heard outside of the hull. Moving closer, he could hear muffled voices on the other side.

He'd held on to his weapon through the crash and his first impulse was to use it; none of the other survivors were of any particular use to him now. Clearer thinking caused him to reconsider this hasty course of action and he began to work on his more important need to escape. Kang knew that the British patrol ships would be closing in on the wreckage soon, and the reverberating thumping he heard echoing off the overturned hull was the sound of a helicopter hovering over the crash.

Kang swam over to the opening that led to *Spitfire's* bow cabin. He braced himself in the hatchway, where he could rest and save some of the energy he was now using to tread water. Once comfortably set, he pulled his hands out of the water to inspect his weapon. Until it had dried and was cleaned, it was useless. Kang holstered the weapon and began looking for other tools that he might find useful in evading capture.

The bow cabin was partially submerged and littered with foam bunk mattresses and other items that had tumbled loose when the boat capsized. Light filtered through the cracks in the broken hull, illuminating the tapered space. The ship's smooth hull retained its graceful lines until Kang's eyes reached the port side, where *Merlin* had landed its fatal blow. There, the hull was driven in and shattered. The strong odor of fuel also permeated the air around him.

Kang began rummaging through the items floating in the grimy water and found a large black waterproof bag held partially afloat by the air trapped inside. The bag felt heavy as Kang pulled it toward him, weighted down by its contents. Positioning the bag to prevent its contents from spilling out and falling to the deep river bottom, Kang opened it and found the boat owner's scuba gear.

Kang could scarcely believe his good fortune. Fate had provided him with the means of escape. He opened the valve on the tank; the pressure gauges jumped as the compressed-air mixture filled the lines. The tanks were nearly full, more than enough to see him safely to shore. If he paddled leisurely, the river would carry him far downstream from the accident and out of the immediate search area.

The chill of the river made him shiver as he looked through the dive bag. The owner's fins, mask, and wet suit were all there. Kang stripped down to his underwear and placed the rest of his clothing in a plunge bag used for collecting artifacts from the sea. The brightly colored wet suit was loose-fitting on Kang's lean frame; it obviously belonged to a man of substantial size. Still, the wet suit didn't bind or restrict his movement, and it would insulate him from the cold of an extended river swim.

Kang suited up quickly, not knowing how much longer he had before the patrol boats arrived. He strapped on the tank and checked the regulator, blowing it clear of any water or debris before inhaling.

Just as he prepared to slip under the water, he noticed a fluorescent red pouch floating in the cabin. The bold black letters read EMERGENCY FLARE PISTOL. Kang retrieved the watertight package and checked its seals. Everything inside the waterproof pouch was dry.

Quickly, Kang pulled out the flare pistol and loaded it. He then slipped down into the water, leaving only his eyes and the hand with the pistol above the surface. Kang aimed at the point where Spitfire's bow tanks were slowly leaking fuel, ducked his head beneath the water, and fired. His hand slipped below the dark water just as the flare struck the fractured port side of *Spitfire*. The leaking fuel immediately erupted into flames.

Kilkenny heard a loud thumping from inside *Spitfire*'s hull, as if someone had swung a sledgehammer from inside. Grabbing hold of one of the fluted contours on the ship's hull, he hauled himself out of the water and onto the capsized craft. He looked around the perimeter of the ship for the source of the noise, when a flash of brightness caught his eye.

"Everyone into the water!" Kilkenny shouted. "Grab anything that floats and push off! The ship is on fire."

The others wasted no time heeding Kilkenny's warning. Roe and Yakushev pulled cushions and life vests from the water and helped Stone swim away from the wreckage.

Kilkenny took one last look before diving in, when he caught sight of something moving beneath the surface of the water. He paused for a moment to get a better look at the strange multicolored object. Kilkenny recognized the large cylindrical shape of a scuba tank and knew immediately that someone else had survived the crash, someone who didn't want to be rescued by the authorities.

The diver had emerged from beneath *Spitfire* when Kilkenny first spotted him. Kilkenny sprinted across the ship's keel and made a running dive into the water as the bow tank exploded. Shards of flaming Kevlar rained down from the fireball that ballooned up from the ship. The shock wave from the blast rocked Kilkenny just as his arms opened a hole in the surface of the water.

The diver was now a good fifteen yards ahead of him and Kilkenny knew that he would have to swim flat out in the choppy river to catch a man wearing fins. The sound of the explosion masked Kilkenny's entry into the river, his body churning the water in a flat-out freestyle sprint. Kilkenny was closing the distance, but the diver's form was darkening. The man was moving deeper under the water.

The waterborne shock wave from the blast punished Kang's ears with a sharp, painful ringing. The pain increased with each foot he descended underwater. At ten feet beneath the surface, the pressure against his ears was a full third greater than on the surface. The agony pounding in his head was almost more than he could bear. Any deeper and he ran the risk of passing out from the pain. Still, he had the disk with the American codes and he had a way out; all he needed to do was keep moving.

Kilkenny cleared twenty-five meters of his open-water race, about where he expected to overtake his submerged opponent. He stopped and studied the water carefully; it seemed to be the same uniform murky brown all around him. Then he saw a flicker of color muted by the silt, then another flash of hazy color. It was the diver.

Breathing deeply into his abdomen, he filled his lungs with air and plunged beneath the surface. Once under the water, Kilkenny entered the murky darkness as a blind man fighting against an opponent who was better equipped for this environment. Better equipped to swim perhaps, but six years with the SEALs had taught Kilkenny that he didn't need his eyes to fight underwater.

Using a deep flutter kick, Kilkenny pushed himself through the water with his arms extended ahead of him.

He aimed his body in the direction that he had last seen the diver heading, hoping to intercept the man's torso on the way down.

His estimate of the diver's depth and speed was a little off, and Kilkenny swam down into the man's legs. Kang's right leg brushed past Kilkenny's hand, gliding up his arm before striking him in the shoulder. A heavy rubber fin slapped against Kilkenny's chest. Kang shuddered when he realized that he'd touched something solid in the water.

Kilkenny, still pointed head-down, wrapped his right arm around Kang's leg and trapped it against his body. Gripping the neoprene-covered calf, Kilkenny locked the joint and struck the side of Kang's knee with the flattened palm of his hand. The knee dislocated with a gratifying snap that echoed in Kilkenny's water-filled ears. The deafened Kang felt only the numbing pain of his throbbing leg, which now hung in the water at an unnatural angle.

Kang rolled to protect his injured leg and turned to face his attacker. His pain and anger gave way to a moment of absolute fury when he realized that his opponent, the driver of that devil boat, was Nolan Kilkenny. Kang was still bitter about the assassin's failure to eliminate Kilkenny when he first became a problem. This troublesome young man was all that stood in the way of his escape, and Kang swore that Kilkenny would now die.

Kang saw that Kilkenny wore no gear and, even now, was straining against the oxygen-depleted air within his lungs. He struck where Kilkenny was now most vulnerable, his solar plexus. The water slowed his punch, but Kang only hoped to knock the wind out of him. At ten feet underwater, that would be enough to drown the man.

Kilkenny felt Kang twist in the water and, sensing the attack, angled away from the blow. Kang's punch landed late, glancing off Kilkenny's back. Only a few bubbles escaped from Kilkenny's mouth.

Kilkenny had only a few seconds left before he had to return to the surface for air. When he returned, the injured Kang would be waiting for him, able to breathe and able to see. Kilkenny had to even the odds.

Kang's head was nearby, within striking distance if he could find it. Guessing his way, Kilkenny lunged out and dislodged the scuba mask from Kang's face. The river poured in against Kang's eyes, obscuring his vision with water and silt. Kilkenny's lungs screamed for oxygen as he reached to strip the scuba mask from Kang's face.

Kang stopped Kilkenny's arm and pushed the clutching hand away from the mask. Both men were now blind in the water, and each had taken hold of the other. Kang twisted Kilkenny's arm back, forcing him to release the damaged leg. He then swam away from Kilkenny as quickly as he could. Kilkenny, now desperate for air, raced to the surface.

Kilkenny's first few gulps of air didn't get much past his mouth. His body seemed to suck the oxygen out of each breath before it even reached his lungs, the demand was so high. Gradually, his skin flushed and took on its normal color. With his immediate, physical needs met, Kilkenny's thoughts returned to the man below.

After Kilkenny's withdrawal, Kang took stock of his situation. He reset the dislodged mask and purged it of the sight-robbing water. If only he could repair his leg as easily as resetting the mask. Dispassionately, he inspected the lifeless limb. It bent awkwardly away from the joint, connected to him only by the pain that radiated from his damaged knee. Without the use of both his legs, he would be forced to rely on his arms for propulsion in the strong river current. His nemesis floated above him like a wraith, a dark shadow against the diffuse light of the sky.

Kilkenny remained at the surface, fighting to catch his breath as Kang watched from below. Before trying to swim again, Kang checked his belongings to make sure everything was in order. The plunge bag was still securely fastened to his weight belt, next to another object he hadn't noticed before—a dive knife. Kang unbuttoned the clasp around the handle, pulled the knife free of its sheath, and held it in front of his mask. The knife had a dimpled rubber-coated handle and a long blade with a serrated back edge. He might be wounded, but Kang now held a decisive advantage in this battle.

From above, Kilkenny could barely discern the multicolored figure in the water below, just at the edge of visibility in the murky river. With a dislocated knee, Kang wasn't going anywhere quickly, but that didn't make him any less of a threat. In fact, he was more dangerous now that he knew Kilkenny was coming after him.

Kilkenny took each breath in slowly, deeply, bringing a calmness to his body and mind as he prepared to do battle. His heart rate fell and his body became fluid, yin. He would be one with the water, allowing his opponent to define the attack while he flowed around Kang's offensive. He would remain in this fluid state, striking hard, yang, only when an opportunity presented itself. He took a deep breath and slipped below the water without leaving a ripple on the surface.

Kilkenny approached Kang in a near trance, seeing the man with his mind rather than his eyes. He moved his arms in sweeping arcs to clear the water ahead of him. At three meters, he could almost feel Kang's presence waiting in the darkness. Kilkenny slowed his descent and waited for the attack.

Using his good leg, Kang turned and moved his body above his opponent. Kilkenny was upside down in the water, floating, with his hands outstretched in search of an enemy just beyond his reach. Kang brought his arm up above his head and prepared to lunge down into Kilkenny's exposed back.

An eddy rushed across Kilkenny's face. Something disturbed the water nearby, moving quickly enough that it generated a minivortex as it passed. The direction of the turbulent flow let Kilkenny know that its source was now above him. Kilkenny twisted 180 degrees and crossed his arms just as Kang's struck down on him. The knife sliced the underside of Kilkenny's left forearm, opening a gash from his wrist to his elbow. The blood from Kilkenny's arm issued forth in reddish clouds, but the wound didn't prevent him from taking hold of Kang's arm.

Kilkenny performed like a weightless gymnast, twisting around his body's center of gravity to gain an advantage. Holding Kang's arm firmly with both hands, Kilkenny turned himself and ground the fragile bones of Kang's wrist together. The nerve bundles running through the carpal tunnel in Kang's tortured wrist quivered with pain until his entire arm went numb. Kilkenny grabbed the knife before it fell away from Kang's deadened grasp. He gave another half turn to Kang's wrist, doubling the man over as his arm twisted back against the scuba tank. Kang tried to resist, but each kick sent a wave of agony through his useless leg.

Kang struggled against him, but Kilkenny countered each of his moves easily. Kilkenny knew that he had no more than a few seconds of air left before he had to return to the surface, and this time Kang must go with him.

With the knife in his free hand, Kilkenny followed the contour of the scuba tank until he found the octopus of lines that emerged from the top. He released Kang's hand, grabbed hold of the line feeding Kang's regulator, and severed the thick black hose. A surge of bubbles exploded from the pressurized tank and the air line whipped about like a frenzied snake.

Kang was in midbreath when his regulator filled with silty water. He choked, and there was no controlling the spasm of coughing that doubled him over as he spat the regulator from his lips. The only thought in Kang's mind now was the blackness that came with drowning.

His coughing slowed and he lost consciousness as the river filled his lungs. Kilkenny grabbed him around the chest and dragged him upward. Kang's mind was so far removed from his body that he didn't notice the easing pressure against his shattered eardrums.

Kilkenny broke the surface with Kang's limp body, only to be sprayed by the prop wash of a Royal Marine Search and Rescue helicopter. *Eagle* had followed Kilkenny on his pursuit of Kang, tracking his position until help arrived. Two wet-suited marines jumped into the water from the helicopter to assist Kilkenny with his prisoner. Kang went up first in the hoist, while Kilkenny relaxed in the water with the aid of a marine diver.

British patrol ships had already pulled the others

from the river. Kilkenny's shivering shipmates stood blanketed, with cups of hot tea, waving to him from the deck of a patrol boat as he dangled in midair below the helicopter. For Kilkenny, what had started out with the flick of a switch on an experimental computer ended with the Thames swallowing up the flaming wreckage of *Merlin* and *Spitfire*.

Chapter 61

Medics aboard the Royal Marine helicopter successfully revived Kang en route to the hospital at the naval air station. The nearly drowned spy alternated between half-choked gasps of air and violent spasms of coughed-up water and vomit. The medics placed a splint on his damaged leg, immobilizing it for the rest of their journey to the hospital. Kilkenny sat back in the jump seat next to one of the navy divers, keeping a wary eye on Kang, while a medic attended to his arm.

Among Kang's personal effects they found his soaked clothing and a sealed optical-disk cartridge containing the stolen cipher files. Kang Fa's operation to capture the new American encryption technology had come within a few hundred meters of success.

A pair of ambulances met the helicopter at the landing pad; one staffed with an MP escort took charge of the prisoner on his way to the base infirmary. The marine doctors treated Kilkenny's laceration with thirty stitches and a mild painkiller. A steaming-hot shower and some dry clothes were prescribed as treatment for a mild case of exposure from the cold river. Kilkenny had just finished suiting up in the duty uniform of a royal marine when Mosley and Axton arrived at his room.

"Will you look at that, Mosley. First this Yank of yours bungles up my operation and now we find him impersonating an officer in Her Majesty's marines. You could get twenty years for that, Kilkenny."

Kilkenny grasped Axton's hand and returned the man's warm smile. "And here I thought they looked rather good on me. Compliments of the base commander."

"They look damn good on you," Mosley admitted while happily shaking Kilkenny's hand. "After what you did today, I'm sure they're proud to have you wear their uniform. I do have one question for you, though. Why the hell did you run off with Yakushev? Axton's people are on the warpath—they've been trying to find him all week." Axton's eyes rolled as Mosley asked this question, a gesture that spoke volumes about the frustrating chase that Yakushev had put British Intelligence through. "For all you knew, Yakushev might have been working for the other side."

"I don't know. Instincts, I guess. Something told me I could trust him, and from what he told me, I think he once worked for both sides."

Axton glowered for a moment. Kilkenny couldn't have known that his remark about Yakushev's past was considered a serious breach of the Official Secrets Act. Knowledge of Andrei Yakushev was one of many things that Kilkenny would have to be sworn to secrecy about before he left Britain.

Mosley just shook his head with a smile at the young man he'd come to admire over the past few weeks. "Well, given the way things turned out, I'm kind of glad you followed your gut."

"Thanks," Kilkenny replied. "How are Stone and Yakushev?"

"I received word that both are doing fine," Axton replied with great satisfaction. "Stone is in surgery right now and expected to recover completely. Yakushev, that stubborn old bastard, came through with nothing more serious than a bad case of the chills."

"What about the others?"

"Those who survived this afternoon are in custody. Roe and Kang are both under guard in the prison wing of the base hospital. Parnell is still missing and presumed drowned. We're dragging the river for his body."

"Best of all," Mosley added, "we got the whole transaction from Chicago to London covered and verified, right down to the computer in Parnell's office. The case against them is airtight. Thanks to you, we've just shut down a major player in the world of industrial espionage."

"I'm just glad I could help," Kilkenny replied modestly. "Say, when can I get out of here?"

"Your doctors have informed me that you can leave the base hospital now. If you like, we can have a car come around to take you back to your hotel." Axton's demeanor subtly became more official. "We would like to take your statement regarding today's activities."

"No problem," Kilkenny replied with an understanding nod of the head. "My plane doesn't leave until Sunday."

*   *   *

News of Kilkenny's heroics on the Thames was spread across the front pages of London's Saturday-morning papers, with eyewitness accounts and dramatic action photos of the flaming boat wreck and the helicopter rescue to titillate the readers. A few patrons in the hotel recognized Kilkenny as he entered the restaurant for breakfast and congratulated him on a job well done. Kilkenny blushed with embarrassment at his sudden notoriety and took the praise politely. Nothing like this had ever happened after a SEAL mission.

His waiter brought over complimentary copies of the morning papers and even asked for an autograph after Kilkenny had ordered. Though different in style, both papers told essentially the same story about Parnell's industrial-espionage activities and the investigation that had ended with a fiery boat race down the Thames. Neither paper mentioned Kang Fa and the U.S. ciphers, nor did either report anything about Yakushev and Roe. Only Parnell and Kilkenny were mentioned by name, with Kilkenny being portrayed as a consultant to British security forces who had bravely jumped into action when duty called and aided SAS officers in preventing Parnell's escape.

A car arrived at ten o'clock to escort Kilkenny to the American embassy, where he would make his official statement. His story, from beginning to end, took the better part of two hours, followed up by another hour of questions to double-check details surrounding his involvement with the whole affair.

"Ready to go home?" Mosley asked as Kilkenny emerged from the conference room where he'd given his deposition.

"I thought I was finished with debriefings like that when I left the navy."

Mosley gave Kilkenny a sympathetic nod. "I've been on both sides of these question-and-answer sessions, and it never gets any easier. As long as you're involved with these kinds of situations, there will be questions when it's over."

"I've got a couple questions of my own."

"Shoot. I'll answer them, if I can, but anything I say is off the record."

"What's the story with Kang Fa? It's as if his whole part in this mess has conveniently disappeared."

"It has. Kang will never stand trial because our government won't allow the cipher files to be admitted as evidence. In a secondary development, Kang Fa has been officially disowned by the government of the People's Republic of China; he's a man without a country. For the next few years, Kang will reside in a maximum-security facility while discreet negotiations for his return to China drag on. He's a blue chip, so our people and the Brits are going to want quite a lot in trade. I assume that your next question has to do with Yakushev and Roe."

"Yes."

Mosley cracked the knuckles on his right hand and shook the fingers out. "Officially, Andrei Yakushev died back in 1991. He was murdered by order of the KGB chairman, and you never met him. There is, however, an elderly gentleman with an Eastern European accent currently enjoying his retirement in the English countryside. As for Ms. Roe, both the U.S. and British governments had no choice but to grant her immunity from prosecution; she simply can't be put on trial in connection with the theft of the Spyder, Cole's murder, or anything involving Kang Fa's intelligence operation.

However, this immunity does not come without a price, and it's a steep one. Roe must provide a thorough and accurate report on all her activities as a spy, both working for the Russians and on her own. She must also assist us in dismantling Parnell's organization. This is going to take her out of circulation for a number of years."

"So no charges will come out of all this?"

"A lot of Parnell's clients and associates will end up in jail on industrial-espionage charges, but no one will be tried for crimes specifically tied to the cipher files or the Spyder. But don't be too disappointed. On a different level, justice has been served."

Epilogue

May 17

Sean Kilkenny leaned back against his Ford Explorer, crossed his arms, and shook his head the way fathers do when their children get out of line. "I see you just couldn't stay out of trouble."

Nolan reached the curb and dropped his carry-on bag at his father's feet. "You know me, once a trouble-maker, always a troublemaker. Mom always said it had something to do with the Kilkenny side of the family."

"And she was probably right. Welcome home." Sean embraced Nolan warmly, his fatherly concern eased with Nolan's safe return.

Nolan ran through the events in London during the half-hour drive to the family farm west of Ann Arbor, omitting only those details that Cal Mosley had asked him to "forget." As they approached the road leading to the

Kilkenny farm, they saw a Chrysler New Yorker limousine heading toward them.

"Must be a prom tonight," Sean commented as he eased his Explorer onto the shoulder of the narrow road, letting the long, dark car move past.

They thought nothing more of the limo until they pulled up beside the barn and saw Martin Kilkenny standing beside a gleaming red Dodge Viper.

"New toy, Dad?" Nolan asked as he got out of the truck.

"Not mine. Let's see what your grandfather has to say about this."

Martin Kilkenny stood next to the car with a devious grin on his face as Sean and Nolan approached. The car bore manufacturer's plates, and, with a careful look at the body, Nolan realized that this car's styling was different from the production Vipers of the past few years.

"Grandpa, whose car is this?"

Martin Kilkenny's smile widened as he dangled a key from his hand. With a flick of his wrist, he tossed the key toward his grandson. "It's yours—at least that's what the man said."

Nolan glanced at the key in his hand and then stared for a long moment at the sleek red sports car. "You're joking."

"I know how you and your father are about cars, so I wouldn't joke about something like this." Martin's thick Irish brogue was filled with sincerity. "Did you pass a long, dark car on your way up the road?"

"Yes?"

"Well, the gentleman riding in the back of that fine automobile left this car for you, along with a note." Martin pulled an envelope from the pocket of his overalls. "He said it would explain everything."

Nolan tore open the envelope with the edge of the Viper key and extracted the letter inside. The stationery bore the embossed penta-star emblem of the Chrysler Corporation. Nolan unfolded the sheet and read the handwritten letter aloud.

"Dear Mr. Kilkenny,

"I read about your exploits in London over the weekend. Bravo! Your name sounded familiar, so I made a few calls. I discovered that your name had come to my attention a few months ago, during the investigation that dealt with an attempt to break into Chrysler's computer network. The FBI said that you prevented the thieves from doing any real damage, and for that I and everyone in Auburn Hills thank you. If our corporate financial records had been damaged, or our engineering research stolen . . . well, I don't want to think about what that would have cost us. You've saved Chrysler a lot of money and we owe you, so I'll get to the point.

"Your efforts to catch the people responsible for these crimes cost you a Mustang. She was a classic, and I ought to know because I built enough of them. The Mustang holds a special place in my heart. By way of a thank-you, I'd like you to have one of our new Vipers. I'm sure you won't be disappointed."

Nolan stared at the signature of Chrysler's chairman emeritus boldly scrawled across the bottom of the letter, still not believing what he'd read. "You mean that was . . ."

Martin grinned from ear to ear now that the surprise was out. "Aye, big as life, cigar and all. Drove this little beauty out here himself, he did. He hopes that you'll like it."

After only a few years of production, the Viper had already earned an honored place in the American muscle-car pantheon.

"I think I can live with it," Nolan replied. "You want to try her out, Dad?"

Sean was already opening the passenger door. "I thought you'd never ask."

Nolan and his father put the Viper through a rigorous test-drive on the highways and side roads between Dexter and Chelsea, turning heads and gathering envious looks wherever they went. Almost two hours later, they returned to the Kilkenny farm grinning like a pair of juvenile delinquents. It was the kind of car that made a definite impression.

"Should we set a plate for you?" Sean asked as they pulled up to the farm's main house.

"No. Kelsey got out of the hospital yesterday, and I'm taking her out to dinner to celebrate her recovery." Nolan noticed a slightly arched eyebrow on his father's face. "What?"

"Nothing." Sean's voice lowered to a sly tone. "I was just thinking about the bounty."

The Newton and Kilkenny families had been close even before Nolan and Kelsey had been born. Once their combined children reached marrying age, the parents began thinking about grandchildren. To encourage those who were already married to have kids, the respective fathers offered a one-thousand-dollar bounty for the first grandchild in each family.

In an effort to create a marital bond between the two families, Meghan Kilkenny and Anna Newton had upped the ante with a five-thousand-dollar prize for the first child from a Kilkenny-Newton union. With most of the Kilkenny and Newton children now married, Nolan and Kelsey were the only candidates left for the big prize.

"For the moment, Dad, your money's still safe."

Nolan parked the Viper beside the old Egan barn, where he now lived. It wasn't until the hot water struck his body that he realized how gritty he felt from the long flight. As he showered, he went over his plans for the evening, preparing himself as if he was going on a mission. He realized that in many ways, he was on the most critical mission of his life. The water refreshed him and brought clarity to his mind. The events of the past few days were forgotten and only the next few hours were important.

Once out of the shower, he wrapped a towel around his waist and studied the fading scars on his face. The gash on his forehead was healing nicely and was mostly hidden by his thick red hair. Nolan wasn't an unusually vain person, but pride in one's appearance was a virtue drilled in by the military, and Nolan felt that tonight required attention to every detail.

He completed the shaving ritual with a light splash of a cologne. With his grooming preparations complete, Nolan dressed in the medium weight blue-gray wool suit he'd bought from a reputable London tailor. From the outside, Nolan was as ready as he would ever be. Inside, it was a completely different story. He felt as nervous as a high school boy on his first date.

Nolan rang the bell and Kelsey's father welcomed him inside and offered him a drink, which he declined. He stood in the foyer making polite small talk while waiting for Kelsey to appear. Kelsey was with her mother upstairs and still getting dressed. Both men waited, half-listening to the evening news while talking about Nolan's new car.

Ten minutes after Nolan arrived, Kelsey appeared on the balcony overlooking the foyer. Her hair was drawn back in a French braid accented with her new gold and lapis hair clasp, and she seemed to glow as she slowly descended the staircase, carefully taking each step one at a time. The shimmering lapis silk dress looked more stunning on her than Nolan ever imagined, flattering every sensuous curve of her body. Nolan's heart began to race as Kelsey approached; she was a radiant vision. In his mind's eye, Kelsey Newton had completely evolved from longtime friend and confidante into something more profound. She now held a place in Nolan's heart that no one had ever occupied before, a vague, empty space that he'd dismissed until the day he thought he'd lost her. The transformation of Kelsey in Nolan's mind, of how he thought and felt about her, was now complete.

"Kelsey," Nolan stammered, finding himself at a loss for words, "you look incredible."

"This is the dress I told you about, Nolan, the one I bought in Chicago. Thanks for giving me a reason to wear it."

"Kelsey, the dress is nice, but you're the one who makes it look special."

Nolan offered a hand and helped Kelsey negotiate the last steps. She was taking the stairs carefully, as if each step threatened to send a jolt of pain through her wounded ribs should she take one too hard. Nolan had suffered rib injuries before and could empathize with her condition. It would take some time before she was fully healed from the accident. When Kelsey reached the last step, she leaned over and kissed him. Her lips lingered on his for a moment and her warmth glowed like a welcome fire.

"Are you ready for a night out on the town?"

"You wouldn't believe how ready I am, Nolan. I'm tired of recuperating. If I don't get out and do something fun, I'm going to lose my mind."

"That's the truth, Nolan," Kelsey's mother commented from the living room. "She's not one to just sit around. For her to be cooped up here is a lot like caging a wild animal."

"Well, I'll take her out for a little fresh air," Nolan volunteered graciously. "We'll probably be out late, so don't wait up for us."

Kelsey's father put a firm hand on Nolan's shoulder. "You two are adults responsible for your own actions. Kelsey has a key, and I expect we'll be fast asleep when you return."

Nolan nodded, accepting the trust that Kelsey and her parents placed in him. He smiled at Kelsey. "Very well, my lady, your chariot awaits."

Nolan carefully helped Kelsey to the door, which her father held open as they both passed through. Arm in arm with Nolan, she already seemed noticeably better. Only when they stopped beside the Viper's passenger door did Kelsey look away from her date and notice the bright red car.

"Nolan, where did you get this car?"

Nolan acted nonchalantly about the Viper. "It's just a car, Kelsey, four wheels, an engine. Something to get you from point A to point B."

"At the speed of light, from the looks of it. It's so cute." Kelsey gave Nolan a stern look; she wanted the truth and not one of his stories. "Is it your dad's?"

"No, it's mine," he answered casually.

Kelsey studied him skeptically, but she sensed he was telling the truth.

"Kelsey, it's a long story, but I'll tell you on the way."

With one arm supported on Nolan's shoulder, she lowered herself gingerly into the passenger seat. The supple black leather interior seemed to wrap around her like a cocoon. Once settled, Nolan closed her door and took his place on the driver's side.

Nolan handed her a pair of Wayfarer sunglasses from the glove compartment and started up the Viper's V-10 engine. The deep-throated growl made promises that only a car like this could deliver. Kelsey waved to her parents as they drove off down the street.

Nolan eased the gleaming red sports car into an open parking space along Main Street, in front of BD's Mongolian Barbeque. Just as the car reached the curb, the owner of the restaurant, an old high school classmate of Kilkenny's, appeared and opened the passenger door for Kelsey.

"Hey, guys," the owner said, pleased to see his old friends. Kelsey accepted his offered arm and gingerly extracted herself from the Viper's low-slung passenger seat. "I've got your table waiting."

"Thanks, Billy," Nolan replied as he followed the restaurateur and Kelsey inside.

The restaurant's interior was decorated in what could only be described as "Ann Arbor eclectic," a mix of whatever struck the owner's fancy. Large black umbrellas were suspended from the metal-pan ceiling and photographs of native Mongolians lined the walls.

Nolan stopped to study a picture of a young man in scuba gear floating beside a coral reef. The diver proudly displayed the restaurant's T-shirt to a colorful school of fish.

"Anyone you know?" Kelsey asked as she glanced at the picture.

"No, probably just some SEAL wanna-be."

They were seated at a table for two near a window, and a waitress took their drink order. There was no dinner menu, the bill of fare being the guest's choice from a varied offering of meats, poultry, fish, vegetables, sauces, and seasonings. In the center of the restaurant, a pair of chefs rapidly cooked several patrons' concoctions in a haze of steam and smoke over a circular cast-steel grill. The effect was a lighthearted and casual dining atmosphere.

After chatting briefly with the owner, they made their way to the buffet and began designing their dinner. Nolan carried bowls for both Kelsey and himself, filling hers as directed while telling her of the afternoon's events.

"So, just as I drop my father off, he brings up the *bounty* again," Nolan explained as he scattered a few sliced mushrooms into their bowls.

Kelsey laughed lightly and pointed at the tofu. The Kilkenny-Newton grandchild bounty was a running joke for them both. "He's just teasing you. He knows that you won't marry until you find the right person."

Nolan looked over his shoulder at her; a devilish spark lingered in her iridescent blue eyes. He smiled, picked up their bowls, and moved down to the seasonings. The same spark smoldered in his eyes, as well; the right person had been found.

"So, Kelsey, how do you like it?"

She let the question hang for just a moment, then smiled and whispered in his ear, "*Hot and spicy.*"